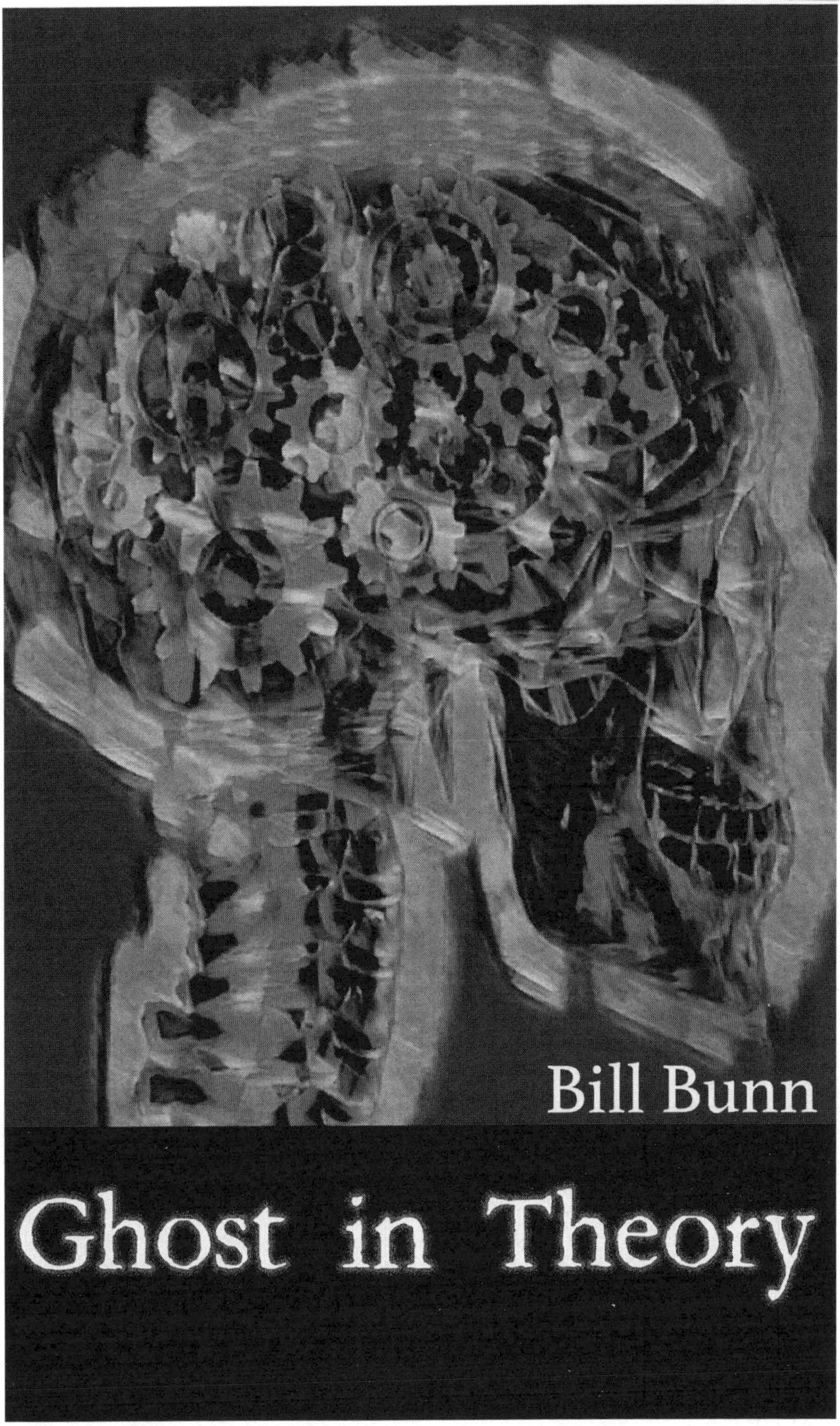

Bill Bunn

# Ghost in Theory

# Ghost in Theory

**BILL BUNN**

BITINGDUCK PRESS
ALTADENA, CA

Published by Bitingduck Press
ISBN 978-1-938463-84-6
eISBN 978-1-938463-85-3
© 2021 Bill Bunn All rights reserved
For information contact
Bitingduck Press, LLC
Altadena, California
notifications@bitingduckpress.com
http://www.bitingduckpress.com

*I'm sorry, Mom. These awful words had to be written, and I was chosen.*

*Yet I desire, even by profane words, if I may not use sacred, to indicate the heaven of this deity and to report what hints I have collected of the transcendent simplicity and energy of the Highest Law.*
—Ralph Waldo Emerson, "The Over-Soul"

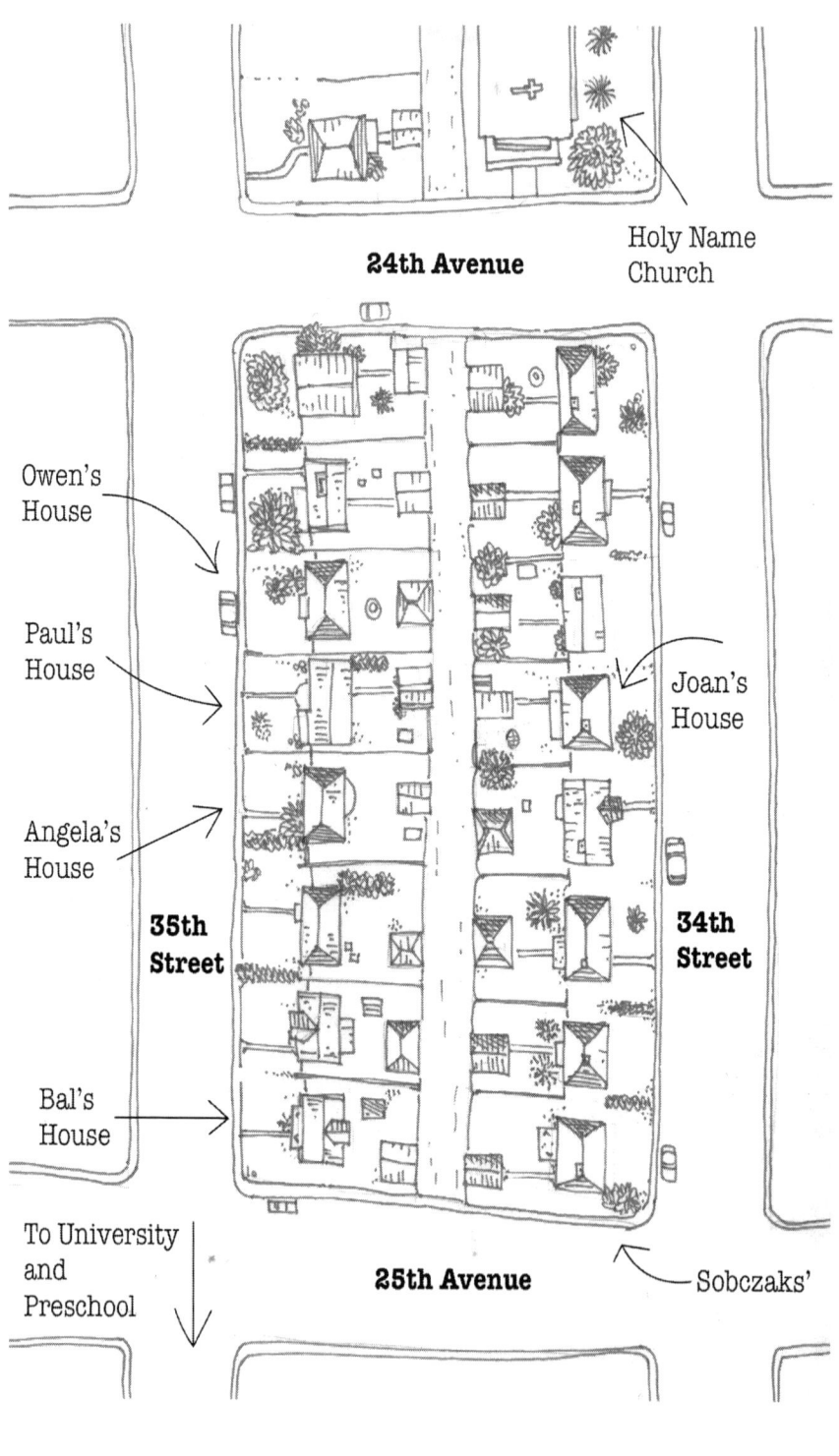

# 1.

"HOW DARE YOU COME BACK. How dare you!" Her saggy, soggy eyelids slowly closed over eyes suddenly young with indignation.

"Joan, I'm not him," he protested. "It's not possible. I just have the same name."

She dropped her paintbrush on the grass, then her gloves, and turned and walked into her house. Bawling.

As for him, he stood awkwardly at her fence where, minutes before, he'd tried to be friendly in a neighborly sort of way, leaned over the fence to begin a conversation.

❋❋❋

JOAN LIVED ACROSS THE BACK alley from his house. He'd been hunched over the ground at the base of a fencepost with a very small saw, hacking back and forth with the vigor of a concert violinist. About halfway through the post, his saw became stuck in the cut. With the skill of a craftsman, he considered his situation and selected his next tool. As he returned from the garage with a sledgehammer he had purchased at a recent garage sale, he'd noticed Joan in her back yard, dabbing a fresh coat of white paint on her wishing well. Her hair was rolled tightly in rollers, and caught and bundled in a translucent beige scarf.

"How's the well, Joan?" he had asked. He prided himself in being an accessible academic. A man of deep community, despite his learning. That he knew his neighbours in an old-fashioned sense was a badge of honour, high knowledge slumming with rustics. A Christ of knowledge, consorting with the ignorant.

"It's bad for water, Tom," she replied, "but good for luck." Interrupted, she glanced at him where he stood holding the sledgehammer like a nine-iron. "You're tearing out the old fence," she continued. "Putting in a new one?"

"Nope," Paul replied, pleased with the folksy way he had engaged her.

"Good fences make good neighbors, Tom," she replied rather sternly.

"Fences keep people apart, Joan, create public and private space. I want the fences out of my thoughts, so I'm taking it out of my yard."

It was a simple way to explain a very complex theory. He could name names—post-colonial theorists, lofty Marxian understandings that implied the general evil of fences, and, yes, this very fence, a scaffold of deduction, built down from sky-borne abstractions to the very fence she had lived next to for thirty-five years.

"I don't know if I like that, Tom." It was the wrong name, and she used it too often, like she was reminding herself who she was talking to as the conversation progressed. It would have helped, however, if she'd used the correct name.

He'd known her for a year by then. In a way her mistake pleased him. To him, a name was a handle on a pot. To move the pot, one had to resort to the handle. It gave him a singular power over her because he remembered hers.

But he did remind her from time to time of his name. He knew she wouldn't remember; her mind seemed resistant to his name, somehow, like egg in a hot Teflon pan. If nothing else, she ought to know that she didn't know his name.

"Joan, my name is Paul."

"Tom Paul?"

"No, Joan. Paul Shreeve."

She looked blankly at him, and her jowls waggled loose like change purses filled with coins.

"So you're not Tom?"

"No, I'm not." She was somehow making a bigger deal of it today than before. *Good*, Paul thought, *I'm getting through.*

"You're Paul?"

"Right."

"Your last name is Shreeve?" Her pronunciation was shrill, but correct.

"That's right."

She opened her mouth as if she were about to talk two or three times, but no sound came out. Her jowls flailed wildly under her chin. The effect of this education seemed immediate and striking, like a Benny Hinn healing.

*Education is like that sometimes*, he thought, as he contemplated her condition, pleased with the effect.

However, the educative shock seemed to extend itself to unhealthy lengths. Was she choking? Was this what a stroke looked like? She didn't seem to be breathing. He began to panic because he'd never taken a first aid course. Finally, her head snapped out of the trance, and she looked at him, horrified.

"What's your last name again?" she asked, sharply.

"Shreeve."

"Are you sure that's your name?" she asked. "Paul?" Her eyes squinted at him and she squared her stance, kicking her little plastic tub of paint into the grass. He watched her step in the spilled paint. *She could use a coat or two herself, after a brisk sanding,* he thought.

He nodded. "It's definitely not Tom," he said in tempered tones. His voice carried a confident flourish that had made him worthy of his college professor title. If he'd been at a chalkboard he would have turned around, written the correction on the board and circled it for emphasis. Or, a specially selected PowerPoint animation might make the point clear. He imagined his name gliding in from off screen, bouncing twice and settling into the screen's center in a startling 72-point font, timed with an authoritative entrance sound.

"How do you spell it?"

"Like it sounds." A pinch of condescension.

"P-A-U-L?" She spelled it and examined him letter by letter.

"Yes." A hint of outrage. Was she humiliating him by dragging him through the spelling of his own name? Of course. He crossed his arms, and strengthened his stance.

"S-H-R-E-E-V-E?"

Oh God, the last name, too. The pause between each letter made the spelling seem all the more childish. And if there was one thing this English professor knew for certain, it was that he was not a child. His grown-up ego swelled and blocked his senses. He couldn't perceive the terror in her eyes as every letter slipped like a combination into its inevitable place. She noticed the overturned paint tub.

"Damn it." She cursed the paint, moving the toe of her sneaker out of the white pool. "That's very strange, very strange." Her face soured as she stepped back and away from the wishing well, crossing her arms. "You're a ghost."

"How so?" he asked, knowing that her thesis was unlikely.

She took another step back. "There was a man with your name who lived in your house."

"And his name is spelled the same way?"

"Yes, it was."

"I should have bought a lottery ticket when I moved in." It was a variation of the classic. Even in a tough class, most of the less clever students would giggle at least.

She heaved forward, bending in half. Her eyes widened and her mouth broke open, as if she might vomit. He changed his stance to avoid having to clean his shoes. She covered her mouth with her fingers and swallowed carefully several times. Once she had achieved a tentative stability, she spoke.

"He killed himself."

"Oh," he replied. "How strange." It was his turn to be silent. He felt something hovering in his nostrils. He rested a bent index finger under his nose. "But perhaps you didn't know—I have my PhD. I'm a doctor. So my name's different. I'm Doctor Paul Shreeve, officially." He ended off with a jerky laugh that smoothed with a rising confidence as it went along. Education always makes a difference.

"Oh, my God," she squeaked in dread, and slapped her hand over her mouth. "So was he."

"It's spelled the same way?"

She paused to think. Sometimes spelling matters. "It's identical," she said in a hushed tone.

He could feel a sneeze coming on. It was a big one.

"My husband and I knew him quite well. He really was a lovely man. He was friends with everyone. He whistled too. God, how he whistled."

The sneeze blew him to pieces, but she did not bless him. Instead, she continued, plying the tissue of memory. Her rib cage heaved up and jerked inwards, creating an odd squeak in her throat.

Her eyes reddened, and a tear fattened on the corner of her left eye. It launched from the corner of her eye and skidded down the side of her nose. Another one plumped itself, waiting its turn to fall. Fat tears on a skinny woman. Irony. Actually, more of a contrasting juxtaposition, which hinted at irony, that a skinny woman might feel a fat pain. (Even under pressure, he couldn't stop analyzing everything. This, to him, was the Cartesian foundation of his existence. He analyzed; therefore, he existed. It worked the other way, too: he existed: therefore, he analyzed).

"His wife was sunning herself in the back yard. She was never much of a gardener. And she started looking for her husband. She called into the house. I can still remember the tones of her calling him. She sang like a doorbell. She came over to our yard in her big hat and sunglasses. Ed was in the garage. She thought he was at our house. Then she headed up the alley, looking in other neighbours' yards to try to find him. She came back a few minutes later, and she was already crying and quite frightened. 'I can't find him. I can't find him,' she kept saying. So I walked with her to her house and went inside. I remember the radio playing and bass tones of the announcer's words. She searched the rooms upstairs. He wasn't there. I sat her down in the chair. She was a mess. Then, I went downstairs. I went down the steps into the rec room. He wasn't there, but it smelled like poop in a tin can. I went to the room with the window facing the Yearwoods, and there he was. He'd hung himself. He'd taken sleeping pills. He'd soiled himself, and he'd cut one of his wrists, too, and the room was covered in blood. Big black drops grew on the tips of his fingers and balled slowly to the floor. Oh God...." She was crying now, weeping. "I can't get over it. I can't...the blood and the shit."

"Ah. That's...ah. Oh." The fluids that transported words to the tip of his tongue where he could spit them forward dried up, as if his mouth was cotton-stuffed.

She slowed down to a gentle, staccato sobbing. "Nothing was the same." And then with a sudden anger. "Nothing!" She looked at him with menace. "How dare you come back. How dare you!"

His university wit, sharpened by years of accumulated banter and classroom repartee, inadequately prepared him for this moment—which seemed hardly possible for a university professor who had a guitar in his office.

Sixteen years of post-secondary education (for which he was still paying) rose in his throat and stopped midway: no idea would step forward to furnish an explanation. He wanted to talk her out of her accusation, out of her emotion, talk her back on to the flat horizon on which good houses were built.

Where were the words? Something was gone.

"Come on, Joan," Paul begged. "This doesn't make sense."

Her eyes, fire-wild, looked at him.

"I don't believe it," he said finally.

"Don't believe it?" she said in an emotion-strangled yell. "Go downstairs and look in the goddamned wall. His ashes are in there. He was a suicide, so the church wouldn't take him." She gulped air to fuel the words and pain that deflated her. "His wife wouldn't take the remains. She was too distraught." She paused as a new look of terror and pain overtook her. "So we put him in the wall, right where he killed himself. Check it, Paul." She heaved a few more times. "Oh, my God."

Suddenly, he needed Joan's fence. Fortunately it stood only three and a half feet off the ground. He bent forward, first on straight arms; then, when strength waned, he lay on the hidden ball of his belly and pillowed his head on the width of white two-by-four capping her fence. He rested on her cool white planks, struggling to shoulder this new crush of night. He was glad Joan had maintained her fence well, over-painted it actually, with gelatinous coats of soft, cool, white paint. He heard Joan's rhythmic sobs move away from him. The sound of her back door. He turned to watch. Joan's back door swayed open, wide as an April spring. She hadn't closed it.

The lengthening silence leaned on him with its own weight. He tried to whistle to shed the darkness, but he couldn't. His lips were dry and he hadn't a spare breath. Instead he thought of his guitar, imagined both hands clasped around the neck, and clung to this thought.

# 2.

THEY WERE "OUR LADY'S" BEADS, worn by the young Polish fingers that fingered them now. His plane landed in this new country, new city, to take his first assignment as a priest at Holy Name Church, leaving a Polish enclave of the Jesuit Order of monks. The monastery had been his second refuge from all, from everything. He was sad to leave it behind. He felt ill equipped. He spoke excellent English, and yet he would be, within days, offering mass to native English speakers in their tongue.

His superior had laughed when he reported his trepidation. "Say mass in Polish instead," he joked. "The body and blood will carry more mystery, which is the substance of all holiness." Mystery, maybe. But Father Joachim's hero was David Hilbert of Hilbert space fame, and so he was biologically arrayed against *Ignoramus et ignorabimus*: We do not know, we shall not know. The credo of the young priest's mathematical mind and training was instead, "We must know, we will know," the very words (in German) chipped into the headstone of David Hilbert's grave.

Joachim, in his bosom, nursed a secret desire to lay open the mysteries of God, a sense that some penetration was possible. His mind hounded the holy mysteries, chased them back into the shrouds of shadow and fog. Mystery transformed by science into a holy quest of sorts, like a holy grail. His mind would not submit to a lack of understanding and was, in fact, the altar on which the wafer and wine was most often tendered.

He longed to hear the Pope speak long and loudly *ex cathedra*, and wondered what a voice uttering words *ex cathedra* would sound like. Perhaps it sounded musical. Perhaps one only heard equations. The vocal tone must be sonically deeper, at least. Truth, when uttered in its purest form, must mark the voice somehow. Could it transcend language, too? Perhaps mass offered *ex cathedra* would mean each would understand in his or her own language.

His finger worked through the beads, though his mind was far from his Hail Marys. He caught his fingers praying without his mind, and stopped them. Could fingers pray without the mind? He was taught that they couldn't. But fingers seemed more faithful than any part of the mind he had uncovered. He cupped the swinging cross in the palm of his hand. It seemed odd that he clung to the cross which, on these beads, seemed so unfixed. Wouldn't he be wiser to cling to something buried in the ground? How could beads be prayer? Beads were perhaps the lumps of existence threaded to God on a steady string, between knots.

# 3.

In the back yard, over a bucket of water and soil, toiled what appeared to be a baby Buddha. Rolls and jowls made his little body seem aged, perhaps even wise. His focus followed a shovel full of clay that he had found in an abandoned posthole and dumped into a bucket of clear water taken from the garden hose. This little god studied the clay as it melted into the water. It seemed to him a contest, which the clay had obviously lost. He stuck the shovel into the water and stirred the clay into brown clouds, which made him grin: it was the water's turn to lose. And this was the little god's joy, to preside over contests, to muck in others' affairs.

He turned from his work, and as he scanned the yard, he noticed his dad lying prostrate on the neighbour's fence, visible between two blooming lilac bushes.

"Daddy," he called. The prostrate man lifted his head, which was facing the opposite way, turned it toward him and set it down again, gingerly, on the top of the fence. "You hurt?"

"Sort of," said Dad quietly. He spoke softly so as not to arouse the ax blade of a headache resting on the side of his head.

"You need help?"

Dad was silent as he surveyed the back yard and sized up his son.

"Are you feeling strong, Lou?" The child's name was Steve, actually, but somehow, Lou stuck better.

"I'm strong, Dad."

"Why don't you bring your wagon over here, Sonny. Park it next to Daddy."

"OK, Daddy," said the boy. He put his bucket of brown clouds into the red Radio Flyer, next to carefully piled dandelions, or wishes, as he called them. He sorted the wishes into two piles. The yellow kind could be wished by flicking the heads off. And the white-headed weeds could be wished by blowing the seedy dander into the wind.

"Bring it over right beside Daddy, please, Sonny. Daddy wants a ride."

Lou, inflated with a sense of responsibility, promptly responded. The undertone of urgency in his dad's voice meant his dad wasn't patronizing him, as he normally did. And this real task brought him a real sense of meaning. He brought the wagon into the alley and parked it in the middle, as carefully as if it were a car.

"No, Lou. Can you park it right under me? Right next to the fence I'm on. Can you make the side of your wagon touch the fence? I bet you can."

Lou, in a mood most earnest, re-parked the wagon right underneath his dad, so the side of the wagon side touched the fence.

"Good boy. You are an excellent boy."

Paul rolled off the top of the fence and fell into the wagon, slamming his head on the wagon's handle, which he had forgotten to instruct his son to put into the down position, crushing the dandelions, both piles, with his rather large ass, knocking the brown cloudy water over so poured into the bottom of the wagon as he lay in it. His fall awakened and angered his headache. He could hardly talk.

"Dad," Lou screamed. "You broke my wishes and chocolate milk." He began to cry.

"I'm sorry, Sonny. Daddy didn't mean to. Daddy's really sorry."

"Get off my wishes, Daddy!" Lou commanded, and began to wail and thunder in his big rubber boots.

"Daddy can't right now. Daddy's sort of sick. And Daddy needs a ride."

"I'm going to tell Mommy," Lou said, when he realized that justice was not to be won through argumentation. "Mommy!" Lou shrieked and repeated as he stormed into the house.

"Sonny? Lou? Lou! Help me, please." But his words did not stop the boy. Again he resorted to silence to conserve his strength. But Mom did not respond to Lou the way she might have. Instead, the two remained in the house for an incalculably long time.

He felt the water slowly soak its way through the seat of his pants and spread slowly up the back of his shirt. A goose egg slowly matured on the back of his head, which he hadn't the strength to nurse, so he lay there, in dwindling comfort, holding, in his thoughts, to the neck of his guitar.

How long he lay there, he couldn't tell. The thought of his guitar seemed to hold him firm, somehow. It must have been noon, finally, when the pre-recorded electric carillon belled the arrival of Saturday noon.

※※※

THERE WAS A CATHOLIC CHURCH up the street, a cinderblock building with a cinderblock steeple, and in that steeple was a loudspeaker which had cost the diocese a handsome 500 dollars when it was installed in 1957. The speaker was attached to an electric carillon that did not require the services of a bell ringer, which was considered a modern arrangement. The speaker was, unfortunately, installed facing the prevailing westerly winds, and filled with all the precipitation the west wind carried. The installer had thought he would point the speaker heavenward so as to perhaps catch God's attention with some of the louder peals, perhaps impress him with the electronic carillon, which to be fair, sported a 12-bell count, with 123 different ring tones imitating famous bells around the world, and a library of 4,500 various peals and free, downloadable changes. However, the speaker's upward mien meant that the speaker also functioned, in some ways, like a cup, catching and holding moisture, God's precipitous reply. The bottom of the speaker, which used to resonate clearly, had succumbed to rust and was, though the Father and his congregation did not know, mostly eaten away. No one had bothered to check the speaker since it carried a lifetime warranty, and the deacons reviewed the file once a year, and finding the lifetime warranty card, assumed the speaker was well. For, they imagined, no sensible company would warranty a speaker that would rust. However, those who listened and contemplated the speaker's tone, as Paul was doing at this moment, noted that the speaker sounded tinny, and thin, like someone had installed a fast-food drive-through speaker to host the bell's sound. A fitting way to announce lunch, thought Paul.

※※※

SOME LONG TIME PASSED. THE back door of the house opened, and out came little Lou. He looked around the yard for a moment, confused, and then remembered what had happened. He came slowly out to the alley where his dad lay.

"Hi, Son," Paul said with a bright, brassy tone, hoping to polish over the distress he caused in the last interaction.

"Hi, Daddy," Lou replied, a little solemn still. "You sit on my wishes."

"Say, I've got an idea. Would you like to make some money?"

"Um. Okay, Dad."

"I'll give you a dollar if you pull me into the back yard."

"OK." Little Lou went around to the front of the wagon, and pulled hard on the handle. But the 85-pound 4 ½-year-old was no match against the potential energy required to pull the wagon with a 200-pound man draped and inert in the wagon's bed.

"Lou, could you ask your Mom to come and help me? Could you tell her I said pretty please?"

"Can I have a dollar?"

"Yes, of course. If you get Mommy out here, you can have a dollar."

Paul began to panic as he lay there. He and Bonnie hadn't been on speaking terms for a while. His formidable intellect was interfering with their relationship again.

# 4.

JOACHIM, THE NEW PRIEST OF Holy Name Church, circled his new office, stopping to adjust the level of a picture he had been considering from his desk. He nudged up the left corner with his right hand. The picture had prevented him from processing some parish paperwork. Level was proper. Level was right. Level was axiomatic. The system of straightnesses in his office, connected things that hung on the walls, the shelves, the walls themselves, work. His judgments, he worked and reworked between these parallelisms and perpendicularities, and with one off, the whole system collapsed. The system corrected, he returned to his desk, glanced one more time at his correction, and returned to his paperwork.

If he hadn't become a priest, he would have been an actuary. His love of applied calculation and machination nearly swayed him to the dark side. But as it was, much of his love he had applied to theology. For this reason, he loved to watch American Christian television broadcasts. Jerry Falwell. Benny Hinn. Jack Van Imp. Rick Joyner. So many. He loved them all—not for their content, but their form. These men's theology was a network of cause-effect relationships, equivocations that enabled them to do theological/ontological calculations on any subject, beams of thought that they could store in his eye for any occasion that required explanation. Most of them were available on YouTube. Done with the paperwork, he rewarded himself with a short Rick Joyner video.

GIVEN HURRICANE KATRINA, WHERE:

*Homosexuality = sin*
*Mardi Gras = sin*
*God = prosperity*
*Prosperity = money*
*Sin = God's judgment*
*Judgment = not prosperity, or damage to prosperity; and,*
*New Orleans = Homosexuality & Mardi Gras*

THEN:

*New Orleans is the sin capital of the US, and, therefore, deserving of God's judgment and a worthy target of a hurricane.*

No need to hoot with wonder at God's antics on that one, said Joyner. It's a fairly simple computation. Despite the faulty conclusion, Joachim admired the math.

Though Joachim was repulsed by some of the man's ideas, the calculative medium caught him by the heart. He wasn't so sure that all the mysteries were so mysterious. Many seemed fairly plain. The Trinity. Like an egg, or like the number one divided into three equal parts. Sure a little infinity here and there blurred the idea, but the general principle seemed pretty clear.

He refused to make himself wonder. It either happened or it did not. Truly mysterious things ought to solicit wonder automatically from the individual, he reasoned. It wasn't like a spice that could be added in to flavor the meal. He could not conjure wonder. As a Jesuit. As a mathematician. As a man.

Joachim walked from his office into the sanctuary with the chalice and matching plate for the bread. He walked out before the sanctuary and genuflected before striding to the ambry to remove a chalice, matching paten, cruets, and purificator. He straightened and smoothed the clean altar cloth until its edge followed perfectly the altar's wooden edge, and then placed the chalice and paten precisely two thirds from the left end of the altar. Down the stage stairs, he spun at the bottom and genuflected again. Then he stepped back to survey the entire arrangement.

His gaze circled over the detail and came to rest on the cross. The cross. The center of it all. He took a slow seat in a pew as his mind machinated. The American Christians, he thought, their cross holds no Christ. Christ does not interfere with the cross's trigonometry. Their theology held no mystery, nothing unknown, and he had visited their churches and heard them reveal the secret logic behind some of the least logical biblical moments. Their cross promoted a bare two-dimensional angularity which was in their theology, too.

American Christians must show up in church to check the cross, to make sure Christ is gone. The absent Christ seemed to fuel much of what their church was about. Much of their theology depended on God's gaping absence and the cross's two-dimensional simplicity.

Completely different, the Catholic cross. He studied this giant crucifix before him. The nails, he noted, seemed to hold Christ to the right angles of the cross. The angularity implied by the wood was a contrast to the Christ, who seemed perhaps fighting the angularity, but somehow helpless. It's true that anyone can crucify Christ if he wants to, he thought. Though perhaps Christ rose, a man may nail him there again, and keep him there if he likes, nailed onto straight, wooden thoughts.

Christ nailed to the Cartesian plane. Christ in two dimensions. Christ nailed to the nexus of the x and y axes. Hands nailed to the dependent axis. Feet to the independent. Maybe the hint was the difference between the two crosses. Maybe the American cross was the empty graph, and the Catholic cross was a sketch of a celestial formula, some explanation of a celestial turning. He paused and frowned. He wished he had his pad of graphing paper, his pencil, and a long silence at this precise moment.

"Father?" Startled from his reverie, Joachim turned to the originator of the sound. Mrs. Beata Sobczak, diocese secretary. "You have a call on line two." Beata, like Joachim, mediated the sacred and practical worlds. However, it was her job to side with the practical, which is why she was the secretary.

"I'm coming," Joachim replied.

American Christians would probably feel safer with a Catholic cross. Bloody safe to have him nailed there, he mused. Like a vicious dog chained to a pole. Some parishioners like to come and check to make sure he's still nailed there every week, ready to shred all evidence and deny all accusations if they should come in and find him gone. Truly, the American cross and the Catholic one were two sinner's crosses. And, somehow, between the two, Christ had been killed.

"Father?" Beata repeated, patiently.

The young priest rose from the pew to follow her back to the church office.

# 5.

THE PRICK OF THEIR FIGHT centred on his latest research. She had gone out with their son to a birthday party one day, and when they returned all the interior doors had been removed from the house. Paul had unhinged them all and dragged them out to the back yard.

The missing doors were connected to a conviction that he had hoped to preach with some kind of authenticity to his classes as he discussed the theories of community and (dis)integration. In fact, a paper he was currently working on, <u>Public and Private Interiors: a Marxist Perspective on Doors and Interiority</u>, had been accepted at the 102$^{nd}$ Karl Marx bi-annual conference, beachfront in Costa Rica. He'd already received a promising sign from a journal that had remarked on the originality of his ideas. So in a quest for authenticity he had removed all the interior doors and had hoped to burn them before his wife came home.

However, the lighting of fires was one of Paul's poorest skills. Though the fire-pit in their back yard had the room to take a stack of doors, he had only managed to burn oodles of newspaper as he attempted to catch his bedroom door on fire. In fact, he had blackened most of one side of the door, leaving it structurally sound but horribly scarred. To the rest of the doors, he took an ax, which he was not much good at wielding either, and with the ax he marked the doors enough that he was certain they could not be used again as doors.

When Bonnie had returned home, she was outraged. Paul had tried to soothe her by pointing out the subtle allusions he had used to foreshadow his actions. He had counted on her ability to properly read their conversations. The accusation of her lack of acuity had severed marital relations for some weeks now. But he had known she was a strong woman when he married, for she had hyphenated her last name, and she came from a family of hyphenating feminists. Officially, she was Dr. Bonnie Birtwistle-Honigsblum-Shreeve, her husband's appendage added to the train of her pedigree. Perhaps if his son was able to convince her of Daddy's indisposition, she might help. However, he was doubtful. It had been several weeks, now, and resolution still seemed impossible. The scarred doors were neatly stacked against the garage where they had weathered several weeks of violent weather.

When she came into the back yard, grim and spiteful, she grimaced when she saw him.

"Get out of Lou's wagon," she ordered.

"I can't. Something's wrong. I can't move."

"Sounds like another mid-life moment to me. Get out of the wagon."

"I can't."

"You will."

"I can't."

She walked over to the wagon, pulled the handle perpendicular with the side, and tipped the wagon towards Joan's fence. Paul rolled toward Joan's fence and bumped on the ground.

"Oh, God," Bonnie said, rolling her eyes.

"See all my wishes?" Little Lou said, happily, pointing to his father's backside. Besides being soaked in brown, muddy water, his ass had several crushed wishes stuck to it. "He broke them. And my chocolate milk."

"Daddy's fat ruined them, didn't it? I'll help you pick some more." The two of them left for the yard, leaving Paul lying in the gravel, facing Joan's fence.

※ ※ ※

IT WAS EASY TO SEE why he had married Bonnie. This steam-headed man's only romance had been with ideas. And he refused to allow anything to interfere with his thoughts, especially baser emotions like love and lust. Communism, he noted, had problems understanding love. He'd also read a very well written paper on the psychological problem of love, from a Marxian perspective. Love, he learned, was a metonymy, where one is intellectually blinded and allows a portion of the other to represent the whole. So a woman's breasts or sweet liquid voice, say, come to stand in for the whole woman. Love was merely a trope-induced blindness.

Hence, he married a woman whose faults were easy to see, so as to avoid love entirely. He married a woman whose looks would not cause him to lose his mind, or his perspective on her. Fortunately for him, he could not forget Bonnie's faults, and as the marriage progressed, they had become easier and easier to see. Paul credited his deepening insight to his own intellectual growth. Obviously, his own capacity for insight was only increasing.

Marriage in its highest form amounted to a party-sanctioned Bildungsbürgertum, an anti-imperialist, anti-hierarchical, intelligentsia (prosloyka, if you prefer), perestroikan cooperative. And Marxist sex. Though Paul was a fourth wave Marxist, so the idea of sex for procreative purposes had been left behind when someone discovered how fun it could be. If one assessed sexual performance in Marxist terms, Paul was likely a base Marxist.

❋❋❋

BONNIE WAS A FINE SCHOLAR herself, and she was currently fighting to bring marginalized voices to the attention of popular media. She, in this sense, was a feminist. She had fought for the first several years for the rights of women, and finished her doctorate on pornography's contribution to the rights of women (her doctoral thesis was so popular that three of the five copies in the Library's collection had been stolen. The other two had numbers of pages torn out).

Pornography, because it displayed feminine sexuality, actually helped to liberate women in their relationships with men, she argued. As a circumspect, fat, and rather unattractive middle-class woman, she, of course, investigated this relationship between pornography and feminine freedom academically. Her classes were quite popular in those years because she believed that classes needed to be exposed to a certain amount of pornography in order to shed the shackles of a middle-class mindset. It was her way of correcting the horrible job that students' parents had done.

She loved the shock. The quick metastatic jolt that she gave students the first day when she projected the film of a woman masturbating onto the screen. Or the lesbian porn videos she would show once in a while to keep them awake. She would grin as the students gasped at her audacity, which many academics, in those days, felt made good scholarship and pedagogy.

Lately, however, she had turned from what she had come to call her "early work" because she realized that when she put up "her ladies" on overheads, and showed videos and films of lesbian sex, she gave her mostly male student cohort boners that put them beyond the reach of logic. Plus, she'd found herself bored with the routine. So she had been turning from the study of pornography, to the study of a new field broadly termed "trauma literature."

After a sabbatical, where she surveyed most of the trauma literature, she decided to specialize on "incest autobiography." She liked it because few had made academic study of it, and because, though she had never been a victim of this crime, it gave her a cause. And an academic without a cause is no academic at all. Now she championed the cause of "her girls," a group of specially selected, socially marooned texts, which she paraded around with her. They, in fact, became her. Every attack on her person, justified or not, personal or professional, truthful or invented became an attack on "her girls." Her own scholarly stature, more of an intellectual obesity, she used to cover and brood on these victims, hoping to raise them to a point where they—and, of course, she—would be properly recognized.

The fact that she had no life of her own had almost everything to do with the fact that she desperately needed these women to win, so she could conclude her career with the loveliest of epitaphs, spoken to those who thought her cause was wasteful: "I told you so."

Furthermore, she had learned, after reading a paper on the use of trauma literatures in the classroom, that she needed to be careful with sexually explicit material with students. The author of one paper discussed how some students would "read" the material more like "tourists," and that they would be titillated by the subject and treat the whole subject like a collection of confessional letters written to a porn magazine. The authors, with a healthy amount of scholarly funding, had studied the subject and found a direct correlation between discussions of sexuality and some students' libidinous tendencies. The subject, she learned, needed to be read by those who would act more like "witnesses." Witnesses were burdened by what they read, and joined the cause, ignoring the sexuality entirely. She had the zeal and approach of an early missionary. Truly she found herself wanting to beat the culture out of these urban youth. To do this she used a collection of sad and sordid texts.

She even found herself announcing that these books were "truth-telling" and needed to be read—and as she often said, "properly believed"—to achieve their effect.

What was so shocking to her, when she first heard herself say these words, was that in her earlier years she had preached the French school of post-modern thought—where truth, in that jaunty French way, was made into quaint porcelain figurines and smashed. She had never stopped to think that the ideas she once held and her current ones did not connect. She had not embarked on a mental journey, beginning at one set of ideas and ending at the other. She had, like a bored child in a toy store, set the first set of ideas down and picked up another, more interesting set.

Fortunately, she was never one to let her past understandings interfere with her current ones, which allowed her to keep up with the academic pack, and, to tell the truth, remain a few lengths in front. She felt no guilt about this either, because this *is* what knowing had come to mean in her times. It was publish or perish. Integrity of idea, proportion of thought, wisdom, the intellectual journey was so beside the point as to be laughable. Journeys were not in fashion, only destinations. To exist was to publish, regardless of the kind or quality of thought.

✽✽✽

SOMETIME IN THE EVENING, AFTER a good snooze against the fence, Paul awoke, one cheek dimpled with the texture of gravel and dappled with dirt. He crawled back to the house, literally on all fours, and into the house, his trek garnished liberally with porcine grunts born of effort and pain. Up the short flight of three stairs, through the kitchen and into the bedroom. After a long struggle, full of pain and humiliation, he flopped on to the white linens amongst dried scabs of mud and plant.

"The prodigal pig has come home," remarked his wife dryly from the living room. She was reading and scribbling marginalia in a book titled *I Couldn't Cry When Daddy Died* in the living room. Paul didn't reply. "I get the bed tonight. Besides, you're too dirty to get close to it. The sheets are clean." The silence made its reply. "Paul, you'd better not have climbed into bed."

"Sorry, honey," he said weakly.

She stormed to the bedroom and set her book down on the night table. "Get your fat ass out of my bed!" she commanded.

"I'm not well," he protested. She strode to the side of the bed, grabbed his belt on the far side of his body and attempted to roll him off the bed onto the floor. Paul spread his frame widely over the mattress to help hold his spot. More dried mud and dandelion dander flecked over the clean sheets. It worked. She heaved several times. She heaved one last time, then suddenly froze mid-heave and released his belt.

"Oh, shit," she said, and melted slowly to the floor. "Oh, God." She lay on the floor for several minutes, tears streaming quietly from her eyes. "My goddamned back. You dick. You wrecked my back," she yelled supinely.

"I didn't do anything."

"You fake. You academic fraud. You blubbered baby." Her anger melted into a stream of tears. "The goddamned doors. The goddamn doors. What about the academic world do you not understand? Ideas are not lived. If I was the kind of feminist at home that I was at work, I'd have hacked you to bits and stored you in the freezer. And you, you, you're a Marxist. A bloody poor one. You. You. It's a good thing Marx did not include meal suggestions in his writings." She groaned deeply as she arranged her body to suit her spine. "Your ideas ... you're supposed to wear your ideas like a business suit. You wear them to work. You come home and take them off." She adjusted her body position again. "You really screwed up my back this time."

She, very slowly, with the help of the night table, hoisted herself and tenderly set herself on her feet. Shifted her body slightly to the right.

"Ow, Oh God." Then leaned forward and slightly to the left. "Okay. Okay. Okay. Okay," she said to herself. She picked up her book and buried her thumb in its crotch to bookmark the page, then used the edge of the bed like a crutch to hold herself erect, edging towards the bedroom door. As she passed by Paul's midsection, with a great effort she turned her body and brought the spine of her book into his groin with as much force as she could muster.

"Uuunungh." He immediately balled like a hedgehog.

She straightened up a little. "It's called a mid-life crisis, Paul," she bellowed, back pain shortening her breath. "You're an average man, having a typical crisis, but you're screwing it up big time with all your stupid, impotent ideas. Don't mix your penis and your brain, or you'll end up like Freud. If you're going to have a proper midlife crisis, drop your brain and think with your dick. For God's sake, find a college coed, sleep with her, and get it over with. I can't take much more of this." She tested her back's strength, standing tentatively, carefully from the edge of the bed and, finding an angle that afforded some comfort, shuffled out of the room.

# 6.

"Hello," squeaked Beata, as if her vocal cords need oil. As happens with many old women, Beata's midsection has expanded and her torso and legs had shortened, so that her hinder portions now comprised a full two-thirds of her body. Her ass surrounded her like a shelf, as if she were stuck in the middle of a small, mobile kiosk. On top of this substantial mid-section was stuck a set of shoulders and a head. On top of the head a brillo pad of short, wiry white hair. Underneath this midsection, a short but functional set of legs.

In the world of words, emphasis is always used symbolically. Beata's ass was, if one assumes she is authored, some kind of symbol. Perhaps a trope. Probably hyperbole. She was cause for analytic contemplation.

Beata had, unfortunately, marked her husband, Michael, as a "catch" fifty-some years before. She married a man she had come to hate for his resounding rejection of life. Michael did not make a lot of money, and she came from poverty, and so pennies she pinched. She hoarded, holding to things the way she wished her husband held her. And with things she didn't want, she was generous. A generous, open-handed hoarder.

After a candlelight mass at Christmas, she took 500 candle butts from the garbage of the church, shocked that someone would throw them away. She had several plastic shopping bags full of wick and wax, and since Paul and Bonnie were neighbours, she dropped off a couple of bags for them, thrilled with herself that she could be so philanthropic with her find. Or, perhaps, thrilled that she could give something that had cost her so little.

Her house warehoused her collections. And she collected collections, so her house brimmed with curiosities. Two weeks earlier, after Lou had played with her granddaughter for the morning and Paul dropped by to pick Lou up, she forced Paul to her basement to view her old calendar collection. Probably thousands of old discarded calendars. "They've always got the best pictures," she said. She passed him a couple of them to look at.

"These are attention-grabbing," he said, as he thumbed through cute kitten pictures from 1987. "It's true they have big pictures, isn't it," he commented, hoping his neutrality wouldn't be taken for insult. Stacked around her were thousands of calendars piled about her basement, pperhaps the biggest stash of discarded time Paul had ever seen. Once clocks and watches were done with their days, they sent them to Beata. She stored those used minutes. Stacks of tabled days, old and empty, marked now only by a number and a corresponding picture. She ended their visit in her big-hearted way: "You want some?"

Paul was walking the Buddha home from preschool this day, after an exhausting day of teaching, past Beata's corner house. She was in the front, hectoring weeds and coddling flowers.

"Oh, Paul," she squawked in a rusty yell. "I've got a treat for your boy." She put down her spade and shuffled around the side of her house, vanished inside, returning with a cardboard milk carton from which she proceeded to cut the bottom away from the top. She placed the top carefully on her front step, as though she'd save it too. She took the bottom over to her garden and, one at a time, scooped something out of the soil. She waddled over to the pair where they stood at her sidewalk curb, holding the milk carton bottom in her right hand, a garden trowel in the other. "There you go, Steve," she said in a satisfied, giving tone. Steve eagerly received the bottom from her and looked inside.

"What is this?" he asked.

"It's a slug, dear," Beata replied.

The lad was dazzled. And why not? Slugs are remarkable creatures.

Old Man Sobczak strode up the block to his home like a man with a purpose, getting back from a somewhere. An assertion of direction and placeness merely through his stride. Beata noticed him and as he approached. "Michael," she called, pronouncing it with softer Polish sounds. "I met the new priest at the church today." He looked unimpressed. "He's Polish."

"Who isn't," Michael replied.

"He comes from the same town you do."

"Hummmph," Michael grunted. "What is his last name?"

"His last name is Trytchania."

"Hmmph," grumped the old man.

She pointed to a house on the same block but opposite corner. "He moved in there." Beata turned back to Paul and the boy, but kept her eyes on her husband. Her eyes registered a confusion, maybe.

Paul reminded Lou to say thank you. Lou muttered the word absently, fixing his stare at the slime in the milk carton bottom. Paul and Lou headed home with their "treat."

"What do slugs eat, Dad?" Lou asked.

"Plants. They eat plants."

"What do they do after they eat?" he asked. "Do they play?"

"In a way, I suppose," Paul responded. "They're considered a pest."

"What's a pess?"

"PesT," Paul enunciated, steering his son from a ditch onto the road of knowledge. "It's a creature that bothers humans. Or one whose ends run counter to human endeavor."

"Pess," Lou repeated thoughtfully.

"PesT. PesT. He eats plants... er... plants that humans like, you know, flowers and vegetables and things. People don't like them."

"Do people hurt them?"

"Usually," Paul replied. "If you put salt on a slug, he does something really remarkable."

"Does salt hurt a lug?"

"SSSSlug. Yes, it does, son," Paul said in an encouraging tone. "It kills them, but in a most interesting way."

The buddha's jowls frowned as he studied the gleaming trail following the slug.

"Do you want to hurt mine?"

Paul sensed danger he was about to step into. But a Marxist, in his mind, always valued honesty above consequence. "Yes, I would." And the Buddha frowned.

"Lugs are my friend." The Buddha pouted, and his clouded face threatened rain.

"SSSSlug. Okay. Okay." Paul protested. "Maybe we can treat this one like our special guest. What do you think?"

The boy nodded.

When the pair got home, Lou headed straight to the garden and dropped the slug among the early shoots of his mother's vegetables.

"Don't you want to keep it in the carton on your dresser like a pet?" He knew his son would kill the creature within hours if he chose to care for it.

Buddha shook his body back and forth to indicate his disagreement.

Paul, being out of his mind, couldn't fund much compassion for slugs. He fought the urge to salt this one into the void. But he wasn't sure he could murder discreetly, so he allowed it to live as his guest until he could undo its living without being noticed. Instead he watched the slug ooze towards a rhubarb leaf, as if to remember the direction it set out in, so he could trace the critter's slime trail later.

# 7.

He was still sour as he left the house, mounted his cycle and crossed the front lawn. He waved to his son who stood in the window eating a donut. The little Buddha did not return his wave. Paul's happy wave ended with a terse frown. He pedaled slowly up on an old army-green bicycle, one that seemed to him much like a Chinese communist would ride. He pursed his lips and looked at the road through the metal netting of his basket as he considered his son's lack of emotional response to his person. The screech of tires dispersed his crowd of thoughts.

"Hey, asshole." A motorist, in a beautiful new silver Volvo wagon, rolled down his window. A white 50-something hipster. Thick glistening strands of hair combed back above his forehead and behind his ears, a man with the personality of cologne. "You got a stop sign, fag. So stop!" Paul had already crossed the street, his face prickling with embarrassment.

He began a slow climb past his son's school. He struck luck and crossed one of the main traffic arteries without a car in sight in either direction. He toodled down a broad street that finished in a T-intersection, then hopped the curb and crossed several fields, through a community hall parking lot, and into the university's parking lot. The meandering Marxist leaned his bike against a tree that he had come to feel was his own, and walked towards the brutalist university complex.

The exposed concrete that marked the brutalist buildings was itself a philosophy, one that was often associated with utopic socialism. There was a certain "honesty" portrayed in the raw construction, shuttering, and open utility work. Sort of an "inside-out" approach to making buildings. Fortunately, it also happened to be cheap. The socialist bent of the buildings had been long forgotten. Yet socialism thrived still.

The university's brutalist architecture had been scarred as the institution's view of itself changed. The original campus had been designed as a "university without walls," a time when educators felt that physical walls impeded understanding of the connection of all things to one another. So it was originally designed around an open concept. The campus also included a lovely system of water and waterfalls, which flowed through the building to physically hint at the metaphor of the fountain of knowledge.

Waterfalls and pools and jets all emptied out into a pond behind the building. The sound of water on the day the minister of education opened the building was something that many who attended thought to be a lovely background.

Just after the school was opened, professors instantly discovered that the thoughtful expressions of knowledge and the flow of water, when they met exposed concrete, aggregated into something that some would accurately call "noise." And two years later, once the flavours of education had changed entirely, administrators began to brick in the spaces and put in folding accordion walls, baffles to absorb and dampen sounds. They turned the flow of water off and once the water flows had been properly dried, built floors and walls over the cement waterways. The metaphor of water proved far too costly to the daily exchange of learning that needed to take place.

Now that in these late times knowledge, in the light of the internet and other technologies, had undergone a complete devaluing, administrators had realized that the walls they had added made classrooms too small to make money. So they were now beginning the process of smashing them out to make spaces that would make more money, dilute any power that was left in learning, to thin it out to harvest as much money per byte of information offered.

Retention rates were now actively tracked, and the university slowly removed barriers that made students drop out. So things like low marks became frowned upon. Anything, really, that injured the now-hallowed idea of "student success." Nothing, it was felt, should interfere with a student from achieving educational goals. Course names were jazzed up. Dull explanations of subject matter were turned by writers into scintillating, culturally relevant ideas, to draw students into taking those courses. No hindrance could not be overcome —especially not students' lack of ability and interest in a particular subject matter. After all, marks were simply a bourgeois symbol of capitalist intention. One more suspect quality inspection on the assembly line of knowledge.

It was part of the slow transformation of education from a system of cultural progress to the painted prostitute it continued to choose to become. It was at his tree, near this garble of exposed concrete and learning that our self-made communist parked his bike.

In his office, in an uncharacteristic moment, Paul closed the door, and from an office drawer removed a bottle of scotch which he uncapped and from the bottle's mouth took two healthy swigs, to calm his jitters and lubricate his words.

He stopped in at the bathroom to check his visage. One strand of hair stood proudly out of place. "Ah ha," he mumbled. He pushed his hands together into a praying position and placed them under the sink tap. The automatic sensor refused to acknowledge his presence. He waved his hands around under the tap. He unclasped his hands, and pushed the sensor cover. Nothing. He cursed as he switched to the other sink. He repeated his ritual. And the faucet would not bring forth its issue. "Farging Marmuck." He slammed his fist on the top of the faucet, and the water reluctantly poured into the sink. Then back to his office. He closed the door quickly. Took another snog from his office toot-bottle, opened the door and began to prepare for class. Class preparation consisted of him reviewing his notes in his office, door open, until class time. Today's lecture: why grammar should be avoided.

# 8.

"GRAMMAR IS A BOURGEOIS TOOL of oppression," he began. The class, filled with students in their late teens, in some cases early twenty's, begrudgingly opened their notebooks. Most, however, stayed on their phones—texting, watching media, and in one case at least, recording the lecture, defying university policy. The student recording was actually attending class on behalf of a group of five students who all took turns coming to class, recording the lecture, to allow the other four students the luxury of not having to attend to the education they so desperately wanted to be done with.

"When I tell you," Paul intoned with confidence and power, his sense of self-importance inflated with his audience, which he so often failed to see had been forced to attend to his words because the system he participated in made it necessary.

Who controls language?" Dr. Shreeve asked. "Is it you?" He pointed to a young woman who seemed to be paying particular attention, right at the front, right of the 40-seat lecture hall.

When he looked out on his audience, the facial deportments seemed to him to indicate that the audience was receptive, open, listening. Which, to some degree, they were. For most in the room, the name of the game was to learn enough of his terminology and approach that they could spoon back to him a good dose of his own mush. His own words parroted back to him, he would reward them with marks because it seemed to him that they had learned something. In reality, the students had learned to resist any real learning, any real change, but in the process had learned to posture and pose with looks of insight and understanding, like circus bears who dance when the organ music begins, forgoing their authenticity and ferocity until the circus ended.

In some ways, giving up grammar wasn't a big wish to grant. Those who studied the classroom examined change from beginning of class to the end of the semester noted that according to research, the classroom did nothing to help student grammar or writing performance.

Paul's lackadaisical attitude, in a philosophical mask, suggested that in fact the English language had somehow become simpler, which it hadn't. Linguistic intricacy, like muscle in a moldering body, had lengthened and loosened and only held things together in the textbook medical sense, but not in any operational, day-to-day sort of way. Language, like a bad knee, was becoming something that though it still consisted of the constituents arranged in a fashion to meet the definition of a knee, language doctors everywhere advised keeping your weight off it, at least in terms of class requirements. Despite his perceptions (which may have been the result of the Dunning-Kruger effect) language had not changed as quickly or to the degree that his own perceptions about it had.

So to give up performative markers, to give up hope for change, to make the class easy, to give out more As than would be reasonable or had been historically possible, was simply to agree that change wasn't possible or likely. Given the human condition, a fair assumption.

Now the most important thing was to make students feel as though education had taken place. Hence his current lecture, which he not-so-cleverly called "The capitalistic, colonial hegemonic appropriation of the English language." This was a fancy way of explaining to students why he would give them higher marks than he should, why the institution would be complicit, and why there would be many fewer comments on their essays than there should have been. It was a lesson designed to introduce the complicity around which both students and professors quit their compulsive striving. Wokeness replaced work. And effortless candied success would be passed out to anyone who asked, as long as the ask demonstrated cultural sensitivity.

"Who am I to tell you that your dialect, your way of speaking isn't correct? Hegemony of the highest order. Hegemony and cheese. Doesn't then freedom require me to offer you linguistic freedom?"

"I want you to pull out a blank sheet of paper," he requested. "We're going to do a 7-minute freewrite on the subject of grammar. If you've been oppressed by an English teacher, or an assignment, you might use that to spark your writing." The rustle of school supplies commenced. Paul pulled his guitar from behind the podium. "Write when I begin playing and stop when the music ends." The music began.

# 9.

**D**ESPITE THE APPARENT SUCCESS OF his favorite lecture, Paul couldn't shake the idea that he was not himself. Or perhaps, that he had become a self that he believed he had never been. Or perhaps, he had been overtaken by another person by exactly the same name. Possession. Haunting. Supreme emptiness. Mathematical equivalents though different symbols, all.

As the light alcohol buzz wore away, Paul's insides felt untethered, gastric, and a-tingle. Joan's accusations undermined his confident Marxism, and he had to give the same lecture to another class in an hour, so he decided, for the first time in a long while, that he'd stoop to coddle his Marxist self with a capitalistic coffee from a chain. He wandered down the central hallway in the main building, known as "main street," to a coffee shop, where he bought a bad coffee loaded with a generous amount of cream to smother the artlessness of the beverage.

As a popular academic, he sometimes sought to retreat from people. He took the open two-chair table tucked behind a brutalist pillar.

As the heat radiated slowly through the waxed paper cup, warming his cold hands, the sensation knocked him out of his senses for a moment. He relaxed, overhearing a table of students talking.

"It actually sucked," the woman intoned with vehemence. "He is like the worst teacher ever. The only reason I took it was because my roommate gave me her notes and assignments. It was like super easy. I just had to show up and stroke his ego a little. I did get an 'A' but I lost a little of my soul to get it." She laughed emptily. "I did get into nursing though."

"You sure I'd get an A?" a male voice asked. "Sure. Just make sure you go to class. Make sure you laugh at his jokes. I said stuff like `You're the doctor.' He also likes cleavage. I showed him mine twice. These babies bumped my mark. Make sure when he brings his guitar to class, you seem to enjoy it. I'll give you my notes and stuff. The notes aren't worth much. The assignments, well, they're personal, you'll just have to change the pronouns, or declare that you're experimenting with your gender using pronouns. Actually, now that I think about it, I'd say you wanted to experiment with gender. It'll be easier and you'll seem way cooler to him."

Paul couldn't handle it any longer. He got out of his chair and rounded the brutalist post, but by the time he'd rounded the corner, whoever had been talking had dissolved into the sea of humanity coursing through the surrounding space. The woman, the probable speaker, he only caught a glimpse of—her squat body and a flash of dyed black hair and a maybe the blue of a bad tattoo sleeve.

Who was this doctor who had a guitar? It was outrageous to think that someone had the audacity to copy his pedagogy.

*It is my intellectual property*, he thought. *I own it.* The irony of this thought wafted away without examination, like a fart in an outhouse. *Though it sounds like the fool doesn't know how to use it properly.*

He reviewed his colleagues and who among them would be drawn to guitar use in class. And then, his second painful dawn in less than a week. Time for another couple shots of scotch.

"It actually sucked," the woman intoned with vehemence. "He is like the worst teacher ever. The only reason I took it was because my roommate gave me her notes and assignments. It was like super easy. I just had to show up and stroke his ego a little. I did get an 'A' but I lost a little of my soul to get it." She laughed emptily. "I did get into nursing though."

Paul found himself delighted and disgusted. Delighted to overhear such gossip. Delighted at the thought of how he would compare to such a teacher. Disgusted that the morals of education had fallen to such an estate.

"You sure I'd get an A?" a male voice asked. "Sure. Just make sure you go to class. Make sure you laugh at his jokes. I said stuff like "You're the doctor. He also likes cleavage. I showed him mine twice. These babies bumped my mark. Make sure when he brings his guitar to class, you seem to enjoy it. I'll give you my notes and stuff. The notes aren't worth much. The assignments, well, they're personal, you'll just have to change the pronouns, or declare that you're experimenting with your gender using pronouns. Actually, now that I think about it, I'd say you wanted to experiment with gender. It'll be easier and you'll seem way cooler to him."

Paul couldn't handle it any longer. He got out of his chair and rounded the brutalist post, but by the time he'd rounded the corner, whoever had been talking had dissolved into the sea of humanity coursing through the surrounding hallways. The woman, the probable speaker, he only caught a glimpse of her squat body and a flash of dyed black hair and a maybe the blue of a bad tattoo sleeve.

Who was this doctor who had a guitar? It was outrageous to think that someone had the audacity to copy his pedagogy.

It is my intellectual property, he thought. I own it. The irony of this thought wafted away without examination, like a fart in a woodplank outhouse. Though it sounds like the fool doesn't know how to use it properly.

Judging from his student evaluations and his own estimation, Dr. Paul Shreeve was the best teacher around. He was a solid even performer in the classroom. Pedagogically, he was known as a pedagogical innovator, according to some. It said so in his website bio.

Part of his success, he knew, depended on the fact that no one else knew how and what he actually taught. Or how effective he was. Certainly, he was evaluated. But the evaluation points were known and marked. So with a bit of gaming, like the students did to his courses, he did to the system which managed his employment.

He returned to his table to review his colleagues and who among them would be drawn to guitar use in class. He checked the clock. 15 minutes until his next class. Time for another couple hoots of scotch.

# 10.

Up two floors on the elevator and down a side hallway to his office.

He stopped at Veto's office. Dr. Veto Swansea was slumped, staring stone-eyed out of his office window at the parking lot below. A self-made catatonic.

"Hey, Veto," Paul said blandly.

Veto turned slowly from the window. "Oh." It took a moment for a spark of life to ignite his dull gaze. "Hi, Paul," he said slowly, with a flat tone.

It took a few seconds for Veto to shake off the rest of his comatose look, one of the effects of his overall experiment.

While his PhD was in educational leadership, Dr. Swansea had explored for the last few years the outer boundaries of tenure. His grand idea had come like a thief in the night, one June evening, in a drunken rage at a department get-together. Omni-drunk colleague, Catherine, sparked his rage with an all-too-direct confrontation: "Come on, Veto. You don't really expect me to believe you work hard. You do nothing for anyone but yourself. You're the laziest guy in our department."

"I may be lazy," Veto slurred, "but it's part of my academic approach."

"Hah, the cow is made of ham."

"I'm doing a social experiment. I'm trying to see how little work I can do before I get fired." He realized his retort had value, but it was far too bald to be useful. "I'm going to write a paper. The working title is," he paused to confer with himself, "`The Crisis of Labor and the Limits of Capitalism.'"

❋❋❋

Veto engaged in a series of social experiments to investigate the idea of labor and such. For his first experiment, he got a job a fast-food restaurant as a clerk. He wore a big blue uniform, with a baby-blue visor, and a plastic button that read, "Hello, I'm Veto, how may I help you." The entire text was covered with clear tape and on the tape were written the words "I'm in Training." He invited the department to watch his experiment; Paul was the only one to attend. Paul stepped up to the counter. Veto's salt and pepper hair stood out among the youthful teens swarming around him.

"Hello Doctor Swansea," Paul said. "I'll take a ..."

"Shut up about my academic qualifications," Veto hissed. "I told them I was a high school dropout."

"You should have been," Paul said with a grin. "Give me a hamburger."

"Would you like fries with that?" Veto sang out, revelling in the ironic authenticity with which he could speak the words.

"Supersize me," Paul replied, with equal gusto.

"You'll want caffeine with your meal, I'd assume," Veto said, knowing Paul's preferences well.

Veto went and got the food, loaded onto a tray and passed it to Paul, without charging him.

Paul glanced around, trying to determine any consequences from taking the tray.

"Put your money back in your wallet," Veto ordered. He pushed the tray close to Paul. "Take it quickly."

"This is food that offends my palate in every possible way," Paul said, taking a solidly Marxist stance on the pureed pulp of capitalism. "I should get it for free. In fact, I should be paid."

"I can't remember how to open the till, so I can't oblige you yet," Veto replied.

Veto then stood motionless behind the counter. As Paul took a seat at a table that afforded them a complete view of the experiment, another customer stepped up to the counter. Veto waited silently, looking at the customer. After half a minute had passed, the customer, a woman, began to get a little agitated.

"I'd like to order, if I may," she announced.

Veto smiled. "I would like to help you, but I can't," Veto replied.

"Listen" the woman squinted at his nametag, "Veto. Would you like to find me someone who can?"

Veto moved away from the counter, cutting through a sudden swarm of employees near the drive-through window, and stood by the French fry machine. An ardent, pimpled youngster slung a new batch of fries under the heat lamps and salted them. Veto stuck his fingers in to the heap of fresh fries and removed a handful. The teenaged boy looked shocked. Veto held one up, winked at the boy and took a bite.

"Ow, ow! Hot. Hot. Those are hot," he said, spitting out the remainder of the fry in his mouth and dropping the handful onto the floor as he clasped his mouth.

"I have to throw those fries out," said the teen. "You touched them."

"Of course, they're on the floor."

"No," the teen replied. "I mean the ones you touched in here." He pointed angrily to the freshly deep-fried fries in the fry hamper.

"I washed my hands," Veto offered.

"These aren't supposed to be touched by anyone except the customer."

"Is that policy?" Veto squinted at the boy's nametag. "Liam?"

One of the managers had noticed the spill of fries and came over. He squinted at Veto's nametag. "Ah, Veto. I think you were assigned to the counter."

"Oh, right," Veto replied. He wandered over to the counter, leaned against the ice cream dispenser, and folded his arms.

The manager followed Veto over to the ice cream machine. "Veto, you're taking orders."

Veto smiled. "Smiles are free," he replied. "Though, if I'm honest, they do cost me a little."

"Veto have you ever worked in a fast-food restaurant before?" the manager asked.

Veto shook his head.

"We require everyone to do his or her part. Everyone is a piece of a machine that delivers satisfaction to every customer."

"I understand your metaphor," Veto replied briskly. "Trite but true."

"Great." The manager waited for Veto to move. Veto unfolded his arms, and stood without leaning just in front of the ice cream machine. The manager seemed to be confused.

"Veto?"

"Can I take my break now?" Veto asked politely.

"Weren't you scheduled to start at 11:30?"

"Yes."

"That was," the manager checked the watch on his wrist, "12 minutes ago."

"Wow, time flies," Veto replied.

"You cannot take break until you've worked two and a half hours, according to company policy."

"Can I take it now and then work off the time afterward?"

"No, you may not." He pointed to his till at the counter. "You have a customer who would like you to take her order." He pointed to the annoyed-looking woman.

"Why would you assume she's a she? Seems a bit sexist," Veto chided. The woman seemed a little offended, as did the manager.

"Veto!" the manager barked. Veto smiled and nodded, turning towards the waiting woman.

"Would you like to order?" Veto asked.

"You know damn well I would," said the probable woman.

"Honestly, I didn't really think you needed any food." His hand swept across the woman's fairly substantial belly and ended up pointing toward her obese daughter's midsection. "If I could advise you to avoid eating here, I would, just for your own good. And I mean that as sincerely and wholeheartedly as I am able to do. The nutritional information will back me up here." The manager swallowed hard—his eyes, sleepy with routine, suddenly widened in fear. "Where do we keep the nutritional information? Though I hear the caloric counts are a bit low because of the way we calculate such things. So you should double the fat counts on all our listings. Did you read that article in the paper?"

"Veto, I'd like you to take your break right now," said the manager, pushing Veto aside. "I'm terribly sorry, ma'am. Can I take your order? I'll reduce the cost of your meal because of the poor service."

Veto shrugged, headed over to the French fry machine and grabbed a couple of containers of fries, then shuffled to the burger station, removed two sandwiches and headed to the back of the food production area and out the back of the building. He came around and sat in the customer area with Paul and began to eat. The manager, after he had taken several orders, came out and stood near Veto. "Veto, we don't eat out in the customer area. You compromise our retail space when you do that." The manager renewed his anger. "You must eat and relax in the employee lunchroom."

"Just a second, I'm almost finished," Veto replied as he shoved a handful of french-fries into his mouth, leaving several poking out between his glistening lips and chin, pulling them slowly inward as he chewed. Grains of salt clung to the sheen of grease, posing like stubble on Veto's face. "Okay." He looked up at the manager. "How can I help you?" he replied with a boxed-cookie sweetness.

"Please go to the lunchroom," the manger ordered.

"Sure. All you have to do is ask," Veto replied. "It is merely a matter of asking."

Veto sauntered off, the manager trailing him, and returned to some unseen place in the restaurant's bowels behind the machines. The manager approached the counter and talked to another manager, who talked to another manager. The group whispered earnestly while dishing up nervous smiles to those at the counter. A few minutes later, Veto meandered to the counter. He stood motionless by the heat lamps at the sandwich station, moving his hand in and out of the heat lamps' rays. The two managers eyed him for several minutes.

They approached him where he stood.

"Wow," he said to the two of them. "I bet you could get a tan under these lights. They're very hot."

"Veto," said the manager, "you haven't done a stitch of work since you've been here. And we need you to get going."

"Yeah, I know, well-oiled, fast-paced, team and so on."

"You're not working."

"Actually, technically I am. At this moment, I am employed by your company and I am almost one hour into my shift. I'm working."

"You're not working," repeated the manager, wincing with exasperation.

"I have no idea what you mean."

"Working means you do stuff—stuff that we ask you to do."

"No, I'm quite certain you're wrong," Veto replied, taking an academic tone. "From a legal perspective, the one that applies to this discussion, working simply means employment. The tax system is based on the idea of employment, not work. It's the only sensible platform upon which to build a sensible tax system. Employment is quantifiable. Work is not. This is one of the interesting problems of labor."

The two managers looked at one another. "This isn't working out, Veto," one of them said.

"It seems fine to me," Veto replied, as he slid the ice cream machine's dispensing arm sideways and watched some ice cream coil softly into the dripping tray. "It's sort of a miracle," he said, speaking of the ice cream.

"Veto, this isn't going to last long if you keep doing this stuff," one of the managers said, putting his hand on Veto's and pushing the lever to halt the ice cream's flow.

"What the hell are you doing? You touching my hand like that, according to law, constitutes sexual harassment."

"You're fired," said the other manager, atremble with rage. "Please turn in your uniform immediately. If you don't you will be charged a uniform fee."

"You'll be hearing from my lawyer," Veto replied in a haughty tone, as he checked his watch. "Sexual harassment is against my human rights."

"Please leave the premises immediately."

Veto stared at the chest of the manager. "Felmud, you will receive a letter from my lawyer for sexually harassing me." Veto looked at Paul. "Forty-seven minutes, Paul."

The two managers pointed to the back of the restaurant, the employees' entrance and exit. "Get out or I will call the police," one of them said. The other signalled to the two guards the restaurant employed to keep the homeless off the premises.

Veto shrugged, glanced at his watch, and ambled toward the back of the building and out the door.

"Forty-seven minutes here," he screamed at the top of his lungs. "And twenty-two years at the university."

Veto's experiment, however, was taking a larger toll on his life than he had planned. His experiment required him to renounce initiative and in doing so, he became a priest of inaction, stupefied. Fortunately, it qualified as scholarship.

***

PAUL LEFT VETO'S OFFICE, THEN stopped at his own to drop off his coat and the things he was carrying, including his cup of coffee. He sauntered down the hallway to the English Department's kitchen area. He noticed a ravaged box of donuts nearby, and chose one that had some kind of nearly bitter filling. He closed his office door. He sat in his seat, and raised his rib cage high to let out a sigh. An overpowering sense of sleep washed over him in his chair.

Among his books he felt safe. Today they felt strong and dense, sure and solid as brick. Safe he was. Safe he would be, here. Yet agitation worked him like an accordion at a polkafest. The TV only partly worked as sedative, which reminded him he needed to make an appointment to ask Vadim for a sleeping pill prescription. Here, in his fortress of thought, the wave of exhaustion caught up to him. He put his head down on his desk, chuckling to himself as he thought of how he'd loathed putting his head down on his desk in school as a child. Just as I could appreciate it, he thought, they took it away from me. Then his mind fell still as his whole body fell asleep.

He awoke later, how much later he did not know, to a small knock. He rubbed his face and fluffed his hair, stood and opened the door.

"Hello, Paul."

"Come on in, Tanya."

He worked at a liberal arts university, around young people, and young women flirted with him frequently. He knew, however, that they didn't flirt with him because of his beauty. They flirted with him because of his power—the power of their grades in his hands. A Marxist benefit of power. So they sometimes, not always, dressed down or up in an attempt to influence their grades.

Unfortunately, given the fact that things at home were tense and had been for a while, he was prone to enjoy such occasions. He knew that a good teacher disliked the sexual advances made on him or her by any of his or her pupils. But he liked it a lot. It wasn't that he went out of his way to promote those kinds of relations, but he didn't do anything to discourage these things. He merely basked in them.

"Can I come in and talk to you about my essay?" she said sweetly. The essay she clutched to her bosom like a baby.

"Sure," Paul replied weakly. She walked in and closed the door behind her. Thank god he had put a small desk between him and the students who came in. She smiled at him while she set down her things.

"You gave me a B on this paper," she said airily. "I think it's much better than that. I'm a pretty smart person, and I've never got a mark this low before."

Paul nodded but said nothing. B, he realised, was a coward's D. Despite other shortcomings, Paul knew essays. He read at least a thousand student essays a year, and another couple hundred professional essays. He knew writing, and for him it was a personal point of pride to mark essays and award each an accurate mark, even though he would hold his nose and upgrade that mark.

She shut the door gently and turned around, sporting a delicious smile. She wore a tight, low-cut white muscle-shirt and skin-tight, low-hipped blue jeans with the waistband of her thong panties showing an inch or two above waist of her pants.

"Do you have your essay with you? Sit down. We can go through it."

"Let me show it to you," she said with a wink.

She refused to take the seat he offered. Instead, she bent over from the waist, and laid the paper down on the desk between them, offering Paul a sustained and wonderful look at her breasts—which Paul had come to understand were magnificent, an eye-level, down-the-shirt-front vista. The waft of her perfume softened his resolve; long, spiraled strands of her brown hair dropped and framed her loosely cupped breasts.

For a man like Paul, this was an excellent trick in the magician's sense of the word. She was inviting him, he guessed, to either choose engaging her paper, or looking at her fine breasts: tits or text. Eros or Error. He inhaled deeply, holding his seat silently. There he basked, drinking it in. Drinking, but yet knowing it was nothing more than a trick. A wonderful, wicked trick.

But what would Marx do? Would he give in to this base desire, and forfeit an opportunity to resist one of the prime tools for the extension and promulgation of capitalism?

He thought of his most recent intellectual ideas. The door, he thought. Always the door. His salvation. His professionalism.

"Would you mind opening the door?" he said quietly to her after a few minutes of silence. "It's politically appropriate."

Her smile faded. She stood, turned and opened the door.

Yes. The door changed it all. He was right. Delight, desire, and his cold professionalism churned within him and exploded into confusion. Yet the open door encouraged his professionalism. Closed doors allowed for the reign of baser desires. Open ones championed comradery, in the Marxist sense.

"Let's review the comments I wrote," Paul said in a voice that slowly grew colder.

Several minutes later, after a detailed, one-sided explanation, she ripped her essay out of his hands. "Bye," she snarled, and strode out.

Paul leaned back in his chair, placed his hands on the back of his head, and pleated his fingers. He noticed he was panting heavily, that he felt warm. He forced his shallow breath deeper to help shed the encounter's effects.

Paul found himself finishing the bottle of scotch with his door closed. He was feeling a little tipsy, as the tendrils of another self, though now softer and more relaxed, probed for soil in which to root.

His own reaction bothered him. Global warming. His icy professionalism seemed to be melting today. The thaw of a polar cap here meant rising tides elsewhere. Maybe medical science could help.

# 11.

VADIM PLACED HIS STETHOSCOPE ON Paul's chest. "Breathe deeply." Paul inhaled slowly. "Exhale." Paul released his breath.

Vadim dropped his stethoscope and sat in his chair. "You are totally normal."

"I'm not. I'm not well."

"I mean to say that your body seems consistent with what I know of how it operates." Vadim grinned. "What caused your distress?"

Paul launched into the long story. Joan defied all the logical tentacles of his entire, and vast (as he assessed it), knowledge. If he had not experienced Joan directly, himself, he could have denied it. He needed, he felt, some kind of explanatory grid to help him cope, so he sought out the smartest man he knew: his doctor, Vadim the Russian Physician. Paul was seated on the cracked vinyl of the examination table. The doctor tore the blood pressure cuff from Paul's arm.

"So she told me I have the identical name." The last syllables of the story fell against the doctor's pancake-sized ears. "And suddenly I couldn't move. I was temporarily paralyzed." Vadim said nothing, but his lips curled in a slight smile. "And I overheard another student say my class was a joke. MY class."

"What an interesting predicament," he said simply.

"What, that's it?"

"I mean, it is an interesting ingredient in experiment of your life."

"My life is not an experiment."

He huffed a laugh. "You're an expert theorist. What is it?"

"It is a struggle," Paul said. Vadim rolled his eyes and drooped his shoulders in disgust. Paul read his body language. "What?! It is a struggle," Paul insisted.

Vadim poked Paul's stomach with his index finger. "This is a struggle?" He shook his head and poked it again. "No, it is fat. It is a job and defined benefit pension plan."

"Well, I'm not a scientist!" Paul snapped.

"Oh, but here you are quite wrong," Vadim insisted. "Life is not a theoretical existence. It is real. There is you, your inexplicable essence, and the cloud of confusion surrounding you. Marx cannot solve the enigma of you. It seems unlikely Marx ever had a suicidal neighbour of the same name. How can you borrow Marx's explanation of things? As far as I can see, you are an ongoing experiment."

"Experiment?" Paul laughed sarcastically. "If I'm a fake Marxist, there's no more to life than a good job, decent holidays, and retirement, with the hope you haven't been overly exploited along the way."

"A little exploitation never hurt anyone," Vadim said carefully. "I exploit as frequently as I can. You need to exploit at least once a week."

Paul sighed. "Are you commenting on my life here?"

"Friend, it is a prescription. I note you are distressed. I am attempting to be gentle. Do not make me cut any closer than I feel I must."

"You are not much comfort. I want a pill. Prozac?"

"You are not so much fun. And no. No pills for you."

"What about my back? It needs surgery."

Vadim snorted. "Your back is sore. It gave out for emotional reasons, not physiological ones."

"I need help. I need something. I'm starting to come undone with all of this."

"Undoneness is not a medical condition." He replied with a smile. "I'll tell you what. We'll do some tests."

"I want a prescription. Now."

"My prescription is that you exploit once this week."

Paul felt a circus of angst swing through his ribcage. "I'm going to switch doctors. You're a bloody poor one."

Vadim grinned and shrugged. "You're a low-quality patient. You bring down the value of my practice."

# 12.

SOBCZAK HAD AN INSATIABLE DESIRE to walk. Why, he did not know. He had no direction, no place he really wanted to go, just a mad desire to walk. So he put on a t-shirt and his brown polyester walking pants. He'd recently acquired several t-shirts from the Catholic Thrift Store, a block away from his home. Today's t-shirt read "And Your Point Is...." He headed out to the kitchen. His wife was already watching her copy of the *Sound of Music* again. She was a sucker for the sappy, happy ending. He made himself a cup of instant coffee, and headed out to itch his urge to walk.

Old Man Sobczak left the house through the front door, saying nothing to his wife, and she nothing to him. He stood on the front step waiting for impetus to move. A story made Old Man Sobczak old, older than he needed to be, yet curiously immature. A story stole everything except his existence. One story invited him back to nourish his homunculus. It was this story he conjured now, a battery he used to get his 70-year-old bones moving.

His brother, a Polish peasant, had fallen in love with a middle-class girl and had devoted his entire life to service her pleasures. His brother had been twenty-three and had, in pursuit of this woman, forfeited all that would have been necessary to make him sturdy.

He had worked to afford the gifts she deserved, he had leveraged his life in such a way that if he never won her hand, he would be bankrupt. His brother believed in a good God and prayed earnestly, fervently, and daily that God would, in His mercy and grace, assign him his inheritance through the bestowment of Malgorzata. All good things would come to those who wait. A life was like the grass, and what was necessary would fall upon the meadow to give that sward its sustenance. Everything was there for its success. It was not a matter of striving, but of recognition. And Malgorzata, God had surely supplied.

Though he had no money, he came from a large family, a close family, one could furnish everything he needed through barter. His family had no education, but they had a heart-driven work and play ethic. He was related to almost everyone in the village, he was related to the universe. And, hence, Piotr thought, since he had fallen in love with such a wise woman, she would surely choose his family over riches. This was, in fact, his special theory of relativity, which was Piotr's firmest belief, and in his mind was only a collection of words that he had heard once from a newspaper-reading uncle. When he had heard his uncle speak the words, the syllables somehow clicked into place and made instantaneous and complete sense of village experience. Truly, relatedness brought meaning. Family was all, and she would choose him because of it. Orbiting bodies only have meaning when they are causally related to one another. Simultaneous existence is not enough. He was related to enough important people that she would surely marry him.

When Michael found Piotr in his bedroom, the hunting rifle had only recently separated the back of his head from the front, and in that split, cut himself out of life. His brother was his hero, and he so desperately wanted to be one reason his brother did not choose this option. His brother could wish the rest of the world dead, but not himself.

Michael had seen it coming, and warned him, in fact, that his doom was certain unless he had changed his ways. There was a new family in town, one with money and education. Malgorzata had, without a thought, left Piotr for the eldest—a dashing, educated son of a banker. Love is sometimes an investment that cannot be withdrawn and otherwise, elsewise invested. His brother found himself bankrupt, and decided to withdraw his life from his existence rather than live indebted the rest of his life.

The end of the story stirred Old Man Sobczak's ancient anger.

The story gave him energy. He cursed. Then he was off. Stride after stride. Boot before boot. He would be nowhere very soon.

So he walked fiercely. He strode up the street, as a man with direction. For in truth, once he began to walk, he had direction. He noticed a ladybug striding across the sidewalk and stepped on it, daring the superstition to engage him.

He found himself at a park, a dry pond, bordered on all four sides by trees, and did this morning what he had done so many other mornings. He picked a pocketful of rocks from rock bed near the community center, and then he walked under the late spring trees with their first greens, listening for the sounds of birds or squirrels. A black squirrel flashed in a quick spiral up a tree trunk, chased by a mottled brown one. He pinched a rock from his pocket and hurled it at the trunk of the tree, hitting just above the mottled squirrel's head. The animal noticed the stone hit and abandoned its chase down the trunk, heading off to another tree. Sobczak whizzed another rock at the little creature, and hit it in the side of its gut. It wheeted an angry cry of pain, the squirrel articulating something

Michael could not. The squirrel sat stunned for a few seconds. The old man regretted choosing a small stone. He hurled another, but it hit the grass just above the creature's head.

"Beast," he yelled. "Rodent. Too stupid to dodge a stone," he said with an anger that hardly befit this creature he had only just met. His eyes bulged with rage. He did not see the incongruity of his emotion as he vented, for he carried this anger everywhere and always. He paced on through the trees. A magpie.

"Carrion," he said, salivating as he spoke. "Goddamned filthy beast." He threw a flat stone sidearm, which arced expertly towards the magpie's head. "Let me hit you with a stone and do the world some good." The magpie was far too wise to give satisfaction to such a man, and hopped up a branch as the stone whizzed under him and tic-tacked through the young poplar leaves. It turned its head to eye this raging old man, assessed him, and flew away. As it flew, Sobczak trailed it with stone after stone, hoping to catch it mid-flight.

Paul cycled by him on his way home, catching him mid-throw.

"Hello, Michael." Paul called.

"Oh, hello," Sobczak replied, dropping the last couple of rocks from his hand to the ground as discreetly as he could. Paul nodded at the magpie.

"How's retirement today?" he asked.

"Terrible, just terrible," Michael complained. "I do nothing all day long."

"You torture the animal kingdom," Paul quipped. A week earlier, on a particularly warm day, Paul had found Michael walking around the neighbourhood shirtless with a fly-swatter in each hand mashing every bug he could find into the great beyond. A moment of silence. "Why don't you do some volunteering?"

Michael shook his head. "People don't like me."

Paul pursed his lips. "Why don't you get another job?"

"Nobody wants me. I'm too old. Though I work hard."

"Somebody somewhere needs you."

"No one needs me."

"Sure they do."

"I cannot find them."

"What do you really want to do? You have all this time, you could do something really wonderful with it."

"I hate life," he replied. His voice lowered and grew coarse as he spoke, as if a demon had used him as a medium.

"Aack! Aack!" The magpie said, filling the pocket of silence following Sobczak's simple declarative sentence.

The thrift of Michael's reply rankled Paul's own weltschmerz; the groundswell rolled into a deep, polluted wave. Paul could feel a thrill of panic birth in his groin. "Ah, well... I should be going. See you, Michael."

Michael waved and smiled. The conversation always began and ended the same way. The cul-de-sac ended every conversation Paul and Michael had ever shared. Paul walked away wondering, as he always did, whether Michael meant what he said. Some of it had to be hyperbole, didn't it? Surely a man who continued to choose to live could not fully mean what he said.

He turned around to see Sobczak throwing rocks into the trees. "Stupid robin. Worm eater!" Remains of his ranting, rock-throwing Polish accent wafted like a carnival scent over a sick world.

# 13.

PAUL RETREATED TO HIS OLD recliner, angled into a corner amid the darkness of the basement. As he sat alone, the torments of his encounter with Joan descended upon him. He replayed his remembrance of the encounter, stopping at critical points during the exchange, looking for a loophole to allow his tattered psyche any respite. Her inexplicable revelations shadowed and teased him like a schoolyard bully, hoping for a fight, one where the bully knows that the other is entirely unprepared to defend himself.

The tyrant towered in his thoughts until an idea offered rescue.

"I shall go and talk with Owen," he said to himself with glee, knowing that his thoughts would be eased by a man who would most certainly undermine Joan's story. He realized Joan was only jealous of him and what he had—his position, his self-possession, his degrees and clarity of thought, his academic standing. She staged it all, he thought, just to hear my soul rattle. Then he noticed he'd used the word "soul," which for a material Marxist like himself, would have led to an instant self-correction. But he allowed it to stand, thinking that this time, he'd only used it as a metaphor for the coordination of consciousness.

He heard the tones of a car alarm engaging, and knew from the threatening chirp that Bonnie was home. Paul hastily folded the footrest under the recliner and headed up the back stairs to the back door. As Bonnie stepped through the front door, Paul yelled, "Just going to see Owen next door. Back in a couple of minutes." Before she could reply, he closed the back door and headed up the side of the house, around the hedge, through the low wrought-iron gate, and up the back steps covered in a deep green astroturf to the back door of Joan and Owen's house. He glanced toward the rear-view mirror that was mounted outside of Owen's kitchen window, facing Paul's back yard. The cool glow of two old eyes met his. Paul waved, and pointed to the door. An upward thumb appeared in the mirror.

The back door was perpetually unlocked, so Paul unlatched the screen door, rolled the brass knob of the inside door, and headed inside.

Owen was stuck in his kitchen chair. Age nailed him there. He sat there in his chair drinking Pepsi out of a small, communion-sized glass and eating Oreos. A care aide he had hired would help him dress and move to the kitchen each morning. She would come back late in the afternoon to help him undress, go back to his room and get into bed. His chair was conveniently located next to the fridge at the kitchen table on which sat a toaster oven. He made his own meals—which usually consisted of taking a frozen TV dinner out of the refrigerator and broiling it on low until the ice deserted the entrée, then one quick blast on high to add some texture and heat.

He liked to watch the Shreeve house, but it sat behind his chair. He hired a handyman to install the rear-view mirror from an old truck on the side of his house so, as he sat in his chair with his back to Paul, Lou, and Bonnie, he could see what was going on.

Owen was not the kind of man who'd mention anything about the suicide of a man who happened to share Paul's name. He was far too old for that. Nailed to his seat, he wanted to be as nice as refined sugar. He depended on the world coming to him. Sometimes he shared a Pepsi and an Oreo with Paul. Owen's personal Eucharist.

"Thanks for the visit," Owen said, his voice skidding out of disuse with a scrabble of phlegm.

"How's the world seem today?" Paul returned.

"I think words are the only thing I don't have anyone to help me with," he commented as Paul walked in the door. "I've lost everything else. Can't even tie my own shoelaces." In the end was the word. "Feels like the words are comin' out sideways today, cuttin' my throat. Have a cookie?" He asked the question in earnest. Paul knew there was no refusing. To take the cookie is to take the Pepsi, too. There is no middle ground. Paul was eager for the cookie. "This is the body..." Paul heard him say. He took. He ate. He took the Pepsi glass. "This is my blood..." It is time to drink. A holy shooter.

Paul belched discreetly and asked about the other Paul Shreeve, relating the story of the mistaken identity. "That old Joan isn't doing so well. She isn't quite right. Dementia maybe." He finished with a contrived laugh. The embellishment of Joan's degraded mental condition designed to draw out an easy "Oh, yes" from Owen's lips.

Owen shook his head. "Joan's sharp. Just like her to tell you, too," he said with a cough of pain. "Damn words." A long sniff. "She thinks you're the returned Paul Shreeve?"

"Yeah, she does," Paul replied, adding another long laugh, long enough to invite Owen to join in. He didn't.

"It *was* your house. And it *was* suicide. That man loved his job. Everyone loved him. I used to hear him coming up the alley, his whistle helping my day along." Owen stopped. "He'd whistle up the alley until he got to his back gate. He'd call to his wife from there in his singsong way. Made no sense. No sense." He paused, marking the change in his story. "Maybe he grew old, like me, and wanted a quick exit." Owen rolled his eyes, the left one milky and focused on Paul, and pointed a knuckle at the rear-view mirror hanging outside his kitchen window. His reverse image of the outside world, of Paul's back yard. Objects may be closer than they appear. "The day he retired, he never whistled or called to his wife again. Never. It was the damnedest thing. All the money and time you could ask for, no kids, nothing."

The tide of anxiety rode high and shoreward. "She seems to think his remains are behind one of the basement walls in our house," Paul added. The play was simple. If he couldn't get a dismissal of the overall case, he could finagle for a minor improvement. The thought that the remains were somewhere in the house was profoundly distressing.

"Yes, I think that's true," Owen confirmed. "She ran his body through the fire and put the remains in the wall, the house he loved." Owen paused for a long moment. His gaze dropped to the table as if to summon strength.

Paul stifled a geyser of nausea.

With a great deal of effort, he met Paul's eyes. "I don't know why you're here again." His voice faltering with emotion. "You let me die so slow when you left. I've been waiting to die for a long while, and you come back. I'm waiting for you to finish what you came for. Then maybe God'll let me out of this chair."

"I'm not him. I cannot be. It is not physically possible and all of science supports me," Paul protested, as earnestly as a used car salesman. A heated roll of dread twisted up from his groin through his chest. Tingles of terror. *Hold it together. Hold it together,* he told himself. "Owen, I'm not the same guy as the one who killed himself."

"That's what you say." His eyes narrowed as he measured Paul again. "You might even think you're telling me the truth. But Joan's right. You're going to finish off what you came for. Do it quick. My ass is sore."

Paul forced himself to chuckle, hoping that a little levity would help him the way Teflon helped an egg in a fry pan. "Don't wait for me," Paul retorted, with a lighthearted tone. The solidity of his knees melted. His arms felt like they might fall off. "Do it yourself."

"I don't see things that way," Owen replied, rejecting Paul's humour outright.

"I'm joking, Owen. Lighten up." He had enough energy for one last attempt. "I'm back," Paul growled. "And this time it's personal." Owen lowered his head in a sulk, leaving Paul to drown without a lifejacket. Paul's back twinged and threatened to give out.

Paul somehow let himself out and got himself back into his basement chair. He sat down in the chair. He sat for about thirty seconds. He grabbed a book from the bookshelf beside the chair. "Too heavy," he said as he gauged the book by its cover. He thumbed through for something light. He cursed as his mental state collapsed and smothered him like a tent without tentpoles.

The TV remote was close. He flicked it on. He surfed for a channel that demanded his entire attention. It happened to be *Family Fear Factor*. "So you're all going to have to stick your head in this clear goo, and then roll it in this tray of live cockroaches. Are you ready for this?" The commentator addressed his question to a family of four, who looked ready to do anything the show asked. It wasn't enough. Paul surfed, changing the channel every couple of minutes. Never had he been so glad to have as many channels as he had. The surfing itself seemed to steal his attention. "This is a fire-hydrant chopper, dedicated to those who died in 9-11." The picture collapsed and immediately re-inflated with new content as Paul changed channels. A cop stood over a man who was lying handcuffed face-down on the trunk of a metallic orange car. He was shining a flashlight on an open wallet. "You want to tell me what you've got in your pockets?" said the shaved red-headed man with badges on his sleeve.

"Oh God," Paul whispered, nearly losing consciousness at the sight of the image, hammering his thumb deep into the remote's supple rubber button.

"Daddy." Lou came downstairs carrying a Lego ship he had just created. "You shouldn't watch TV after school 'cept Friday." He squinted at his dad and stepped closer. "You 'K?"

Paul stretched his lips wide, the way he would if he was smiling. "Daddy's okay. I just have to watch TV for homework." Bonnie materialized, standing behind Lou. She rolled her eyes as she overheard his excuse.

"You want to go to the store with Mommy?" Bonnie asked with a sweetness that sugar resented.

# 14.

Paul planned to lie in front of the TV through supper, into the evening and through the night. The media's nattering helped him stay away from hoodlums that waited for him in the neighbourhood of his thoughts. He drifted in and out of sleep, in and out of terror and emotional incontinence for the entire night.

He found himself alone in his tan-and-orange checkered recliner in the basement. This chair, the TV, and the disarray of unused living equipment was where he felt most fully himself—next to his University office, of course.

When Paul and Bonnie bought the house, the basement was bedizened in fake pine paneling with a dark mahogany trim, which marked a progressive decor. Fortunately, Bonnie was handy with tools and had drywalled over the pine paneling, then painted the room a calming white.

Paul lay in a fugue upon this recliner, feet in the air. Eyes darting, scanning the drywall for hints. Adam's apple pumping up and down, hands dug into the rolled arms of fabric and foam. Before him the TV blared. He'd turned it on hoping it would call him out of a growing mental tornado. At the moment, the TV show blared an old episode of the cigar-chewing Columbo.

"I want you to hear the tape," Columbo said.

"Yes, I'll hear it. By all means. Go ahead," replied the murderer.

Paul tried to discipline himself to follow the shades and blades of logic, but couldn't, thus he could not relish the surgical blade of justice as it fell, cinematically at least, on the guilty.

In his thoughts, a dysphoria of disposition, a plurality of Pauls, perhaps. His mind fighting to sort out his own Paulness as it blur-blended with a Paul he was fairly sure he wasn't. How could he know? This was the critical question. Nothing in Marxism could help here, as the theory had more to do with the complexion of a society than one, possibly two, of its struggling members. This was the realm of psychology, of which, Paul knew practically nothing, though as an English professor, he was sure the opposite was true.

The razor-edged thought he'd used so often to critique capitalism and its tendrils now turned on him with the violence of critique saved for the worst of things.

Then a thought: Paul in the wall. He replayed Joan's words, or what he thought he might have heard her say. He boiled it down to "Paul in the wall." And this kernel of an idea flaked into a larger plan. Then he replayed his recollection of his doctor's consult, experiments and proof. Though his mind was far too jumbled to piece together the sense of what he was about to do, it boiled down to this: If Paul is in the wall, the problem exists. If Paul is not in the wall, all is well. It would be a matter of scientific proof.

He left the room for his wife's toolbox, which he knew she kept in their garage. After a futile fling through her collection, he found a hammer and a pry bar, and with those, bounded back to the basement. He picked a spot across from his recliner, slammed the hammer through the drywall, then proceeded around the room, stud by stud, looking for Paul in the wall. Smashing, peeling, tearing.

Clouds of drywall dust filled the air. Drywall rubble covered the room and its contents. Paul had trashed most of the room, hurting his hand and his thigh once or twice in the process. Oddly enough, his manner and mood improved as he moved through the room, his hopes rising that in fact Joan was a crank, a lovely liar, that this whole story could be chalked up to hijinks and distilled, with enough time, to psychology and hilarity.

That was his mood until he had to move his recliner. His hammer went through the drywall first, and another punch and the hammer's head punched a neat hole in the pine paneling. He levered the head of the hammer in the hole and yanked a large hole to the studs. Resting on the nogging, in a part of the wall just behind his chair, mere inches from his head when he reclined, was a black plastic box. On it rested an envelope. First horror. He began to weep. His inner emptiness dripped through the corners of his eyes.

With a gentleness born out of muscular fatigue and despondency, he lifted the box and the letter from the nogging, placed it in his arms and collapsed in his chair. And reclined. Thrills of terror bolted from groin to crown. With everything he had, turned the black box carefully, until a white mailing label appeared on the front. It read as follows:

Shreeve, Dr. Paul, PhD, M.Phil, B.A. Honours (Magna Cum Laude), CTC, C. Mgr, C. Dir, Plog. B. Re., MPHR, CLTR, D. Phx., MRE, CCD, F, Cert. Mat. Planner, ISO 9000 Cert.

And, at the end of the train of certification, Paul passed out.

# 15.

Paul and Bonnie's next-door neighbour to the south was a whore, sort of a suburban one. It had taken them several months to figure out what she did for a living. He wondered for a while if she was a slutty executive, with her stiletto heels and a mini-skirt that barely covered the Holy Land, promoting the settlement of the Gaza strip.

Honestly, he thought, there isn't much of a difference between sexing a john and pleasing the boss. There's just a matter of how one advertises and whether one takes cash or direct deposit.

However, the hours she kept helped him clue in to her profession. Paul admired her for her business approach; she'd seemed to turn her one-night stands into a subscription. She worked out of home, and the clients came "courtin'" in the late evening to stay a little or a lot.

Paul called Mondays *green Mustang day*, since her Monday "regular" drove a green Mustang. A big, fat, black-haired, pore-fed, Greco-dark lard box, loud, full of yesterday's lines, gums with two pews of whitened teeth. Tuesday was red and white, window-reno guy. Lanky, un-swanky, a pencil in each pantleg (eraser down), spaghetti noodles dangling in each sleeve, a meatball head, and a salt, mostly salt and pepper mullet. Wednesday brought a stiff-walking actuary, blue pinstripes, furtive, a neat shaver, trim in every way. A giant leather brief case he held motionless, mid-thigh as he took hurried steps, steps that made it look as though he was in a hurry to get somewhere, like the shareholders had requested an audit and he had funny books. He would stride up the walk with a tenting woody. Sex had been camping on his loins all day, Paul supposed. Thursday seemed to be freelance day, or, perhaps, sample day. Different men, mid-lifers all. All of them like men on the sinking side of the Titanic, going down, band playing final bars, angry and out of time, desperate for one last dance. Friday, twin three-hundred-and fifty-ish-pound brothers who arrived in a sagging, sorry Toyota Camry. As they walked to the front of the house it looked as if each of them was kneeing a pair of basketballs that they kept in the front of their pants. Paul always marveled at their size.

He wondered if she kept a post-it note like a bookmark in the flabby folds so she knew where she left off last time.

The weekend seemed to be time off, with occasional off-site work.

It was a formula for success. She had a routine clientele, and she didn't depend on anyone too dearly, so that one john switching customers wouldn't upset the finances. She could get a business loan with a strategy like that.

The mom brought her daughter in on the family business from time to time, a way to help her earn extra money. Sometimes the daughter greeted clients at the front door in a bath towel, and helped them in. For her, it was a hobby that paid.

The mom, Angela, was a fading flower. She lounged in her early 40s maybe. Hard to tell. Hard living can age a person quickly. She was a reasonably attractive bottle blonde. Paul had watched the daughter—maybe 16, maybe a young-looking 20—a week before, drinking rum and Cokes while talking on the phone in the back yard, her mom conducting business in the house.

The daughter freelanced, too. The day before, a roofing crew shucked the old shingles on their house and added new ones. She was on the front step, talking on the phone while mom did the books inside. She strutted up and down the block until they picked her up, and the roofing crew left with darling Jennifer sitting in the crew boss's lap, doing her sweet wiggle. She didn't come back for two days, but then she could afford a new cell phone and cigarettes—probably got twenty percent off the roof job, too.

Angela seemed to take a break from her work now and then, when instead of her regulars, her Baptist parents came to visit her from Saskatchewan: a place called Forget. She stopped her swearing, stopped smoking. Her customers often drove by but never stopped. She lived cleanly for the visit.

One night, one of her gentleman callers couldn't wait any longer. He stopped by and wondered if he could bother her for help with an errand. She got into his green Mustang. They drove around the corner and she gave him a blow-job on the spot. A little money later, she was back inside her house using that same mouth to talk garden trivia and memories with her parents.

# 16.

ON A BED, IN A house just up the street from Paul's, lay Bal. Bal was short for Balthazar— a dry mouthful of name, one his mother had thought distinguished. Bal flopped onto his back, his body aching for a change in position as he lay in bed, waiting for his wife to come home. After he turned himself, he lay back on his pillow and touched his toupee, making sure it was still properly tacked to his bald head. He still felt clean, and smelled as good as a bottle of Aqua Velva would let him. Next to him on the bed lay a glowing window-square shape of moonlight, holding her place. He'd masturbated, but masturbating didn't scratch his itch any more. He wanted to know his wife again. It'd been months since she'd even had reluctant sex with him.

He'd always felt she had sex with him because she felt sorry for him, never because she wanted to. He was always trying to transform the moment of sex from the normal pity-pork to a vibrant sexual moment. But it was difficult. It was hard to feel like a sex object as a plastic click-pen of a man, with a tremendous chin and a toupee. He'd tried the sexy underwear, the more dramatic sexual moves, dirty suggestive talk—but on such a man, like on most men, these things seemed ironic. He had the type of sexuality that could only get a woman to lie still for ten minutes while he did his thing, if she felt sorry for him.

His wife denied his advances, which mainly consisted of him touching her at all. And the more she denied him, the harder and more obsessed he seemed to get. It seemed to him as though he was the tree-thin woody looking for anyone and anything to get him off, but that existence (his in particular) was one long unsatisfying hard-on. One so hard that even when it legitimately got off, it would rigidly ask for more. He, Bal, was a circumcised hard-on, with a toupee stuck to his tip. And so, next to the window-framed square of moonlight, lay this hard dick of man, with his toupee arranged as erotically as possible.

It was 2:37 a.m. when he heard the soft click of locks and the gentle thunk of the deadbolt. She swept into the house with a faint hum and a quick, quiet step. She brushed passed the bed to the ensuite bathroom. He could smell pork, cigarettes, and deep-fry oil that had licked its way onto her skin. And he waited, limbs atremble as she prepared for bed. In his mind he played tapes where she craved him the way a female porn star craved any old penis at all, with the constant craving that stiffened his love limb that caused him to walk erect to work, that made him desire not just women, but everything and everyone.

Oddly enough, as he thought of it, his penis would more properly be reflected if it had been a gaping hole instead. A hole seemed to properly announce a need better than a pole. For that is all an erection ever meant to him: there was a hole that needed to be filled, and that this hole actually had the audacity to protrude made him smile at this particular moment. He had one of the most outgoing holes he'd ever met.

He could hear her brush her teeth and sweep back into the room. In the moonlit window she undressed swiftly—in a single movement, her shirt lay on the floor. In a second movement, she stepped out of her skirt. She popped her bra off, and shrugged the device from her shoulders to the floor. Then she turned to the bed and rolled into the moonlit covers next to him. She'd turned from her prudish insistence on pajamas some months back, and taken to sleeping semi-nude. She turned her back toward him, sighed in a satisfied way.

It was now that he made his druthers known. He groaned, as if asleep, and turned towards her, as if he was turning in his sleep, and flopped his right arm over her midsection.

"Not tonight, Bal," she said immediately. "I'm too tired."

"Huh?" he replied in a sleepy way, hoping if he didn't seem like he wanted anything, he would lull her into complacent, accidental sex.

"Not tonight, I said."

He pretended he had fallen asleep again. However, the idea of sex was captivating and caffeinated. Completely awake, contemplating any way he could think of to open up her hole, so he could satisfy his hole with hers.

He lay awake for another couple hours afterward. Odd, he thought. One of the perfect moments of peace had to be after the legitimate orgasm, the meeting of a legitimate erection with a legitimate hole. He thought about how the world would act if everyone lived in a post-coital reverie. Drivers would be much kinder, he thought. Prices would be lower. Ideas softer with rounded edges.

He lay quietly, and realising he wouldn't be sleeping anytime soon, imagined a rosary, and with his mind moved the beads of thought around the string of sanity. Hail Mary, full of grace. After a few rounds, sleep extended its friendship.

And with that, he removed his toupee, placed it gently over his alarm clock, so as to cover the red glow of the numbers, and went to sleep.

# 17.

IF THE LAST FEW YEARS of a man's life were good for anything, he thought, they were good for walking and TV. This thought was thunk by Old Man Sobczak, now 72, as he lay in his bed at 5:30 a.m., waiting for his clock to strike 5:45. He waited patiently, not thinking of his grandchildren, or his children, or his wife, his wife who lay beside him snoring. He was thinking of the television programs he would experience in the line-up of a Wednesday morning. His program strategy had already been worked out some weeks before in consultation with the September version of the television guide. He'd worked out which channels to switch to and when, carefully devoting some time for channel surfing in case something occurred in the day which required his viewing attention. Some of it he would capture on his Personal Video Recorder for later, which would accommodate his walks and rocks. He reviewed the calendar dates in his head to make sure no statutory holidays, American or Canadian, would cause him to adjust his schedule. He was delighted to conclude that this week would, in fact, be a predictable viewing week.

This was his seventh year of retirement, all of which he'd devoted to the television set and his aimless pedestrianism. He worked with the plots he saw there, and at the same time worked backward through his life to see if, somehow, the pixelated theories of life corresponded in any way to his reality.

He was a scientist, of sorts, and his subjects were the TV and his own life. And as science works its way up from instances and occasions to the grand theories which run the universe, so Sobczak, for that is what most called him, did with his viewing. He had embarked on an investigation of the TV set and a few ideas began to form around his loose experiment, ideas which one could call Set Theory.

He felt as though his life might end as unresolved as a soap opera, the episode ending and the big mystery of the installment left unsolved. That lack of resolution seemed to make sense of his own discordant existence. But he puzzled over the high drama that soap operas presented—every episode, though unresolved, ended in a precipice over which the entire show seemed to hang, and this was the one piece of the soap opera that did not fit his existence. The local cable channel hosted several shows that offered the critical lack of drama that seemed to mark his life, and in doing so, attracted his attention. The guests on the local cable talk shows he had never heard of, and the camera angles were always wrong. These shows inspired a lack of attention and deserved to be no more than the filler of the sizzling sausage that TV had become. Still, local cable felt like his life, except that on TV there was always some glib resolution, which of course did not suit what he knew.

He wondered if it was possible to blend TV genres and invent the theory of his existence. If he took a soap opera, and cast it with the feel of the local cable channel, that would about amount to the sum of his existence. Sort of an unresolved, uninteresting show with no cliff-hanger. Truly, that was his life. Absolutely uninteresting. Most snapshots that he carried in his own albums had been a waste of film. All of the drama of his life happened off camera, and truthfully, his life had only amounted to one moment ever.

Then there were his dreams, the TV shows he dared not compare his life to. There were the Hollywood movies and sitcoms. Places of assured happiness, which under threat, both resolved and attained new heights of bliss. This surely couldn't be any of the fodder of existence. These were men's dreams, dreams of other men's lives. They were an invitation to contemplate heaven, a kind of earthly existence that existed for no one. But each offered twenty minutes to two hours of relief from existence.

Even better yet were re-runs, shows he had seen before and knew the happy conclusion before the show began. His happiness was guaranteed, risk entirely averted. Resolutions were complete and total, a kind of redemption he refused to hope for.

He was a lapsed Catholic, which didn't say much for his life in any remarkable way, for he had been a lapsed employee, a lapsed friend, a lapsed husband, a lapsed father, a lapsed citizen, and had in every way possible led a lapsed life. He had taken to calling himself an atheist. His reasons he could explain in terms of a television show.

His life was such a piss-poor show, all 70-odd years of it, that he was certain that God couldn't be watching. Who would watch his life after a half an hour in his Polish presence? Plus, if God was not only a viewer, but a writer, he felt sure that God had scripted his life rather poorly, that there were scant ingredients for any sort of watchable plot. And plot was supposed to happen, a person wasn't supposed to have to create it. Sobczak was not a man to usurp the lines he felt he ought to speak. He just couldn't find many lines at all. And he hadn't the energy to write his own. He waited for the inner impetus to speak, which hadn't arrived just yet. The fight and sex scenes in his life were so poorly done that no sort of adult warning was necessary; the scenes themselves would certainly be seen as warnings, even to young children, that vitality and sex are not beautiful and lead nowhere. His life was a poor script, acted by a poor actor, under poor direction, with a poor budget. In sum, then, he really did believe in God, but he ignored God as a way of getting back at Him for his terrible, Polish destiny.

# 18.

"WHAT IS THIS?" HIS WIFE screamed. He awoke to these words with his nose in great pain. "What have you done to our basement? All my work?" Bdelygmia. By her work, she meant the drywall she'd carefully sheeted over the fake pine paneling. The corner work. The taping and mudding. Thank your favourite deity he hadn't put the hammer through the drywalled ceiling.

"What is this?" she shrieked. She wasn't leaving time for an answer, an obvious case of erotema.

A warm liquid flowed from his nose, over his face, and down his chin. A quick touch and visual inspection revealed it was blood. "I had to find Paul," he said weakly.

"What? What? What?" she shrieked. One could argue her utterance was an instance of epizeuxis. Despite her use of device, a white-hot anger burned in her face. "You destroyed our basement. All my work." Her anger melted to howls and tears.

"I had to find Paul." He paused. "To see if it was true." Brachylogia.

She returned to Paul's chair and punched his crotch. He hedge-hogged into a fetal ball, obeying instinct. His body curled around the remains of Paul and the envelope, as Bonnie's well-placed fists dropped rhythmically on all his sensitive bits. An effective three-minute sample of argumentum ad baculum. Paul fought to stay conscious.

"How could you? How could you?" Probably conduplication, but given the current amount of body pain, an extra second of thought would be needed to confirm. Intuitive but effective given her current emotional state: it captured her internal state with what seemed like accuracy. Animorum motus.

And the peroration. "You're such a," she paused and looked at her bloody fist, "weenie," she said, fighting to keep her language clean, in case Lou was listening.

Paul held his hands up to deflect the blows. "I had to find the –" he said, as she resumed using her fists. The fine filament of consciousness abandoned Paul to bathetic collapse and praecisio.

*Ghost in Theory* | 65

# 19.

PAUL WAS OUT IN THE back yard mowing and trimming. Angela was out in her sweats, mothering her flowerbeds, coffee in hand.

"Nice irises," she said, pointing to the white iris plant that had been growing out of control. "I love those white irises."

"There are a few different kinds, are there?" Paul asked.

"Oh, yes. Many, many kinds. I'm a member of the Iris Society. I study them. I grow them." Her focus shifted from the flowers to Paul.

Then she noticed Paul's face. "Oh, are you okay?"

Paul remembered his injuries. "Oh, this." Paul pointed to his own face. "Construction accident." She seemed unconvinced. "Drywall, panelling, that sort of thing."

"Oh, that's awful."

"It looks worse than it is," Paul insisted.

"I hope so."

"You seemed to have injured yourself," Paul rejoined.

Angela's gaze snapped down to her wrists. A bruise circled each of her wrists. And a blue-black wreath ringed her neck. Instinctively she brought a hand up, as if to remember her bruise.

"Oh, that. Forgot about it. I had jewelry that got caught on some furniture... um... after I tripped."

"Ouch," Paul replied in sympathy.

"Yeah, ouch."

"Interesting," Paul replied. "I've got to cut the lawn. I'd better get to it."

Paul was about to step away, when Angela's father came to the fence for a chat.

"Cuttin' the lawn, eh." Starting the conversation with the classic opener: redundancy.

"Yes."

"You're mulching?"

Paul smiled. "Yes. It's a little easier and better."

"I'm just out visiting my favourite middle girl." He winked. "She was always the one who wanted to move to the big city. She's doing all right now."

Paul smiled and nodded, resigned to the conversation's direction.

"The city is sure noisy, not like home. I'm having trouble sleeping. It always seems like there's a siren going somewhere. And hot. Have to sleep with the window open all the time, which makes the noise a little worse." The old man's eyes glossed over as he chatted, forgetting Paul entirely. His piece of property at home, his 36-year-old "baby" girl in Moose Jaw. His oldest boy in Edmonton. His withered Baptist words worked to a lengthy burble of one-sided trivia; obviously a man who didn't get listened to very often. Apparently no whiff of his daughter's successful business sexploits, unaware of her innovative subscription approach, her pecker-poker career to pay the bills. She's a businesswoman, a sexecutive, a lost-monkey organ-grinder. His Baptistness, it seemed, had overwhelmed his ability to see reality.

"Well, I guess I should let you go," said the man as his head returned to him. "I do like to talk. Glad Angela has good neighbors."

"Well, it's nice to meet you," Paul tagged. He looked towards the house. Bonnie's face mooned in the window. This would not go well. Though they'd never discussed Angela, they both knew what she did, and though Angela sought friendship with Lou, with Bonnie, with him, Bonnie was stand-offish. Paul stroked his bruised cheek.

"It was nice to meet you," Paul replied. "I've got to finish up, here." Paul walked away to uncoil the extension cord he used for his weed whip, wondering if he had just given the man a free word-job.

# 20.

"I CAN'T HAVE THIS IN MY house anymore," Paul said to the new young priest. He held out the black plastic box of remains to Joachim with a palsied hand. Under the box, the unopened envelope. It was a historical moment, as Paul was willingly speaking for his first time to a member of the clergy. "The remains do not belong to me, and they were left behind by the previous house owners."

"Your name is—" The priest began, assessing the man before him carefully.

"Paul Shreeve." Paul felt naked for a moment.

"What happened to you, Paul?" asked the priest.

Paul was confused for a moment. "Oh, you mean the bruising?" pointing to his own face. Joachim nodded.

"Construction. Wall problem. Drywall. Crowbar." The priest's eyebrows furrowed with confusion. "I had a problem with one of the basement walls."

"Ah," said the priest, as if he wanted to hear no more. "The name of the deceased?" the priest gestured to the black box shaking slightly in Paul's hand.

"Paul Shreeve."

"No, please. The name of the person whose remains you brought with you."

"Paul Shreeve."

"Okay." He steepled his fingers and tucked them under his nose. "What is your name, then, sir?"

"Paul Shreeve." Paul, sensing the nature of his struggle, continued. "It's kind of a who's-on-first-situation, except it involves death, not baseball. We're both named Paul Shreeve." He met the priest's eyes, which were widening slightly. "But we're not related. This is just some random accident, a chance thing." The priest seemed doubtful.

Paul pushed the dusty black box and letter, passing them to the priest. The priest finally accepted both and set them down on his desk. The priest read the tag affixed to the box.

"Quite a train of certification, here," he commented. A lot of certification, Paul agreed with a nod. Too much paper. Certifications probably caught fire. No wonder he was cremated. Paul then dug for his wallet, in his front right pocket and produced his driver's license. "Same name," he repeated, "but no relation."

The priest read both documentations carefully. Then re-read them. He picked up the driver's license and held it next to the box label. He pulled his head back and cocked it to one side, and scowled. "From an actuarial perspective," he said finally, "The chances of this occurring are infinitesimally small. Desperately, desperately small. So, small, in fact, that one might call it divine."

"Oh no, not divine. I'm not religious," Paul protested. The priest closed his eyes as though he were tired. "I'm a Marxist. This is an accident. A random moment, whatever the odds may be. I don't want to argue the point." Random somehow made the whole thing far more acceptable. If the incident was divine, the horror was overwhelming.

"You say he was a member of the church?" Joachim asked.

"I'm told so."

"May I have a moment to consult our church records?"

He returned moments later with a file. "He was a suicide. And the previous priest refused to bury him or give him a funeral. But that is old thinking." The priest stopped and looked at the box. "Usually suicide is an order of operations problem."

Paul frowned at the priest. The priest offered a thin smile. "In mathematics, processes need to be done in a certain order. This is true in life as well. If a person gets the order wrong, it can lead to the wrong conclusions."

"Order of operations?" Paul said.

"PEMDAS," the priest replied. "Parentheses, Exponents, Multiplication and Division from left to right, Addition and Subtraction from left to right. I think of suicide as an order of operations issue. It's the final parenthesis in the bracket of existence. It's to be waited for, supplied by our creator." He gestured beatifically towards the roof. "Some choose to alter the natural order of operations. He was also cremated. The church used to frown upon that too. But I understand the widow's predicament. Cremation would be the only option. The funeral equivalent of getting a body 'to go,' I suppose." He paused. "I think we can help you out, Mr. Shreeve."

"It's Doctor Shreeve, actually," Paul said automatically, and once conscious of what he'd said, regretted his utterance.

The priest's eyes widened quickly, and he looked down to the sticker on the box of remains again. "This is an uncanny situation, Dr. Shreeve.

Uncanny indeed. The odds would be in the many multiple millions, low billions, I'd estimate."

"Unlikely, but not impossible. Someone always wins the lottery," Paul retorted quickly. "My driver's license?"

The priest, lost in thought, came to three seconds after Paul asked the question. "Umm. Yes. Yes, of course." He plucked the license and passed it to Paul.

"I'll take his remains and we will say a funeral mass for this poor soul, but you must attend that mass and you must invite the grieving neighbors." Joachim picked up the sealed envelope that accompanied the ashes. "This is not for me, however." He pointed to the envelope's addressee. "As the children like to say, 'finders keepers.' It has your name on it." Paul's breath caught in his throat. His heart began to pound.

"But it's not my name," Paul protested, his voice neared panic. The priest raised his eyebrows. Paul tamed his voice. "Well, yes, it's my name. But, I'd be breaking the law, technically, by opening that envelope. It's a matter of intention, not the mere spelling of a name." He hadn't the capacity to appreciate the irony of his invoking of authorial 'intention,' which had been sold, part and parcel, by progressive North American English studies back in the 1970s.

The priest dithered a moment. "It may not be your letter, but it is most certainly not mine." He paused and an imp of a smile crossed his face. "I will do my part. I will also hold on to this letter. For now. I will properly commit this man's remains to God, if that is what you wish. I will then return the ashes to you, or to whomever may be interested in claiming them."

Paul sighed. "Please, don't give me the box back," he whined. "I have nowhere to keep it. I don't want to keep it. I can't keep it. I can't…"

The priest held up an open hand until Paul's agitation subsided. "First things first. We'll observe the proper order of operations, and see where we go."

# 21.

Paul returned from work on Tuesday. This day he was not on his bicycle. Instead he walked, as it was his turn to pick up Lou.

Paul dropped by the daycare for gifted children where Lou spent his days. He was a little early, and he watched the teacher work on colours with the children. She held up a green handkerchief.

"What colour is this, children?"

"Green," they replied in unison.

She held up a plastic frog.

"And what colour is this?"

Responses differed. "Frog." "Blue." "Green." "I don't know." The teacher smiled in a way that seemed to say "How stupid can you be?" She held up the green handkerchief again.

"What colour is this?"

"Green," said the class.

"Then, what colour is this?" she asked, holding the frog next to the handkerchief.

Part of the class said, "Green." The rest of the class spread out across the range of possibility and answered. A blond-haired girl sitting at the back asked a question: "How could a frog and cloth be the same colour?"

"Madeline," the teacher said in her patronizing tone. "Do the handkerchief and the frog look the same, somehow?"

"Yeah." Madeline, said dejectedly, knowing already how to fall into the funnel of education. "They're both green."

"That's right," the teacher exclaimed with plastic glee. "Very good, Madeline."

"Wait!" Paul said, interrupting. "I mean please."

"Yes," Miss Honey replied.

"There is a problem here. I just want to point out you did not teach this class what the colour green is. All you did is point to a green swatch of colour and say the word green. You are building an assumption in them—not teaching. This is Pavlovian conditioning, not education. This is not a proper foundation for thinking about green things."

"Yes," she agreed and nodded. Miss Honey seemed confused but agreed, perhaps hoping that the encounter would end. But Paul, latching

*Ghost in Theory* | 71

on to the issue at hand, was able to leave his problems behind for a moment and so continued.

"There is no essential sense of greenness that you can offer them besides making them look at this particular object, and having them associate their impressions of that object, their experience, with the word 'green.' I mean, how do you know whether her sense of green is the same as her students'," he said, pointing at Madeline. "Perhaps one student sees this swatch as blue. Yet she is taught to say the word 'green' whenever she experiences a colour she sees as 'blue.' Maybe someone here is colorblind. Have you thought of that?"

Miss Honey seemed only tolerant on this point.

Paul continued. "Here is a major problem of education. There may be large differences in how we see things, but we teach ourselves to use the same words. So, standing in front of the 'green' swatch of colour, everyone in the room, except the colour-blind kid, will say the word 'green' when she holds up the swatch, regardless of whether there are any differences in the way each perceives it. Do you see? Do you see the problem? It's a thin, data-free approach to teaching."

Miss Honey smiled at him and turned to the class. "It's time for our goodbye song, children."

The children launched into their goodbye song with a thoughtless gusto born of routine.

After the class was over, Paul cornered Miss Honey as she moved to her desk, to organize her things. "Do you see what I'm trying to say?"

"Not really, Mr. Shreeve."

"It's Doctor, actually." She didn't seem to repent or recant, so Paul took her on as a challenge. "A few kids believe that green has to do with the swatch you hold up each time you teach them about green. But you're a good teacher and realize that the children have to be taught to abstract the quality of green from just the paper, and apply it to other areas of their experience. You show them a frog. You show them a car. You show them a sticker on a banana, a sweater, a tree. And they expand and abstract, they generalize the sense of green from the paper to all green things. Who knows what they see when they see 'green,' and green becomes one of the world's untried assumptions."

She smiled blankly. "Steven was a good student today," she said. Paul struggled to make a connection. "He didn't take advantage of his size and hit the others like he usually does. I gave him a Good Behaviour Award. It's usually given to students who do good things, but in your son's case, what he didn't do was very nice."

Lou ran up to Paul shouting, "Look, Dad, look." He shoved a piece of paper into his dad's hand. *Good Behaviour Award*, it read at the top. *For stopping hitting others.* Paul looked up. Miss Honey smiled. Lou grinned, and snatched the piece of paper out of his dad's hands.

"Steve," Miss Honey said, "if you stop using the eff-word, you could win another good behaviour award." Paul had 'liberated' his son's vocabulary a long time ago, to protect him against petit-bourgeois morality preschools tended to promote. She turned from the conversation to her desk and began to organize.

Paul smiled blankly in return.

"Hey, Paul." Another man waved to Paul as Paul stood there, not quite finished with his thought. "We wondered if Steve could make our party this Saturday." A small compliant little blonde boy stood beside his dad, hanging onto his dad's leg.

"I have an issue with the way green is taught in this school." Paul wagged his finger at Ken, ignoring the boy on his leg. "Students are learning to separate colour from all objects. In other words, the whole object, rather than maintaining its wholeness begins to divide: objects separate themselves from their colour. Each of the students, after passing the unit on colour, can now say that the piece of paper is green. And, in saying so, have divided the colour of the thing from the thing itself."

"The party is going to be at that new indoor playground on the south end. I think it's called 'Let's Play.'" Ken continued. "Could Steve come?"

"Daaaad!" the little boy interrupted. "It's called 'Play Time.'" Ken patted his son's head and nodded to Paul.

"Life for the child begins as an unbroken unity an inexplicable, inarticulate whole," Paul replied, partly to Ken, mostly to himself. "Here begins science and knowledge, literacy and abstraction: the business of separating. The business of separating things just expands from the colour unit: the universe splinters as they learn. Knowledge, like our cells themselves, divides and divides and divides, and forms the corpus of all human knowledge. A big, blood-fed, tumored bundle of pieces, based upon sets of uninvestigated assumptions. Like the assumption of green." He looked at Ken, who with a tin smile and raised eyebrows, waited. Paul raised his voice with his index finger and wagged it as he finished. "Just wait until these kids learn how to count. In fact, they need to learn to count because, through teaching, their knowledge fragments."

"Divorce is the goal and result of most technology. The technology of the roof, the simplest roof, for example, divorces a person from some aspects of the elements. This person must no longer live with the consequences of rain, for instance, for the rain hits the roof, but not the individual. It's a form of divorce, isn't it? The door, the door, my friend. The door, the fence, the wall, private property, grains of the grounds for divorce. Think of the television and how we need not get together at the theatre to watch a spectacle. Think of how, as we watch, we need not contribute to the set, for it is indifferent to us. It separates the very people in the room from one another, and prevents their discussion. In other words, all inventions, all gadgets, have this slow and inevitable effect on community, on our initial and necessary dependence on one another and our world. Utter individuality, in the American sense of the word, means that a person can meet all of his or her existence needs without meaningfully engaging another human being.

"So, is that a yes or no?" Ken queried again.

"Ah, sure. I'll bounce it off Bonnie, but it should be fine."

# 22.

He sat marking in his office for a few hours, with the door open as was his habit. It was about 8 p.m. before he came to his senses and realized he should have been home long ago. He got up, got his coat from the back of the door and stepped into the hallway. As he moved through the door's threshold his knees gave out. He found himself unexpectedly lying on the floor.

"Fuss mother of cool!" he cursed. A security guard happened to be sauntering up the main hallway, and heard his jussive outburst, skirted the corner, and saw Paul lying on the beige and black carpet tiles outside of his office. He unbuckled his holstered can of pepper spray and approached slowly, his hand resting on the can.

"Sir, sir. Are you all right?"

"I'm not sure. Something's wrong. Can you help me back into my office?"

The security guard attempted to help Paul up.

"Can you just drag me back into my office?"

"You sure, sir?" the guard asked.

"Yes, yes. Weird as it sounds, I'll be fine if I'm just back in my office. Just grab my ankle and pull me..."

The guard stepped into Paul's office, grabbed his ankles and dragged him over the carpet tiles back into his office. The drag across the floor untucked Paul's shirt, hiked the tails up around his neck. Once back in his office, Paul sat up, slowly. Then stood.

"Thank you, kind sir," Paul said to the guard, who had wheedled his way around his body to the door again. Paul pulled his undershirt down and began to straighten his button shirt.

"You just need to be in your office to stand?" The guard complained.

"It's like I don't have a spine when I step out the door."

"That doesn't make any sense," the guard argued.

"I know. I know." He raised a hand to the side of his mouth, as if to speak privately, behind his own back. "Believe me I know. I'm out of my coffee muggin' mind. Something's cuckoo, if you know what I mean." He used the index finger of his other hand to circle an ear.

The guard backed away slowly, and began backing up the hallway.

"Goodnight, my good fellow," Paul called. "And thank you."

He sat for a few minutes and thought through his office. The basement deconstruction incident had been added to the "door" problem. It's not like he'd be missing a sleep in a warm bed. In fact, he had a sweater and a couple of suitcoats in his office. Maybe he'd office camp tonight. Might as well. Good a place as any. And he'd stay more or less safe, cozy, comfortable. He'd scare the hell out of the cleaning people, no doubt, but he wouldn't make it home until his spine firmed up somehow. Who knew when that would be?

# 23.

"It's your funeral," Bal said with a grin, as they entered the building. Paul smiled and nodded to mask his near nausea at precisely that thought.

Anyone who was in on the "Paul Shreeve stunt double scandal," as it came to be known, attended the funeral. Bal and his wife, Virginia. Joan. Owen and his 'helper' Moody. Michael and Beata. Angela. And bruises. Paul, and fading bruises. There were two others. One woman with a veil over her entire face. The other some wrinkled prune from outside current social circles, meaning the old man lived across 26$^{th}$ Avenue, an entirely different neighborhood. All had waited years for this unhappy moment. All were there because Joan had phoned half the neighborhood to insist they come.

The mass commenced. At the front of the church, on a TV tray that the priest used to eat his TV dinners, sat the box of ashes, perfectly placed in the centre of the tray, on a doily that the priest's mom had inherited from her mother. The priest had improvised these arrangements in haste as he realized that very morning that he had failed to make arrangements to properly display Paul's remains.

Bal, most at home in church, took a seat next to Paul. He immediately unfolded a small bench from the back of the pew in front of them, and knelt on the padded black Naugahyde. "Paul!" Bal exclaimed in a whisper. "On your knees."

Paul was suddenly aware that everyone around him was kneeling, except Owen, who couldn't. A communist taking to his knees in this den of delusion? What would Marx say?

"Paul. Knees, now."

Maybe just this once. Paul slipped forward onto the padded bench.

"Ya damn communist, just do what I do."

The priest called the service to order: a mass to be said for the departed brother.

Then began the callisthenics of the service. Up. Down. Up. Mumble. Down. Up. Shake hands. Mumble. Finally, the group was left sitting and at peace.

Young Father Joachim stepped up to the podium for the homily. "I'm going to take a few liberties, because there are no loved ones here today. Most of you seem to have resented this man for having taken his own life, which is reasonable but should be confessed. The end of his life is dark, by human standards, and is a beacon of unresolved tension and pain. He committed suicide in a moment of bad health, which is a dark deed. And he was cremated, which puts his body beyond any rites I could have offered it. Not much light. Not much hope. It does put a priest in an awkward predicament. How do we find something life-affirming here?

"I will do my best to build a case for hope today. I will take certain liberties to find light. I am going to call the man whose life we contemplate today Saul, borrowed from the biblical narrative, so as not to confuse him with your friend and neighbor, Paul, who as you know shares the same name and essential credential.

"My main indulgence will be to use math to make a point. It says what the Bible says but with more force, I believe. Many people struggle with the biblical texts these days, so let me use a mathematical concept instead, something simple. Though I suppose people are not familiar with the biblical texts nor are they familiar with math ones." He held up a Protestant cross, one without Christ's body adorning the front.

Paul raised his hand to ask a question. Bal, wide-eyed, grabbed Paul's hand and tried to pull it down, but it was too late. The priest noticed his raised arm. Mass stopped for a moment.

"Paul, we don't ask questions in a Mass," the priest told him.

"Sorry. I can't ask a question?"

"Of course, but not here. This isn't like a class. I'm not here to answer questions. This is a ritual, where we quietly contemplate our questions and bask in the mystery of God."

"Well, it isn't a question about God. It's a question about math."

The priest sighed. Simple calculation. Mass times acceleration equals force. Mass derailed. Acceleration stopped. Force lost.

"Today I will entertain your question, Paul. Since you are," the priest stopped to select the appropriate word, "connected to this situation. But this is not how to behave in church. Please, what is your question?" He suddenly seemed bored.

"What about math suggests that this is a good place to introduce it?"

Once the young Pole absorbed the question, he seemed to energize. "Actually, a fine question. I will digress briefly to explain. I will suggest two connections. First, a lot of cognitive theorists believe that the only way cognition works is by analogy. These analogies mirror our reality quite closely.

"There is a correspondence between math and life. For example, there is the parabola. Take a baseball and throw it into the sky on a windless day. The ball's trajectory will be closely reflected by a parabolic equation. Sine waves are useful to map heartbeats and rates. Basic math symbols share congruence with life. According to some, Newton's ideas were accurate to one part in ten to the seventh power. Einstein, one part in ten to the fourteenth. And accuracy continues to improve.

"Though math is an analogy, it approximates reality closely. Theology is also an analogy. Of course, there is no way to estimate how accurate theology is to reality, as it's not the same sort of system. Godel's ideas are related to mathematics but I want to apply them to the problem of the existence of God, abductively. Theology, the stock market, and living lend themselves to abductive thought. Nothing wrong with this sort of thinking, and it's appropriate to certain subject matters."

Bal elbowed Paul. "What does abductively mean?" he whispered. The whisper was loud enough that it caught the priest's attention.

"It's a best-guess type of argument," Paul muttered. Bal's eyebrows furrowed, asking for an extra helping of explanation. "It's like when you go to a doctor," Paul continued in a whisper. "The doctor listens to your list of symptoms and then makes an educated guess on how to fix them." An image of Vadim flashed in Paul's mind. "Or not," he added. The priest's stare intensified on Paul. Classroom or not, Paul knew what that meant.

"Mathematical systems rest on a series of truths called axioms. Axioms are assumed true without any proof of them. If a=b, and b=c, then a must = c. Or, perhaps, any two points can have a line drawn between them. If these axioms are part of a system, then some of these axioms will be true but unprovable. In other words, regardless of the system, parts of the system will be unprovable, and the proof of the entire system will remain 'incomplete.' Hence, Gödel's ideas are sometimes referred to as 'Incompleteness.'

"This is not entirely different from the idea of convergence, a basic mathematical concept related to Cartesian coordinates. I want to apply it slightly differently, though the concept is somewhat the same. We can approach the truth, say in a mathematical system, and attempt to prove the consistency and validity of the entire system, but some of that system will always remain outside of the provable scope. Gödel's First Incompleteness Theorem says any sufficiently expressive math system must either be incomplete or inconsistent. And mathematicians are loath to think that a system is inconsistent. Instead, most choose hope—they are forced to hope, instead, that their systems are incomplete. Otherwise every mathematical idea is invalid. So an element of faith and hope underlies all mathematical systems, not unlike theological ones.

"Gödel's second idea to do with incompleteness declares that a math system cannot prove its own consistency. Which means that system is either incomplete or inconsistent. Mathematicians choose to believe that the system is incomplete because if they chose to believe a system was inconsistent, math should be abandoned.

"For those of us who choose to live in the world of theology, we labour like mathematicians. Like math, the system of theology is either inconsistent or incomplete. Saint Paul suggests it may be incomplete. Like mathematicians, we choose to be optimists: we choose to believe our understanding is incomplete, and labour to complete our understanding.

"An extension of Gödel's idea is this: a system cannot be used to demonstrate its own consistency. In other words, a system cannot be used to prove itself, which makes a certain amount of intuitive sense.

"This has a few important ideas, two of are worthy of mention today. First, systems, and our need to invent them will be endlessly recursive. For every theory or system we invent, we must invent a new system to prove and interpret the previous system, and Gödel's Theorem suggests this is an endless, recursive process. So, perhaps it isn't best to invest too much in chasing the next theory to explain the one we have currently. Perhaps it's okay to rest with a system that's only partly explainable.

"If Gödel permits us a slight misuse of his ideas—and I'm not sure he'd approve wholeheartedly, as he didn't approve of abductive leaps—this is what becomes possible. This is why I have been using mathematics to explain theology, of late. Math is a system outside of theology that I can use to help think through the axioms that theology presents to us. In other words, math is a system which, used recursively, theologically, may shed theological light, and help confirm the theological system.

"Secondly, this God system that we have, which we call theology, Catholic theology, rests on a set of axioms. If Gödel's ideas are correct, and if they can be used outside of the realm of mathematics, then here's my point this day: some parts of the theological system must be assumed. They are true, but cannot be proven. Some of them cannot be proven, and the system that we live within cannot be used to validate the theological system itself. We are forced to hope, that our system is incomplete, rather than despair that it is invalid.

"In terms of the world in which we find ourselves, we live, I'd suggest, in what Gödel would refer to as an inconsistent system. It means that any idea or its opposite could be proven at any time.

"As to living itself, mathematical signs show some correspondence with actual existence. The equals sign, which was invented in the 16$^{th}$ century, is an example. Sometimes we encounter a situation where one situation equals another. We believe there is an equals sign when we buy something, for example. I buy a hamburger for five dollars, my assumption is that the hamburger and the amount of money are equal. And perhaps they are.

"Inequality signs were invented in sixteen and seventeen hundreds, because life and math systems hinted that such symbols were necessary. It makes some degree of sense. Sometimes things are unequal. Think of the man whose son is murdered. The killer is caught and brought to justice. Many people think of justice as an equals sign, an eye for an eye, a tooth for a tooth. But no matter what happens to the murderer, can there be equality in such circumstance? I do not think so. An irreplaceable life is lost. The crime will always be greater than the punishment, even if the murderer is executed. Our situation today, as you will likely agree, is one of those unequal moments. Saul left behind more pain than he carried with him when he left. This is a fundamental inequality of which you are the evidence."

As the priest returned from his cloud of thought to the front of the church, he noticed a dull glaze in the eyes of most people, except for Paul, who was rapt, hanging on every word. "But I digress," Joachim finished. "Let me continue, please. And no more questions." The priest cleared his throat and resumed the homily, holding up the Protestant cross.

"This bare cross makes my first observation clear. The cross suggests the Cartesian plane. Here is the origin." The priest pointed to the intersection of the crosspiece and the upright post. "The upright post is the y-axis, or the dependent variable." He ran an index finger up and down the upright. "The crossbar suggests the x-axis, or independent variable." He paused and turned the cross to face his gaze. "The cross represents our current dimensions, the standard Cartesian existence which, at this moment, the group of us share. When you walk into the church, you know to make the sign of the cross. One way to look at that sign is to see it as an affirmation of the Cartesian dimensions we inhabit." With his free hand the priest crossed himself. "To put it colloquially: X marks the spot." The priest lay the bare Protestant cross on the podium and picked up a Catholic one with the corpus easily visible. "Here is a cross from a Christ who transcended the Cartesian system. As you can see, he is nailed to the intersection of the X and Y axes. We are not given units or scale for either of these axes, so we are left guessing as to the independent and dependent variables. But that is beside today's thrust." Bal giggled aloud at that moment. Startled, the priest glared at Bal for a moment.

"What I'm here to draw your attention to today is a subtle point. If I take this cross of Christ and turn it sideways," Priest turned the Catholic cross to its profile, "you can see that Christ himself dimensionally protrudes from the Cartesian plane. I want to suggest to you today, that this subtle reading of the cross hints at an inter-dimensionality which is a concept that can bring us some light and hope to the darkness of Saul's dark and dreadful passing." On a white board, he scrawled a formula:

$$x^2+6x+5=0$$

"Let me give you a simple example of hints of another dimension, using something simple, like the roots of a parabola. Sometimes a parabola, which is a thing found in nature, cross the horizontal axis. The places where it crosses the x-axis are places where Y equals zero. The zeros of this function are x=-1 and x=-5, real numbers. But what about this equation?" He added another beneath the first:

$$x^2-3x+10=0$$

"The zeros of this parabola are not real. They are complex: they have an imaginary part, which is a realm of numbers which may be imagined and calculated, but which do not belong to the realm of numbers which make sense, Cartesianally speaking. But sometimes, using the quadratic equation, we can find zeros that aren't plottable on the Cartesian plane. They exist, but they are beyond Cartesian understanding. There is an existence, but it's outside of our framework."

The priest lingered in silence and assessed his audience. As if to respond to the glazed resistance, he rewound his thesis a little. "Let me restate this idea: if the zeros are plottable on the x axis, they're real." He paused. "If the zeros fit into this plane, we consider them real. If the zeros cannot be explained in terms of this plane, we call them imaginary. We can try to visualize imaginary numbers by creating a separate plane, called the complex plane, and the zeros of this equation can be seen as intersections of that plane." He paused. "Real or imaginary. It's an interesting distinction. All that is meant by that, mathematically, is that things cannot be coordinated Cartesianally. They certainly exist, so they are not imaginary in the sense that they are figments of our imagination. They are imaginary in the sense that the Cartesian dimension has no room for them, so to speak. In other words, it's something like Mary and Joseph—they're real enough, but there's no room in town for them to stay. Real and imaginary. Not unlike a fundamental distinction we like to make in our own world."

He stopped to look around the room again, which seemed to him in a perplexity. Paul was puzzled but still entirely engaged. The priest pursed his lips and let out a gust of breath. Lifted a hand in a stirring motion.

"Death, friends, is maybe something like the quadratic equation, where one undergoes a process of transformation and ends up with an existence outside of the planes we ourselves exist in. A transformation from real to imaginary. A transformation from our plane of reality to an alternative one. Saul has a self-inflicted Damascus experience. There is a decent possibility that Saul set himself free from our Cartesian existence and let himself loose in another one.

"Experientially, we may encounter these dimensions during regular life, perhaps when we sleep, for example, as there is a profound mystery surrounding sleep and what it is. But sometimes dreams seem to me like a dimensional knot. This is the landscape we inhabit, which is the intersection of a multiverse of all possible universes predicted by the various manifolds, with our universe as just one small point among many.

"We do know that energy cannot be created or destroyed. So Saul, when he escorted himself to his end, could not rid the universe of the energy he was, and still is. He punched the ticket he had in this world only to be ushered into another. Saul—the energy, the quantum we all knew—has been removed from this world. His energy quadratically removed and evaporated from our dimension and absorbed into dimensions around us and beside. He may be looking down on us, he may be beside us, he may be behind. I must also mention there is a certain quantum of 'entanglement' between the life of the deceased and the life of the man who now lives in his house." Paul froze. "There is an undeniable correspondence between lives, so much so that one might wonder whether the divine had his hand in this event." Paul groaned. There was more than one audible groan in the tiny audience as well. "Unpleasant, perhaps, but I could not be honest without acknowledging our creator's statistical hint.

"How can we begin to understand these other dimensions when our most extensive tool, math, will only insinuate their presence? All I can suggest to you today, using the analogy of math with some help from science, applied theologically, is the quantum we called 'Saul Shreeve' has transcended our dimensional entrapment and been loosed elsewhere. And those who the Son has set free shall be free indeed. Amen.

"I will offer a small prayer on behalf of Saul Shreeve. The mathematician Sir Roger Penrose suggests that the brain is a quantum organ. Though he would object to my use of his idea in the way I will apply it, I will do so anyway. If the brain is a quantum organ, prayer may be a quantum technology. Reaching not to a heaven that is up there," the priest gestured to the cinder block cathedral's roof, "but laced between and around our existence. Now. Here. Or, if we place 'now' and 'here' close together, perhaps now-here. Nowhere. As a few church fathers would say, 'Closer than thought itself.' Our dimension layered and interleaved with many others. And communication made with our quantum brain could travel much further than we know, in a much shorter distance." He paused to gather himself. "Let us pray."

The homily and prayer done, the priest hosted communion. The liturgy led to a moment when the alter girl rang a set of bells. Paul, who was following the procedure with a sharp attention, lurched when a small girl with a pageboy haircut held out a trio of bells and rang them loudly. Like someone had set an alarm in the service, and the clock's time had come. The bells jolted Paul.

"What was that?" Paul whispered to Bal. "What are those bells?"

Bal shushed Paul with a finger to the lip. Paul waited for an answer, and so Bal whispered. "Sanctus bells. They ring when the wafer and wine become the body and blood," he whispered. "The moment of divine invigoration. The spirit is joined with the body. Consubstantiation."

"Divine entanglement?" Paul asked, in the spirit of the priest's talk.

Bal looked at Paul. His blank stare soured to disgust. "Don't take communion. It would be a mortal sin for a postmodern Marxist to partake of the body and blood," Bal admonished. "Believe me, I've committed enough sin to know."

Finally, after a few more ups and downs, the affair was ending. The priest motioned the sign of the cross. His blessing: "God is X, friends. Solve for X."

After the funeral mass, Paul tried to leave quickly to resume his Marxist life. He shook the priest's hand as he stood by the exit. "Thank you, ummm, Father," he finally conceded. Father Joachim nodded in reply.

And so Paul walked down the steps with Joan, to head the half-block home. Her permanent of tight brass curls glowed in the light of noon as the electric carillon buzzed a noon-hour tune over the neighborhood. She seemed stooped with a greater weight than she had when she'd arrived. Whenever Paul encountered her, she seemed aflame with rage.

Joan turned to him and snapped, "That was the weirdest funeral I've ever been to. What a weird priest! Math, of all things. Desecrating the temple with math. And you asking questions. And what kind of homily was that? What the hell was he talking about?"

"Doesn't mass use Latin? Do you know Latin?"

"Course not!" Joan spat.

"Then you're used to not understanding what's going on," Paul quipped. His steps were steadier than when he'd set out for the funeral.

"I'm used to not understanding Latin, Paul." She shook her tightly curled head. "I'm not used to not understanding math." She winced as she thought through her own words.

"You mean if you're confronted with your ignorance of Latin, that's okay. But if someone clarifies your ignorance of math, that's offensive?" Checkmate.

"Math is for schools. Latin is for church." Then a bone-bundled fist raised in frustration. "This was not right. It was math. I'd quit going if I wasn't Catholic. And, if that was your funeral, I'd be embarrassed."

# 24.

"YOU CARDBOARD WHORE," HE SAID, spitting his venomous words toward the box. *Honeycomb is an excellent source of 5 essential nutrients* read the audacious box of cereal, standing on the table before him.

"Frigstricken lot of good, you are. Prostitute of sugar. Prostitute of taste. Using the sacred symbol of the bee comb for your flow-munching lie." He paused to spoon some sugared shapes to his mouth, and masticated the lumps away, until speech was politely possible again. "You'll take anything that is sacred, anything that is precious to human existence, as the comb of the bee, which to the shame of humanity, has never been copyrighted in any way, and use it to sell your wares which have nothing to do whatsoever with honey." With the end of his spoon, he contemplated poking the box, and, wishing to poke the box in the crotch, he tried to decide where the box's crotch was. "Not only have we stolen the bee's honey, but we have stolen what you are and what you make and plagiarized you, made you entirely ours." The stiff wooden exterior was obviously some kind of erection, the bag seemed uterine, or perhaps bladder-like. The French had something, he thought, when they assigned a gender to all objects. There's a great wisdom in that. The bag had been slightly opened in a vulvic fashion.

*Is this a penis or a vagina?* He wondered.

He paused and fondled the box more tenderly, as if he might get it to talk with a gentler touch. A broad grin broke as he realized the truth.

"You are both, you slut-box. You are willing to be whatever I want you to be. You are both a female that doesn't matter, and an inconsequential male hardened only by consumption. You are a throw-away hermaphrodite. A one-morning, two-sided stand." He puckered and set the spoon on the outside of the pucker. "Hard and wet, that's how I like them."

"Stop swearing at cereal boxes," Bonnie said striding into the kitchen. "Lou was listening to you. If you aren't going to stop talking like that, I'm going to make you stop. Someone needs to protect his ears." Her comment was a not-so-gentle reminder of when she asked Paul to stop using the eff-bomb around their son. She'd beaten Paul nearly senseless until he'd agreed to use a creative swearword in place of a more evocative cussive.

"From what? Vulgar though my analysis has been, it is nevertheless the truth. You want to trap him in the guilt of some petit-bourgeois mindset. Let's not build a fence around the lad's mind too early."

Bonnie sighed, and turned around, her eyes hot with menace. She opened her mouth.

"I have a theory," Paul continued, stopping her words in her throat. Looking down at his bowl, he spoke. "Language is only good for telling the truth. I mean, language really sings, really speaks when a person tells the truth." He herded the limp cereal around the bowl with the spoon. "Politeness is usually some kind of lie, and thus innocuous, inoculating the speaker and the hearer. If the hearer accepts the politeness, against reality, he guarantees that nothing of the truth can be present, causing a failure of language. Truth is something like a ghost that only haunts words when they are truthfully uttered." On the edge of his spoon, he held up a flaccid piece of cereal. "It's losing its erection." He let it flop back into its bowl. "That's the secret of all consumerism: early ejaculation."

"Stop it, you analytical freak," she said, levelling balled knuckles towards his mouth. "You are a disgusting, analytical pig."

"So much for the dialectic mind, free speech, and the dialogic. Ah, it's probably the trouble with words themselves. And the fact that truth is always vulgar and in poor taste. Language is only good for telling the truth, and when it is used properly, you wish it had never been invented." He rested a finger in the cleft of his chin. "I will limit that pronunciation to social truth, and to any truth spoken about any human or human existence in general. Yes," he added, thinking of newspapers, "the truth is edited in every way by every media, and it is politeness, polity, and general good will that hinders the truth from being spoken. Hence, fry-flog politeness. It is my enemy."

As he finished speaking, he noticed that the tightening, whitening knot of knuckles was now level and parallel with his mouth. He bowed his head, awaiting his punishment, and silently began to scoop the cereal. Lou entered the room, and Bonnie's fist unfolded into an open hand, which she used to pat Paul's cheek. Paul winced and closed the eye above the cheek of her open hand. She turned and scooped up her son in a loving embrace.

Paul turned his attention back to his ripening philosophy of cereal. He turned the box on its side, reviewing the nutrition information.

"How much fibre? With milk. Without milk. How much iron? Milk is a good source of vitamins A and D. 26 percent of my daily intake. The cereal box is offered as a contemplation for the breakfasting person. These are ideas to dwell upon while one eats. This is the new salvation. The new pillars of religion. Truly, how trivial this life has become," he muttered quietly, noting a swelling emotion. A quick spoon of shaped sugar. "This box's philosophy: Life is a series of nutritional decisions, based on information provided by the companies as demanded by the government. This information was made public because the government believed if people would make better nutritional decisions, the government would be required to pay less to maintain that public's health." He smacked a mouthful of cereal into a cheek. "Too mundane for me. Wouldn't a better world have cereal boxes with philosophical insight printed on it?"

And without warning, he found his eyes tearing up, liquid working up into blubbered balls tucked away in his eyes' inside corners.

"Is there a cereal box out there that sings? Is there one? Please do not destroy the world, if there is only one cereal box that speaks. Let me find that one. Let me find it. Let me find one thing worth my career. No, let me find one thing worth my life."

"Oh, my God," Bonnie said in a derisive laugh. "You're crying over cereal. You're nuts."

"Yeah, daddy," said the Buddha and his jowls, as dry coins of cereal clanked into his bowl. "You're fuckin' nuts." He giggled.

"Steven!" Bonnie said sharply. The little boy sheeped to the shepherd. She turned on Paul. "This is your fault, you Marxist prig." She turned back to her son. "You want milk, sweetie?" Bonnie added. And the pair shared a giggle.

Paul floated his spoon in an open pool of milk and watched as it slowly sank into the white sugar swamp. And a new wave of emotion pushed firmly at the backs of his eyes and gut. He stood and left the room.

# 25.

After classes finished, Paul left his office and walked the back route to his doctor's office on the far side of campus. Partway there he lost his rigidity again, but managed to flop into a cement chair covered with an annoying orange fabric. From there, he called Security requesting a wheelchair escort.

"I tell you, doctor, something is seriously wrong," Paul pleaded. He was seated in a wheelchair that he had borrowed from Security Services.

"There's nothing physically wrong with you," Dr. Samsonov insisted.

"But I know I'm exhibiting the classic signs of anxiety disorder. I'm entirely falling apart."

"You know how to learn things off the Internet. You have simply plagiarized a list of symptoms. That is all. You are truly fine."

"I only feel fine in my office. I'm afraid any time I leave it. I'm coming undone."

Vadim huffed. "How can one be fine in one's office and not fine outside of it? It defies rational thought. It's is psychology, not medicine."

"It's medicine. It has to be."

"You stepped through the door, and could not walk?"

"Right!"

"That's your head."

"Which is why I want medicine for my head."

"You do not. Medicine won't help with your psychology. This is not a prescriptive ailment. You are … um" He paused for a moment. "What is the idiom?" he asked himself. "Kookoo." Vadim pointed a finger at his ear and spun his hand in circles. "How you say in English? Nutso?"

"Nice. Thank you, Vadim. Nothing like a professional diagnosis. I feel helped." Vadim shrugged. "Academics are a specific type of insane. It cannot be medicated."

"Okay, then. If not for my mental health, how about for the sake of my marriage. It's falling to bits."

"Is it falling to bits for medical reasons? I can prescribe Viagra."

"No. I don't need a three-hour woody. How would that help anything?"

Vadim sighed, looked at his watch, and frowned. "Okay. I will ask then. Why is your marriage falling to bits?"

"It started with my research."

"Research?"

"I began researching doors."

"Doors? What is this about doors?"

"I've been experimenting with doors. Today unwillingly. At home more formally."

"What is this? Are you locking them? Closing them? Opening them?"

"Removing them. Today was confirmation of the power of the private made public. If a public system can reach into private contexts, then the system prevails. If the system cannot reach into a space, then the system fails."

"Where have you been removing doors?"

"My home."

"You mean you took all the doors off?" Vadim, the Russian Jew, rolled his eyes as he spoke.

"I took them all off," Paul replied. "Except the front and back doors, so as to keep our home heated."

"What for? I don't understand this. Беспредел!"

"It's to counteract a small problem I see with Marxism. Sort of an experiment."

"You removed the doors from your house to experiment with Marxism? This makes no sense to me. Maybe you do need a prescription."

Vadim took the stethoscope he was holding and flipped it over his neck and took a seat. "This is so ridiculous, it's interesting. Continue."

"I took them off because I think doors prevented Marxian system from penetrating the private human existence."

"I don't get it."

"Marxism is an ideal, a system of thought that accounts for people's public behaviours, but what brought the Russian experiment to its knees was that the system did not reform the person within the system. The system held them in place, but the private spaces were ones that undermined the system's reach, and, hence, individuals nursed private greeds and malicious intentions that, had the system reached into private spaces, would not have existed."

"You're mad."

"I'm not. A few days ago, another example." Paul launched into a telling of his encounter with his female student in her quest for a better grade.

"First of all, communism did not fail because Russians had doors. Communism has never existed, and never will. This is a fact." Vadim set his index finger on his lips and closed his eyes. "Russia was only a Nazi Germany that turned into a Paraguay."

"What if Marx had somehow dealt with the individual, the being one becomes when one is by one's self? It was the door that separated an individual from the system, and when one separated one's self from the system, no good would come of it. When one closes the door, the base emotions run rampant. It was the separation of the individual from the system that allowed for utopic disintegration."

"You're suffering from the vapours."

"The people needed the system to keep them aligned to the goals of the state."

"And you would eliminate privacy in order to accomplish such a thing?"

"It makes sense. I'm just experimenting, that's all."

"Why don't you use cameras, the way capitalists do? Better yet, the Chinese. Big Brother is what works the capitalistic ideal into every western citizen. But that's not the same as removing the doors. Removing the doors means that everyone sees everything, and that idea is abhorrent, disgusting. Not everyone should see everything. People won't tolerate it. Do you really want me to see your wife on the toilet? She would not wish it, nor would I. However, if a discreet all-seeing eye, someone who is not revealed, sees all—even your wife on the toilet—that would be okay, especially if those being viewed have the sense that the eye is benevolent. If, for instance, the eye acts as a security camera, the person being viewed may well believe the eye to be benevolent. The eye acts to protect and extend the system. The all-seeing eye is permissible, but not everybody seeing everything." Vadim shook his head. "That idea is a steam locomotive on a gravel road."

"The problem with the all-seeing eye is that the seer has far too much power, and that power can become a means of production. One all-seeing eye is totalitarian. The power instead of being de-centralized is taken from everyone." Paul noticed Vadim's grimace. "But you at least agree with me that privacy has been a problem."

"Yes, but I think that idea is well understood. It is, in fact, a modern assumption. Generally speaking, public life is one in most systems that presents the unblemished ideal of citizenry. Private life is the wellspring of all sickness and disease. Although that is changing, of course. A porn star for example."

"Yes," Paul agreed. "So the ultimate Marxian quest, if utopia is ever to be achieved, would be to make life entirely and always public."

Vadim rolled his eyes. "Your marriage is in problem because you are an idiot. Your wife, she is Гром-баба." He studied the ceiling briefly. "A thunder woman. You're such a base Marxist, with a healthy dose of Bentham and hedonic calculus. These systems are amoral. And this is a stupid conversation."

"You provided half of it," Paul replied, with a half grin, "and amorality is the problem. The system must make a moral stand." The two were silent for a moment.

"I think you have delivered your insight upside down. If I turn the box over," Vadim said suddenly, "you have discovered existentialism. Finally! There is proof that existence precedes essence."

Paul pursed his lips, then frowned in thought.

"Since we are wasting each other's time," Vadim began, sitting forward, and placing his elbows on his knees and folding his hands together. "Do you think pigs have souls?" he asked. Paul considered a response, in silence, glad for the distraction. "Fish don't have souls," the doctor added with certainty.

"They couldn't possibly," Paul said almost grinning. "I'm surprised you'd even consider ascribing such properties to pork. How do you know fish don't have souls?"

"Fish don't have souls because they were created earlier in the process, and the idea of soul grew the closer God came to creating the human."

"Religious proof?" Paul asked.

"Right. You Marxists don't like that gauze. No, my favourite philosopher says so. And I don't really like fish."

"Do you think that soul makes an animal better to eat?" Paul asked, mockingly. As he buttoned up the front of his shirt. "Maybe it's a kind of internal marinade."

"Cannibal," Vadim replied in a rebuking tone.

"The only thing that comes to mind is the story of Christ casting the demons into pigs."

"Yes." Vadim nodded approvingly, as he considered the new information. "However, that only proves that they have the capacity for souls, not that they actually had them."

"Are you only allowed to eat meats with soul?"

"Cannibal. It's not about eating at all, but a philosophical discussion."

"How could it be philosophy? It's speculative religion," Paul protested.

"Where I come from, those who live ideas are not inferior to those who merely know them. It is possible to be a holy man and a philosopher. Here it is a sin to believe an idea. When one believes an idea, one is known as religious rather than philosophical. And religion, here, is a pejorative term."

The conversation fell into silence for a moment.

"What about worms?" Paul asked.

"The soul is indivisible," Vadim declared flatly. "Some worms can be cut in two and both ends grow into new worms. They must not have souls. But some worms won't regrow both halves. So maybe those worms have a soul."

"They are hermaphroditic, but still need another worm to procreate. Does that affect soul capacity?" Paul asked thoughtfully. "I'll have to check on that. The conversation has been, um, distracting."

"Paul, there is nothing wrong with you." The doctor offered a hand to pull him out of his wheelchair. Paul took it.

"Doctor, something is broken, something is wrong," Paul replied, sliding forward on the vinyl seat of the wheelchair, twitching to his feet. He juddered upright, as though he were balancing on stilts.

"Look, you are healed."

"I can't walk from here."

"You don't have Parkinson's. For God's sake man, steel yourself. Have some self-respect. If you must, use the wheelchair to help you walk."

"Self-respect?" Paul's anger boiled up, and the quavering stopped. Vadim gestured towards him. Paul was stunned for a moment, observing himself. "I am going to charge you twice for today's visit," Vadim declared. "I find your delusions disappointing."

# 26.

A DAY LATER, PAUL ENCOUNTERED THE rock-throwing Michael Sobczak on his way home from work.

"What do you really want to do?" Paul asked. "That's the key question." He paused, sliding into a groove he'd used with students. "You must want to do something."

Despite Dr. Shreeve's fourth-wave Marxist philosophy, he suggested some adaptive illusions he thought might help a lost man, just like it seemed to help lost students. Hence his recommendation wasn't a good communist idea, it was a life navigation question. Not celestial navigation. Basic compass work. Orienteering maybe. Or a kind of evolved eco-locating.

Michael seemed confused, and took his middle finger and carefully scratched a hole in his thinning hair. "I dunno what you talk about." He stopped scratching, but held his finger on the top of his head. Then he pulled his hand down to see what he'd captured under his fingernail.

"Is there something you really want to do in life?"

"I don't think that way."

"You've never thought about what you really want to do?"

"I do not... I have... what do you mean?"

"I mean, there must be something you have always wanted to do, but you haven't had the time. There must be something."

"I don't know." He scratched again. And stopped.

"Have you ever wanted to do something, even as a young man, or a boy, perhaps, something that you wanted to try or do, but couldn't?"

"I don't know," he said in a genuine puzzlement. "This is something different. This is something. I'm not sure."

"Can you think of anything?"

"You must stop talking now," Michael ordered. "I must walk home for lunch."

# 27.

It was like encountering a cave man in a wheelchair, every time he stepped on to the Alzheimer's ward. Paul felt a warm release spider through his chest as he stepped towards the man in the chair. With every footfall, his wobbly step steadied.

"Unggh. Urrrrrr. Ubbb blubber," said the hunched, shriveled, hairy man in the wheelchair. Furtive blue eyes were hemmed by the large gold frames of his glasses. Bonnie stepped close to the man as he flailed with priestly gestures. She pushed his arm out of the way, so as not to be hit, and pecked him on the cheek. "Gnerrr flubber butts."

"We're here to visit you, Dad," Bonnie announced to no one in particular, not even Dad. The little Buddha stood behind her, in a bland state, perhaps blithe, using his mother's body for protection from the old man. "Come and kiss your Grandpa," Bonnie said to the Buddha, grabbing his arm and pulling him forward under the protective arch of her armpit. Bonnie grabbed her flailing father's wrists and held them for a moment. The little boy leaned onto his grandpa's lap, accidentally putting his hand in the old man's groin for support, and kissed him.

"Ahhhh," screamed the old man, and bent himself in two before Bonnie released his arms. "Screed malick cold gart." Paul smiled to himself. The old man slowly straightened up and sat still, apparently still recovering.

"Mom, can I watch TV?" asked the Buddha.

"Give Grandpa a cookie, first, son," Bonnie said. The little boy went to a dresser in Grandpa Don's room, and chose an Oreo for Grandpa, and took two for himself. Then he walked over to his grandpa.

"Open wide, Grandpa," he said. Grandpa didn't respond. Andrew waved the cookie in front of Grandpa's eyes. Grandpa's mouth opened almost automatically, and Andrew shoved the whole cookie in the opening. Grandpa gagged, half coughing, half spitting the cookie to the floor.

"Can I watch now?"

"Yes, you can."

"Can you change the channel for me?"

"Sure, Son." Bonnie left the room with her son and headed up to the TV room at the end of the hall. In the room sat sixteen seniors in various states of death or decay, watching Dr. Phil blasting into the room. "What kind of wife are you?" he barked through the TV's speaker.

Bonnie walked to the front, to the TV, and turned the channel to a cartoon of some surly-looking robot boys sitting on dragons. Hunches of flesh groaned and stirred as the tone of the TV's blare changed. Most of the aged in the room did not expend the effort to get up and leave, preferring to protest with unintelligible mumbling. The group together sounded like unenthusiastic Catholics reciting the Lord's Prayer. Bonnie cranked the TV's volume even louder to drown them out. "Is that good, dear?" she half yelled to her son.

"That's a good one, Mom," Lou replied, slotting a cookie into his mouth.

Bonnie kept the remote with her and sat with her son. She would have left him alone, but he had suffered an attempted assault by a couple of seniors some weeks before over TV channel choices and hogging the remote.

Paul liked being with the raving man. His father-in-law, Don, was a needy, needy soul. He was a hypochondriac. But he wasn't a regular hypochondriac, the kind who moans over aches and pains and finds attention and plays on the faults of medical science. He was a researched hypochondriac. He was the sort who consulted medical dictionaries and books of symptoms and who after a good bit of research would act the symptoms until he got the diagnosis he wanted.

He inhabited one disease or syndrome for a while, getting an insider's view of the treatment regimen, and then decide whether he really liked it or not. If he didn't, he'd experience a "healing" and he'd be off to the next disease. A scholar and tourist of ailment.

Paul had grown used to the pattern. Really, Don's hobby was his own health, and he played with it the way some grown men play with train sets or army figurines. Paul supposed it was a better one than collecting mugs, something his aunt did. Literally every surface in her house was covered with stupid bits of corporate propaganda. She always delighted with surprise when someone, hosting a garage sale, let one go for ten cents. Diseases generate better conversation and require a greater art and skill.

But Don was a complex figure in a complex set of relations known as the extended family.

"Don, how you doing this week?" Paul asked. He waited for a few minutes. "I'm sorry about Steven hurting you. Are you okay?"

"I'm not bad," Don whispered, slightly hoarse. Paul passed him a fresh cookie from the drawer. Don took it and downed it in a single bite.

"Have they been treating you well?"

"Not bad. We have beef for supper tonight," he wheezed. He glanced around the room carefully, making sure Paul was the only one around. "Bath day tomorrow."

The Alzheimer's phase of Don's hobby marked the most intense role he had ever undertaken. Paul understood him perfectly, however. Don hadn't had sex in thirty-five years, a similar trajectory to Paul's current one. Don was too moral to consider divorce, girlfriends, or prostitutes, even pornography. He hated his wife and she him. Together, they had dragged each other through a miserable home life and a bitter retirement. This Alzheimer's ward, Paul imagined, was a kind of heaven for the old man, with churlish, obese angels thundering around in pastel uniforms and bearing a wonderful array of drugs.

And no one would quiet the old man. Don had been able to yell the replies to a lifetime of insult his wife had thrust at him over the years, and to which he had never responded. So though the words of the argument were not important, Don's expression was. An argumentative glossolalia. A force of form over content.

"Hey, bath day," Paul repeated. "What would it cost me to get one?"

Don rattled a laugh. "It's going to be a good one. Laura's on."

"Which one's she?"

"She's the pink one." He raised a gnarled finger to clarify.

"Ought to be good."

"Hum," he said gleefully.

At that moment, the bigger blue one walked in to give him a dose of medication. Don immediately glazed over. She pulled his chin up, pulled his mouth open, dropped three pills inside, and closed his mouth, holding it closed with her hand while he swallowed.

"He sure is calm with you around," said Big Blue. "You're like Prozac."

Paul winked at Don, and the corners of Don's eyes flickered with a smile.

The Alzheimer's diagnosis was a difficult one to get from a decent doctor. The ultimate hypochondriac quest. They went through six or seven doctors to get the right diagnosis. The problem was he had all the symptoms, but none of the causes (as was perpetually his problem). A causeless effect. He wanted the diagnosis, and his wife did too. It constituted an emotional answer to their relational equation. It was their way of accomplishing a medically funded, sanctioned separation. And so, he came to live in the care of nurses in the Alzheimer's ward. Paul rarely found him ranting and incoherent; he found him sad and alone, craving to be manhandled by a buxom new nurse as he went for his weekly bath.

"Listen, I need some advice," Paul began. "I've got a problem with my neighbors." Paul took a few moments to explain his situation, knowing that the old man couldn't talk without undoing his diagnosis: a practical instance of Communication Accommodation Theory.

Bonnie re-entered the room with the Buddha, who was still twitching with the violence of the last cartoon. "It's time to go now," she announced. Paul stopped mid-sentence. "I'll think on it, Paul. We'll talk next time," Don growled.

"What did you do to him, Paul? Why's he growling like that?" Bonnie kvetched. She whacked the back of Paul's head with an open hand and leaned in. "You shit," she murmured. Steve bounced up to her backside.

Bonnie pushed Steve towards her Dad. "Give Grandpa a kiss goodbye." She replaced the TV remote at the front of the room.

Buddha stepped towards the listing old man. When the child was close enough. Grandpa suddenly sat erect and yelled in a menacing way: "Griven snobby right smart."

Little Stevie shrank away from the old man. "Grandpa scary kissed?"

Bonnie frowned. "Kiss me, then," she said to the lad, "On the lips, and I'll give both of our kisses to Grandpa." So the boy slobbered on his mother, who wiped away his kiss discreetly, before she turned and planted the kiss on her hand and gently slapped her father's face. "Bye, Dad."

"Gribber hobby puck."

"See you, Don. Good chatting," Paul said, patting Don's knee. Bonnie turned to face him directly with an angry stare.

"You're such a dick. Dicks are people who make fun of retards. Now, get out to the," she noted Steve in the perimeter, "effing car."

"Don, widen your vocabulary," Paul advised. "You're overusing 'G' sounds today."

Paul waited to see if any of Bonnie's limbs suggested a threat before he quickly scooted past her into the hallway.

# 28.

For some reason he stayed in the room, he dared to stay as a granddaughter began to watch a children's cartoon movie. It wasn't that she wanted him there. His interaction with her had been so limited that she had come to treat him the way she would treat a door. It was that for some reason he didn't leave, a reason he couldn't identify. One of the main characters was blue and shot out of a bottle from time to time. His granddaughter was transfixed, bewitched by the character, though she'd probably seen the movie fifty times. Beata came into the room and raised her eyes in surprise when she saw him watching with his granddaughter. She set a tray of cookies and milk in front of the granddaughter, and took a seat. If he was watching, she would too, even though she'd seen this movie more than thirty times. She sat there, head facing the TV set, but her eyes on Michael, marvelling.

He was slowly sucked in by the story, which moved a little too fast for him, using idiom he couldn't follow. A beige-faced character came to a crisis in the film, where the blue and beige character began to discuss how to extract themselves from the Disney-trouble they were in. In a perceptive clearing, when he could follow the dialogue, he heard the message of life.

"Follow your heart," said the blue character.

"I can't—she'll never believe me," said the beige.

"Common. Follow your heart. That's the secret."

"That's what Paul was saying I should do," Michael muttered to himself. He slumped back in his chair.

Then the dawn. "Of course. Of course. Of course. It is simple." He looked out the window. "I understand you, Neighbour Paul."

"What do you understand, Michael?" his wife asked suspiciously, noting the smile on her husband's face.

"Follow your heart. That is the only way to work." He laughed, a gut-deep belly laugh.

"What's wrong, Michael? You are acting sick," the shrillness of her question conveyed her feeling. "Stop it."

"I must follow my heart," he repeated and slapped his knee. "And I shall." He sat in his chair and watched the movie through to its end.

Beata watched him nervously.

His heart soared with the blue and beige characters as they achieved apotheosis, and won the hearts of female blue-faced and beige-faced characters, one each. As the credits started to roll, Beata watched him dry tears from his eyes. "So simple," he whispered. "I almost missed it." He noticed his wife staring at him. He smiled at her. She covered her mouth. "What was the name of the new priest?" he asked.

"Ah," she said slowly. "Joachim Trytania."

"That's what I thought you said," Michael said. "I knew the Trytania family long ago. This must be the youngest of the Trytania family. They give the last brother to the church."

"You knew them!" Beata exclaimed. "You must come to hear him." She'd been inviting him to church, to renew his catholicity for years. She wanted, more than anything in her whole life, for her husband to meet her first love—the church. The theological mothership that suckled and succoured her once a week.

"I shall come and meet him."

"Really?" she asked. Her heart rejected the meaning of the words she'd just heard. "Why?"

"Of course," Michael said. "It is time."

"Time for what?" Beata asked.

"To follow my heart," he said and shrugged. "It is inevitable."

"Oh, Michael. You make me so glad," she said, her tears finally arriving, minutes after the end of the movie. The blue and beige characters were doing outtakes as the credits rolled. "I'm so happy." She stood, and went to the kitchen, embarrassed that she had so easily believed him, mistrusting this emotion that she swore she would ever indulge for the rest of her life.

# 29.

Vadim entered the examination room holding a basket of fruit. "Why are you here?" he asked.

"I am here because I am in need of help. I've had about ten hours of sleep in the last week, most of them last night, in my office."

"Didn't we discuss this last time?"

"Yes. But I'm asking you again."

"You want some fruit," Vadim said, holding the basket towards Paul.

"I do not want your fruit. Fruit disgusts me."

"Oh. How is this?"

"It is because fruit is the reproductive element of a plant."

"You are sick."

"It is a simple fact. If an apple tree wants to procreate, to make other apple trees, what does it do?"

"I don't really know."

"Of course you do, you old Jewish bastard. The tree grows apples. Apples are its form of sex. To eat an apple is to eat an apple tree's orgasm."

"You rootless white bastard. Is that fellatio or cunnilingus?" Vadim said as he pinched a grape from the stem. Paul shrugged. He studied the grape for a moment. "But this grape has no seeds." And with some satisfaction, he popped the grape into his mouth. As he bit down on it, though he fought his own reaction, Paul could still see his eyes widen slightly with surprise as the grape exploded in his mouth.

"Ah, the most pleasurable fruit of all. Fruit without the threat of reproductivity. Welcome to the age of the pill, the condom. Seedless sex. The purpose of the grape is still to bear seed, whether it has it or not. It is an exact parallel of the current cult of sex. Something where the seed-bearing point of the fruit has been removed."

"Bigot. I could complain to Human Rights about what you imply here."

"Polygamist."

"I am not. The law says nothing about the number of vines I fornicate with. And it just so happens that I am committed to none of them. Nor am I faithful to any one vine or variety." He plucked another grape and held it up between his index finger and thumb. "In fact, I have no idea where the mother is now. And as for the apple tree in my back yard, I never have eaten from it. Not once." He grinned. "I have inadvertently kept myself a moral man, apple-wise." He set down the tray of fruit on the corner of Paul's desk. From the tray he chose a banana. "I think Freud would agree with your theory of fruit. If anything led to the sexual revolution and our current growing titillation." He looked fondly upon the banana, and caressed the banana's nub. Gently he broke open the banana's neck and slowly, and as seductively as he could, peeled the banana's yellow jumpsuit to reveal its tender white flanks. Then with a moan, he pushed it into his mouth, slowly closing his eyes. Paul looked on at him over the tops of his glasses. Bite after bite he took until his mouth was stuffed full of white mash.

"Are you quite through?"

Once Vadim has swallowed most of the mash, he looked at Paul and smiled. "Could I borrow a cigarette?"

"I might as well start smoking today, so when I've purchased my first package, I'll give you one."

"I must say though you are not sleeping well, you are an excellent conversationalist."

"I cannot sle..."

"I do not want to talk about your sleeping problems. Why don't we talk about your weight problem instead."

"Yes, I'm fat," Paul agreed.

"Yes, I know," Vadim replied. "You teach English. I read a book and a man calls another man a 'fat head.' What is this mean?"

"Fat head?"

"Is this intellectual obesity?"

"Brain fat?"

"Too much useless thinking?" Vadim asked with a grin. "Fat head?"

Paul did not join him in his mirth. His focus shifted inwards, and he began to try and talk the demons out of himself.

"I still can't sleep. I have had about four or five hours sleep in the last week."

"You're exaggerating. You said ten hours a minute ago. What is intellectual fat?" asked Vadim, laying the banana peel on the side of the basket, like a pair of folded pants. He plucked another grape, slowly biting down on it until it exploded in his mouth, which made him blink again with surprise.

Paul sighed, but allowed the current of conversation to draw him in. "I suppose intellectual fat is made of ideas that are never going to be used." He stopped for a moment as the ideas began to carry him out of himself. "They've been processed by the intellectual mill, deep fried, ingredients added, and marketed. I'm reading the same intellectual pap that all others in my discipline are reading."

"Yes?" Vadim replied, hinting that Paul should quickly come to his point. "Your fruit theory is quite original. I'm certain no one has written that one down."

Paul ignored him and continued. "What do I do with these ideas?"

"I don't really know," said Vadim, plucking another grape.

"I store them. I remember them. Do they do anything for me?"

Paul raised his eyes and connected with Vadim as he bit into another grape.

"I don't really know," Vadim said in a flat tone.

"Nothing." Paul said with a bit of a disgusted laugh. "Nothing at all. I read a supposedly intellectual book and I have a bunch of stored, unverified ideas in my head that I'm never going to use. I act, as I always do, as though these ideas have substance, a merit of their own. But I must act. Some of these ideas are pointless, some are useless, some of them are just stupid. I'm obese because obesity is in. If I were to give up the flab of my knowledge, I'm afraid I'd have nothing to teach. This useless fat is the substance of my teaching. It's the substance of what I do. I am intellectually fat, aren't I?"

"You are physically fat. Maybe you are a fathead, too."

Paul glared at his doctor briefly. "What would I do if I cut ideas I don't use? What would I do if I only taught ideas that I believed in, that I believed were true?"

"I think you would not say much."

"You're fumbumbling right. And shut up." Paul sucked in a deep breath and let out through his nose. "Maybe you are right. Maybe I am a fat head. Maybe I should start on an intellectual diet. If I can't live by the idea, if I don't need it to live, I'll dump it. You're looking at man who will live a slim intellectuality."

"I am doubtful you can do it. You have hundreds of thought-pounds to lose."

Paul turned from thought to menace the doctor with his eyes.

Vadim smiled sweetly, while he blinked with surprise at the bursting of another grape. "This kind of exchange is why I quit obstetrics."

"I cannot sleep. Every night I am overcome with such terror, and I must use the TV to fall asleep. I have started to whistle, not to mark my happiness but to draw my consciousness out of my head. My head has become a living hell. I need a prescription for sleeping pills. I want to be able to shut it off without having to go in there."

"Let me reiterate my examination. Were you sleeping well before all these incidents?"

"Yes, I was."

"Then I will not give you a prescription."

"What do you know?" Paul shrieked. "I am very nearly losing my mind," Paul said with a sudden jet of tears. "I can't hold it together." He began to shudder as his grief broke loose within him.

Vadim put an arm on Paul's shoulder. "No prescription will help this malady, I am sure," his words were soft.

"I need to go to a clinic and get a prescription from another doctor."

"You are welcome to do so," Vadim replied pulling his hand from Paul's shoulder. "But you would be going against my medical advisements."

# 30.

It had been a long time since Old Man Sobczak had confessed. So, in his return to a cinderblock Catholicism, a special confession was required. However, it almost didn't happen because the new priest so busy marrying and burying people, blessing this and that, working his smells and bells, that he could rarely make time for the basics, despite the profound and documented psycho-spiritual benefits. Very few new recruits were going into the priesthood, which meant Father Joachim was doing the job of two or three priests. The personal confession, though an important element of faith, was too demanding and costly, timewise, so the priest preferred a general absolution rather than a specific confession. But Beata's persistence won out. And so Michael Sobczak found himself in the priest's well-aligned office on this particular day, at 9.30 a.m.

"My friend the university professor told me last week I should follow my dreams. And then I watched a movie with my granddaughter, and the princess in the movie said that 'a dream is a wish your heart makes.' These things make me think of my life. I have not followed the heart that I have. I have not obeyed my dreams." Though they both spoke Polish, and both knew the other did, they continued in English. When in Rome.

"I have heard this many times, but until the professor said it, it did not make any sense. I have thought for many hours since that day, and I know that my first step is to begin to be Catholic again, then I should invite you to cleanse and bless my house. But maybe I should tell you what my dream is, and you can tell me if it should be followed."

"Michael," the priest began, intoning the old man's name with the softer spirants of the Polish tongue. "This is a good thing you do. You do not explain such things to me. They live between you and God." But in truth, he did not have the time or inclination to take in the old man's words.

He'd even started going into the seniors' homes to which he was assigned and when he found one or two on their last legs, he'd given them their last rites while they were sitting in their wheelchairs staring at him. The priest was even too busy for death. He could not wait for death to make its late-night, last-minute appointments. His appointments and appearances were lined up by his secretary like cars on a rush-hour freeway. So he would sweep in whenever he had a spare moment and do last rites for Catholics who wanted them. It was kind of like a pre-approved mortgage. As he performed last rites over a flesh-pile crowned with a frizz of white hair, which he presumed was an old man, he realized he could help the system by working with a Kevorkian who could administer a lethal dose of morphine just after he'd commissioned the parishioner for death. It would, he admitted to himself, be a whole lot more convenient than meeting death on its own terms. He'd also started grouping numbers of the less-aware seniors together and saying the rite once over them all.

The priest practiced his eye for identifying which ones were going to go next. He thought these things again, as he mumbled the rite over the head of an old, dull-eyed woman in a mint-green sweater, scabbed with food. He'd been halfway through when the woman seemed to come to her senses.

"Not yet, father," she said, fanning him and his words out of her presence. "Not yet." He lowered his voice, finished, and stepped away, so she was "done." He did all he could to stay ahead, but it was not enough. And he was far too busy to hear the confession of just one man.

However, given the devotion of Beata, his secretary, and her insistence on her husband's proper repair to the church, she had insisted. She had insisted, partly, because she was worried if it wasn't done correctly, it wouldn't stick, the way the bond of a glued joint could not be guaranteed unless the surfaces were properly prepared.

So the old man found himself sitting in a pew noting the odd effect that the orange glow, the stippled-rippled orange glass in the windows—because stained glass was too expensive—had on the morning light. Not only did the whole inside of the church glow with an unearthly orange, but the light's hue gave him the distinct impression it was late evening, even though he knew it to be morning. His head said morning, his body said night. This bifurcation toyed with his mental clock, the way two ping-pong players swat a ping-pong ball.

The priest bustled in from the sacristy, with a professionalism that befit his office and schedule. He crossed his arms and invited Michael to follow him to his office. He walked through the sacristy, where the priest was stopped and pulled away for a brief discussion. Michael found himself in front of the control panel for the church's electric carillon. There were a number of switches with names, most in Latin, beyond comprehension. He noticed one titled "De Profundis" and out of some perverse reflex, he opened the protective glass door, reached inside and toggled the switch from off to on, then closed the door again before the priest re-entered the room. He found himself giggling at his boyish mischief, with no clear idea what he'd just done.

The priest returned and without a word, waved him back into a procession that led eventually to the priest's office, which Michael found in pristine organizational form. The priest showed him to a chair, and then left for a few moments to patch a few small diocesan leaks before attending to the confession.

The priest whisked into the room. "Would you like to offer your confession?"

Michael looked up, a little lost. "I am not sure. I don't.... Ah, I used to live in Poland, in a town near yours. I want to confess a heart of darkness..."

The priest held a hand up to silence Michael, and sighed. "Do not worry about your confession. You will get better at it with practice," he said. In theory, the important thing wasn't the specific list of sins. The important thing was that the church offered forgiveness. The rite could be shortened, even if it meant forgoing some of the good nutrition of the confession for the confessor. "Let me pray for you." He took Michael's head in his hands like a ripe, grocery store cantaloupe, and prayed a general absolution, and then a general blessing on the forlorn senior. He fought an urge to keep going and do the last rites. Michael stood and the two shook hands.

"Is it true you're from Polansk?" Michael asked.

"Yes. I'm from a small town called Siedlisko."

"Hmmm. My family lived nearby," Michael said. "Trzcianka."

"What is your family name?"

"Sobczak."

The priest shook his head. "I know of several Sobczak families, but none from Siedlisko."

"What is your family name?"

"Trychania."

"Oh yes. I know your family. Do you have an older brother Joseph?"

"Yes, yes," said the priest, his tone warming for the first time in several days. "He is much older. I am the accident."

"Thank you, father. I am restored. My wife wants me to book an appointment to have you come and bless my house."

"Yes, yes. Please talk to your wife and she will book a time for that."

He turned from the conversation, and let his mind run to his first contribution to the diocese: the Gold Mass, his special project.

His mind was already on the Gold Mass he had just planned. It would be the first of its kind for this diocese. The alchemical call overwhelmed his cautious sensibilities. He aimed to host it on Saint Albert the Great's feast day.

# 31.

Bal studied the bottle of Viagra he held in his hand. He took one of the pills after getting the prescription at a walk-in clinic. He had decided to try Viagra not because he needed any fibre in the woodiness of his member, but because he hoped it would help him achieve a suave sexuality that seemed to elude him. He felt his loins grow, and grow, and grow. Interesting, he thought, as he studied his own feelings. He hadn't had a sexual thought for a couple of hours now, as he worked on his tomato plants, but he'd taken the pills as described, and was sporting a large woody as he cucumber-crawled doggy style around his plants.

The timber in his pants disappointed him: There was nothing sexual about the erection, and he realized that the pill only provided a hard-on. Not sexuality. Not a well-bred, worldly, sexual broadcast. His erection might as well have been a worm as wood. Like carrying an eggplant home from the store in his pants. The pill did not offer any erotic insight or advantage. Bal had offered his sexuality to the pill the way the five loaves and two fishes were offered to Christ. He sighed. In this case, however, no miracle. Nothing in life seemed to work as advertised.

He began to imagine the world again after everyone had had sex. Not the cheap kind, the kind that satisfied only for a short while, but the deep, inside kind, the kind that would keep a person satisfied for a lifetime. It seemed to him that the one problem with humanity was that the effects of sex never lasted. Which was one of sex's disappointments. If God and heaven existed, he thought, heaven would be after some kind of big, celestial sex. The Big Bang. Sure, sometimes a cigar was just a cigar, but not very often, and likely just after a good round of rumpety-bumpety boom.

If anything could bring desire, in the cosmic sense, to flaccidity it would take the Big Bang, a cosmic coitus that would that would take the intensifying crescendo of this world, this aching hole, to the calm after bliss.

He left his tomatoes and headed inside to make himself some supper. His woodland member had led him slowly out of thought into long strings of sex acts that he contemplated over and over until he sat down with his supper before the TV to watch the evening news. As he watched, he noted the nearly orgasmic tone of the news hosts, one male and female.

The fear, the absurdity, the giant tease of life. The short stroke of the news stories, faster and faster, blood lust and loss, beasts, scandal and war. It was clear the world was already out of its mind, like a body most of the way to a climax. Reason could no longer break through.

As he stood there, waiting, he noted again, that the world was entirely screwed, beginning to end, in, on and around every hole. In fact, humans had the delightful ability of locating new holes and sexing those as soon as they found them. It was the little sexes that led him, again, to postulate, from another angle, the existence of the Big Bang. It would be a big bang, the giant, mother orgasm that would bring the world to rest again.

If the big nooky brings the world to its senses, he reasoned, then we are in the pre-coital phase now. The world is a teenaged boy, surfing porn. Horribly hot, and nowhere to spend it, nothing to spend it on. This is a pre-sex problem. Oh, the glory of the sex and post-coital phase. Oh, the glory of this shivering, shooting apocalypse. The world is a man tied to a bed, heaving with desire, waiting for anything to satisfy.

He imagined a post-sex world where the world lay exhausted and loose like the droopy, rubberized Salvador Dali painting he had once seen, where the world's woody had finally gotten off, and for a little while afterward, desire did not exist.

The news confirmed the Big Bang: the world is coming to some kind of orgasm. The Big Bang is coming.

A cosmic orgasm would bring the world to rights again.

***

AFTER PUTTING HIMSELF TO BED, and trying to calm his pole-hard penis by himself, he could no longer sleep. Bal, aching for some kind of sexual contact, pulled himself out of bed, dressed and headed out into the night, to surprise his wife at the restaurant. He'd insisted she get a job to help pay down the mortgage on the house. His tiny pension did help, but it was not enough. She was a quiet, mousy girl, who had no idea how beautiful she was. In fact, she was shapely and voluptuous, and since she'd taken the job at the restaurant, she'd seemed to slowly realize that fact.

He pushed his toupee a little forward, to help cut the cool wind that bore down on him. It was only about a 6-minute walk to the restaurant. "Restaurant" was hyperbole. This was a drinking dive with windows. As he pulled into the light of the sign, *Pegasus Schnitzel House*, he could see the lordly of the lower income bracket sitting next to the window. He stopped to watch a man finish a point, probably on a political subject, pointing his finger across a cheap wagon-wheel table at another group of men who seemed to snarl in return. As he watched them, a sudden light seemed to light the faces around the table. Angela had arrived with the next round. She lowered the jugs of beer on to the table and all eyes were not on the beer, but on her fantastic breasts, which seemed, as he noticed now, to almost pop out of her blouse. She herself seemed to enjoy the leer, for she stuck her hands on to the edge of the table, squeezing her breasts with her elbows causing them to swell towards the drinkers as she slid the bill onto the table between them. The money came onto the table. Lots of it. No one seemed to bother to consult the bill's total. They stared at her breasts and forked over the money. She put her breasts away and scooped up the money in a single motion, smiling to herself as she did so.

Bal was aghast. He watched her as she turned to walk away. But she didn't walk. She flounced. Her body swayed and bounced this way and that, and men's heads everywhere turned to eye her sexy swagger. He stood out near the walk, on the sidewalk, his mouth open. Where was her modest catholicity? Her demur nun-like self that he'd quit his job for? He'd never seen her walk like that ever. She was like walking sex act. Occasionally she'd throw her head back orgasmically and laugh as she talked with a patron. Bal had to adjust his stance to accommodate his still-substantial woody.

He stood outside in the light of the sign and watched her most of the evening. The Viagra left him, but his wood remained. She was sex personified. Oddly enough, though, no man laid a hand on her. They stared and put their hands to their mouths to catcall. But no one patted her behind or fondled her at all. Odd, too, he noted, that the restaurant was mostly, if not entirely, men.

He stood outside in the light of the sign for most of the night, gazing at this woman, a good, penitent Catholic, a woman he'd slept with, who laid beside him for several years, a woman he obviously didn't know. He waited until the drunken patrons left, smelling of pork, cigarettes, and beer. He waited and watched his wife clean the tables, hoist the chairs, invert them on the tabletops, vacuum the floor, while her swarthy boss towards the back of the restaurant drank, counted money, and polished glasses behind the bar.

# 32.

PAUL STEPPED INTO THE WAITING room and took a seat. The waiting room was empty. The receptionist-slash-nurse was filing her nails carefully, and as Paul watched her, he guessed that she must have played the violin at some point in her life.

He walked over to her. "Yes?" she asked. Continuing to concentrate on her filing, she did not look up "I'm here to see Dr. Samsonov."

"You must be pregnant," she replied.

"I'm a man," Paul replied, suddenly offended. "How could I be preg…"

"Of course you are," the Nurse replied in a nasal tone, with some kind of eastern European accent. "I joke. Dr. Samsonov used to be an obstetrician. Can you briefly describe the problem you would like to discuss with Dr. Samsonov?"

"I am still having troubles sleeping," Paul replied.

"OK." She stopped filing for a moment, and gestured to the waiting room seats. "Please take a seat and read one of our many lovely magazines." She disappeared from the office, and returned fifteen minutes later, straightening her skirt. "Doctor Samsonov will see you now."

She led him down a narrow corridor to his normal waiting room. He took a seat on the papered surface of the examination room and waited. He heard some intimate laughter in the hallway before Vadim burst through the door and sat down.

"So what seems to be the problem?" he asked.

"I told your nurse."

"She did not tell me."

"Same as before. I am having trouble sleeping."

"Oh," Vadim replied. "What does that have to do with me?"

"I wondered if you had any medical solutions to this issue."

"We have spoken on this topic a few times."

"Yes. Yes. But I need help. I've slept even less since we last spoke. I'd need a pill."

"You do not."

"But I do," Paul whined. "I can barely hold it together. I haven't slept since this whole thing began. That's ah…maybe six weeks now."

"Given your temperament and what has happened to you, I declare you to be completely normal. Your lack of sleep given these circumstances is understandable."

"But I need to sleep. I need to stop thinking."

"Yes."

"And I can't."

"I know this."

"Then I need a prescription for sleeping pills."

"You do not. You are sleepless for perfectly sound reasons. To medicate you is not right. Your body will begin to sleep again. I assure you. I reiterate: you are normal, except you are an academic, which is a sort of abnormality, but it cannot be cured any other way."

"Are you one of those hippie doctors—I heard you used to be an obstetrician. I bet you denied your patients anesthetic." Vadim immediately frowned at the word *obstetrician*. "Why won't you prescribe anything to me?"

"I was an obstetrician, but I gave it up because the hours were crazy and I was tired of being insulted. I did, for your information, prescribe anesthetic frequently."

"I have to teach my classes," Paul blurted. "I can hardly hold a single thought in my head."

"I'm certain you'll have a greater educative effect in your current condition."

"I can't teach. I can't even read my notes properly!" Paul said, snapping like the dogs who chased him in his thoughts.

"I think sometimes intentions get in the way," Vadim chided gently. "What you mistake for education is your intention to get one point or another across. When something is intended, it is education. I think no. Education is only openness. And educational intention devastates openness in most cases. A humble ignorance is preferable. Ignorance assigns beauty and respect generously compared to someone who believes he sits on a throne of understanding.

"Education is a transformative. They need all the information I can give them, and I have to help them understand what they need to know and why they need to know it." Paul's defensiveness backed its way into anger.

"Tsk, tsk, tsk." Vadim wagged a finger before his globular nose. "One only needs to learn enough information to suspect it all. Or at least educated enough that one begins to doubt what one knows. This is what it means to be educated well. Imagine your mind is a refrigerator. Do you slam the door on that refrigerator and leave it closed once you think you have all you need?"

"Ah...," Paul's anger started its engine, but Vadim had already begun a reverie that would not end until it had its way.

"Of course not," Vadim answered. "You daily inspect things to make sure they haven't gone off. You use them. And once in a while, you pull everything out of the fridge to clean the whole thing. This is a good mind. Not just good grocery philosophy." Vadim was thinking through his ideas as he spoke. "This is where you are at, my friend. You are cleaning out your mind fridge, whether you know it or not. This is why I won't give you prescription. A pill just slows your hand."

Paul raised his hands in protest. The rev of anger ended with a sputter and choke. He took a breath which he intended to spend on speech, but Vadim continued.

"Knowledge is groceries, not a destination. In fact, knowledge is only a means to learning. It is not learning itself. Knowledge is necessarily generic, which is to say, meaningless. Learning is when the person comes to see that knowledge has some kind of personal relevance."

"Knowledge is power."

Vadim sighed and shoogled his head side-to-side, then looked up with a frown. "You are a secret Catholic, no?"

"Of course not!" Paul barked.

"But, you still believe that knowledge is a eucharistic celebration? I shall switch ... how you say... metaphors." He held up elements of an imaginary Eucharist. "If a child ingests twelve years of education she is transformed into a citizen." He placed the imaginary wafer on his tongue, and held up another imaginary wafer. "If she eats another six years of information in the sciences, she is then a scientist." He placed the second imaginary wafer on his tongue. "But I know enough people who call themselves doctors, or biologists, who are merely idiots, not even citizens. Information does not transform a person. That is ... обман ... a lie." He crossed his arms, and stroked the end of his nose with his fingers. "Do you think I'm a good doctor because of the courses I've taken?"

"I ...," Paul began.

"Don't answer. I know what you think. If I have taken 20 courses to do with food preparation, would you eat the food I made? I hope not." He snorted at his thought. "You are what you know. It is a Eucharistic thought. And I know it to be false."

"Am I going to have to pay extra for your educational insight? Or will you write a prescription?" Paul blurted, finally.

"Philosophy instead of pills, friend. Let your mind find its salvation. Suffer, please, until you don't. Then you shall be cured."

# 33.

At a pedestrian-controlled crosswalk, the Buddha pushed the crossing button, which peeped, and Paul watched as the cars in both directions paused to leave the white-lined crosswalk open. Buddha pleased with his own power, like Moses, parting a traffic sea for his people.

Paul studied Lou's button pushing. "When you push that button, Lou, you're asserting our existence, our egos. And look what happens." Paul gestured to the lines of idling cars. "These cars stop for us. And this tells us something. This tells us that whenever and wherever the ego is asserted, energy must be expended."

Lou had learned to ignore his dad's academic spouts, tugged on his arms drawing him forward into the white parallel lines, without a muzz of a thought.

"Actually, it makes sense," Paul said, as he followed a path of thought. "The most ecological thing I can do is kill myself, isn't it?" Lou led his dad across the street as traffic resumed its course. "So it makes sense that any assertion of the ego is un-ecological, an expenditure of energy. Like the cars must idle while you and I cross the street, energy they spend accommodating you and me as we cross the street. The ego is not eco." Paul chuckled to himself, and the simplicity he'd tripped into. Lou, who understood laughter, offered a fat, loose giggle.

Lou managed to steer his dad to the sidewalk and set him in the direction of their home. Paul, caught by an idea, obeyed.

"Pollution is a strange idea, Stevie. Everyone thinks of it as a form of dirtiness, which it is, sort of. But it's actually more of a form of purity. Like a plastic bottle. Its problem isn't its dirtiness. Its problem is its purity. It's made of rarified ingredients that profoundly resist a reintegrating to nature. Pollution is more like a weird salad of purity. Nature is not purity. It's all things mixed. Pollution is things unmixed."

# 34.

PAUL HEADED FURTHER UP THE corridor to his own office. The sun slopped over his desk in a thick warm syrup. He rolled his office blind to stem the flood of light. His coat he hung up, and replaced it with one of three sport coats he kept on the back of his office door. He hung up his coat and donned his sport jacket. Two tone green hound's-tooth. Then he sat in his chair, booted his computer, hunched, with both elbows on his desk, and began to conjure the mind and resources he would need for his day, while he massaged his temples. A gut-load of fatigue spread through his body as focus on his lecture shooed the ghosts away from his thoughts for a moment. He yawned broadly. Teaching distracted enough that his spine was fine.

❋❋❋

HE WAS IN THE MIDDLE of class and Paul had just finished leading the group through a Marxist/gender reading of Edna St. Vincent Millay's poems, "I Too Beneath Your Moon, Almighty Sex" and "I Shall Forget You Presently, My Dear." A surly young man with a tuft of black hair, named Noah, stuck up his hand.

"I see what you did to that poem, and that is utter bullshit."

"So what are you trying to say?"

"What you did to that poem is bullshit." Noah seemed near anger and had missed Paul's joke entirely. The rest of the class tittered, resisting a bigger laugh because of Noah's seriousness.

"What was bullshit about it?" Paul asked.

"The whole thing, beginning to end."

"That's a very specific criticism." The class laughed.

Noah, now huffy, tore a piece of paper out of his binder and passed it to Paul. "Here are the notes I took on your lecture." It was blank.

"Whoa," the class countered in unison. But Paul was not daunted. He looked Noah straight in the eye.

"Young man, what you do not realize is that everything means something." He met his eyes. "Everything means something!" he yelled. "Why did you pass me this paper? Why?" Paul looked at Noah, to demand and answer.

"Cause it's empty," Noah replied contemptuously.

Paul laughed condescendingly. "You passed it to me because it means something. You think you passed me something that is empty, void of meaning. But you cannot pass me anything without it meaning something." He smoothed out the slightly crumpled paper. "Do you think the paper you passed me comes from nowhere? Do you think it carries no history?" He wagged his finger at the class, which had suddenly begun to listen intently. "You are foolish if you think this piece of paper means nothing."

"First of all, does anyone know what this paper is called?"

The class bantered a few names around, but with Paul's affirmation, they settled on a word Shelley used for it: fullscap.

"It's not fullscap. It's fool's cap, or foolscap." Paul turned to the board and wrote it down so they could appreciate the spelling. "Does anyone know anything about foolscap?"

The class fell silent. "It's called foolscap, named so after a watermark of a fool's cap that became associated with a particular size of writing paper. Do you think that means something?" The class groaned a yes. "Do not trivialize this point, or you'll piss me off even further." He stole his gaze from the class and put it back on the paper for a few moments as he assessed the page. "As I gaze on this white paper, I notice that it is not completely blank. There are thirty-four horizontal lines, robin's-egg blue, on each side of the page. At the top there's a one-and-a-quarter-inch blank space, with no lines. And on the left-hand side of the page, there's a thin red margin line, one inch in from the left edge, stretching from top to bottom. In the margin, there are three holes.

"I can read this paper as a symbol—of, for instance, the unlived life. Youth. Ignorance. I can read this sheet as a philosophy: It is form without content. Existence without essence. Or the tabula rasa—almost. Painted with hints as to how it wants to be used.

"This paper makes certain suggestions to me, as I look at it. It is writing paper, clearly. The pale blue lines are there to guide my words, to organize words, not just for me, but for those who might read after me. If there were no lines on the page, I might think of it as drawing paper, perhaps. But this is writing paper. The primary message was this: Write. And to suggest writing is to suggest a certain individual agency. Paper is not given to a dog, is it now? And foolscap is common—it is a democratic suggestion that all should write. It is a small protest against the printing press, a medium begging for a message. An undermining of the capitalist machine. A miniature subversion. Calling for some kind of demonstration of the individual. This individual must have certain skills, must read and write. This paper therefore implies widespread literacy. There's an implication of government, the kind of government and citizens that would be required to make sense of such a piece of paper. You would only make available such paper, if you were certain that there was no serious threat caused by it.

"There's a bulky blank at the top of the page. Which gives a person the sense that there ought to be a title at the top: that writing needs room for a title, perhaps. The paper has holes, so it can be slipped into a binder. It is something that implies the writing instruments that could be used on it. It anticipates the pen or the pencil. This is an expanding story, I think, and I need to house it in a binder so it can grow and the order can change. It is a temporary medium, and suggests that the words written upon this page will not be worth very much, nor will they last long. To use this paper is to automatically devalue the message. The paper, too, is one primarily used in a school setting. There's a required sense of openness, an attitude of learning that this paper asks of me. I should be listening and taking notes.

"Now where is my analysis coming from?" Paul gestured to the class. "Where is all this bullshit coming from?"

Hayword raised her hand. "From your head, sir."

"Right, and precisely true," Paul said with a vehemence that startled the group. "Meaning is in the eye of the beholder. So, what is the problem," Paul gestured towards the class, "If someone believes a page to be empty?"

The class was silent.

"I'll tell you what it means," Paul said in a menacing tone, as he leaned towards the class. "An empty page is only empty in the eye of the beholder. The emptiness is in one's head." He paused. "Nothing on the page means nothing in the mind. And here is the ironic truth: there is no such thing as nothing. You see, perception and knowing paint everything you see. In fact, one of the problems with human science is that it's entirely dependent on the senses. If I ask myself, for instance, what colour my front grass is, at this very minute after I've fertilized it and conditioned the soil, I would say that grass is green. However, green is simply the way I sense light: Light hits most objects in unique ways. Most objects absorb some of the spectrum of light, and reflect others. If every object reflected all the light striking it, everything would be white. If every object absorbed all of the light striking it, everything would look black. Grass absorbs much of the spectrum of light, but the middle band of light, somewhere between 500 and 560 nanometers, it reflects that colour back to me. One of the easiest things I might say about my front grass is that it is green. What I'm really saying when I say that, is that when a normal human eye gazes at grass under the conditions I am experiencing right now, that human will likely see the similar colours absorbed and similar colours reflected, which most human with normal human colour perception would call "green." Humans are some of the only creatures on the earth that would call grass green. Hence, I must ask myself, as I think about it, is my front grass, really, in its truest character, green? Or do I, as is characteristic of my species, think that the universe and its creatures shall all find grass green?

"The Romans began the idea of cut grass as a symbol of land ownership. Cut grass, then, carries the hint of an economic structure, and economic status, because grass was difficult to cut in those days. You needed a slave or two and a sharp blade. Or a heard of goats or something.

"More broadly, when I look at grass, when I touch it, when I smell it, when I taste it, how much of what I sense of grass is truly a part of that wondrous phenomenon? If grass is green because I perceive it that way, then the question for me becomes this: How much do I paint on the world when I gaze at it? How much smell do I add, when I sniff at a scent? How much of me do I sense when I stroke a tuft of green stuff? What if grass, as I see it now, was like language, my perception of grass, like the word grass, only reflected me back to myself, and nothing else—what then?"

Paul walked from the front of the class to stand in front of Noah's desk. "If this page is empty, it's only a symbol of your mind. It's only because you don't have the intellectual capital to see what's already written on it." He set both his hands down on the front of Peter's desk. "And that is what you're here to learn." Then, like an old preacher, who knows better than to yammer beyond a brilliant ending, he finished his afternoon quickly. "Class dismissed."

# 35.

Owen loved to wear his Oxfords, with the thin, black nylon laces that made the shoes hug his feet. Besides old as dirt, he had no feeling in his feet any more, no more feeling in the bottom half of his body. He had made it to the sitting position on the edge of his bed, which was his daily goal, and waited, doing puzzles until homecare showed up. He had a special cane with a pincher at the end that he used to snap and grab things around him. A mechanical dog. He used his cane to grab a bottle of Old Spice from his dresser a few feet in front of him. He pried the plug out of the hole and carefully splashed a little around his body, and dabbed a little in his crotch, just because it tended to smell a little between baths. He was just getting used to the "darkie"—as he called her—who had been helping him for only the month or so. The previous one had been white trash, and he had fired her and called the agency when he had discovered she'd been stealing his money and rum.

"Moanin', Own," said this gentle woman from Jamaica. "Hour you deday?" her language smooth and soft like a thick towel.

Owen didn't respond. He hated whoever it was who had come to help him, in this case, a woman named Moody. If he could have seen who she was he would have enjoyed her full and generous heart, and a smile that tapped into some fund of unlimited joy. But he could not see her for what she was. He only knew how vulnerable he was, how exposed, and how this woman had come to run important parts of his manhood. So, he hated her.

"My shoes came untied yesterday," he said roughly.

"Oh, 'dats okay. Weel fix 'em deday."

"I asked you to double-bow them. But you didn't."

"Yesse did, Own. Yesse did." She shook her head as she spoke

"Make sure they don't come undone today, or I will call your boss."

Her smile didn't flinch. "I do the bess I can. If I doan stick, you call."

She got him out of his PJs and jerked on his support leggings. Then a pair of freshly pressed pants, one of the three identical pairs he had. A fresh white undershirt. A plaid flannel shirt (but all his shirts were plaid flannel). Then she took his shoes, loosened them up, and slipped them over the swollen bulbs of his feet.

"Easy now," Owen said, anticipating some kind of pain, a pain which never arrived. She grinned. She did up the laces.

"I would like the laces tighter."

She re-tied the laces, a little tighter.

"Tighter," Owen said, wagging a fist and finger in front of her face, pointing at his shoes. She did them again.

"Dat's tight as dey go, Own."

"Good. Now, double-bow."

She let him have his rant, which gave him the illusion of power. This made him happier.

She helped him to his chair in the kitchen. He could hear the muffled sounds of Steve in Paul's backyard. He used his pincher to pull the sheer curtain away from where it covered his rear-view mirror. He wagged his head left and right, to check the angle of the mirror and the view it afforded.

"Adjust the mirror," he said, pushing is luck a little with an imperative. But he had no idea of the broad grace of the woman attending to him at this moment. She smiled.

He waved at the window and the glass as she moved it up and down, towards the house and away. Finally, Owen nodded. She came inside, tidied up briefly and left.

Owen watched the Buddha truck and thunder around his yard. He was very glad for the new lack of fence, the one Paul had removed recently. The lack of fence afforded a much better view. And the view, as small as it would have seemed to anyone else, was better than any of the crosswords and word-finds he did to pass his time. And so he studied the mirror image of this little god as he went about his business.

He remembered being a boy on the flat prairie. His dad farming and building. The son lost and bored, neither in the house, nor in the barn. He poured a Pepsi and dragged the bag of Oreos across from the far end of the kitchen table with his mechanical claw. As he assembled his food, he arranged it on the table from right to left, in order of consumption. Then, like an old video machine, he began to review his favourite memory. It started with dad pounding a stake into the ground, and his mother coming out of the house to push him over to where his dad was working. Owen was an only child and never asked at his five years of age to participate in the work of the farm. So his father's labours were still a marvelous spectacle to him.

He watched the one stake go deep in the ground. His dad stepped a few feet beside the driven stake and pounded another into the ground. Then he nailed a cross member between the two stakes, and winked at

Owen. Owen always slowed the memory's play as his father winked. That particular wink may have been the highlight of his life. How he treasured it.

His mother held him in place while his dad disappeared around the far corner of the barn and returned with a rough-cut pine plank. He placed the plank across the cross member and strapped it on by nailing loops of canvas in place. Owen knew this contraption was somehow related to him, by the squeezes his mother gave him and the looks his father cast him between hammer blows.

His dad sat on one end of it, as happy as if he had found a cure for cancer. Owen was pushed to the far end of the plank as his mother threw a leg over behind him. And they seesawed. For a boy who has very few toys or playmates, this was as remarkable an event as could ever be hoped for. In fact it was beyond his comprehension.

His dad and mom only had a few minutes a day where they could seesaw. But that did not dampen his enthusiasm for this device. Often he would sit on what came to be understood as "his end," waiting for one of them to come along and add the necessary weight to make the device work. He had many memories of sitting alone on one end of the plank, in the dirt. Sitting down and alone, waiting sometimes for hours for someone to pull his ass out of the dirt into a play of balance.

To this playground he returned daily. It was this playground he often saw in Paul's back yard, through his rear-view mirror, and when he died, he planned to live there. Waiting on his end for someone, his dad, God, someone, something to sit on the other. The afterlife had to be different, he reasoned. This life was mighty one-sided. Maybe the next would bring balance.

# 36.

IN THE DYING WARMTH OF the day, Paul was walking home from Lou's preschool after a good soaking rain. Another group of clouds in the west began to fold and roll together, and the sky darkened slowly again. Instead of Lou's usual pugilistic questioning, his little mouth frowned as he studied the wet world. After they crossed 26$^{th}$ Avenue and began up the 35$^{th}$ Street sidewalk, he finally spoke.

"The squirms are drownded! exclaimed Lou. He found one draped over a stone in the gutter, held against the rock by a torrential flow. "Help you, squirm!" he yelled and with his clumsy little hands fished the worm out of the flow, stone included, and chucked him into a flowerbed on the adjacent lot. Lou ran back to the sidewalk found a critter inching its way over the concrete, toward the road. He pinched it away from the concrete. Paul watched the worm twist and buck as Lou chucked it into the same flowerbed as the previous one. "No, don't be drownded."

"Sorry, son. What was that?"

"The squirms are drownded," he repeated.

"I'm sorry, I think my ears aren't working well today. Did you say squirms?"

Little Lou looked up from underneath his Spongebob umbrella and shook his jowls in the affirmative.

"What's a squirm?"

"Look, Daddy!" Lou ignored the question, hunching down over the sidewalk cement. In a small oval-shaped indentation on the sidewalk lay a shoe-sized puddle of water. In that puddle, a single pink, pencil-thin, finger-length creature struggled, for god knows what.

"Oh, a squirm," his dad noted. "That's called a worm, son, not a squirm. Worm." This kind of correction was always important.

"The squirm is drownded," Lou said.

"The worm is drowning," his dad repeated, a detectable, delectable emphasis on the word *worm* and on the suffix-finish of drowning.

Lou bent down and fumbled with fat fingers to capture the creature.

"I wouldn't touch that, son. You don't know where it's been."

Lou, having won the battle with the worm, hoisted the creature as high as he could. The worm thrashed as he pinched it between his fingers.

"Mommy says squirms eat dirt," Lou said. His face twisted. It looked as though part of him wanted to laugh. Some other part seemed sick with agony.

The dark sky above them broke open again and began to drench the world once again. Lou didn't hold his umbrella over his head, and seemed not to notice the rain as it pelted him. Instead carried the worm over to the nearest lawn and underhanded it to safety.

The worm, it turns out, had not been a Marxist concern of any kind. Paul hadn't heard a paper on the subject, nor attended any session, academic discussion, or forum to do with the worm. His son's small gesture opened a new wing of existence and triggered insight, precious insight. Suddenly Paul could see. He could see worms. Perhaps for the first time in his academic life.

Worms had pulled themselves out of the ground, presumably to avoid drowning. They were stretched on the sidewalk, wiggling on the roadway, washing down the gutterways towards the drain.

Paul was instantly overrun by metaphor. They were everywhere! Instantly, he understood their plight: In an effort to save themselves, these brute creatures had worsened their own condition by trying to save themselves. The oppression they experienced by the road building, the cement and asphalt was not unlike the plight of the proletariat! But worms couldn't unionize! Nor could they revolt. They had pulled themselves to refuge in such stupid places. What an ignorant creature! The irony was deep, rich, dirty, and sad. Paul swallowed an urge to weep.

Paul studied his son as he nobbled worms from their places of probable death, to places that seemed to increase the odds of their survival. From the sidewalk (for Lou was only allowed on the sidewalk) he rescued those worms he could, and placed them in gardens, under hedges, and on lawns.

Though the thought of actually touching such a creature repelled him, Paul knelt down and fiddled at a worm wedged in a crack of cement, but determined to head to head into the roadway. Lou stopped for a moment and eyed his dad as he picked at the pink form. Once his finger touched the worm, it writhed in place.

"Get it, Daddy. He's mad, Dad! Get 'em when he's mad. You can save 'em when they're mad."

Paul found the emotional wherewithal to capture the critter between his thumb and forefinger and into his palm. The worm seemed to breakdance in place.

"Oh, no you don't," Paul said to the worm, who seemed to want to writhe out of his hand before transferred to the lawn. It fought against its own best interests! How typical! He held the writhing critter up to his face. And suddenly a torrent of emotion broke open. "You've got more living to do." His words halted and jerked with absurd, disproportionate emotion. Fortunately, fat little Lou wouldn't notice because, like Lou, Paul had abandoned his umbrella, too. And with a slightly understated flourish, much like a good communist who had righted a wrong (not in the moral sense of course), dropped the worm into dirt of a tree well. Lou was pleased.

"Daddy," Lou said sweetly. "You are a superhero of squirms."

Paul turned to him, slightly stunned silent by his son's insight. "You're right, son," he replied. "I never thought of it that way."

For the next several minutes, the two of them worked feverishly as the sky soaked them to the skin. In a moment, after they'd come to their senses again, Lou spoke.

"I like saving worms, Lou," Paul admitted to his son.

"Why do you love them?" the little wise one asked.

"I never knew I loved worms, Lou. Not until today. But I do love them." He realized he was using intangible, capitalist, colonial language. And, that most ridiculous and inarticulate of words: "love." The semiotics of his sentence depended on a word so broad, abused, and misused it could hardly mean less than it did. In his mind he justified it as a language he would use to communicate with the very young, someone like his son.

From the head of his treasure trail, a push of emotion rushed up his throat, asking for tears, but he found the strength to refuse the request this time. "I love worms for their blindness, for their deafness, for their handless groping, for their inability to do anything but love and process dirt." He bent down and retrieved a worm as it arched and pushed down against sidewalk cement, in an attempt to drill its way home. "You don't know where you are or where you're going, do you?" he said to the pink beast in his hand. "In the city, the worm is certainly a lost creature. In a good downpour, they squirm out of the dirt, up between sidewalk blocks, through cracks in roads, between pavement and building, and in an attempt to save themselves, they stretch out on concrete and asphalt, long and thin, waiting for the waters to ebb. And they cannot find their way back to safety. They have no flamdoodling eyes."

"No fuckin' eyes," Lou agreed with a giggle.

The two recovered their umbrellas and resumed their walk home, saving the odd worm as they walked, as the spirit led. Paul led Lou out into the middle of the quiet street they were walking along. In the middle of the street, they stopped and watched as one worm arched heavenward and swung its head around, attempting to sense its way back to his home.

"You need some help, don't you? See, sonny, there's no way he'll make it. Look where he is. He's pulled himself out of a crack in the road, and made about a ten-foot trek to the crown of the street. He's heading the wrong direction desperately, as he feels the moisture leave him high, and ever drying. And if worms dry out, they die. Heaven, for worms, is down, down into the soft moist-mothering bosom of the earth, into the rotten, fecund world of bits that humans care only to call dirt." Paul pointed to a garden near Bal's house as he continued to gaze benevolently upon this lost creature. "I watch him, appreciate his condition, and how very like me he looks as he throws himself into an effort that he imagines will lead to a continued life. But it won't. I can see with my eyes that his aim is off, and death will surprise him shortly." The Buddha stood there nodding as if he had understood it all, but as usual, Paul was talking to himself.

Paul squatted on the ground and found a nearby maple key, and used the flat end as a spatula, sliding it under the worm and pulling the worm off the pavement. As soon as the maple key touched the worm, its defensive instinct kicked in. It twisted, hoping to pull itself out of Paul's grasp. "Whoa, easy, boy." Paul had the creature firmly in the palm of his hand now, holding it low so Lou could satisfy his eyes.

"You see, his instinct tells him I am a predator, I am a bird, about to make him into a meal. Not many creatures submit willingly to the so called 'chain of life.' More accurately, not many creatures will submit to the chain of death.

"He cannot distinguish between a touch, friendly or foul. His assumption is that all touches other than one from the earth or another worm will lead to his death. That response would line up with the odds of worm experience, I'd bet." Paul walked off the street towards the line of tomatoes up the side of Bal's house. He took his son's hand as he lowered the creature into some wet, dark loam. The two of them watched as it quickly nosed into the dirt and pulled itself out of sight. Lou continued to study the worm and attend to his father's words. "You're right, though. I'm like a god to these worms. I can't see much room for providence in how he must see the world. I carry him from the middle of my street to a particularly lush portion of grass, and I set him down. He untwists himself, and pokes his head into the dirt and pulls himself away from view. Down into heaven." He realised that the pronoun 'he' offended the worm's gender self-identification. They were hermaphrodictic, weren't they?

"Right, Daddy. Evans down," he looked at his dad wanting to laugh but trying to see in his father's face whether the joke was worth one. His dad noted his desire and laughed, and so Lou joined in laughing louder and longer than it was worth.

"You see, in the worm's mind, I think he is pleased with himself, pleased at what seems to be him a successful twisting episode. He'll tell his friends about being in the beak of the big one, and how his survival instinct and machismo kept him from death's slicing sickle. How he struggled to dive deep, and somewhere, somehow found the strength to try one more time. And how on that dive, he found home, paydirt." Paul paused and pulled his son off of Bal's lawn and onto the drying sidewalk.

"I don't think worms have the capacity, nor the inclination to recognize a moment of … um… benevolence, or maybe the right word is *grace*. It is inconceivable to them. There is only the struggle to live, and in the struggle, grace, unseen, comes upon a worm like the best part of a story, a story which he will tell but not understand, a story which he will claim as his own, but in his thoughts, he will know that he cannot remember any real reason that it resolved the way it did." He listened to his own words as a student might listen to a lecture. This was a way he learned from himself. As he began to hear himself talk his lecture began to elevate in its tone. He was curious. This thought had come to him with a trajectory all its own. Where was it going? Who was he talking to?

"Perhaps I impugn the worm by writing my thoughts on his actions. Appropriate his story. Perhaps I am right. One thing is true. I am a saver of worms, a careless saviour, but a saviour none-the-less." As the two walked slowly, Paul bent down and pulled a pale worm out of a stream of water following the gutter down to the storm sewer. "How about here?" He chucked it under a hedge. "You know, Lou, only you and I would know that we're trying to save worms. Just the two of us. 'Superhero of worms' would be terms that only the two of us understand. Worms likely view me differently from how I view myself. I imagine the worms would speak of me, not as a redemptive figure, but perhaps as a bad hunter—a vindictive, hungry bird, but sloppy. Any who believed that I was a redemptive figure, which, given my earlier admission is extremely unlikely, would likely be discredited by other, more logical, more scientific worms, who would discount my actions from several angles of worm logic. Any teaching about me or advocating prayer to me in worm public schools would be banned. My attempts to help them would be seen, I think, as failed hunting, or they're think they escaped the clutches of death thanks to their own bravado. A few of them will have horror stories of what I do to them. I have thrown worms under trees or hedges. I just threw one that ended up hanging one over a branch of a tree. Even though most of those worms would make it, I imagine they'd have tales of horror to tell the others." He paused and grimaced as his son unwittingly stepped a worm, crushing it out of life.

"Oops, Dad. That one broke."

"That one broke, sonny." He squeezed his son's hand and bent down again. "Here's one we can save. Should we save it?" Lou nodded vehemently. "Do you want to be saved?" he asked the worm. "Oddly enough, almost all of those I 'save' would have harrowing tales of how they'd been treated, how they'd come close to death and it had mysteriously let go of them, or they'd fought it off. I, to them, would be the figure and specter of death. They'd also associate me with the rain and wet—a worm's weather of judgement—because that's when I do my saving thing, and so most would naturally assume that I am associated, in whole or part, with death itself. None would welcome me."

"I try the next one, Dad," Lou said. He had gained authority over this species in the little while he had watched his father interact with and pontificate over it. Lou bent down to pick up one.

"Dad, they feel wiggly," he said happily, throwing the worm onto a lawn with his short arms.

"Don't they feel great?" his dad replied, having abandoned his earlier disgust.

Lou nodded and bent down to pick up another.

"I think a few of the quieter worms, the more contemplative ones, perhaps the ones that were much more dried up, and couldn't muster much of that instinctive twist to free themselves might wonder at this weird instance that returned them from a most certain death. Perhaps they feel they weren't worthy enough or good enough to eat, and feel less of a worm as a result. The most I dare hope for is that some worm was mystified by my actions, that the whole event made him think, and makes him think, causes him to wonder." He stopped as Lou began to forget about his dad as he inflated with the power of his new job. "How much wonder would a worm wonder if a worm wondered on wonder?"

As Lou skipped from one fleshy victim to another, chucking them wildly on to lawns under trees and into gardens, Paul spoke: "I do think saviors have a difficult time consorting with those they save. For one thing, we're not their kind. Even if we had the power and opportunity to visit with these worms and tell them what we're trying to do, the words I want to use would not be, I am convinced, in their vocabulary. Nor would they like us destroying the unction and myth they've already built. I am convinced that such communications would be useless. I must be happy in the truth: I am despised and rejected of worms."

"I like worms," Lou said lustfully.

"Me too," Paul agreed. "I find it easy to have pity on worms, lost worms. They have no eyes, so when they get into trouble, of course they cannot see their way out of it."

"No flam-fuckin' eyes, Daddy."

Paul smiled. "No flag-fogged eyes. They have no ears, so they cannot hear the truth. Their brain capacity is infinitesimally small in comparison to my own. In the rain, hundreds of thousands in our city who think they are saving themselves, worm their way into a certain death. And they have every excuse to do so: They cannot see what they are doing; they cannot hear things that would correct their choices."

"Are worms better than people, Dad?"

"Humans can see, can hear. But as far as I can see, despite our big brains, twenty-twenty vision, and good hearing, we pull ourselves towards death at an even faster rate than worms. Worms only work themselves into trouble. Humans pledge each other, push each other, prod others to death. Humans build factories designed to promote death and shoot it through water, air, and earth as liquid, solid, or gas. Humans experiment with every conceivable way to bring death to other humans—cold, hole-making devices of various sorts, concussive devices, fire, pestilence, creatures, emotions, food. I'm probably forgetting something in my list. Even death-obsessed lemmings are much less creative in their investigation and exploitation of death than we humans. We've explored, as humans, every conceivable path to death we can think of. We've used our eyes, brains, and ears to make death as available and ubiquitous as possible: perhaps death is the only democracy we've ever achieved. I think this is why we humans have so little compassion on other suffering humans. Humans are the best earthly creature at death. The human race's collective resume, the number one job humans are qualified for, is death-dealing. With such marvellous capacity for death, it's hard to feel sorry when we occasionally succeed at offing one another. It's also hard to feel sorry for a beast who, despite a big brain, two eyes, two ears, and opposable thumbs, chooses to put him or herself in harm's way. Maybe the Romans were right: We're so good at death, it really ought to be entertainment."

Paul found a worm, nearly completely dried, and stuck to the sidewalk, despite the downpour. Lou noticed the change in his father's focus and joined him as he gently pulled the animal from the concrete, being careful to allow his skin to pull away smoothly from the sidewalk's surface. "Slowly, slowly. Easy now." Paul brought him up in the palm of his hand and looked for a sign of life. Its pink had dried into a darkening red. He looked dead. Paul found a puddle and baptized him — full immersion. "In the name of me, I baptize you," Paul said aloud, mocking the ritual.

His attempts a resuscitation failed. The worm's body kinked in a way that only a dead worm's does. Paul buried him carefully under a tree so at least he could rest in the dirt he loved.

Up the street they went. He found a couple of supple, moist ones stretched out in the bald sun, desperately escaping to nowhere. One had small bits of debris—sand and so on—stuck to his skin. He was sluggish, the sun evaporated his thoughts and he hadn't the energy or clear instinct to recoil at fingers. Paul baptized him just to get rid of the debris. "In the name of survival," he said dunking him into the water. The shock of the cold puddle water woke him up and he writhed just as he ought to. Paul found another mostly dried one. He liked the dried ones. He found another puddle, and baptized it. "In the name of the holy wiggle that it had, that I have, too." The water caused the worm to do a sluggish, slow bend. *He's still alive*, Paul thought. He found a patch of dirt, dug a small hole with his hand, placed him under, and buried him alive.

Paul learned that he liked the dried ones particularly because he could find one, every few, that'd dried in his spot, still alive, and he could take him back from the brink of death and re-give him that most holy gift, that big mystery of what we so frequently call life. It was Paul's recreation.

"I'm a kind of scientist," he said to Lou, holding his two mucky hands in the air like a gloved surgeon. "Scientists can't create life. But they can mix and mess with life force, stem cells, say, and make things grow. Like me. I don't create worms. But I can take worms and mess with them and help them grow."

As the two worked, the sky clouded and broke open, and a particularly big downpour filled the gutters and rushed toward end of the street. Paul and Lou took refuge in a bus stop shelter. Water hurried drain-ward in a wide impromptu creek, ankle-deep, four feet wide. In the creek's flow, Paul saw a couple of big worms tumbled by the flow, headed for the sewer grate, destined for a slow drowning death. He leapt from under the bus shelter and into the water, and one rolled into his splayed fingers. Water invaded both shoes. He lifted the worm out, flattened one end, and watched it curl over as if a bird had done this to him. Paul chucked him onto the grass and reached for another. The water brought worm after worm, as Lou looked on from underneath the shelter. Paul's count must have been up near 45 or 50. Enough to worms to start a worm religion, or a good debate among worm-folk.

# 37.

ANGELA SPENT A LITTLE EXTRA time in the shower before bed, sanitizing her body from the occupational stain and fluid, like a mechanic cleaning after working on engines. It was a careful clean, nearly religious in its thoroughness. Her daughter was out, earning a little extra money for herself. Angela was alone. She approached her own bed. Not the one she worked in, but her other one, one hidden in the couch. She removed the cushions and jerked the bed up and out. The bed was perfectly sheeted, waiting. She pulled a couple of folded quilts from a hope chest, made by her father, which she used as a coffee table. The quilts she draped over the unfolded bed.

Then she lit her candle and sat watching the flame, clearing her mind of the day's debris with the same thoroughness as her shower. She believed in heaven, and that she carried heaven with her all day and lived it out all night. Heaven, she believed, was her dreams. And when she died, she believed that she went to live in her dreams. Her dreams served as the frame to which she bolted the rest of her life: it upheld her steady state. They held her firm when all else broke lose. So, she was careful to treat her sleep with a deep reverence. The hot curve of the flame's thigh smoothed itself, lifted high, made itself young — like a promise. She smoothed the creases in her forehead, one by one, like the wrinkles ironed from a dress.

# 38.

PAUL FOUND HIMSELF IN A dither on his way to work. The story Joan told him would not fade. It would not relent. It hounded him day and night. The darkness somehow veiled a bright, light world before him. The front spokes of his bike exploded with winking bars of light as he headed towards the sun in on a bright late spring morning. His breath he exhaled like cigarette smoke. Then, somehow, he felt light. Frictionless. His dark thoughts evaporated as he sought to orient himself to whatever might be happening outside of his mind.

For a fugacious moment he imagined himself as a nun, looking like Sally Field—the Flying Nun. He put his right hand on the top of his head and nodded, just as Sally used to, to try and catch a lifting breeze. His tire winked a little further, the bike suddenly lurched and gentle black clouds flocked over his vision.

Sometime later, the blackness faded into brilliant blue. He blinked several times to cope with the colour. Two cotton-ball clouds scurried across the sky. He lay in pea gravel covering the pavement, between two parked cars. He breathed in slowly. His bike lay overtop of his chest. He pulled his hands to a position in front of him. His right one was covered in dried blood. He attempted to push the bike off his chest. He slid the back of the bike under the back end of a brand-new Toyota Corolla and sat up. Instantly the cars and street began to spin. He lay down again.

His head hurt, as if someone had smashed it with a brick. With some effort, he raised his left hand ,and touched his head where it hurt. He pulled his hand away, and the fingers were gobbed with blood, thick, like ketchup. He raised one of his feet and pushed the bike entirely under the Corolla. In a dizzy crawl, he moved up from the street to the grass of the boulevard. The sky seemed all-searching, all-knowing, and entirely too bright, so he lay facedown, wondering what the sky was looking at, and why it should find him so interesting.

"Flame off, Sky," he said, speaking into the grass. "Leave me alone. I'm not in right now. If you'd like to leave a message, do so after the beep." He paused. The light persisted. "You find me interesting because I am down while you are up. Now, go away." He paused again. He waited. The sky seemed to fade.

"Oh, my God." The silence brought thought. The thought brought a tremor of terror, arcing from his throat through his chest. He was too far inside himself. Thoughts began to turn on him again. snapping like junkyard dogs off the chain. He was in too deep.

"Oh, my God, I've got to talk. Hello, hello is anything out there?" he asked aloud, hoping that the audible sound of his words would pull him out of pit. "Hello, this is Paul, I'm needing help." He laughed as he ran out of things to say. "Blah, blah, blah, blah, blah, blah, blah, blah, blah, blah," he sang, to the tune of Jingle Bells.

He rolled over to face the sky. "Look if you must. Annoy me please. I'm having trouble with my mental balance at the moment. If you would please sit on the other end of the seesaw, we might strike balance. Please. Pretty, pretty please." Then, after a few minutes, he stood, and stumbled up the boulevard to the college. "Fugue this. I need to talk to someone. Got to talk." A quick glimpse of his hand. "I've got to get cleaned up." He stumbled as dizziness set upon him. In an apparently drunken stupor he headed to the college mumbling and shouting to himself. He didn't notice the stares of those he passed.

"Are you okay?" howled a clerk attending the gym's check-in desk.

"Yes, I'm fine, quite fine actually," replied Paul smiling. "Just need a bit of a workout."

"You look like you need medical attention," the clerk said, slightly horrified.

"Nah," Paul said with a nervous laugh. "I just need up a bit to clean."

"I'm going to call security," said the girl.

"It's worse looks than it," he said defensively. He stopped puzzled with what had just gone wrong with his words. "I mean ... sorry, much better than it looks. It's much better. Don't worry about it, please." Paul didn't wait for her response. He headed into the change room. He caught himself in the mirror. He looked like he'd just completed several axe murders, and then turned the axe on himself. The sight of himself stole the strength from his knees, and a new dizziness threatened to wipe him off his feet. He stuck his hands under an automatic sink faucet to clean them off. The water refused to run. "Flag off, Frag off, Smag off," he cursed. "Recognize my sovereign existence, will you, you flute-snooting piece of machinery. He slammed his hand down on the spout, but the water still refused. "You Scottish bum-muddler. I'll find my water elsewhere." He shuffled from the sink to the showers, and struck the shower button with the palm of his hand. The water first hit his head like a pleasant thought, and some poured over the back of his head, and flowed down his inside of his shirt. The rest soaked slowly through his shoulders slowly, the wetness wicking down his frame. The water flow stopped briefly, and he palmed the button again. Then pulled the shower curtain closed and fell to his knees.

A few minutes later, someone entered the shower area. He had big black shoes and black pants. Paul could hear the beep and squawk of radio communication as the water poured and dribbled. He observed the water beading on his pants and then slowly sinking in. The fabric must include synthetics, he thought. Suddenly the shower curtain opened like the curtain on the first act of a play.

"Excuse me, sir," said the man with heavy black shoes. "I'm with security. I wanted to make sure you're okay."

"I'm fine," Paul said, speaking to the peach tiles on the wall near the floor. "I just an accident had, that's all."

"What's your name?"

"Shreevepaul. Department English."

"What kind of accident did you have?"

"My bike car hit, I think," Paul mumbled. "I think. I'm pretty sure."

"I don't understand you, sir"

"Bikecar cident. Hit. Boom. Pow. Ouch," Paul slurred.

"Was it a hit and run?"

"Sister Bertrille." He gurgled on the word 'Sister' and on the word 'Bertrille' as the shower water ran over his lips.

"Pardon me?"

"My fault. Parked car." The warmth worked its way through his pants to his skin. He felt as though he'd pissed himself, which, given his current condition, didn't feel too bad.

"Was anyone else involved?"

"Enthrington."

"Excuse me?"

"Nope." He spit a little as he enunciated the bilabial plosive.

"Do you need medical attention? You look like you do."

"Physically fine. Need a Psychiatrist. Drugs. Nope." He shook his head. A dribble of water, which had been pouring from his upper lip, snaked slowly to the floor as his head moved.

"Sir, I'm having trouble understanding you." The legs bent and the bulbs of two knees protruded beneath the tight black fabric. A few minutes passed.

Paul was crying, suddenly, but the water made it impossible to tell.

"Can I call you some medical help?" The left black shoe stepped into the shower. "Ooooh. You've got a nasty gash there. You need stitches. You should see a doctor.

"I hate my doctor."

"Sir, are you refusing help?"

"Yeppir. Snoop. Solutely."

"Okay, okay," the security guard said, backing away. "It looks like you'll live."

The black-shoed man swept the curtain back into place, and stepped out of the shower area. The static and beep of communications halted as he spoke, presumably into a microphone: "Incident confirmed. No code. Repeat no code. Check back in fifteen."

The shoe retreated, leaving a filthy footprint. Paul studied it as the spray of the shower slowly stippled and blotched the filth, and finally ate it away.

Several hours later he was sitting in his office, feeling a little better, dressed in his workout gear and a baseball hat. His workout clothes smelled of old sweat. The hat covered his new gash. And the matted hair that he refused to comb for fear of reopening the wound again, combined with the eclectic assemblage of dress, brought many odd looks from those who saw him. He was in no state of mind to notice.

He, however, was on the inside of himself rifling through the contents of his interior, as if he were looking for a set of keys. His interior, had it been an office, was impeccably neat. Everything filed. Furniture neatly arranged. But somehow, now, everything had fallen apart. Ransacked. By some unknown assailant who happened to share his name.

※※※

HUNGRY ON HIS WAY TO class, he filched a bag of expired cheezies from the English Society Study Room.

As class began, he held the bag of cheezies aloft. "Before we get to work today, let me show you these. What are they?"

"Cheezies," someone answered.

"Yes." He lifted a puffed corn orange crescent up before the class, the way a priest holds a wafer before transubstantiation. "Have you ever seen any real cheese this color before?"

"No," a couple of students said.

"Right. But we still eat them, don't we? What's interesting is that these are hyper-orange, and hyper-cheese flavored." He stuck one in his mouth. "It reminds me of Dr. Swansea, who complained to me once that his potato chips tasted too much like potatoes.

"So why are they safety-vest orange, and yet still I eat them? It is because this neon-orange is necessary to invoke the symbol of cheese. The color here tells me I'm not eating actual cheese, I'm eating the symbol of cheese." The class was silent. "Think about that for a moment. I am invited not to eat food itself, but the symbol of food. I am eating a bag of cheese flavored ideas.

"This is a transformational moment, not unlike the idea of the eucharist, where food is abstracted from what it actually is—a blend of chemicals and corn—to invoke the idea of cheese. Reality transformed into symbol. Bad for health. Bad. Bad. Bad. But so delicious."

He gave his afternoon class an exercise in the computer lab, which they worked on the entire time. He tried to be helpful, but found he had nothing profitable to say to anyone. His complete lack of style prevented students from approaching him.

And he stared at Jessica's beautiful legs as she swiveled gently on a computer chair. The legs, her legs, which were crossed at the moment, drew themselves together at her perfectly formed hips. A ruffled white mini-skirt prevented him from more carefully examining the join. Despite the feeble powers of his mind, he was able to move beyond this flimsy cotton barrier.

After much of the class had passed, he awoke. He stared into the empty chip bag and noticed he was poking his wet fingertip into the corner of the silver lining to extract the last of the salt and vinegar flavouring. He consciousness snapped back from Jessica's legs and hips into the brown and beige carpet tiles on the floor of the classroom. He raised his eyes beyond the bottom half of the world.

Jessica met his eyes and gave him a mischievous grin. The chip bag, silver lining and all, dropped from his hands to the floor. The quick heat of embarrassment warmed his face. He straightened his posture.

"OK. Time's around. I'd like you to hand job in the exercise," he said. Students milled about as they printed their assignments, stacked them on his desk. One of his better students, Chris, filed to the front and passed in his exercise.

"That was the best class ever," Chris said, glowing. "Your lecture was brilliant, and the exercise was absolutely perfect. Thank you."

"Ah," Paul replied, pushing away the returning thought of Jessica's swiveling legs. "You're welcome." Jessica passed in her exercise and left the room. Paul picked it up. Her essay exercise was titled "Why I like Bad Boys." The first few sentences betrayed a grammatical indecency that went with the subject matter. The warm prickle of his own delight with her topic disgusted him. It was a complete breakdown in control. He fought harder to keep his mind away from her. He tried to think mathematically and alienate these thoughts by creating an environment hostile to these things. He reviewed the minutes from the last English Department meeting, which did help somewhat.

He thought of the calculation of area under a curve. He thought of the extreme violence that math did to the curve to achieve its answer. The perfect swell of Jessica's leg as it reached the hem of her skirt, she was beyond the reach of math. His stomach tightened and tingled at the thought. There was no math to describe her. The problem further complicated as Paul imagined gooseflesh on her thigh. The gooseflesh added volume to the curve and created a problem too complex to bother with. Math faded, and he was left with her thighs. Then himself.

Alarmed again, by how unprotected his mind had become, he stood carefully, picked up the assignments and walked out the lab and back to his office. Where had his resolve gone? Where was Karl Marx? And as he returned to his office, he noticed he'd left the door to his office open.

"Schist," he said to curse his own lapse. As he moved to his office's entrance, he noticed his computer and guitar had been stolen.

"Fark." And with reluctance he called the Security Department to file a report.

***

PAUL CAME TO IN THE middle of departmental meeting with no sense of how he'd gotten there. "I don't think you're entitled to speak on the subject, I really don't." The words, though well enunciated, flew from Allan's mouth into the room with droning, nasal buzz, like a subdued kazoo buzzing with academic precision. He angled the top portion of his pear-shaped body towards the group. The skin beneath his comb-over flashed red with indignation. "Why did we hire a man this time around? I cannot give my support to a white man teaching women's lit-tratures" (this was how he pronounced it). "Now, I don't want to suggest that there was anything wrong with the hiring committee. But, how could this have happened? It's a serious breach of justice." So this pear-shaped, white, self-titled radical spoke. His plodding way had caught up to the meeting's point a half hour late, like a city bus. But he didn't let that stop him. All the ideas he'd ingested over the course of the meeting had suddenly become his own, and he uttered them in an authoritative confidence, as if no one else in the world had thought them until he opened his mouth.

Paul swiveled in his seat, his thoughts still not on the bubble. He felt—not drunk, exactly, just molasses slow, like he had three brains instead of one. The words that were being spoken around him seemed to make little or no sense. Instead of hanging together in lines like they normally did, the words broke a part into nonsensical strings of sounds. Musical. Tonal. Atonal.

"It was the first time I felt as though I didn't want to work here," said Brittany, speaking in support of Allan. She was a thin woman, and almost a radical in her style, for she truly was open to so many more things than the average person. Almost anything, in fact, especially drugs and sex in fashionable positions. She wore her slogans on t-shirts she had made from time to time. The one she wore to this meeting read *Stop Appropriating Voice*. The slogan was stretched tight on thin cotton, stretched between peaks of her breasts. She wore her slogans tight, these days, so she could show off the money she'd invested recently in her breast augmentation surgery. A surgery the department had noticed, but never acknowledged.

Krandall, who had been staring at her slogan for quite sometime, raised his thick glasses to stare at her mouth as it moved. He was a man drawn obsessively to bow ties, but didn't wear one, because he didn't want to be classed in the category of bow tie wearers. He was also drawn to analysis. Why, he wondered, would a post-colonial feminist bother with breast augmentation surgery? What about the breast was enhanced when size was increased? The nipple was never proportionately increased. Why were breasts, in general, fun to watch? If eyes were the nipples of the face, why wasn't he drawn to them as easily? What did it mean to care more of breasts than of slogans? Why wouldn't Brittany sleep with him when she'd slept with a man in sociology, and before that, that long-haired rickydick, Mervin, in Media Studies? His thoughts returned to the meeting occasionally, where his mind tuned into the conversations just to make sure the meeting's social trajectory was on course given its initial coordinates. He brooded over a set of intelligent words he was going to throw into the meeting when they fit. Allan meandered on, and no one was listening, not even Allan. When he paused for a short time, Krandall interjected. "I disagree," he said, and stopped. The breasts had bewitched his active thoughts into oblivion.

Next to him, in a fashionable tussle-haired hairdo, sat a man who was a master of stylish trivia. A man with infinite style sense, yet without substance. Thom was style personified. All relish, no hot dog. His meeting etiquette consisted of a series of postures which he took, ad lib, to follow the meeting's tone. His current fashion in meetings was to sport a pair of small spectacles and to look over the tops of them as people spoke, to occasionally remove them and point to people with the ear pieces as one spoke, and to sigh, recline and rest one of the earpieces over his philtrum. He had the glasses even though they were not required by prescription. Krandall had spoken, and knowing that Krandall made a study of being right, he immediately removed his glasses, pointed the earpieces at him, gently gesturing the glasses towards him. "Hear, hear. Krandall, I concur." Krandall, who was still sloganeering, was startled from the object of his contemplations and looked at Thom with some fear, for he too had lost track of the meeting.

Catherine, who was still drunk because it helped her cope with the department's bald politics, was feeling acutely inclusive and noticed that Paul hadn't spoken. "Paully, what have you to say? We haven't heard you speak," she squeaked in her dramatic drunken tone. There were others in the meeting, fourteen in total. The tenured members of the department. After Catherine's remark, all the members focused on Paul.

"Ah." Paul began, throwing out nonsensical sounds as they occurred to him. "The sky, not like me. Sally, she fell, hurt her flying head." In the fog inside his head, he realized he should stop. The meeting stumbled on the pebbled syllables he uttered. A cough. The snapping sound of a juice bottle releasing its vacuum as the lid was twisted off. He checked to make sure his baseball hat sat upon his head. He rose. "I bladder. More I go soulless." He smiled big, reassuring the crowd with his teeth, gave a thumbs-up and soodled out of the meeting into the hall.

He went back to his office in a complete fog and closed the door, waiting for the feet of his sanity to touch the ground. He sat and spun in his excellent office chair for some time. Then a question entered his mind: which two books in the hundreds crowding his office hadn't likely touched before? Ideas have polarity, don't they? He gazed around. He had a Holy Bible, one he used to look up allusions in the works of authors such as Blake, T.S. Eliot, and Milton. He took the bible off his shelf and spun in his chair. He a copy of the *Anarchist's Cookbook*, which caught his eye. He pulled the cookbook off the shelf with his left hand while holding the Bible in his right. Then, slowly, he put the two together until they touched. There were no sparks. He gazed around his office. No other local effects. That he noticed, he added to himself.

*Who knows what happened elsewhere in the world*, he thought.

He set down the cookbook and swung around to grab his worn copy of Marx's *Manifesto*. He clapped the two books together and looked around. No noticeable local effect. Then he rolled his eyes.

*Of course! These two have touched before somewhere, somehow.*

He took a couple of Jacques Lacan's works down and touched them to the Bible. Then a Baudrillard. A Robert Ludlum novel and Galbrian's *The Prophet*. *Midnight's Children* and *Huck Finn*. G.K. Chesterton. Voltaire and Seneca. The Hardy Boys. Terry Eagleton. Jacques Derrida. Franz Fanon. Homi Bhabba. Freire.

"Aha," he said triumphantly, rediscovering a vein of Harlequin Romances. He touched one of them to the all the books in the growing stack on his desk, finishing by touching the Harlequin to Marx, and then collapsed back in his chair, catching his breath.

*Something's happening somewhere*, he thought fiendishly. *I wonder what it is.*

# 39.

"YOU HAVE HIT YOUR HEAD badly," Vadim reported, after completing his check. "You should have likely gone to emergency to get stitches for your cut, but it would now have to be reopened to be properly stitched and it has already set. You have experienced a severe concussion. You may not do anything for the next two weeks that will cause you to bump your head again, or you could end up incapacitating yourself permanently. I will give you a prescription for a few Tylenol if you need to control the pain. Otherwise you are fine. You may re-button your shirt." He thought for a moment. "Do you want to take time off of work?"

"No, I can't. I'll go to pieces."

"Do you have a helmet of some kind? A bike helmet, say?"

"Obviously, no."

"A motorbike helmet, then?"

"No."

"Give me one moment." The doctor left the exam room. He returned a few moments later with an older, 70s styled, open-faced helmet with a sparkled American flag adorning the piece. He bandaged Paul's head sufficiently. Then slipped the helmet carefully on Paul's noggin and strapped it under his chin.

"I like the sparkle of America on your head. You must wear it. If you get clipped on the head one more time, you'll be a retard for the rest of your life. I mean more retarded than you already are."

"Do you have to use that word?"

"What word?"

"The r-word."

"What? Retard?"

"Yes, that word."

"You afraid of it?"

"No."

"Then I will use it. It means slow. And one more whack on the head and you'll be slow, if not dead. You must wear this helmet for the next three weeks, for whatever you need to do. Don't even take it off at night. Do you understand me?"

"Seriously?"

"Only if you want to continue working."

"I want to work."

"Then wear it, okay?"

"Okay. I'll do it. Okay. What about the rest of me, the sleeping trouble and so on?"

"I'm hoping this knock on the head knocks—how you say—intelligence in to your skull."

"Knocks some sense into me?"

"Right, that is it. Otherwise you are fine."

"How can I be fine? That is a senseless thing to say. My head hurts, but that is a minor problem to the one I am living with otherwise. I cannot sleep. I cannot be alone with my own thoughts. I am in great mental difficulty."

"I am trying to tell you that your problem has nothing to do with your body. Your body is in reasonable condition, besides the dent in your head, given your age and your propensity to certain indulgences."

"I'm not well."

"If you want my opinion, though I am not an expert in these areas, I would say the problem is with your soul."

"The soul? What kind of thing is that for a doctor to say?"

Paul had dismissed the idea of the soul many years ago. He'd dropped it from his vocabulary because it did not exist. It could not be verified in any way. Academically, the word was one to be avoided entirely. It was a word, like "imagination," that created trouble for learners and thinkers. Besides, the soul, as far as he could tell, was merely the binding agent of the senses, the thing that coordinated the data from the various senses and bound them to a particular event. There was nothing spiritual about it. It was physiological junction. Not a spiritual recliner.

"I told you, I'm not an expert in these things. I am expert concerning the body's health, no more. Yes, I understand that the soul, scientifically speaking, is a bit of a problem. It makes no sense to talk of one when it is scientifically improbable. The science of mind, right now, is embarked on just such a journey."

"So, you are diagnosing a problem with a mythic portion of my being."

"You condescend, do you? You obviously know yourself well."

"Point to the soul. I defy you."

"Ok, Mr. Smarty Pants. Where are your thoughts?"

Paul immediately pointed to his helmeted head.

"How do you know?" Vadim asked.

"Because that's where the brain is."

"What an assumption." Vadim said with a laugh. "We got that helmet on just in time. I'm hearing what you're saying and it makes no sense."

"So are you saying that your ears are part of your thought. Or perhaps you merely perceived the thought and it was presented to you by me." Paul thought for a moment and his clear expression clouded. "I doubt very much you could even separate your so called 'thinking' from your perception. Your thoughts may be in your skin. In your eye. In your ear."

"But they feel like they're in my head."

"Yes, that is true. And that is a very odd fact. But there is nothing science can do to prove that they are there. They measure impulses and centres of control, not thoughts."

"So it's a mystery?" Paul asked, about to dig in to an argument.

"I will not allow you to call the soul a mystery," Vadim chided. "You are a Marxist. I understand your difficulties with the soul. But you deal exclusively in science and commerce, and for science, there are no such things as mysteries: there are only things that researchers haven't investigated yet, and to most scientists, these uninvestigated spaces are not mysteries: they are what they call problems. In your world view, there is no possibility for mysticism, no pockets that, without some research and prolonged thought, cannot be explained. The soul, then, is a 'problem,' not a mystery."

Paul opened his mouth, but the words that had congregated for launch dispersed like farts in a hurricane.

"One of the problems that might lead to soul is the problem of centralized consciousness in general. Trillions of individual cells, and one point of focus for this entire being. It's a problem. The problem at the moment is that researchers cannot find a centralized processing location when a person experiences an event. Some think consciousness is a quantum organ. Pretty complex."

"If I were renovating my house, and I hit my thumb with a hammer, I would process the sight of my hammer hitting my thumb through one part of my brain, the sound of the hammer mashing my thumb through another point, the pain of the sixteen ounces swung in anger is processed elsewhere, and the dawn of realization as to what happened is managed in yet another. All of these separate sensations and thoughts bind together somewhere in the brain, and all the parts of this experience come to be associated with the one event. Once we can locate where all these limbs of experience come together, we will, it is thought, find consciousness. Some feel that 'soul' is the equivalent of consciousness. Problem solved. My soul is, science would say, a sensory coffee shop, the place where all the senses meet, smoke, and chat."

"So you're saying I have a problem with my coffee shop? Did I lose my coffee shop?"

"Can a piggy bank lose money?" Vadim replied without a hint of humour.

"That's insane. How would you know if your coffee shop is out of business?"

"You would know," Vadim said carefully. "Though the soul is less than tangible its loss would have an incalculable effect on that person."

"Would it be like the symptoms of depression?"

"No, I would say you are wrong, as usual," Vadim replied. "On another matter entirely, I have a question which I'd like to discuss with you." He looked at Paul over the tops of his glasses, with an unusual gravity. "Do you think dogs can sin?"

"What?!"

"Do you think dogs can sin?"

"What kind of question is that?" Paul replied incredulously.

"A good one, I hope," Vadim replied flatly.

"Do I get paid for answering your questions?"

"You see I think that the dog is a fairly high-functioning mammal. I think they, like many of the higher-order mammals, are capable of altruism. If they are capable of altruistic feelings, then they are capable of making a choice, and, hence, could sin. I think humans, when they train a dog, install a standard of moral behaviour, which a dog could then deviate from. Perhaps we humans poison other creatures with our sin."

"There is no such thing as morality. Morality is a myth used to quell the masses. Dogs are purely instinctual creatures." Vadim grinned at Paul's words. "You make it sound like they might volunteer at a food bank at any time."

"I think dogs are too smart to work at a food bank. But that is really a conversation for another time. If, as you suggest, dogs are purely instinctual, then they can never sin. And this is the problem."

"How is this a problem?"

"I am trying to decide how to treat my neighbour's dog."

"What?" Paul gaped. "So if dogs are capable of sin, you would what? Poison it? Kick it?"

"This is what I am thinking. Yes. But, I have to take my soul's ass to visit another patient. Good bye." He dismissed Paul opened the door stepped into the hallway, his gait surprisingly light for his heavy, hairy deportment. Paul sat for a moment slightly stunned. Then he brought the front of his shirt together and began to button it up.

❊❊❊

"Shore leave," Paul swore, as he stood at his tree. His communist green bike did not lean naturally against the tree, unlocked, as it usually did. It all came back to him. His bike lay under a car on a road a good half a kilometer from where he was standing. He walked a little unsteadily across the road, across a parking lot of several acres, jaywalked across the first two lanes of a busy road, and stood on the grassy median to wait as cars from opposite directions cleared and he could cut across the next two lanes. His head felt unusually heavy with the helmet on. And the helmet did seem to attract lots of attention.

As he stood on the median, his head dropped and gaze came to rest at his feet. And suddenly his lack of soul came to mind, and impressed on his thoughts was the idea that his soul probably knew where he was, and might try to communicate to him. Directly after these thoughts his eyes noticed a piece of paper, which, before he picked it up, he already believed was a message from his wayward soul. He held it carefully in his hand and crossed the second two lanes. A large truck locked up its brakes, skidded, narrowly missing him, and leaned on the horn.

Paul ignored the truck and tucked the paper into his back pocket, then walked across a large grassy park to where his bike lay under the car where he'd left it some time earlier.

"Ah, farking crap snappers," he cursed as he strode unsteadily towards the edge of the park. On the edge of the green lay his bike, now more of a sculpture than a practical transportation device. As art, it was utterly unappreciable. Its pretzeled wheels were a cliché only a vandal could appreciate. The frame was bent oddly, as if it had been driven over, and had nothing aesthetic to say except "bad bike." Alas, the road from useful to art was a short one. He knelt next to the bike's frame. The communist green paint had shelled off in a few places, revealing a republican blue underneath. How faithful it had been. He had developed a deep affinity for this two-wheeled invention. Never pretty, but true and dependable, like Socratic discussion. Like Marxian doctrine. He patted the bent seat tenderly, rang the cheap bell clamped to the handlebars, and stood up and wormed his way home.

❊❊❊

Bonnie had gone to yoga, taking Lou with her, so Paul settled in to make himself a little supper, choosing a box of macaroni and cheese. After his snack, he headed down to his filthy recliner chair, and enjoyed laying his helmeted head on the back of the recliner.

Knowing his wife would take the familial bed, he kicked up the rocker's footrest and turned on the TV. After a couple of hours of channel surfing, he settled on a Colombo episode. Though he couldn't have identified it, the show used the precise modus operandi of his academic existence. The caper and the culprit were known, and you spent the entire show trying to prove what you knew from the outset. At some point, before the final confrontation and arrest, he fell asleep. He awoke about 12:30 a.m. and watched as a man demonstrated a new exercise machine. Then, a showing of *Beverly Hills Cop*. He fell into a lumpy sleep near two and awoke after a nightmare a little after four. He tried a book, but his eyes refused to take to the words. Too tired, and he tumbled back into the rough mix of thought that was preparing to ambush him, it seemed. Before he was overwhelmed, he turned his attention to the TV.

# 40.

BEATA, APART FROM LOVING TO collect things, and suffering from a profound lack of affection from her husband, had taken to collecting cats, for neighbourhoods threw them away like pets they obtained for free. She had an absurd sense of care for all forms of this creature. Currently she housed four or five. It was a difficult count as the cats seemed to have trouble committing to her care.

One day one of her new adoptions, a dirty white cat, caught and began to torture a baby robin in Joan's yard. The motion caught Joan's eye as she washed dishes in the kitchen, and just as the cat was about to snack, it met her sneakered foot and was launched sideways into the fence. With a howl reminiscent of a baby hitting a wall, the cat took to the alley. The young robin seemed stunned. It lay still in her grass, feet folded under its body, resigned, it seemed, to its fate. The bird's fledgling feathers mizzled and clumped with cat gloob. A deep pleasure overcame Joan. The universe had asked for her help again. Maybe she'd been forgiven. Surely this was a good sign. This nameless bird wasn't her first rescue. The bird went into a shoebox, which sat in the grass for now.

Paul stepped out the back door of his house, lugging a garbage bag out to the back bins. His helmet gleamed in the early morning sunlight. Joan looked up from her bird supervision to find the source of the disco-ball-like refractions spangled and jigging over the pale yellow siding of her garage.

"You're going to be fine," Joan said to the bird. "Relax." Paul looked over at her, and held up a hand in greeting.

"Sorry, I didn't catch that, Joan."

Joan's head snapped up to meet Paul's, her face crabapple pink. "Oh. Hello, Paul. What's up?" She pointed to her own head, which at the moment was covered with a green polyester scarf, underneath rows of hair coiled around pink plastic rollers.

"Ah. Small bike accident."

"Oh. But the accident's over."

"Sort of, though I have a concussion. The doctor says I have to wear this helmet until I'm out of danger."

"Seems appropriate," Joan rejoined. Her eyes dropped to the box at her feet. "Oh, dear, get back in your box," she said to the bird.

"What you got?"

"A baby robin. One of Beata's cats almost got him."

Paul shuffled over to her fence to look at her new charge. "You going to take it to the animal clinic?"

"Don't need to. I saved a robin many years ago when I was just married, a baby robin that had fallen out of nest." She reached out to touch Paul's arm, realized what she was doing and pulled it back before she defiled herself. "I couldn't touch him. But I couldn't leave him alone. I was at home by myself all day long, so I found a little tub, put the bird inside and began to care for it." She smiled as she recalled the tub, which she had placed in her bathtub until her husband came home. "I hid that little bird from my husband." She shook her head. "I'm not sure why. This little bird was squawking at me. I felt absolutely helpless. Helpless. I couldn't do a thing." She flipped both of her hands over. "I didn't know what to do. Suddenly," she said shaking both of her hands, "it was like I began to understand what the bird was saying. I knew what it wanted and could sort of hear what it was saying." She reached up to wipe a tear from her eye. "Here I was useless at everything else in my life." She eyed Paul furtively, wondering quickly whether she would continue or not. "I couldn't parent. I was a horrible wife. I couldn't garden worth a darn. But I could hear what this bird wanted. It was a kind of miracle. It was my special gift. I felt like I even understood what it was thinking. It was as if," she said, "I was born with some part of me distantly related to robins." She turned and met Paul's eyes. "Since I understand these birds so well, it was only natural that I began to talk to them."

"I know what you mean," Paul replied. "I talk to worms for the same reason. I chat with them as I pick them up, soothing their fears, chiding their resistance, telling them of the spot I'm hoping to find for them. I talk to them of their own condition, of their ailments and personalities as they evidence themselves in our interactions. This morning, I chatted with a rather dry worm and ended up warning him that I would spit on him in order to revive him, which I did, and so he did."

Joan eyed him with an affection that made her mistrust herself. "I know what you mean," she admitted. "I'm so glad this little fella showed up today. But talking to critters seems a little crazy."

Paul laughed. His head rolled back, making the helmet's disco dazzle jitter around the yard. "I do think I seem crazy to some. Here I am walking around talking and spitting into my hand. Bending down over roads and sidewalks talking to them all. Most passersby would believe I am crazy, just trucking nuts." Joan jumped at his pseudo-swearing. She might have misheard. "I'm sorry," Paul offered, being careful not to trample on the tender connection. Joan nodded her forgiveness. Cursorial theory. Paul continued, "Some might assume I'm on my phone, talking like a schizophrenic to someone who isn't there, really. Others, might believe that I am praying, or perhaps involved in some odd penance or in some kind of severe pain."

"I've been thought crazy for that reason," Joan agreed cautiously. "I had been talking to a robin I'd just released. It was sitting in a tree. I was standing under the tree's branches, gazing upwards chatting at the bird. My in-laws were standing behind me and they didn't greet me. They just stood there and listened. To their untrained eyes," she said with some disgust, "it looked as though I was talking with the tree. Of course," she said, "if I saw someone talking with trees, I'd think they were nuts. My in-laws could never see the object of my conversations."

"That's an important general principle," Paul noted. "If a person witnesses a person talking, but cannot make out the object of the conversation, or deems that the object of that conversation is unable to converse, the witness is likely to disparage the goods and character of the talker. Hence, conversations with trees, birds, worms, cats, or God, are all hard ones to defend. Thank goodness we look a little less crazy with technology around."

"You know, when I saved my first robin, I kept it through the fall and on into the winter. But I didn't think it would migrate like it should." Joan's face grew a widening grin. "So when the bird was strong enough, I called all of the major airlines to see if they would carry this bird to any of the major southern states, just to help the fella get the idea of what its kind did. The airlines were not terribly cooperative, even after I explained the bird's willingness to suffer transport in the belly of a jet. I was willing to pay, too. Part of the problem had to do with the law, apparently. Technically the raising of a robin contravened federal laws, which prevent robins from being raised as pets."

She shooed away another of Beata's cats from the robin's proximity, and told Paul of her aneurysms, four of them, how she ought to turn in her driver's license. Occasionally, as they talked, she'd address the robin.

"It's okay, my dear, your wing is fine," she said, speaking to it patiently. "You are going to have to use it soon to get away from these dreadful cats." She shooed another cat away from the bird. "I won't be here forever, dear," she said with a warning tone. "You must learn to live on your own."

The bird looked at her in an understanding way. Paul crossed the alley to his own yard. Joan picked up the box and bird. "That's it, wee one," she said in an encouraging tone. "Let's go to tea." She and her four aneurysms went into the kitchen to make a cup of tea.

Paul turned back to his yard, drunk with thought. So drunk, in fact, he stumbled on a posthole and dropped face first into the dirt.

❋❋❋

"Oh, there you are," said the voice of a man who came walking around the side of the house. "I tried the front bell but no one answered. Figured you must be out back." Paul smiled, his face darkened with a dusting of loam.

"Ah," the man began, when confronted with the spectacle of Paul. "Um. Nice helmet. How'd it go?"

"Earthworms have only one sense: touch," Paul replied. "Touch is all they have to do all that they do. It is true that they prefer shade to sunlight. However, their entire experience of sunlight comes through touch: like the sun on my back as I, shirtless, rake the yard, and the sun presses its yellow heat onto my skin. What's odd to me is the kind of sex they have. Earthworms are hermaphrodites and carry both of what is necessary to produce other earthworms—sperm and egg—in themselves. This, you might think, would make them independent, pioneers in the art of masturbation, productive masturbation. But they don't, apparently. They get together in twos and help fertilize each other. How odd."

"So they had a good time then?" the man replied.

"It strikes me as odd because the worm's touch is so highly developed that he can tell the difference between my finger and another worm: worms never attempt to have sex with my finger. They can sense the touch and movement of their own kind. Fantastic. Their sense of touch must be a type of touch that is light years beyond the rudeness of the human touch. This is the earthworms' gift: they were given a glorious, sensitive grope at the universe. The grope balances on that one beautiful, complete, well-used sense."

The man surrendered his attempts to get an answer from Paul. "I'm here to pick up my son. Did you kids have fun?"

"Aw, Dad," the youngster complained. "Just a few more minutes."

"No, we need to get going right now, son." He turned back to Paul as Paul continued to talk.

Paul continued forward. "Human may well have been the starter kit, the prototype, the test case for the senses worldwide. We have only the most rudimentary of each of our senses. Other beasts' own senses often put ours to shame, as does the worm's sense of touch. How primitive we must seem to the worm. How sad, a thinking worm might think, that a human needs so many other senses to compensate for what he or she can't experience by touch. Is it better to have one sense, cosmically tuned, or five failing ones?"

"Paul?"

"Human hands, allowed to touch a small chunk of skin, could not tell the difference between someone's buttocks and a breast. Most of the time, humans use their eyes to help them feel. And so one sense poisons another: touch is overwrought with seeing. In fact, seeing precedes touch. If a man sees he's touching a woman's breast, the very nature of his touch is altered by his seeing. If that same man sees the nub of a football instead of the breast, his touch is altered again. The human web of sense is so interconnected, and the work of each sense bleeds into the others that it is impossible to properly disconnect them and sense each for what it is, what each of them could be. Each of them taints the other, intentionally and unintentionally, like actors in a Shakespearean tragedy that leaves everyone dead and on the floor before the curtain closes."

"Thanks for the playdate, then," the man said, grabbing his son's hand and pulling out of the yard. "Say thank you, son."

"Thank you, Steve," the kid yelled as he was dragged out of the yard.

# 41.

"MY DAD IS IN THE hospital," Bonnie said, making sure to indicate by her tone that things between them were still strained. "He bumped his head on the sink in his room. It's not too serious. He got three stitches. I've got to get to the hospital to be with Mom."

Paul groaned.

"What's the groan for?" she said, ready to turn his comment into the first shot of another war.

"I guess that means we'll be seeing your family again."

"What do you mean by that?"

"You know what I mean."

"You'll see Bruce. And you'd better not say anything to him this time. My mother's under stress."

Perhaps the best place to begin the explanation is with the brother-in-law, Bruce— or Bruise, as Paul called him. He called him Bruise first of all because Bruce never noticed the phonemic difference of the pronunciation. Each misuse of Bruce's name was like an excellent joke that flashed off his brother-in-law's rodeo belt buckle and flew over his head, not that Bruise was a cowboy, just that he liked big, shiny buckles and wished he was a cowboy. Secondly, Paul called him Bruise because his grasp on reality was so tight that his every perception was instantly damaged by his grasp. His failure to perceive was stunning in this sense: that after a lifetime of perceptive failure, he still had not seemed to realize his own issue with reality.

Bruise could not supply for his family, nor did he work very often. When he did it was odd jobs, mostly for seniors who wanted a pile of dirt moved, a fence painted, a drive to the airport. But he had dignity, dignity up the yin-yang, in spades. This is a man with a thoroughly healthy self-esteem. The perfect product of our modern educational system.

"Bruise. Glass-egoed schlub. Retarded mother-lover."

"Paul!" Bonnie said sharply. "Get over it."

Once Paul had gone over to paint his in-laws' apartment. He was willing and determined. He spent a week scrubbing the walls and then painting, to the best of his ability, the entire place. He did it for free, because he believed he was obligated to help his in-laws because they had parented his wife. Once the big part of the job was complete, there was a little patching and touch-up finish a hallway wall. Paul couldn't do it because he had what some like to call "a job."

Bruise, who lived in a house that his mother bought him and who claimed that he was a painter by profession, wouldn't come over to make these few simple repairs unless she paid him. So she did. He was paid five hundred bucks to paint a single wall. He then talked her into a repaint job for another five g's.

Last month, Bruise's wife decided she didn't want to be a nurse any more. She decided she was going to be a real estate agent. So his mother-in-law, because Bruise asked nicely, paid for Careen to take the real estate course. She passed. And Mary, agreed to move out of her house to provide Careen her very first listing. To support Careen was to support Bruise.

Since Mary was moving out, she wouldn't need her stove, would she? So, Bruise, living in a house Mary paid for and who wanted her new stove, took her stove to his house and sold his own, and kept the money.

Careen, after working less than ten days as a realtor (after Mary paid for the course, and signs, cards, and brochures), decided that she didn't want to be a real estate agent any more. Nursing was a better gig. So she quit her real estate job and dropped the house listing. Mary didn't want to leave her house anyways, she said. So she stayed. And so now in the garage lay a stack of brand new signs with Careen's name and cell number.

A month later, Mary called Bonnie and Paul wondering if either was interested in helping her go stove shopping. Bonnie was too busy, of course, so the request fell to Paul. Mary had been eating out of a toaster oven for three months and really wanted a stove. Paul told her to get Bruise or Careen to take her shopping, and pay for the fucking stove. Mary took exception to the word "fucking," which bent the family framework for a while. Oddly enough, she had a greater problem with Paul's use of language than with the lack of stove.

So it was little surprise that Paul couldn't hold his tongue this time.

"When you see your mom, ask her if Bruise could sell her heart on the organ market," he remarked. "Oh, wait. I think he already sold it." With an open forehand, Bonnie sculled his cheek, just below the helmet line. He blinked slowly and raised a hand to the side of his head. "You're so fourth wave," Paul said, speaking of her feminism. He backed away just as her hand windmilled past his nose. "Maybe you'll get a paper out of this."

# 42.

"THE BRUISE HERE, IT SEEMS to me like the outline of hand." Vadim was inspecting Paul's face with blue nitrile-gloved fingers.

"No," Paul winced.

"I have been doing some thinking about your situation," Vadim began. "I think I understand how you are caught."

"Please, go on, good Doctor," Paul enjoined.

"I think you are stuck between the modern idea of knowing and the older idea of knowing."

Paul sighed.

"Friend, I put up with your bullshit all the time," Vadim said, responding to the sigh. "You can put up with some of mine."

"Okay. Fine. Go."

Vadim nodded and his eyes looked toward the roof as he drew down his ideas. "One of the great flaws of intellectual knowledge is the level of abstraction that has come to be associated with knowing. Abstraction is the idea that knowing can be had without letting an idea have its full grip on one's life. Knowledge, and education, has become a way of collecting curiosities and oddities of a particular discipline and explaining a cursory knowledge in that discipline."

"Look at me, Paul," Vadim commanded. Paul had let his helmeted head droop to conserve energy. He raised it enough to meet Vadim's gaze. "Machiavelli was one among many who, along with the technologies of the day, promoted a lower investment in the things that we know in order to know more things. We lowered our investment in a specific area by renouncing the claims that a particular knowledge had on our lives. Existentialism, for example, became not a way of life, but a perspective that one could adopt if one chose to. To be a properly trained philosopher, one would be required to collect and `understand' a number of perspectives, one of which included `existentialism.' But the claims of existentialism, the difficulty of knowing and of being, are things to be avoided because that would `bias' the knowing of other systems which made competing claims on the knower's life. So to be acquainted with the knowledge's breadth, we renounced a specific knowledge's claim to our lives, which is some of what Vadim meant the other day. We abstracted ourselves out of the true philosophic lifestyle, we abstracted ourselves from a truly human perspective.

"So when one decides to operate one's self as a moral being, which means that one has adopted a particular philosophic outlook and has allowed the particular knowledge to root in living, one automatically impugns all other `perspectives' one carries, by refusing the claims of that system.

"It is much more fashionable to think this way: `If I were an existentialist, this is what I would do in this situation.' Or, `If I were a stoic, this is how I would think here.' Yet again, `If I eres a Brahmin, here's how I'd see this situation.' Instead of adopting a single system entirely, one has a rotating carousel of perspectives, like a revolver, with a bullet in every chamber that can be used when appropriate to undo the truth or the knowing of another perspective, or to make a stronger point if one chooses to do so. But to know many perspectives is to know nothing at all. It makes for scintillating conversation, a conversation that pleasantly occupies time, without the difficulty of truly ever understanding an idea."

Vadim stopped to make sure Paul was tracking his loops of logic.

"A $6^{th}$ century man decides that God exists. He then decides that his worldly ideas interfere with his relationship to that God. He then acts on his belief and renounces everything he owns and lives penniless moving from village to village, living on the strength of his ideas. Then, imagine a religion student in a religion class studying that same man's ideas. He would learn that it merely a perspective. If he was a good student, he would go away understanding this $6^{th}$ century life in some detail, remembering the man's name, where he was born, the general movements of his life, and his end. But he would also clearly understand that his religion teacher did not mean him to seriously contemplate or invite him in any way to consider living on those same ideas in the same way. Could the $6^{th}$ century monk and the religion student be considered equals in terms of their knowledge?

"If one offered both an exam, and both took it, their answers to the multiple choice questions might be the same, as might be their short answer sections. In fact, they might write similarly styled essays. Do they know the ideas in the same way? Is there an assessment technique that could reveal the difference? I think the exam would only reveal problems with the $6^{th}$ century education, and spectacular curricular gaps. When the $6^{th}$ century monk got to the next question on the exam, where he was asked to describe, in four sentences or less, the Hindu idea of the afterlife, and the final, short essay on the tenets of Mormonism, he'd be unprepared.

"But in living with a single point of view, Machiavellian detachment is lost, abstraction is lost, and one drops to a lower level. It is impossible to be moral and intellectual in today's sense of the word. One must always renounce one's intellectuality, and be satisfied to drop to a disdained level of practicality, the brass tacks of implementing one perspective in one's life, that makes intellectual heights of abstraction impossible.

"So it is with most of our knowledge. To know it is intellectual bliss. To live it, an intellectual sin. Like in this country, where nationally employed men of religion are told that it's okay to pray, but a sin to name a specific deity. It sort of promotes religious promiscuity. We have an abstracted religion where one can pray to great beyond, and embrace all knowledge at once, and screw all knowledge at the same time. Intellectual monogamy is not popular. Can I get an awomen? This is, in a sense, the intellectual big bang. The explosion of knowledge, and at the same time, the fornication of all knowledge, with the giant abstract phallus that has come to stand for smartness."

Vadim looked at Paul, who seemed to represent an argument. "Ironically, some would jump on the idea that the abstract phallus is a `male image' of knowledge and that the image ought to have been more inclusive, or that it stands for the male domination of all knowledge, but it none-the-less seduces most educated westerners, suggesting that further abstraction in one's language is required in order to be properly fair in one's intellectual pursuits. It is the selling of the human soul for the sake of knowing."

Vadim took a breath before he finished. "I think you're trying to know Marxism from an experiential point of view. It is a perfect viewpoint to use as a plastic plaything. It is the sort of idea that ought to come free in a box of bad cereal. But don't try to live it. It won't work. Quit taking it so seriously. I used to live in Moscow. I can tell you with authority that no Russian, past or present, has ever taken Marxism too seriously. Let it go. It's just a theory. And a bad one at that."

※※※

BONNIE RETURNED THAT EVENING. PAUL was sitting in his saggy, sad recliner in the basement, reading. Helmeted, as though reading might injure.

"We've decided to invoke his living will," she said in a flat tone.

"What do you mean?" Paul asked distractedly, his eyes trying to hold to the lines in a Terry Eagleton text he was re-reading.

"We've decided to invoke his living will," she repeated.

A moment passed while her words soaked in. Paul suddenly snapped to attention.

"What? He had three stitches, for God's sake. You can't invoke a living will."

"Mom sat down with the doctors and told them what he wished and showed them the legal documentation. And they agreed to abide by his will."

"You cannot be fracking serious."

"I am. It's the humane thing."

"You're murdering him."

"It's what he wanted."

"You let this happen?" Paul asked incredulously.

"It's the right thing to do."

"Right in what sense? But he's not even ill."

"The doctor says he is."

"Three stitches do not constitute a life-threatening illness. You're going to allow it?"

Bonnie sighed and looked away.

"His living will is a joke. You know it."

A few years before his attempt at an Alzheimer's diagnosis, Paul's father-in-law had suffered through a particularly lonely spell and a bout of depression. Most of it was over his son, Bruise, who has sponged off his parents his entire life and despoiled his parents' estate so he could sit at home and run his "business." In Don's depths he decided to stage another family event and invited two estranged daughters, and the third not-quite-estranged Bonnie, and the life-sucking son to a grand event where he announced that he had made a "living will." If, he said, he should ever have an injury that would lead to death, he requested that he not be revived or put on life-support to artificially sustain his worldly presence.

"Let me go," he said with a firmness worthy of Moses walking off the mountain. It was a grand moment, but given that his son sucked money out of him, and his daughters were alienated, he was articulating an acid undertone that had been present for some time. Even his wife, Mary, tired of his health hobby, longed for his demise—actually, she wondered a few times aloud, while visiting Bonnie, whether she should have ever married him at all. Not much of a man, she had said. Don's "living will" wasn't really the grand revelation it was supposed to be. It was the articulation of almost the entire family's secret and not-so-secret wish for him.

Paul had attended his father-in-law's announcement, and recognized Don's depression and loneliness for what they were. His living will stooged as another stage in the health hobby. The message was that he was trying to tell his family that he wished to be cared for. Paul noticed the lack of interest in the room, as did his father-in-law. Don seemed somewhat surprised to see every member of his family agree so readily to the terms he'd set out. Don had used the living will to suss whether there was a shred of care left in any of his family or not. Within the sacred walls of family he found no shred of hillbilly bunco.

This was a man who had picked at the plaster of his life, and finding rot underneath, sledgehammered at the punk looking for a hale and healthy bones. But he never did find them. The anger at his discoveries let to a fury of destructive energy, until the house of his life collapsed around his ears. At the end of the process, without energy to renovate, he sat like Job in the midst of the rubbled remains of his 64 years, in sackcloth and ashes.

"Oh My God." Paul clasped the side of his head. "How did this happen?" He paused and dropped his hands. "Your brother had something to do with this, didn't he?"

"He did suggest that we might use the living will."

"I'm not surprised. Then whatever cash remains can begin to flow."

Bonnie raised her hand as though she would strike him. "Paul, this is thin ice." Paul balled himself in his chair, and rolled away from her onto the floor. He didn't need to hear any more.

"Why do you even care about my Dad? The way you make fun of him, I'd have guessed you'd be the first to pull the plug."

"First of all, this isn't 'pulling the plug.' This is more like beating a man to the verge of death and then refusing to plug anything in."

"You mean it's a mercy killing."

"I mean it's a murder—not much to do with mercy, I don't think."

"It's about mercy."

"Mercy! It's about convenience."

"He's not happy." Bonnie tried to lift a foot into Paul's stomach, but missed. Paul took to his feet and moved to the open part of the room.

"I believe he's the happiest he's been for many years."

"He's a vegetable."

"Not as vegetative at all. He was happy there. He's worked hard to get there."

"You smartass. This is no joke."

"I am serious. He wanted to ditch the battle-axe, and this was the only way he felt he could."

"What are you saying about my mom?"

"I'm saying she's a miserable, entitled cow." Bonnie set her teeth, and clenched her fists. "I'm also saying he has a family that depresses the hell out of him."

"You self-righteous prig. How would you even know? Do you talk to him?"

"I do."

Bonnie's eyebrows raised a little with surprise, perhaps even fear.

"And he tells you these things?"

"Yes, he does. And I think you know that already."

"But, He's MY dad."

"So you can do to him whatever you like."

Bonnie raised her fist and stepped towards him.

"I'm tired of you hitting me." She took another step towards him and sunk a fist into his stomach. He doubled over.

"You're losing weight," Bonnie remarked and left his fetal form on the basement floor.

# 43.

"Is it even legal?" Paul asked, after setting up question with a ten-minute overview of Don's existence. "To end a man's life over three stitches. God, I hate it."

Vadim shrugged as he did up the helmet strap under Paul's chin. "It depends on how you look at it. I mean, if he's pretending, and everyone knows it, it's murder. If they don't know—they genuinely believe he's ill—then it's humane. It sounds like the word of an English teacher against a medical doctor." He shook his head in disgust. "Use the helmet strap. One more good knock and you'll make full professor, if you know what I mean."

"I'm not joking. I don't really know about his quality of life. I certainly don't accept the ideas of a doctor on this issue. Nor the insight of my brother-in-law. He thinks life without rational thought is not worth the living. If you can't think you can't live. I'd argue he's pulled off a rather pleasant pseudo-rationality for his forty-two years of living. He's proof that one need not think, really think, at all. For some, the mere capacity of thought serves thought itself."

"You surprise me here. I would expect that you would agree, as an academic, as a Marxist. Once rational thought leaves the building, once Elvis is gone, the show is over."

Paul sighed. "Yes, I'm being inconsistent. I see that. But there's still a bee in the brew here." He stopped and his eyes looked around the room and his head bobbed as he added and subtracted his sums. "Bruise's emphasis on capacity reminds me of my own dad. His love of tools. He's built a few things around the house, but his real reverence is for capacity. He's older now and almost never uses his tools, and let me tell you his woodworking collection is fairly complete. My mom harps on him to give me his tools, since they sit idly while he ages. Not that I could use them. Bonnie could, I guess. But for him, he collects tools not to use them, but to enjoy the understanding that he could, if he wanted to, do something with them. In short, he collects capacity, and extensions of his own capability. In some ways, his tool collecting has become fierce in his elder years. I think his tool purchases are a compensation for his waning human capacity. Just a few weeks ago, he and my mom went and pre-purchased their own headstones, plots, and funeral arrangements. A day later, my dad went and purchased a brand new cordless drill and an extended set of router bits. He seriously contemplated a metal lathe, but found the price, in the end, too prohibitive."

Vadim nodded his agreement. "It's more common than you think. My girlfriend goes to a gym, and so I am there sometimes, by circumstance. Weightlifting and muscle growing. Gyms. Many there are trying to gain something. I saw a muscle-bound woman one whose muscles were far larger than my own. I watched her has she heaved huge weights one way and another, and positioned herself in the oddest of ways to make sure every muscle had its own little workout. At the end of the day, however, her muscles aren't much good to her except as display units. What is the display about? It's about capacity. It's a demonstration of capacious strength that she takes the trouble to wear on her body. She's creating a living advertisement for unrealized potential."

As the two men kibbutzed, they they were both invigorated.

"What about the stupid SUV craze?" Vadim offered. "People driving around town in these humungous metal boxes, belted to tremendous horsepowers, belching fantastic amounts of hydrocarbons in to the air, what is this about? To me, it is a demonstration of capacity. A feast of potential becomes the means and the end."

"I mean, think of sex," Paul said.

"I do, believe me," Vadim agreed.

"Perhaps the most audacious demonstration of capacity is human sexuality. The sexual revolution, brought about by condoms and the pill and other ways of preventing sex from its end. The utter celebration of frustrated capacity. And capacity, I believe, is always meaningless in the end."

"But it's quite enjoyable meaninglessness."

"It reminds me of Auguste Rodin's sculpture *The Thinker*. Did you know that the first version of this figure was part of a larger work called *The Gates of Hell*, a door commissioned to celebrate the work of the great writer Dante? On the top of this door sits the very first version of *The Thinker*. In the original, the thinker is looking down and contemplating the fates of those in hell—in other words, he's thinking about something. Rodin never completed the door he was working on, but he pulled out many of the figures from his door and exhibited them individually. *The Thinker* was one of them. Actually, it was originally titled *The Poet*. The figure, apparently, is supposedly the likeness of Dante himself. Rodin achieved a lasting fame from his figures, the most famous of which was *The Thinker*. But the thinker was abstracted from the door. Sitting on his own, bent with thought, his gaze cast nowhere but down, as if to focus on deeper recesses of thinking, the thinker becomes an icon of capacity: the grunting stoop of a man engaged in thought. Capacity without a focus."

"Makes me think of Mexico when I was there last," Vadim said. "Some poor Mexican kid who can't get a decent job or a decent education, who can't go on holidays anywhere and would just sponge off the social system, if there was one, he might as well be dead. The smile on his face as he walks down the heap of garbage, with a fragment of food he's going to call supper, is just his own ignorance, right? Not even the good sense to hate his own life. Might as well be dead. We know he's poor because he has no excess capacity to display."

"So this man, Don, who adores the touch of the nurse," Paul continued, "loves the taste of his food, and the heat of his bath, is condemned to death, as justified by his lack of ability or his refusal to demonstrate capacity, when compared with the greed and minor successes of most of us. If Don's life is compared to that of a middle-aged man—a man with one home, two kids, and a pickup truck—it'd be tempting to find Don's life inadequate. It doesn't look as glamorous; it lacks demonstrations of useless capacity. Therefore, the life is deemed inadequate.

"Oh, and his family," he persisted. "A great raucous group of morons who never let the man wake up enough after hitting his head to let him speak for himself. And Bruise nattering in the doctor's ear until she capitulates. So we stopped giving him food and, especially, water. Instead we gave him morphine, and drugged him away, away, away, into the beyond. The family always insists that they just followed Dad's wishes, but it's not true. They euphemize. They euthanise. More properly: murder."

Paul's eyes seemed to glaze as he spoke. "I protested. But I have no legal standing, so the doctors wouldn't measure my opinion into the mix. So I held his hand for a while as he was on his way out. It was Monday and he was scheduled to die sometime on Tuesday. He was on some heavy doses of morphine so he couldn't talk. But several times he gripped my hand with surprising strength and looked at me with terror in his eyes, confused and frightened. So I talked over him and into him. I talked to him words of love and tried to help him remember better times that were and the better times that have yet to come. 'He's not terrified,' said Bruise, as I talked to him about his dad. 'He's lost his mind. How could he even have a sense of what's happening?' Here's what he meant: he has no capacity, and, hence, no worth. And, this, Bruise insisted, is what we ought to do with these sorts of people.

"And I was too weak at the time to make anything more than a few comments. Shame on me. Shame on someone who knew better. Shame on the system, on the doctor, who, like Pilate, agreed to his sentence out of social pressure. Shame on the family. That sweet, sick, ugly family, who made a nurse a more attractive option than his own flesh and blood."

"You rant. I hardly talk." Vadim declared. "At least I get money to listen."

# 44.

BAL WAS OUT IN HIS yard, tenderly farming his tomatoes doggy-style. He had sculpted the earth into conical heaps around the plants' roots and smooth, weedless troughs for the water to follow, far enough from the root mounds to lure the roots into growth. It was the roots of tomato plants he was contemplating as he absently stroked the loam, as if he were petting a dog.

Paul came sauntering up the street.

"Hello Paul," he said. "Where's the bike?"

"Ah, it was destroyed when a car drove over it."

"Oh," Bal said, startled by the reply. "But, you were not on it."

"Fortunately, no," Paul replied. He carefully walked up Bal's walk to where Bal knelt at the corner of his house. He surveyed Bal's work. "That's some nice gardening you've done there. You need a magazine here to take a picture. And those tomato plants are huge."

Bal seemed pleased. "I grew these all from seed, you know."

"That's amazing. I kill tomatoes. We buy the seedlings from Walmart and plant them. And they always turn brown and fall over."

"How do you water them?" Bal asked.

"I just water them. I don't know."

"No, Paul. You must be careful. You cannot water them too close to the root. These plants like to be teased."

"So I need to insult when I talk to them," Paul quipped.

"No," Bal replied, tolerating the humour because of his great need for company. "You see the roots of my plants?" He stretched his hand toward one of the conical heaps. "I plant them high on top of a heap, to keep the water off the plant directly. Otherwise they get root rot, right here." He pointed to the collar of the root, where the stem met the earth. "The stalk thins and the plant falls over."

"That's what's happening to mine," Paul said, with a hint of amazement. "So you don't water them directly?"

"No, they're a female plant. They need foreplay, they need to be teased."

Paul laughed. "You think that's a female trait?"

"It is to me," Bal stated seriously. "Women don't need sex, at least I don't think so. So the only way to get them to want it, is to tease. If the teasing works, they'll grow tomatoes for you."

"Women?"

"Tomatoes."

"So how's that different from a male plant?"

"Men, we need sex. We're not tomatoes. We're more like zucchini or pumpkin. We don't want to be teased. We want everything and lots of it, now."

"You're making me think about gardens erotically."

"I do. They're very sexual places."

"Oh," Paul replied, intoning his reply flatly so as to stem the tide of unwanted information that seemed to growing.

"She's cheating on me," Bal said, looking away to his row of tomatoes.

"Sorry?"

"Virginia is cheating on me."

"I'm sorry to hear that," Paul said, suddenly looking for a polite way to end the conversation. He looked at his watch very obviously. Bal's problems grew like cataracts on his eyes, so he missed Paul's hint.

"She's having an affair with her boss at the restaurant." He sniffed. "I left my job for her."

"Oh, that's too bad," Paul replied, offering as little as he could to encourage the conversation, but enough so as not to offend.

"I should never have sent her out to get a job," Bal said. "I cannot tease. I am not good for tomato plants. I cannot make a tomato plant like me." He smiled sadly to himself. "Except real ones, of course." He patted the heap of earth around the base of a plant. "It is not enough to understand tomatoes." He looked up. "She doesn't know that I know. And I don't know what I should do." He looked pleadingly at Paul.

"That's a very difficult situation."

"What do you think I should do?"

"I don't know, Bal. I've never been in your situation."

"But what would you do if you were?"

"I don't know."

"Please, just answer the question. I need to hear your answer."

"I don't know." Paul dropped his eyes to the ground. "I just don't know." He let a moment of silence develop between them. "Ah...I'd guess I'd probably talk to her about it. I would want to find out why she's doing it, and find a way to fix it."

Bal's eyes teared over, and he pinched the tears from the corner with thumb and forefinger of his right hand. "Thank you, Paul. I needed to hear your answer."

"I'm sorry to hear about it," Paul said gently. "That's sad to hear. And I wish you good luck as you sort it out." Luck? What sort of a Marxist wished anyone luck?

"Thank you, Paul."

"I've got to get to work now," Paul said defensively.

"Of course. Have a good day."

## 45.

THE PRIEST LOOKED OUT FROM his office windows, which afforded him a view of rows and rows of asphalt shingled roofs, piqued, stationary and afraid. Grey parishioners before him. The very sight of these houses caused his stomach to turn. How lost this architecture was. How lost the people who would tolerate such design.

Truly, he thought, how lost is this world, marvellously lost. Suburbia was full of the anonymous damned, who hoped to not be what they were, scratching their way into higher living. It was a smoldering, fecund ground that both birthed and denied anything but middle living. A boiling vat of desire for anything except what was. Most believed life should be better– take them farther, lead them higher – and spent their lives swinging between desire and reality, struggling to bear what was and what could never be. Suburban folk sizzled and seethed, hot with motive and stood up by opportunity.

His secretary, Beata, hobbled into the room with a copy of the bulletin for his review.

"Got quite a view of the neighbourhood, eh, Father?"

Joachim turned from the window to study her.

"Yes," he replied in a way that ended the conversation.

# 46.

"I saw you polishing the Pope with that guy who owns the restaurant."

She suddenly swung to face him. "What?"

"I saw you polishing the Pope with the guy who owns the restaurant."

"His name is Mateo." Her confident answer shook him.

"OK. I saw you polishing the Pope with Mateo."

"I love him." Her answers were as firm as her body.

"I love you."

"Ah. I don't love you. I'm not sure I ever did."

Bal flinched as if he'd been struck. "What?"

"I don't love you. I don't think I knew what love was when we married."

"Oh. Oh. Oh." Bal said. He sat down in a chair. "I want to fix us."

"You know what?" Virginia asked, her voice razor-sharp and steel-strong. "I don't." She folded her arms over her chest. "I was a victim when I met you. I wasn't myself. The assault changed everything." She paused. "I married a father-figure. But I've healed. I've grown. You haven't."

"I left everything for you. Everything," Bal hissed.

She shrugged. "I'm grateful for your help, don't get me wrong. But that was your choice."

Bal's shoulders dropped slowly and hunched forward. His arms crossed and folded back on his body—a self hug.

"Yes," she sighed, as if a burden had been lifted, and her face became radiant, beatific. "I am in love with Mateo. I never understood the power of love until I met him." Her glowing expression soured. "Until I met him, I never knew how I felt about you. I think I married you because I was afraid of everything. I also felt sorry for you. Yes, well, yes, look at you. If sex is charity work, your face would be on the poster. You are pathetic to a degree that inspires the nurse in me. I thought love was nursing. But it is not. That can't make a good marriage."

"Oh, Virginia. Please don't say that. I want to fix things. I only want you."

"I don't want you. Not anymore. I think I want to leave." She paused and looked at Bal. "Yes. Leave. I'll leave tonight."

She went to the closet ran her hand over the short rack of clothing hanging there.

"I don't think I want any of this, either." She stormed over to her purse, plunging her hand into its contents. "Here are the keys to everything. I don't want any of your money. Nothing. I just want out. Right now." She grabbed her coat, swung her purse over her shoulder and strode out the door.

He followed her out the door.

"Virginia, I'm sorry. I was wrong," he pleaded. "Don't leave me. I don't care if you're having an affair. I promise I won't bring it up again."

She turned to him in the dark. "Bal, you're so pathetic. Truly pathetic. I can't believe you'd settle for this. It's why I'm leaving you. Get back in that house and find your life."

# 47.

"SINCE YOU GUYS WERE AT the last one, I'd like to invite you to my next one." It was Veto, who'd just informed the group that he'd been hired by a major department store, as a sales associate in their menswear department. "I think I've got a better thing here, because I'll be able to move around. That should keep me employed for a longer period of time."

"What's the shortest time ever?" Paul asked.

"Was it not that twenty-seven minutes at the cow meat restaurant?" asked Allan, another tenured English faculty member asked.

"You mean forty-seven minutes. And, no, the shortest one was working as a carpenter's helper. I lasted thirty-one minutes. It was sad because I even purchased a toolbelt, hammer, and a tape measure for that job. I still have them somewhere." Veto paused to think for a moment, and then shook his head back into the moment. "I just haven't tried retail before. I was going to work at a CD/DVD store, but I was worried that I would be sucked into working just because I like music. Don't want that."

"No, you don't want that." Allan agreed with a grin. "What a perverse exercise."

"Actually, I disagree," Veto rebutted. "Though I think your comment marks a certain problem with my researches."

# 48.

IT WAS A SMALL, YOUNG magpie. To Paul's eye, there was nothing wrong with him. But the circling flock of older, larger magpies sensed something wrong. The young one fell from the tree to the ground, where it stood there, dazed. Then slowly the group of older birds dropped into a ring around it, and one at a time they took turns pecking at the little bird. They pecked the young magpie on the head, and it seemed to Paul that in such a condition, the little creature had no chance. Though terrified, the little bird acquiesced to the punishment, and seemed through its compliance to agree with its aggressors. Paul was overwhelmed by the bird's low self-esteem. How the dominant class had repressed this lowly bird, and were going to peck it out of existence because it was not meeting their definition of normal. The working class was always under the knuckle. "I believe in you, little one," he said to the bird tenderly.

He watched a particularly fat old bird take a swipe at one of the young one's eyes. He found himself suddenly overwhelmed with emotion, and he strode over to the ring of birds. Perhaps his newfound love of worms had warped his understanding of his place in nature.

"Fub off," he yelled. His arms he flapped as he stomped like a chicken around the young bird. "Don't let them do this to you," he said, to try to coach the young impressionable magpie. "Where's your sense of self? You're being complicit in your own murder." The old birds backed off, but just far enough to stay out of Paul's reach. It was obvious that this parliament had convened for this task and it wasn't going to fall off the agenda. This was some kind of deep ritual beyond Paul's ken, and they weren't going to leave until they had done their job.

"You filthy sinners," he yelled at them all as he noted their unrepentant demeanours. "You smutty sinners. How can you do this?" He found he was weeping as he spoke, and his emotion was preventing him from cursing further.

He jumped over the still-dazed bird to drive away the big old fatty that had hopped a little closer, hoping to peck the little one in the head again. He lunged at the big bird, who hopped lazily further and then took to his wings for a short flight away. "You fat capitalist. The fat get fatter." Paul was screaming uncontrollably now. He turned and as he did so, the rest of the birds closed in on the little one and another took a peck at another eye. "Ah, ah, ah…" Paul screamed, running back to the little one. He got down on his knees close to the little creature. His eyes blurred and he couldn't easily follow the movements of the birds any longer.

He had one goal, and that was to save this little bird. He stood on his knees and waved like a hellfire-and-brimstone preacher at the ring of birds around him. Waving, ranting, gesticulating. The young magpie submitted underneath him to what must have seemed to it a much more terrifying fate than the pecking death he had been promised.

And there Paul remained, kneeling, waving the other birds away, following the ruffled bird as it attempted to step away from this satanic moron, and back to the peck- fest he was expecting.

He stayed with the bird most of the day. In fact, he called his department secretary to inform her that a 'family emergency' had occurred and he would not be in to work. After about an hour and a half, some of the birds began to disengage and set out in search of anything edible. The remaining birds hopped into the branches of a green-leafed poplar tree and waited, squawking a protest every few minutes —which to Paul sounded very inarticulate. In a moment he fled over and grabbed an empty cardboard box and returned to the bird.

"Stop it. This one can't matter to you," Paul repeated. At one point he set the box down on the street and threw rocks at the birds, but being an Arts major he was almost useless at hitting a target, so the effect was laughable. The noise of him walking up the street did, however, attract the attention of Old Man Sobczak, who was out for one of his full-speed directionless walks to the park. He approached Paul from up the street with a knowing look. Today's t-shirt had a picture of a clown on it. Underneath was printed the words "Do I scare you?" Paul turned to him and suddenly was overwhelmed with self-consciousness, realizing suddenly he'd been ranting like a lunatic. Sobczak's confidence in his understanding of the situation was slightly undermined by the magpie in the box, which confused him. So he focused, instead, on the part of the situation he did understand.

"I will get those mother-effing birds." He waved Paul on with a hint of pomposity, like a don dismissing a grateful mafia supplicant. "I will take care of them for you."

Paul took the help gratefully, though now somewhat embarrassed by his actions. The old man lofted some practiced shots at the birds, which came much closer than Paul's. He took over the cursing of the birds, too. "Mother effing beasts," he yelled confidently at the magpies, as he had done hundreds of times before. But this time his voice carried a confidence. Rocks whizzed, loud words flew. And the two progressed towards Paul's house in a short parade, with a vulgar ending.

When he got home, Old Man Sobczak stood guard outside the front of his house throwing rocks and swearing at the top of his lungs. His life had suddenly found purpose, which he was revelling in until Paul approached him where he stood on the front walk, thanked him for his help, and asked him to leave. Then, after cutting the box into a bit of a shelter, Paul began to try to nurse the bird back to health, feeding it bits of things he found in the fridge, which the bird seemed to ignore entirely.

The bird had recovered somewhat. Paul felt gladdened. He bent down to lift the box and carry the magpie to a better part of the front yard, and as he scooped the box, the bird took flight and flew up under the spruce tree. Paul's heart soared with the flight. He'd saved the bird's life! Until the bird hit the picture window at full speed. And fell, neck broken, into the poorly tended flowerbed below.

# 49.

"Morgan-Bessler Funeral Homes," said a sweet, slightly sad woman on the other end of the line.

"I'd like to attend the cremation of John Donavon Honigsblum, and I wondered when it is?"

"The cremation is later this morning, sir. I'm afraid, however, you are not able to attend because of the express wishes of the deceased." Don had explicitly barred all family from attending any funeral rite as part of his living will.

"Oh, yes, I'd forgotten about that. Um. Would you mind giving me an exact time, just so I can think of him at that time?"

"Yes, sir, I understand. He will be cremated at 11 a.m., this morning, in full and proper honour."

"And just for my own peace of mind, where is he going to be cremated?"

"All cremation... excuse me... your father's ..."

"He's my father-in-law."

"Excuse me, your father-in-law's cremation will be held at our home, located off of 17$^{th}$ Avenue."

"Thank you very much. I find that information consoling."

"I'm very sorry for your loss, and thank you for choosing Morgan-Bessler Funeral Homes."

"Ah...." Paul wanted to point out the inconsistency on a slight logical clash between her sorry-ness and her thanks, but he let that go, realizing it was likely a scripted sign off, generated by some witling MBA. "Thank you," he replied instead.

He hung up the phone and looked at the clock on his computer: 10:05. He grabbed his coat, informed the department's secretaries that he did not feel well and was going home to recuperate, so would they please cancel his classes for the rest of the day. The happy one frowned. The sad one smiled.

Then he moved quickly out the doors to the main area of the campus, where all the busses swarmed carrying students to and from school. After a few conversations with the various bus drivers, proletarians all, he found a bus headed in the right direction and struck off downtown.

The neon sign for Morgan-Bessler Funeral Homes glowed in the afternoon grey. He found the "customer" entrance, but decided quickly that he wanted another entrance. A man was polishing the hearses and processional vehicles in a large garage, with the door open.

"Ah, hello," said Paul approaching the jeans-wearing, sandy-haired man. "Where do they do cremations here?"

The man nodded in understanding. "You'll want to go into the main entrance of the funeral home, right on 17$^{th}$." Suddenly his face clouded over. "But I don't think we have one scheduled until this afternoon."

"Ah, well, there's a cremation scheduled for 11 this morning, the receptionist told me so on the phone earlier."

"Do you mean a cremation without a funeral?"

"Yes, that's it," Paul replied.

"You're picking up some John Doe ashes, are you?"

"Yes, I think so."

"OK. You see that white sort of clinic-looking building over there?"

Paul could see a grimy white-colored building that sat on an adjacent lot to the funeral home, surrounded by a chain link fence topped with three rows of barbed wire. "Yes."

"That's where we do our cremations."

"Oh."

"Yes, were one of the only company in town that offers that service, so we're quite busy."

"Is there a cremation scheduled there for eleven?"

"We really don't schedule cremations there. It's first-come, first-served."

"So it might be taking place right now?"

"Could be. It depends."

"Thanks for your help," Paul replied quickly. "That's where I need to go."

"No problem," the man replied, and began to polish the black surface again.

Paul walked as quickly as he could, and once the garage was out of sight he broke into a run, running through the open gate and into what seemed like the main door of the building.

The inside of the building was the same colour as the outside, the floor covered in a dull green mint tile. At the far side of the building, there was a youngish man, perhaps in his early twenties, sitting at a badly battered desk, reclining in a tattered, cushioned seat, with his feet on the desk. He was reading the city's tabloid paper. When the door closed with a bit of a thud, the man looked over to see who was coming in.

"Can I help you?"

"Yeah, I'm here for a cremation."

"Do you mean you're here to pick up some ashes?"

"Ah...yes. That's what I mean."

"Are you from another home?"

"Ah ... Yes."

"We've done a bunch this morning already. Which home are you picking up for?"

"I'm here about one particular cremation?"

"Oh. What's the name?"

"John Donavon Honigsblum."

The man set down his paper, stood, and headed a clip board hanging on a nail in the wall. "You're early," he said. "We haven't done him yet."

"I was told he'd be cremated at 11 this morning."

"Yeah, I bet our front office told you that, didn't they?"

Paul nodded.

"It doesn't really work that way in here, but they don't want nobody to know that." He tapped the clipboard with an index finger. "I've got two more to torch before him. So that'll put him at around..." He studied a clock on the wall. "More like 11:40. You might as well come back."

"I don't have that luxury. Can I wait?"

"I'd do him first, if I could, but we have two out-of-towners that have to be done, packed, and on the plane by 12:30." He pointed to two urns on his desk. "They got priority."

Paul took a seat and watched the clock for a while. The man got up from his desk "Got to let 'em cool, and box 'em, and get the next one in the oven." The man left the room, and returned a bit later. "Man, she was not a light lady," he said, wiping his forehead and reaching for a can of cola. "But she will be soon." He winked at Paul. Almost a half hour later, the cola man left the room again and returned after completing some kind of routine. "The convicts always burn well," he said thoughtfully.

An idea contorted the man's whiskered face for a moment. He looked at the clock again. "Actually, if you're waitin', maybe I could ask you a favour. I just started this burn. If you don't mind holding the fort for a minute, I'd like to get somethin' to lunch on." He pointed out the window to the deli across the street.

Paul nodded.

"Great. The burn won't be done for another twenty or so. I just put him in. And if the phone rings, don't answer it."

"Sure."

The lanky youth patted his back pocket to confirm his wallet's whereabouts, and strode out of the building Paul watched him head to the corner and wait for the orange Don't Walk signal to turn, then wandered past the desk and through a doorway, past a sign that read "Authorized Personnel Only." Down a narrow corridor, he followed a hulking growling sound to a room where three caskets lay, parked like cars at a strip mall. He followed the row. There were three plain pine boxes in a row.

On top of each casket there was a paper form. Paul picked up the form and looked at the name. "Forbes, Tim," read the name on the first shiny casket. "Macks, Theresa," read the next. Paul surveyed the caskets for a moment spinning in a slow circle between them, and slowly walked to the unfinished pine casket. The paperwork lay face up, and he read the words "Honigsblum, Donavon." He examined visual qualities of the casket for some time, his eyes blurring over with tears from time to time, some of which fell like a Disney movie, from his eye to the top of the casket. He stood and sobbed. He held the paperwork in a trembling hand.

"You were the best of your family," he said to the closed wooden door. "You were the best. If you were a scientist, you were a fine one. You found your meaning in the bare cupboard you called life." He stopped for a moment and contemplated the casket lid, and without really thinking let his hand slide to the top of the lid and lift it slowly. Slowly. Slowly. He lifted it up. Inside, cramped between planks, lay John—a green-white, awful-looking John. He lay so pale he seemed almost green. He was naked, and though peaceful enough in the face, slightly contorted in body. Three stitches over his left eye. An almost olive roll of fat circled his upper hip. His feet were bent oddly at the heel and his legs wouldn't stay down. His body, naked, covered unevenly with sickles of hair, all of him done, discarded. Nothing more could diminish this man. Paul's blubbering deepened, and he reflexively elongated the vowels in which he howled as the grief dropped beyond his stomach into his loins.

"I'm sorry," he said to the man in the box. "Don, forgive me. I didn't know what they were doing." He dropped the paper work to the floor as he talked. He bent over this green, oddly bent, shrivelled hairy body and kissed him on the cheek. "Goodbye, friend." He slowly stood again.

"I already checked," said a voice behind Paul. Paul suddenly straightened up suddenly, grief evaporating. "He's a John Doe from the hospital and they always send 'em that way. The others are dressed, but there's nothing good." Paul wiped his face carefully with his sleeve and then turned around, slowly.

"You better put the lid back on, in case someone from the office drops by."

"Oh yeah," Paul replied, and turned, happy to hide his face from the cola man, to slowly replace the casket's lid.

"Hang on a minute," cola man said, and disappeared for a while. He returned a few minutes later. "Just put him on the rack for a minute or two to cool. Can you help me load him in?" Paul nodded. "Can you wheel him over here?" Paul pushed the casket over to the oven door. "You got your side?" he asked as he opened the oven door. Paul nodded, bent down, and the two lifted the casket and slid it into the oven door, onto a metal conveyor belt. Cola man slammed the oven door and punched a red button to the left of the door.

Paul watched through a little thick glass window as the casket slowly moved towards another opening and into the orange-white heat of the oven. "Oh, God," he whispered. "May you burn like gasoline." Suddenly a wave of nausea overcame him. "Do you have a washroom in here?" he asked, fighting to hold himself together.

"One in the front near the door."

\*\*\*

FORTY MINUTES LATER PAUL LEFT the crematorium with a small black plastic box, still warm, one that looked as though it could file business cards. On the box's outside, a white card that read "Honigsblum, Donavon," printed in a dot-matrix font and stuck with packing tape to the front of the box.

Without much of a thought, Paul got back on the bus and headed back to the college. As he headed back up the stairs, blasts of bright light cut long angular blocks across the staircase. The light was laced with the fine filament of dust that added fibre to the light's shape. It seemed to him as though his father-in-law mingled with light were trying to re-form somehow on the steps before him. But the ash, the sediment, was too fine and hadn't the will to come together again. Paul studied the sunlit dust: "I think I read about this in *Midnight's Children*. Education has had its effect on you, friend."

"Shaboodle nubs," he said quietly to himself as he mounted another exposed aggregate step, for he had intended to go home. He stopped and raised his eyes from the steps back to the column of fibrous light. He thought about leaving. But his office, because it was four walls and a door, seemed to call to him.

The ashes were still warm in the box by the time he snuck in through a less-used hallway and into his office and closed the door. He sat in his chair and pushed piles of paper aside to let the black box sit clear, in its own little space. He leaned back.

"Ha, you old bugger," he said to the box. He stood and reached for a pile of books, from Derrida, Terry Eagleton, Jacques Ellul, a few Harlequin romances. He stroked his philtrum and considered his choices a little longer. "I'd better get a few more of the older guys," he thought aloud. Stanley Fish. Walter Benjamin. Marx. Augustine. Cicero. Vygotsky. Hegel. Aurelius, Haraway, Freire. These and many others he placed on his chair. He shoved a few of the piles very near his computer, back behind the monitor to make a place for the books, which he stacked neatly beside the cooling ashes. He took his seat again and cleaned his glasses. And peering with the intensity of a scientist, he watched as he carefully lowered each book onto the plastic box containing his father-in-law's remnants. Each book he lowered slowly to the top of the black box's surface to see if any spark, any fire jumped the gap. "Mind the gap," whispered to the box as the first book hovered over the top of the box. He ran his eyes back and forth between the space, watching for sign or spark. Then he threw it to the floor and grabbed another one. He dropped each book on the floor when he was done.

"Damn," he said, lifting the last book off his father-in-law, dropping it to the floor. He reclined again, sitting way back, putting his feet into the clearing where the books had been, staring and contemplating the black box.

"Ha, black box. The ship is down. Get the black box, let's find out what happened. If anything will tell us the truth it will be the black box. Captain was drunk. First mate sexing a stewardess in a bathroom in the aft of the cabin. The human is too unreliable to consult on such matters. But the black box, the black box won't lie."

He sat longer, sometimes chuckling, sometimes tearing as he reviewed some of his fonder memories of this man. Then the phone rang, kicking him out of his repose, almost dumping him backward on the floor.

"Did you pick up his ashes?" snarled Bonnie's voice on the other end of the phone.

"Yes, I did."

"I thought so. The funeral home has been freaked because they didn't know where the ashes went. But one of the grief counselors interacted with a man of your description who picked up the ashes."

"Yeah, that was me."

"OK. I'll let them know what happened. But next time, you should let someone know you took them, eh."

"Ah, next time? Yes, by the way, what are we going to do with his ashes?"

"He just wanted them scattered."

"Anywhere in particular?"

"Nowhere. Anywhere."

"That's two places," Paul quipped. "Which is it?"

"You dick. Don't get fresh with me."

"Who's supposed to scatter them?"

"No one."

"Don't you mean no one, or anyone? We'll have anyone drop them anywhere and no one finish by dropping him nowhere. That'll take care of him."

Bonnie ignored him. "No one who is family."

"What does that mean?"

"It means he didn't want anyone who was family to scatter his ashes."

"He didn't mean that, I don't think."

"Don't try and start this argument again." Paul could hear the foaming sea of saliva approaching his ear. "His living will actually states that he wants us to pay a stranger to pour his remains down a gopher hole and cap the hole with a rock."

"Oh. That makes sense."

"What are you saying?"

"Nothing."

"Really? Bruce doesn't want to hire a stranger. He doesn't see the value in it. Mom agrees. And she doesn't consider you to be family, so you might as well do it."

"Don't you want to?"

"No. It's in his living will."

Paul sighed heavily. "You make me so tired with that reply."

"Oh, God. Are you starting up?"

"No. Just making a point."

"You take care of it."

"Are you sure? He's your father," Paul spoke tenderly.

Bonnie laughed as if he had told a joke. "That bastard wasn't strong enough to be my father."

"What do you mean?"

"I never considered myself his daughter. He was part of a speed bump that I like to call my childhood. You take care of his damn ashes. Let the loser bury the loser."

Paul felt a burrowing grief sweep up from his loins, make a circuit in his chest, throw shards of pain into his thoughts, before it headed back behind his crotch.

"I'll scatter his ashes," he yelled into his office phone, recycling a few of his tears with his tongue before he slammed it into its cradle.

# 50.

"It's called analysis," he announced to his class. It was a remedial university composition course so he assumed the students knew nothing. "Analysis literally means to pull things apart. To take things to pieces." The class exhibited a docility that befitted their unknowing estate. Paul was pleased, and therefore,continued. "Taking things to pieces has long been a method of gaining control over a subject area. Aristotle was one of the most recognized for his ability to take things to pieces. He took speaking and writing and divided up into its constituent parts—schemes, tropes, and argument into its parts. Propositions and conclusions, and labeled different kinds of logical constructions. He was doing all of this to gain power over language. Mechanics learn their art by taking vehicles to pieces. Business majors, by taking companies to pieces. And so it goes."

A timid, thin, Mormon-looking boy raised his hand.

"Yes, Tyler?"

"How do you get power out of taking things apart?"

"Well, it's kind of like a recipe. To gain power over a cake, you must learn both the ingredients and how those things are combined. You have the recipe, you have the cake."

"But isn't the whole always more important? Like the cake, isn't it more important that the pieces make a cake, than that the cake is made of pieces?"

"You're saying the same thing," Kyle said, speaking through his poorly haired chin.

"No he's not," Paul rebutted, and slumped against the chalkboard in heavy thought. "It's different. Listen carefully, and I'll transpose the thought. Do minutes make an hour, or is an hour made of minutes?" He shook his head. "Is a life made of minutes or minutes made of life? That's not the clearest of examples, probably. I'm losing the thought. Sorry, Tyler. I'll try and think of a better example. I'll come back to that in a moment, okay?" Tyler nodded.

"Separation is a way of gaining power. Science has so consistently pointed out almost everything can be separated. For instance, the oils in canola can be divided out, or extruded, from the canola with hexane.

The oil can then be bottled and sold, or turned into margarine. I actually know someone who did hexane extrusion for a living. He worked at a margarine factory. Hydrogen can be separated from oxygen, energy from matter, electrons from nuclei, genes from cells, identity from identified, man from wife, sperm from penises, desire from hard-ons, embryos from wombs, time from living, and a man from himself. What God has joined together, let science split asunder." Paul smiled. "The atomic weapon is one of the greatest examples of the power of dividing, the power of nuclear divorce. This divorce can power or powder towns, cities, provinces, countries. For better or for worse, if you show me an area of knowledge I will show you signs of divorce."

"Are you saying divorce is good?" asked Tyler.

"No. I'm using as a metaphor for the facts." Tyler's eyes clouded, but he refused to ask any more questions.

"Is this on the final exam?" asked Kyle.

"It's on the exam of life, for sure. But it's not necessarily on mine." Then without warning, Paul burst into tears and began to weep like a baby. Several times he tried to steel his frame in order to contain the outburst. The students looked at one another.

"Sir, are you okay?" asked Vanessa. Paul attempted to try to communicate with her, but he could not stop his blubbering. So, one by one, the students gathered up their materials and left.

# 51.

The Housekeeping Department called.

"Paul, we've been receiving complaints that you have been using permanent markers on the whiteboards."

"Are you sure it's me?" he asked.

"On two of the whiteboards the words 'Feck capitalism' were written. Along with numerous other obscenities."

"That's my thesis statement all right. Capitalism, though apparently successful, is a massive, terrifying, death-dealing failure."

"Ah ... okay. We don't mind the words or the expletives. We do mind, however, that is not easy to remove. It takes sometimes as long as forty-five minutes to remove some of your lecture materials from the boards, and we cannot afford that."

"I'm tenured."

"Ah. Um. Great. Good for you," the housekeeping voice replied. "So?"

"Tenure protects my teaching approach and intellectual property. I use those markers to make a point."

"Yes, right. Could you use erasable markers instead?"

"So you're objecting to the permanence of my words?"

"Ah, yes, I guess in a manner of speaking."

"You're saying writing in space, but not in time."

"Ah... not sure about that."

"You're saying that my words are not good enough to be permanently on the board."

"Ah... I don't think so."

"Is there any word or sentence I could write that I would be entitled to write in permanent ink?"

"Ah... Paul, um, sir, I think you're missing my point here."

"This is the very point," Paul snarled. "This is the very feckled point. This is the essential mother-forging problem."

"Sir, I'm not appreciating your tone."

"You are censoring the truth, the big capital *T* truth. You are preventing me indicating to students through form that some things are more important than others, that some things are worth permanence." Paul raised his voice to a scream, and pulled the earpiece away from his ear.

"And for that reason I must ask you to completely fob off." And in a magnificent slam he smashed the receiver into the cradle, cracking the digital face of his phone.

In his rage, he instantly picked up a permanent marker and took his chair and began to write slogans on the walls of his office, mostly in discreet out-of-the-way places. He wrote things like "Knowledge is power: educate the masses," "Farm Capitalism," and other articulate epithets. He was particularly proud of one he managed to get in the high far corner of his office by standing on his filing cabinet. "That'll show those mother fathers," he said to himself as he climbed down.

For his afternoon class he loaded up on permanent markers and planned to write some of the most outrageous truth he knew on the board.

# 52.

At about 1:45, as Paul sat in his office, the fire alarm bell began to ring.

"Ah," Paul cursed, as he hunched over an essay with his green marking pen. After the bomb scare a few weeks back, he knew how to respond. He grabbed his car keys and wallet from beside the computer and pulled his coat from the back of the door. He considered the stack of essays he was working on as he raised his hands to cover his ears. He could suddenly hear the rustling of thought stirring in his head as he pushed his fingers onto the flaps of his ears to block out the bell.

"Frame it," he said to himself, and the muffled bass tones made the expletive sound especially close and wet. He strode under the fire bell and out to the stairwell. He released his ears as he headed down the stairs, and clasped them again as he walked under the last bell. He released his ears quickly, slammed the release on the door, and stormed out onto the common, between buildings. Though he was one of the first to leave his own building, there was a large commotion outside of the building on the far side of the common. Several emergency vehicles were positioned outside and on the lawn. Emergency personnel lumbered over the lawn in large white suits. Students and faculty were lined up as they emptied the building. Each of them stepped into draped areas where a person in white suit hosed them off from head to toe on the front, made each face the opposite direction, and hosed off the back.

Paul stepped towards the building as streams of soaking people, some running, some walking, some disgusted, some giddy, left the cordoned areas. Paul had crossed almost half of the lawn when several police officers ran up to him, fending away several gawkers who were drawn to the scene.

"Sir, please clear the area." His sunglasses winked with sunlight.

"What's going on?" Paul asked.

"Anthrax," he replied. "The building will be closed the rest of the day."

# 53.

"VADIM, I CAME TO TELL you—to brag, really—that I don't need sleeping pills any more. I am now so tired that I cannot think. My mind is so stuffed with the TV I watch as I fall asleep, I believe I've demonstrated some serious progress. I wanted to tell you, you mother-fodding, good-for-nothing doctor, that I am much, much better now, and no longer require sleeping pills."

"So why are you visiting me today?"

"I would either like some kind of heavy-duty antidepressant, or I would like to commit myself to a psych ward. I am losing it. I'm completely fucking gone in the head."

"How do you know this?"

"My knowledge keeps dissolving."

"Hmmm," Vadim said thoughtfully. "What liquid dissolves it? I have patients who could use such a liquid."

"I'm serious,"

"I am too."

"Molasses, or corn syrup, feels like. Something thick and gooey. But my interest is not in the liquid but in what happens to my knowledge. It keeps fragmenting into smaller and smaller pieces. Literature lost its gravity and became a series of books. The books lost their cohesion and became essays and stories, which became a set of conjoined paragraphs, which became a series of schemes and tropes, which became sentences, which became grammar, which turned into linguistics. And the linguistics turned into, I don't know, strings of ape sound. At the end of it all, I'm left with meaningless detail. A sour porridge of thought. I can no longer think."

"I see your problem, though I would have compared it to Cream of Wheat."

"No matter what knowledge I begin with, I end up chopping it up into smaller and smaller segments. And when it's too small to chop, the pieces begin to break up by themselves."

Vadim studied Paul's earnestness for a moment, and with a large swallow avoided another smart-ass reply. Paul took advantage of the pause to further unburden himself.

"I started out on what I thought was a rock, which became a beach, which is now quicksand."

Vadim winced as Paul spoke. "Please constrain your metaphors."

"And this bothers me because, somehow, I intuit that knowledge ought to be a unity. That rather than moving towards pieces, I ought to be moving towards bigger and bigger truths. But I'm not. I move from big truths to smaller and smaller splinters of knowledge, and I have less and less to stand on." He turned and stared desperately into Vadim's eyes. They seemed solid, like black rocks, and Paul anchored himself to them for several moments. "Do you know the one truth?"

"I do," Vadim replied, without blinking. "The truth is that you are sick: you are rational. From this truth all others will make sense."

"Stop kidding with me. I'm on the verge of mental health issues."

"I am totally serious," he replied stolidly. "Let me diagnose you." He set down his book and placed his hands upon Paul's shoulders, patting them lightly. "Just relax." He continued, patting from the outer shoulders to the base of Paul's neck and up. "You have a tumor," he said mechanically. He massaged Paul's head. "And now I shall find it." He patted the top and sides of Paul's head gently. "The tumor sits on your shoulders."

"I am standing on edge of a precipice and you're going to belly-buck me over?"

"Don't debase me in such ways. You offend me by not considering my diagnosis." Vadim pulled his hands away from Paul's head and retreated to the door of Paul's office.

"But the problem is with the knowledge."

"What is splitting things? Knowledge, if it exists outside of you, is a noun, is it not?"

"Yes. I suppose."

"And this splitting is an action, is it not?"

"Yes."

"Which is a verb, correct?"

"Yes."

"Only beings can act, perhaps only humans."

"Yes."

"Therefore, the action that is being done is being done by someone. Who then is splitting your knowledge? Is it me? Is it your wife?"

"Hmmm," Paul grunted. His face frowned deeply as the weight of his thought increased.

"It is your rationality that is splitting things. Put rationality in its place," Vadim declared.

"What do you mean?"

"How aware are you of yourself? How big is the window of rationality?"

"How do I begin to assess that?"

Vadim paused and rested an index finger across his lips, and then pointed it at Paul. "Do you have to remember to breathe?"

"No."

"Do you have to remind your kidneys to remove impurities from your system?"

"No."

"What about your heartbeat?"

"I get your point."

"Is it fair to say that your entire existence is managed without your knowing or understanding it?"

"Yes."

Vadim smirked. "My dear Phaedrus, how much of your action every day do you understand?"

"Very much, I would say."

"So you know, of course, that you are twitching your foot at this moment, do you?" Paul looked suddenly at his foot and as he looked at it, it stopped. "Do you remember the hallway when you walked to class this morning?"

"OK. I see your point."

"Do you agree with Freud's invention, that there is an unconscious?"

"Yes. Yes." Paul sighed and slumped again.

"So, what percentage of what you do are you aware of?"

"Well let me go with the amount of brain capacity I apparently use and say ten percent."

"I should think that extremely unlikely. I would say no more than 1 percent, and this would be very high."

Paul soaked in Vadim's statement for a moment and nodded. "OK. I agree."

"If you are only aware of one percent of existence with your rational mind, why assign it all authority over your existence? If your rationality could be compared with an apartment building, it might have one hundred floors and there is one window in the entire building. And it is on the tenth floor facing north. Who would base all their decisions on what they see from that window?"

"That does seem rather limited."

"Let me be more pointed."

"Please."

"How much do you actually know about Marx?"

"Rather a lot, I should think."

**Ghost in Theory | 189**

"How do you know these things?"
"I read them."
"Are you sure of Marx's existence?"
"Yes."
"How?"
"It's an established historical fact."
"Who established it?"
"We have his writings."
"Maybe he plagiarized."
"Absurd."
"Yes, but possible, no?"
"Maybe he never existed, like those who doubt Socrates' life."
"I can't win on these grounds."
"No, you can't. You can never win because you have accepted the boutique equivalent of gossip—verified, indexed, and commonly thought to be true. You are the accumulation of a great many unexamined assumptions and a torrent of second-hand, half-remembered knowledge. Very little of what you know is rationally verifiable."
"What does 'rationally verifiable' mean?"
"Mindful, first hand, documented experience, of course."
"I have never experienced Marx first hand."
"Then you cannot know him in any rational sense. You may only rationally assess second-hand reports."
"That's the historical version of rationality."
"That's faith. If Marx ever existed, if he lived as others say he did, then perhaps it's true. This is of course giving great credence to your belief that things existed before you were born, and that you were born at all."
"I was born. I'm here." Paul protested quickly.
"Do you remember your birth?"
"Ah, no."
"Neither do I. I do hope your mother wasn't lying."
"All humans are born, and I'm a human. You would know. You were an obstetrician."
"I can only tell you, scientifically speaking, that some humans were born. If you like, I can give you a list."
"Oh, you are a ridiculous doctor. I don't know why I come to you."
"I do not know either."
"Of course I was born. Of course I am human," Paul bawled.
"For both assumptions, I must ask how you know."
Paul stopped suddenly. "I could ask my dad."
"He was probably in the waiting room."

Point taken. Paul frowned. "My birth certificate?"

"Must you rely on the government to exist?"

"I'm cornered."

"I agree," the doctor said, and brought an index finger up to the tip of his nose. "To live at all, you must assume your life. Life is nothing more than a fundamental assumption. But I think if you insist on building houses of ideas then build, at least, from the ground up, like most builders do. Building from the sky down never works." He closed his eyes and sighed. "I must go. I have more important things to do than to discuss philosophy with you."

Paul returned to his office. Splinters of thoughts lunged and thrust into consciousness. Paul parried with a modern move: computerized distraction. He opened a solitaire game he found on his ancient loaner computer. He played for an hour and half, until the beginning of his next class.

# 54.

U P THE BLOCK SAUNTERED PAUL, passing Bal as he was pounding a tall steel post in to the edge of his lawn, where it met the sidewalk. His toupee was laying in the grass beside him as he worked with a frenetic energy to drive the post into the earth.

"Hey, Bal," Paul said with a smile. "How are things?"

Bal looked up suddenly, and anger filled his features. "You jackleg. Stay away from me. Go away."

Paul's eyes opened wide and he stopped his step. "I'm sorry, Bal. It's me, Paul."

"I know who you are, scapegoon. I'm not blind."

Bal took a step back. "Why are you upset with me? What have I done?"

"You told me to confront Virginia. You told me." He stepped away from his work and pointed a skinny finger with a marble-sized knuckle at him. "It was you." His face suddenly blazed red and his facial muscles tightened. Then he melted into a blubbering heap and fell on the grass. "She... she... she left me. I couldn't stop her," he wept. Then the tears suddenly stopped, and anger tightened his facial muscles again, and he stood up, and accidentally put a muddy shoe on his toupee, which had heeled like a faithful dog beside his right leg. "I shouldn't have listened to you. I'd still be with her today." His pronunciation became difficult with an abundance of saliva, which began to spill out of his mouth. "She'd still be sleeping in my bed. She'd still be there."

"I'm sorry, Bal," Paul said. The attack seemed to warrant an apology, even though he couldn't remember doing anything directly to precipitate the event. "I think I was just telling you what I would do if I were in your situation."

"Chuckheaded tombstone. You told me to confront her, so I did. And she left me because I confronted her." The rain of spit continued. "I'm all alone. Nobody but me." As his rage descended into sorrow again, he held out his finger again. "You. You did it." He melted again and collapsed onto the lawn, this time sitting on his hairpiece.

The urge to leave the situation welled up earlier in Paul and finally he began to obey it. "Goodbye, Bal. I'm terribly sorry."

"I'm not finished with you. You, you, you dog. You filthy dog."

Paul passed him and once he passed him, began to walk quickly. Then trot. Then run.

"How can you run from me?" Bal howled, standing atop his toupee. "You're a bad, bad man." Once most of the way up the block, the howls and abasements spangled the air. Paul could only feel the syllables beat the drum of his ear. So he lumbered on, now mad with dread, drowning dreamlike in a monstered sea.

## 55.

"I DO WANT TO DIE," OWEN said plainly.

"I'm not going to kill you," Paul said. "Not happening."

"You could at least get me a gun. Your rifle," Owen said.

"I'm a no-gun guy, Owen, no gun to lend."

"You definitely have a gun in the house," Owen insisted.

"Nope."

"Have I not told you the story?"

"What story?"

"Joan's son, John. He uh… had mental health issues. Nice kid. Very bright. Too bright. There was a couple of things that set him off on the wrong track. Anyhow, he somehow felt he was suddenly in a war with China. We used to have a good Chinese restaurant called The Pagoda where the strip mall is on 37th, near 17th. So John took his dad's 30.06 and headed down to Woolco — that's what it was called then—and bought some shells, then walked down to The Pagoda and shot the cook. When he came home, Paul met him in the alley where John was excited and waving the rifle around. He was nervous with the rifle. It was loaded, of course, and he had a box of shells. Paul was very fatherly toward John, so he asked for the rifle, nicely. And John offered it to him. He took it and put it in his house somewhere. When the cops came, they arrested John and took him away. For some reason, it changed the court case that they didn't have a weapon—his sentence would be lighter or some such thing—so Paul kept the rifle and didn't tell anyone about it. He told me about it a few years afterwards. Apparently, no one knew he had it. The cops assumed he'd ditched it somewhere. But Paul told me he'd put it in the attic."

"The rifle is in my attic?"

"Think so."

"Not sure it's there. I seem to recall Bonnie got extra insulation blown in to the attic. So if wasn't removed before then, it probably was during."

"Maybe. I feel like you probably would have heard something from the insulation installers if they'd found a weapon, don't you think?"

"So you think I should check."

"I wouldn't be surprised if it was still there, Paul."

"Great. Not like I can get it. I don't really know where to look. The attic is a big space, and now it's all full of insulation."

"Well, it would have been vermiculite, if you sprayed anything. Very thin stuff. Easy to find a rifle. Probably right around the attic access."

"Attic access?"

"The little square wood panel in the ceiling of your main floor somewhere."

"Oh. Right. I know what you mean. When did he shoot the restaurant guy?" Paul asked suddenly.

"1983. August 20."

"I thought he was around when Paul, ah, you know. Wouldn't he have been in prison, and then couldn't help you do anything."

"Oh, yeah. He was given a lighter sentence because he was, you know. Not right in the noggin, if you know what I mean."

"Well, I can promise you this, Owen. If there is a gun up there, and I find it, I'm not bringing it for you."

"If you're not man enough to do it yourself, then the least you could do is bring it to me so I can do it."

"I don't want any part of it, Owen."

# 56.

"YOU WANT ALL THESE CLOTHES?" It was his portly mother-in-law, her second chin waggling below her mouth, probably mouthing the opposite of what she had just said. She was standing over a bunch of Don's old clothes.

"I think they'd fit you." She held up a plaid shirt, one of Don's favourites, and pinched it to Paul's shoulders. "I think you and he had something in common."

"You mean you wish we had something in common," Paul said with a barely masked menace.

"You read my mind," she replied in elegant, oily tone.

"You must be so happy to be free," Paul added.

"How could you say such a thing to a grieving widow?" she said with a thin smile.

"I'll take these clothes. I'll take them all. I'll take them because I cared about the man. I'll take them because these clothes were offered to Bruise first, and he didn't take them because they weren't good enough for him." Her lard-lidded eyes flinched a little on that one. "I'll take them because I hope for as much success as he found. You're not good enough for these clothes, either."

He pulled the box away from her, and took it to the basement to his new room. He came up and found Bonnie and her mother speaking furtively in low tones. Buddha was sitting on Grandma's knee.

"I'll pay to replace the doors," she said with a volume that was meant to be heard. Both women eyed him.

"Fugpeddling Mugwarmers..." Paul began.

"Don't use those disgusting words," his mother-in-law demanded. "Use the word 'farm' instead."

"Alright," Paul said, drawing a little breath. "Farm you, then. Farm right off."

The thick, heavy lids of her eyes lifted a little in surprise, which pleased Paul.

Shocked, Mary turned to her daughter to see what she would do. Bonnie was making a fist with her right hand, holding it low below her thigh so Paul could see it and her mother couldn't.

"Paul, that's extremely rude," Bonnie said, her tone marking outrage. "Apologize."

"I don't give a fat farm," Paul concluded in a huff of disgust, and left the room. He knew, of course, he would pay later.

# 57.

"COME ON, PEOPLE. WHAT'S KIND of sentence do we have here?" The crowd shrank away from him. Paul had just walked into class and popped a compound-complex sentence onto the computer projector. Given the remedial work they'd been doing on phrases and clauses, he thought the group should be able to answer the question.

Katie, a nice young woman with only an acute brand awareness, no moral compass or cultural understanding, stuck her hand in the air.

"Katie," Paul called.

"I wanted to ask a question, Paul, not answer yours."

"Ah, okay."

"What the hell happened to you?"

Paul sighed. "It was a cooking accident."

"What kind of cooking accident does that to a person?" Michael interjected. He was a basketball-playing journalist, who liked running his fingers through his thick, shoulder-length hair. "Is that like you 'fell down the stairs'?" Some of the class tittered.

"That's about it. These injuries were all related to a common kitchen utensil. Stairs had nothing to do with it. Is there anything else about my appearance you'd like to comment on?"

"Nice pants," Jessica quipped.

"You guys don't want to work today, do you? Don't give me a hard time for my pants. I just got these."

"You didn't buy them, I hope," she added.

"No. No, I didn't. I actually inherited them from a man who just died." Paul struck a fashion pose and pointed to the pants. "These, ladies and gentlemen, are the pants of a dead man."

"Gross," Katie said, instinctively clutching her Guess purse. A few others groaned.

"Leave my pants alone. I like them. Let's get back to the sentence," Paul commanded. He walked over to the opaque blinds blocking the natural world's distraction on the classroom. Paul hauled up the first blind, and the sun from hot afternoon poured in around him. He turned his back to the window, leaned up against the bottom of the window's sill, and raised his hands. "Come on, people. Don't stress me out here. I was under the impression I've been teaching for a few days. If you haven't been learning, then I haven't been teaching."

Nicole, a jittery, Prozac-tamed divorcee, tittered. "Raise your hands again, but say 'God loves you.'" Paul raised his hands. "Now everybody watch," she yelled.

Paul raised his hands. "God loves you."

"You look just like Jesus Christ," said Ling.

"Jesus Christ," laughed another.

Paul immediately stepped out of the light. "Stop it. You'll give me a complex. Plus, I don't have the hair for it. Next thing you know you'll be asking me to heal you of your bad grammar."

"You look sort of like a Mormon Jesus, I'd say," said the portly, droopy Vanessa. "Tight hair, but the same kind of holy light."

"Do you know what you're saying?" Paul asked in a joking tone. "I'm a communist. Jesus is an opiate."

"Maybe you're a user," Vanessa replied.

"Hmmm. Nice." He halted briefly. "If you don't mind, though, I'm closing the blind." He pulled the blind back down.

"Grammar is powerful. You know the new automatic taps the university has installed in all the washrooms? Do you know the difference between the old taps and the new ones? The old hand-turned taps meant you had to act, to do something. You were a grammatical agent, a verb, and you had to be just to wash your hands. But these new taps, you're not a creator of action, you're not enacting a verb, you're a noun. You have to wait until the tap senses your 'noun-ness,' if you will, before it will turn on the tap for you. As a verb you're free. As a noun you're not. And the essence of all convenience and luxury culture is to emphasize noun-ness. But the interesting part of life is to be part of a process—a verb. A noun does nothing for itself or others. It is something that action gets done to. As a verb, I'm an actor. As a noun, I'm a victim. In one case I am asked to act as a noun, which I despise, and in the other, I am asked to be a verb, which is much preferable. I want to be a verb, don't you? Now, let's get off this Jesus Christ thing, and get to work.

"Can anyone tell me what's going on in this sentence?" The class sat quietly again. He gently smacked his own forehead. "You're going to make me answer my own question, aren't you?"

"Face it, dude," Jonos said in a gentle tone. "You might as well. You have a saviour complex. And saviours get to make the questions, but they must always provide the answers."

# 58.

"So, there I was in front of the window as I opened the blind," Paul was mid-sentence. "And this kid asks me to say 'God loves you.' So I do, and they accuse me of being Jesus Christ."

"Oh, God," Vadim said with a laugh, rubbing his forehead. "At least they know who Jesus Christ is. A young person in my office today announced that Winston Churchill was his favourite American President." He laughed and sighed at the same time. "But if I may say so, you look like hell. What happened?"

"Construction accident," Paul said quickly.

"Construction accident?" Vadim questioned. "Didn't you use that excuse two times ago?"

Paul shook his head. "A wall thing. I was dismantling some drywall, and hurt myself in the aftermath."

Vadim's eyebrows pinched together to demonstrate his confusion. "It was a concussive event, entirely my fault. But I'm otherwise okay," Paul added to address the confusion and doubt.

"Don't have me over for supper," Vadim quipped. "I'd hate to be responsible for how you'd look afterwards. Bonnie takes care of you?" Vadim half-asked, half-stated.

Paul grinned. "She's planning to."

"Good," Vadim replied, missing the undertone entirely.

"Are you sure that's what happened? This bruise here looks like a set of knuckles," Vadim said gently as he inspected Paul's head.

"Yes," Paul answered quickly. "No."

"Be careful unless you enjoy wearing my helmet. Your skull is still healing," Vadim admonished. Paul met Vadim's eyes. They seemed to register a sorrow. "Many a mighty Jesus has ended in frustration because the world would not listen to his message. Often, he cannot get the world interested enough in him to even bother with crucifixion. He's enraged. And his revenge is to excitedly plan and await his own crucifixion," Vadim said slowly. "He kills himself to remove his own saving power from the world." He paused and caught Paul's wavering vision with his own, and waited until Paul focused on him. "Be careful, sir."

"Yes, yes. Of course," Paul agreed, snatching his focus away from Vadim's. Vadim stilled him with a hand on the shoulder.

"I did not retire from obstetrics. I was forced to quit. I was working late one night, and a baby girl was born to this woman, but she came out struggling. She had inhaled her meconium. She was calm, her health significantly declined already: she had not long to live. I thought I could probably sustain her life for a short while, but I am certain she would have died. As I stood there, with the baby in my hands, the mother relieved and overjoyed, I had the overwhelming sense that I should not help this little one, that I should let her go quickly without my aid. I attempted to pass the mother her baby and reported to the mother that her baby girl was not doing well. The mother promptly passed out. The nurses were prepared to do all they could, but I called them off. I recognized, as I have seldom done in my life, that this was a holy moment, one that should be passed in silence, as this little one visited and left this life. So I did. I held this little girl in my arms until she departed, a matter of ten minutes, perhaps." Vadim's eyes teared up a little.

"I am not sorry for what I did, still. I was sued, and part of the outcome of the suit was that I was not allowed to work in my area of specialty again. But you realize by now, I've violated that request, so you must not report me." He grinned sadly.

# 59.

AS HE SAT AT HOME, pleased with the anthrax scare and the gift of time it had suddenly awarded him, he was disturbed by someone ringing the front doorbell of his home. Then an aggressive knock. "Dr. Shreeve," a voice yelled through the door. "This is the police. Please open the door immediately or we'll knock it in."

The front door was mostly glass, covered only by a thin layer of sheer curtain embroidered thinly with butterflies, and as he approached it he noticed two men out front. He opened the door quickly.

They were policemen. "Yes, officers? How can I help you?" Surprise and compliance mingled filled the tone of his reply, like the inside of a jelly donut.

"Are you Paul Shreeve?" demanded a man with big chopper-quad glasses and an absurdly well-trimmed moustache. Their black uniforms sucked the heat and light out of the afternoon sun.

"Yes. Yes I am." His words shuffled out unsteadily. "Dr. Paul Shreeve."

"Sir, we need you to come downtown and answer a few questions." Paul caught a faint red glint in the officer's glasses. He looked away from the officer's windows and noticed that there were four cars parked at odd angles in front of his house.

"Ahh. Ah. What's this regarding?"

"I'm sorry sir, but we're only here to escort you downtown."

"Any idea at all?"

"No, sir. Please step outside and we'll take you downtown."

"Ah. Um. Could I get my coat?"

"No, sir. Step outside of the house right now, please."

"My keys?"

"Outside now, sir." The officer moved his hand to the handle of his holstered Glock.

"Ah. Yeah. Sure."

"And, sir, if you'd kindly turn around. Policy requires us to handcuff you." The officer's lip sneered up like Elvis's.

"What? I haven't done anything. This violates my rights."

"Sir, it's just policy."

Paul pulled his hands against his midsection, automatically.

"What if I don't want to go with you?"

"I'm afraid, sir, that you don't have a choice. You must come."

"Oh." Paul shrunk into himself and then, with some effort pushed his wrists in front to receive the cuffs.

"Turn around please, sir." The officer gently pulled his left hand behind his back and clicked the cold steel into place. Then, a little more roughly, he grabbed the right elbow and pulled it back and clipped the two together. Then, sunglass Elvis man turned him around gently and pushed him to the car.

Angela was on her front step with a watering can, a trowel. She followed Paul's perp walk with a puzzled expression. Neighbours stood around the scene. Old Man Sobczak and Beata were walking the block together. Joan was walking home with a bag of groceries from Walmart.

"They got you, eh?" she cackled. "'Bout damn time."

Owen leaned forward in his wheelchair and gazed through the gauze of his sheer front curtain. Joan looked a little relieved. Owen, twisted with warring emotions, like a man whose life-saving operation has been cancelled. In the middle of all this, Bonnie pulled up in front of the house and stepped out. Her nostrils flared as big as quarters. Still stickdoodled about the anthrax scare.

She walked up to Paul where he stood, handcuffed and held from behind, and brought her hand across his mouth in a broad and painful slap. Her heaving damp body stood in front of him, like a hockey player wanting a fight. Her nostrils swelled down from quarters to dimes as she sucked air out of the atmosphere, then quarters as she pushed the air back into the world.

"Ma'am," the officer said, opening the back door of a nearby cruiser. He pulled Paul back and lay his right hand on top of Paul's head, like a priest giving a blessing from behind, pulled him towards the car's rear seat, and folded him in half like a chair. His head wasn't quite low enough and he caught the side of the cruiser above his left ear.

"Ow. Frappé furgwater, that hurt."

"I'm sorry, sir," said the Elvis.

❋❋❋

"So the anthrax, you're saying, was really the ashes of your recently deceased father-in-law John Donavon Honingsblum."

"That's correct."

"You poured some his ashes into an inter-office mail envelope and placed that envelope in the inter-office mail system."

"That's correct."

One of the detectives grinned. The other frowned. "Why did you do such a thing?"

"It's long and complicated."

"We'll make time."

Paul explained, in as clear a manner as he could, the history of his relations with this family and how the situation had come to be.

"I was very angry with the flippant manner they displayed towards this lovely man. They didn't give a damn. Not a single damn. They weren't even going to pick up his ashes. So I did. I think Don would have appreciated my idea. If he's watching from somewhere, he'll be thrilled with how it's gone. Sort of an appropriate send-off. Some in the inter-office mail."

"Some in the inter-office mail," the detective repeated. "Where did you put the rest?"

"Ah. Um. Oh." Paul realized that the officer had done a neat trick of noticing his use of the determiner. "I don't think you're going to like this."

"Try me," said the unhappy interrogator.

"Well, the reason I put some of his ashes in the interoffice mail, was, ah. Well. I ran out of postage."

"You ran out of postage?" said the other. It took a moment to sink in. "Do you mean to tell me you mailed this to people?" He thundered incredulously. The happy cop snorted, trying to control and release the gust of his laugh.

"Just a few people. Close relatives only."

"How many exactly?" said the frowny cop, tilting his ear towards Paul. He took a pad of paper and slid it towards Paul, and rolled a pencil across the metal table. The pencil's sides striking the table made the pencil sound musical as it rolled.

"Ah. Bruce. That's the son. The mother. And one sister who lives in the Toronto area. So I guess three."

"Did you pack these ashes properly?"

"What do you mean properly?"

"Describe how you included the ashes in these mailings."

"Eh... well. I addressed the envelopes and affixed the postage. Then, I poured some ashes in each."

"Stop," ordered the frown. "Do you mean you poured the ashes into a plastic bag, or some kind of box?"

"No, sir. Just a regular envelope."

"What do you mean regular?"

"I mean a number 10 business envelope."

"And nothing else?"

"It was just business. And nothing else. I had nothing else." Paul looked down at the pad as the officer began to write the names. "I'll have to get some of the info from home. I can't remember all of it."

"We'll call your house right now. Will your wife have the information?"

"She will, officer, but this is going to spoil the surprise." The good cop laughed heartily. The bad one frowned.

"This is a nightmare of paperwork." The frown motioned to the smile to make the call. The frown pulled the pad from Paul and passed it to the smiling officer, who took it and left the interrogation room.

"Ah. Sorry?" Paul offered.

"For someone who works in a university, this was a pretty stupid move," said the frown.

"I didn't mail all of him. I kept about half of him in my office. The good half," Paul said defensively. "I just wanted to send a little personal visit. They deserved it…them."

"Based on what you've reported," said the frown, "there will likely be some charges pending. The postal system does not permit the mailing of any powdered substances, like cocaine or cremated human remains. You have committed an offence there, and will be charged. You will either pay a fine or end up in court. The university's inter-office mail, you'll probably get off on that charge, because the university, it turns out, has no rules about sending ashes through their mail system. Though I'm sure they will after this incident."

"Maybe I can get on the Interoffice Mail Policy Review Committee," Paul thought aloud. "I could spice up those minutes, I'd bet."

"Sir, please don't joke. This is quite serious."

"Far too serious not to joke, officer," Paul replied.

# 60.

Paul was reclining in his old La-Z-Boy, snoozing under the faint heat from his halogen reading light, when Bonnie came downstairs after her mother had left. Paul was stretched out and didn't notice her arrival. She had a small pot with her.

"You bitch," she screamed as she brought her hand down on his crotch.

"Twud," was the sound her hand made as it hit something solid.

"Oh fuck," she screamed. "My hand. What did you do to my hand?"

"I should have invested in a hockey can a year ago," Paul said. "Great invention, isn't it?"

With her other hand she plunged the pot into his gut.

"Twang" rang the sound of something solid on the bottom of the pot.

Paul lifted up his shirt. "Ah, that's where I put the atlas." He slid the large atlas out from under his shirt and glanced at the page she'd just hit. He'd expanded the book's protection by opening the atlas, so it would cover all of his chest. "You just hit Newfoundland. Those east coasters. They're always the hardest hit. They always get the worst of it."

She picked up her pot and whacked Paul's head.

"Pang." Again. "Pang." Paul was no longer conscious, but she did not stop. She beat him with the pot until she her anger was pacified. And then she began to weep.

*\*\**

Paul woke up in pain on the back step of his house. He got to his feet slowly. The back door was locked. He knocked. And waited. The night sky was littered with stars and wonder; an invitation to wonder. But Paul couldn't. His balls hurt. Seriously hurt.

He hobbled around to the front door. Tried the lock. The doorbell rang, but no one answered. His balls hurt. But it was a kind pain, and he enjoyed it.

He couldn't think. Not in the pain he was in. He could only cope, which is just what he'd needed. Physical pain offered him a little thought holiday.

A clock on the far wall of house read 11, probably p.m., he deduced. And Bonnie wouldn't be opening the door any time soon. He looked up and down the street. There was still a light on next door. He stood shivering in the cool evening air, under a magical sky. He rang the bell until someone inside turned the ringer off.

He felt his pants gingerly. A lot of pain down there. Moisture of some kind. No wallet. No keys. No getting into the university tonight, not without ID. No sleeping in the car or garage.

He looked next door. A shadow splashed the gauze of a window covering. Someone was home. And for some reason, as the clock struck 11 the electric carillon broke into a chime. De Profundis, had he known the shenanigans his friend Old Man Sobzcak had committed. Such mischief! Its tones rang out in defiance of the noise bylaw, as defined in sections 29-36 of the *Community Standards Bylaw*. The flagrant disregard of community standards could only indicate the decline of the general moral state of the community.

Paul finally gave up, and seeing no help, used a ginger limp to make his way next door. Finding no bell, he gently knocked on the door. Angela cracked the door open carefully.

"Hello!" Paul said. He was distracted momentarily by the bruising on Angela's face. "What happened to you?" he blurted.

"A little storage problem. A bunch of things fell on me while I was trying to warehouse them. Logistics. Return to sender. That kind of thing."

"I shouldn't bother you. You're in pain. I'll just …"

"Why are you here, Paul?"

"Ah, oh right. Ummm. I'm locked out of my house without my keys and wallet and I really don't want to …"

Angela inferred what he was asking and opened the door wide. "Come on in."

"Are you sure?"

Angela grabbed his hand and pulled him in.

"Easy, please. I'm not doing so well myself."

"Sorry, Paul. What happened to you?"

"It was an atlas. The world, you know, No coasting for east coasters you know. It just … I don't actually know. I was unconscious for a while. I woke up and I'm in Spain. Pain, sorry. There isn't enough light for me to see what happened."

"Oh, my God, Paul. Your pants." She pointed to his crotch, where a large patch of blood had soaked through his crotch.

"Oh, fudgemother godfrey," Paul swore. "I have to go."

"Maybe to the hospital."

"Would it be okay if I checked it out first? Can I use your washroom?"

"Sure. Sure. Um. Sure. Let me get you some paper towel, maybe. And some hydrogen peroxide."

"Oh God. Hydrogen peroxide?"

"Just to keep any wounds clean."

"Right. Right. I just can't imagine…"

"No, but if there is a significant wound, you'll want to keep it clean."

"Right. You're absolutely right. Sorry to impose on you like this."

"No problem. It's …"

Paul looked at his own crotch. "Oh, my God. What the hell has happened, little buddy?"

"Little buddy?"

"Yeah. That's my name for him. Sorry. Inappropriate. Not in my right mind at the moment."

"Is that from Gilligan's Island?" She fought a smirk.

"Sorry. Yeah. If there's any part of me who's likely to cause shipwreck, it's my first mate."

Angela snorted. "Insubordinate?"

"Understatement. Insubordinate and incompetent. He doesn't feel like part of me. He feels like he's independent. I talk to him sometimes."

Paul pulled the front of his jeans forward for a peek.

Angela closed her eyes.

"Jeemus bluestreak."

"Is it bad?"

"I don't think it's good to be bleeding in that general area."

"How does your little buddy feel, right now?"

Paul looked at Angela. Then at his crotch. "Not good. Like someone's kicked me in the crotch severely several times." He paused. "Which is of course not what has actually happened. I mean that metaphorically. It's just an expression of my pain."

"Not literal, got it." An awkward moment set in as the two of them looked at each other. "Better check on your little buddy," Angela eventually offered. She held out a roll of paper towel and a brown plastic bottle of hydrogen peroxide.

After some commotion and a mighty, high-pitched scream, Paul emerged a few minutes later.

"How is it?" Angela asked.

"Ah. Well, I think it will be okay."

"No hospital?"

"No hospital."

"I think just from your pants it needs attention."

"Honestly, if little buddy doesn't recover, it'll be fine. He's been trouble my whole life. Trouble. There's not a damn bad idea I've had that he hasn't been part of. Seriously. What am I supposed to do with him? There's not a person on the planet that can explain why he's attached to my body, and what I'm supposed to do about him. Marxists say nothing! Feminists get angry at it, but not in any helpful way. I don't really know any philosophy besides the hedonistic ones that bother to include him. But hedonism is a bad idea, it seems to me. Imagine the child support.

"It's this primal piece of equipment that refuses to evolve with the rest of me. It's leftover of the primal drives of millennia ago. Like an alligator in your pants. The dick was doing what was good for the species 133 million years ago. What the flugelhorn solo is a dick good for? Babies, right? Pleasure. Babies, sure. Propagation of the species and all that. But seriously, pleasure seems weak. If you take all the moments of pleasure I've experienced and added them all together, I doubt I've had more than a couple of hours of pleasure in a lifetime, all told. How much of my focus has he stolen? I'm guessing, minimally, seventy-five percent of my focus. And that's being quite optimistic. How much of my thinking has he stained? I don't think it could be any less than one hundred percent.

"I don't know if damaging him hurts his influence or helps it. If it hurts it, okay, I'm glad he got hurt. If I end up thinking even more about him?" Paul shook his head. "I mean I love him. But, I don't even want him. I didn't ask for him. I can't manage one. I don't know what I'm supposed to do with it, and I have not heard once sensible person on the subject of what to do with it. It's like having an insubordinate employee in a fast-food restaurant. Seriously, I nearly hate it as much as feminists do. But they aren't attached to it, are they? They don't have to live with a drunken lecher in their pants, do they? Fugbunches of nougat. No they don't."

"Let me get you something to change into so you can sit down while you wait."

"Not necessary. I can stand." Angela left the room anyhow.

Paul rambled on. "If a woman has a bad idea, let's say it goes to 4, and 4 is really bad. This little buddy I have has nothing on that. I can think badness to a level so far beyond their understanding it would literally terrify them to hear my thoughts. I'm a Spinal Tap 11 and I'm not close to the worst of my gender."

Angela returned with a pair of sweatpants and a belt. "These'll work. They're clean, but you'll need a belt with them."

Paul disappeared into the washroom again and returned dwarfed by the sheer volume of the sweatpants, which he'd held in place by a tatty vinyl men's belt, wrapped twice around his waist and buckled.

"Have a seat, Paul," Angela offered, gesturing to the hide-a-bed couch beside him.

"I'm sorry I can't be as helpful to your wounds as you have been to mine," Paul said. "Thank you for your help." Angela nodded. "I will go after a short visit."

"Paul," Angela chided. "If you can't get into your house, and nothing changes, are you going to sleep on your front step all night? That seems like a bad decision."

"Ah. Um. Well, it seems too much to presume I can stay here. Your daughter...."

"My daughter's away for a few days. I won't likely sleep much anyways. I'm feeling my troubles." She pointed at her bruised face. "You're not exactly a stranger, so stay here, please."

Paul looked at her carefully. "Fair enough. I won't be sleeping much tonight either."

"How about a cup of tea?"

Paul would have normally said no. Especially because he knew that tea only leaves the body through one orifice. "That sounds great," is what he heard himself say.

Moments later Angela emerged balancing a china teacup in each hand. She set one down on the end table on either end of the couch. A pair of Tylenol on each saucer. She pointed to his at one end.

She sat down on the other and turned on the TV. "I'm watching Columbos. I'm most of the way through Season Two."

"Love Columbo."

Paul palmed the Tylenol and slapped them into his mouth, and swigged a scoof of tea. Angela took each pill separately, followed by a delicate sip.

The two sipped and watched. Refilled and sipped and watched. When Paul had to visit the men's room, the pain was indicated by a healthy roar.

"That's the last of the pot," Angela announced as she upended the teapot over Paul's cup.

The two sat for another episode before Paul looked over at Angela, who had teared over for no obvious reason. He reached over and covered her hand with his.

She looked sideways at him for a moment. Paul just returned a smile. She looked at Paul's hand and broke into a sob.

He tore a square of paper towel and passed it to her. She wiped her eyes and blew her nose.

And when both had settled again, Paul held his hand out toward her, inviting her to take it. She did. And so, together, they passed the night.

❋ ❋ ❋

Though Paul had family members who had leapt from earth to the belief in a god, Paul himself had resisted. His own theoretical god wouldn't permit anything but condescension to all things religious. Which was odd, in a way. When cornered on the subject, he would admit that theory was in fact theoretical, and that in all cases, theory was just a stunt-double, a walk-on for the idea of truth. Under debate conditions, he would also grudgingly agree that theories needed support to continue. The difference between theory and religion, in his mind, was this: one was much more concerned with the truth than the other. The problem with religion was that though its tenets were theoretical in nature, there was no mechanism to collapse the old and replace it with the new. Even though the educated guesswork used in theory and the educated guesswork that shored up religion were similar in intent and method, in Paul's mind they were profoundly different, which in fact they were not.

Like most humans, Paul liked to maintain a distinction that allowed that some ideas of how the universe operated were better than others. He believed that his ideas of how to close the gap between what he knew and didn't know were far more "objective" than others'. Another odd fact that he used to justify his biomechanical viewpoint was its utter bleakness. The bleakness made him feel oddly warm, that he was somehow facing something so ugly and real that it must be true, that he was one of the few who could tolerate such difficult truths. It also allowed him to condescend to his own existence to the point where he could allow it to be mundane, which as Marx rightly pointed out, was a form of opiate.

The one thing about life and humans was that humans always thought they had it all figured out. They knew everything there was to know about everything. That's where mythology came from.

But, in truth, it was all theory. All of it mind-stitched comforts used to prop up existences for which, truth be told, there was no accounting. But oh the theories. Theories of this, theories of that. Mental gap-spackle meant to smooth a wall, so the wall would take some paint. Theory in all its forms was the worn recliner that allowed everyone everywhere to sit comfortably. And Paul was only beginning to writhe in the stark discomfort and uncertainty.

# 61.

It was Friday. Blake and Jake slowly broke free of the insides of their sagging Toyota Camry, pulled themselves free of the interior, and stood as the corpulence to which they'd become accustomed fell back in place. So Blake stood outside of the vehicle as his two hefty, bowling ball-sized lumps of flesh, mounted on either side front of his groin, sorted themselves out in his pants. His brother made no noise, but lumbered up the walk to the front door of the house.

Blake was the leader of the two twins, and his immense presence, almost 400 pounds of it, had put him into a rather surly mood. He was excited, for this was his time of the week to shine, but he was also angry at the expense of Angela's services. His corpulence swayed around him, pulling at his frame as he walked. There was a certain joy he felt as his body boiled and bounced around him. He felt snug, like a child wrapped up in a sleeping bag, protected like a boy in a blanket fort, secure as a turtle with his shell on his back, home always with him.

Jake, his brother, did not have that same feeling. He was the second born, behind by four minutes, and the smaller of the two. As such he was born without a personality, perhaps without a soul, and hence depended on his elder brother for everything. From his elder he had gained the model for his deportment. From him he learned how he should think, how he should feel. He was thirty-five pounds lighter than his brother, but had to work very hard to keep the weight on. He was in a light and excited mood, though feeling a little unsettled because he was walking ahead of his brother, and without Blake in visual range, he was always unsure of himself, agitated.

Blake turned to his brother, as Angela opened the door to let them in. "Hello Angela," Jake ejaculated. "Can we tie you up today?"

Angela frowned. "I know you pay me extra, but the last couple of times you've gone too far. So maybe not today."

"Come on," Blake cajoled. "We'll behave better, I promise. Plus, I can double the danger pay."

Angela sighed.

"Please, baby," he pleaded. "We're very good customers, aren't we?"

"Okay, okay. Double the pay, but not as far as last time."

"Sure," Blake said, his throat pinching his reply. "That's fine with us. Jakey, here's been doing a little dreamin'. So's we might accommodate his dream, right, Jakey?"

"Sure," Jake replied compliantly. "That's what I've wanted for a long time now."

"So you want the regular job with a tie up?"

"Yeah. Let's go with that. We'll put the tie up at the end, can we?"

"Sure. You're the bosses."

Angela did her dance, and stripped down the way the two boys liked it. But she noticed as she did her thing that Blake seemed fidgety, distracted. Jake, bless his soul, wedged in his skivvies, was transfixed with her. She pulled her bra down to reveal her sumptuous chest, watching Jake very closely. He wasn't engaged. His mind was somewhere else.

The rest of the routine went off without a hitch, until the tie up. She allowed herself to be tied to the bed. The soft bulbs of skin hung in rows above her face, as Blake struggled to get a knot that would work to tie her up. Strapped to the bed, helpless, she waited.

Once she was secure, Jake began his speech. "You're an old bitch. You ain't the best lookin' we've seen. But you're in our price range. That's why we come to ya."

"Would you mind untying my hands, Blake? I don't really like your tone."

Jake stepped towards the bed to untie her, but his brother stopped him.

"Jake, don't do that. Don't listen to her. We're not going to take her shit anymore."

"Ok, Blake. We won't take it anymore. But did she do everything she s'posed to do. She didn', did she?"

"She missed something, Jake."

"Sure she did. She been shortchanging us a little bit every time we come. And she is getting' uglier every time too. She depreciating. She should be cheaper every time. But she's not. Here's what you deserve." Blake stepped up beside her, raised his hand in a fleshy fist, and brought it down into her stomach. Jake stepped up to her face and brought the same fist down on her jaw. Jake saw how he could please his brother and stepped onto the bed in a hurricane of fat and fist and pummeled Angela where she lay twisting and contorting with pain and reflex. Jake brought his fist down on her jaw one more time, and she lay still, while Jake continued to do his worst. After a few more minutes, Jake turned from the bed. "Come on, Blake. We should go." The two of them checked their clothes and zippers in the front hallway mirror and left, leaving the door open behind them.

# 62.

PAUL WAS MOWING THE LAWN. Angela pulling weeds in the garden. By chance they met around the side of the house and looked at each other. Both immediately intensely self-conscious.

"Ah, I had a cooking accident," Paul began. "It was a pot. I wasn't watching. Kinda freak accident." Paul was wearing the helmet again. Angela nodded and took her cue from him.

"I fell down the stairs." As she opened her mouth Paul noticed a few chipped teeth.

"Wow, you fell hard," he commented with compassion. "Those aren't kind stairs."

"It was two sets, actually," Angela said. He noticed an extra sibilance on her s's and some trouble with t's. A cute new lisp. "The small set, I just fell funny, and the small set was worse than the big one."

"Wow, you really whacked your wrists," Paul said, noting the bruises looping her hands.

"Ah, yeah. I was carrying a heavy load, and it fell on my wrists, and pinched my wrists against the corner of a stair as I fell."

"What are the odds of that, eh? That's awful." Angela searched Paul over for a minute or two. Her search implied her question.

"Ah, pressure cooker, with me." Paul said. "Standing around the old pot and something blew, I don't remember much else."

"Good thing you weren't burned as well," Angela added. Paul touched his face automatically.

"You know, I never thought of that, you're right. I must be the dab-flabbingist man alive. Lucky as the day is long."

"Me too," Angela asked. "It could always be worse, couldn't it?"

"Yes," Paul agreed. "Heaven is always now, because there's always another Hell below."

Angela smiled sweetly. "I think the ability to breathe is the kind of success that I enjoy right now. I can still see flowers," she said, gleaming carefully through her one open eye, the other shut firmly with a swollen shiner. "And I get the rest of the week off from work."

"I don't," Paul said. "I can't take work off, even though I probably should."

"By the way, you work at the university, don't you?"

"I do," Paul answered.

"Do you have career type programs there?"

"What do you mean?"

"Well, I'm thinking of getting another job, but I don't have much education. I'll have to keep working but I thought I might try for a change."

Paul nodded. "I'll get you our night-school calendar. There are a number of possibilities you might find interesting."

# 63.

"I WANT YOU TO KILL ME. I was trying to appeal to your sense of life and dignity, but I can see that it isn't going to work. Instead, I'll tell you the truth."

"I'm still not going to kill you, no matter what the truth is," Paul insisted.

Owen swallowed. "I murdered the original Paul."

"Nice try, Owen. Plus, even if you did, I don't care. I'm not the same guy."

Owen took a healthy swig of rum. "I was having an affair with Joan. Her husband was away, he was a welder. Hard-living guy. Anyhow, he was working on the rigs near Fort Mac somewhere. My wife was in Florida, dead-heading home. We'd just had a ... moment, I'd guess I could say. And Paul caught us embracing in her back yard. He was terribly embarrassed. Long story short, we had a small tussle and I ended up hurting him badly, accidentally, and he died. We didn't know what to do, so we dragged his body back to his house. His wife worked, and wasn't home. So we took got him in his basement. Joan's back gave out. We were trying to stage the scene. Joan got her son to help me. After he helped us, he was never the same. Oh, god. Oh, god. Oh, god. How many lives have I destroyed? I thought the cops would figure it out. I mean, it was the worst frameup job. We literally strung him up and set up the scene.

"Of course it destroyed Bess, his wife. She couldn't fathom why he'd do such a thing. And he wouldn't. Of course he wouldn't. He was the happiest guy around. It destroyed her. We did get away with murder. But both of our marriages fell apart. Joan's son went nuts. Started with the drugs. Schizophrenia, probably brought on by what I made him do. Started hearing voices that told him the corner store owner was Viet Cong. Took his 30.06 Remington up to Woolco, before it turned Walmart. Bought a box of shells and headed over to The Pagoda and shot a cook dead. Went to prison. But came home and then, after our little escapade, died of an overdose. That's all on me, my stupid idea. Shouldn't have got him involved. I've loved Joan for a lot of years, and now from my chair in the kitchen. But she won't speak to me. I suppose John told her what I made him do."

"I'm not here to kill you," Paul repeated. "I won't do anything like that. I couldn't do it. I'm not that guy. I won't bring you the rifle."

"You must do it. You will do it. It won't make everything right. But it'll balance things out, as much as possible. Maybe God will find an extra weight that I can bear and that extra weight will right the wrong."

# 64.

JOAN WAS DABBING GREY PAINT on the base of her wishing well when Paul approached her.

When he fell into her field of view, she looked up with an expression akin to Edvard Munch's Scream, with hair rollers, which then settled into an unexplained malevolence.

"What do you want?" she spat.

"Sorry, Joan. Don't know what I've done to make you so angry."

"You know what you've done. Don't play naïve with me."

Paul rolled his eyes. "Listen. I'm just asking about something that I heard in the neighbourhood the other day."

"I don't know if I want to hear this."

"It does involve your son," Paul replied. Joan's head snapped up as if Paul had slapped her.

"Then you get away from me right now. Right now, you hear? Don't say another word. Not one."

"Sorry, Joan. I'm not trying to hurt you."

"You said the same thing in 1992. But it wasn't true, was it. It was not true." Tears began to streak down his face. "Just leave."

Paul held both of his hands up and backed away.

# 65.

"Thank you for helping me," Paul said. "Bonnie's not home for another couple of hours. If we can get this done before she gets home, that'd be good. Steve is having his nap." Paul was feeling useful, pulling Michael Sobczak from off the street to perform a meaningful service.

"I want to help to thank you for helping me," Michael replied, as he took the stepladder from Paul and scissored it open underneath the attic access panel. He wore an LED headlamp Paul had offered him, which he clicked on and cycled through the settings until he settled on highbeam. Then up the ladder.

He stepped up and removed the attic panel and passed it to Paul, who leaned it against the hallway wall.

There was a two-foot chimney of cardboard above the opening, presumably to there to keep the extra insulation from falling down the attic hatch.

"Hold on," Michael said, pointing to the ladder. Paul embraced the ladder as best he could. Michael stepped up the ladder until his upper body was swallowed by the ceiling.

Paul could hear the faint shushing as Michael began to fish through the insulation around the attic hatch. The odd kernel of insulation floated into the hallway.

"Nothing here," Michael announced.

"Fantastic," Paul responded. "I knew it wouldn't be there." A burst of joy opened in his chest.

"Now I check the other side," Michael replied.

"Oh, right." Paul replied. And the potential swallowed Paul's joy with a thrill of dread.

"Umm. I don't think…. I don't see…"

Michael flailed and shushed through drifts of insulation. An occasional thunk as Michael's fingers groped the ceiling drywall.

"Maybe? Maybe…"

Paul's heart shoved itself into his throat and he choked.

"What's this?" He groaned with effort. "It's something, I think." The ceiling drywall knocked and scraped. Michael groaned as he lifted. "Oh.

Wow. It's heavy. Hold the ladder." Michael stepped up another rung and shifted his feet. "There we go."

"Here is the thing," Michael said, as he lowered the butt of a rifle to Paul in the hallway below. A bolt action hunting rifle with a scope. Paul grabbed the stock and lowered it to the floor and leaned it up against a doorframe. Michael stepped a rung down the ladder and began to tidy up.

"Mortified Feldspar," Paul cursed. "It's true. The frappin' story is true. Inculpatory evidence." Waves of dread began to storm against his sanity again. Michael began to step down the ladder. "Why do these stories always have to be true? Michael…" He stopped the old man's descent. "Is there a box of ammunition up there, too?"

Michael harrumphed and stepped up the ladder, began fishing again. After a few minutes he descended. Clutched in his hand was a dusty old yellow and green box, almost full, but with two shells missing. And a Woolco price tag that read "$7.49."

Paul set the box of shells on the floor, and a toe caught the butt of the rifle. The rifle began to slide and Paul reached out to grab it before it hit the floor. As he did, a loud explosion filled the room, with a good puff of gunsmoke, and the smell of ammonia.

"Paul!" Michael yelled.

"Sorry, Michael."

"Am I bleeding?" Michael yelled.

Paul inspected himself, then what he could see of Michael.

"I don't think so."

"The gun was loaded," Paul said.

"Obviously!" Michael replied angrily, as he rung down the ladder. Paul was holding the rifle upright, almost like a baseball bat, as Michael pulled it from his hands.

"Idiot!" he yelled. "You might have killed me." He examined the trigger and snicked on the safety. Then unbolted the action.

"Sorry. The gun fell and I tried to catch it."

Michael shook his head, and noticing a hole in the wall, pointed to it.

"Isn't your son in this room?" Michael asked.

It took a moment for the thought to arrive. "Oh, God. Please no," Paul exclaimed and fell to the floor. Michael put an arm on Paul and crouched down to examine the hole in the drywall. Then he carefully stowed the gun and ammo in a hallway closet.

"I check on your son," Michael said. Paul whimpered on the floor, in typical Fourth-wave Marxist fashion.

Michael opened the door carefully, and peered inside.

**Ghost in Theory | 221**

Steve was sitting on the floor near the foot of his bed, playing quietly with his Lego collection.

"Hi Steve," Michael offered.

"Hi!" Steve replied. "Who are you?"

"He's okay," Michael called. Paul sniffed and raised his head.

"He's okay?"

"He's fine," Michael replied.

"Daddy, that was a big bang!" Steve said, taking to his feet and rushing into the hallway. "You fell down. You okay?"

"Daddy's okay if you're okay."

Paul got to his feet slowly. Michael stepped into the bedroom and followed the trajectory of the rifle shot. A neat hole in the side of the mattress, and an exit hole mid- mattress. A hole in the bedroom wall, through which it was now possible to see a strained pink sunlight through a shag of insulation fibre.

"Oh my God, Paul. Oh, my God." By this time, Paul was standing behind Michael as he followed the shot through. "You are a lucky man, lucky, lucky, lucky,"

"You lucky, Daddy," Steve agreed.

At that Paul wrapped the Buddha in his arms and burst into tears.

# 66.

After the anthrax story, Paul related the gun incident. "So, the gun went off, and if little Stevie had been in his bed, well…" Paul let silence finish the sentence.

"That is crazy story," Vadim agreed. "What happened to the holes?"

"I plugged them," Paul said. "Except for the mattress. I just kind of covered them over with goop and paint."

"Because Bonnie would kill you if ever she knew."

"Oh, I think *kill* would be a nice way of putting it."

"So what happened to the rifle?"

"Michael took it away for me. I don't want that thing anywhere close to me."

"You, a Marxist, are, how you say… squeamish with a rifle?" He sighed. "You know Stalin? The revolution? It was not some woke joke on social media. It was bodies and blood. Not one or two choice ones, but millions and millions of bodies. Nearly a billion killings in communist history. The greatest human sacrifice to a single idea of all time, if you count bodies, and for what? So you can pose with these ideas in your classroom? The gun has always been communism's best argument. Don't talk people into your viewpoint; you point a gun at them and ask them if they agree. So you can find a way to argue that Marx was gender-fluid friendly? All the guns and blood in the world couldn't bring about communism the first time. Not once did it seed utopia. The Russian Revolution was just the beginning of an ongoing bloodbath. At its core, very human thing: power, greed, and money. I don't know many Muscovites who think much of the idea of communism."

"Now you, my friend, if you call yourself Marxist, need to be fine with guns, pro-gun, with a blood-ready focus to destroy the middle and upper classes. Which would be you and your people, by the way."

Paul changed the subject. "Prescription?" Paul asked.

"Stay away from guns."

# 67.

"OUT YOU GO!" SHE SHRIEKED. "You are not welcome in this house any longer."

"But it's half my house, isn't it?"

"Not when a judge gets through with you, it isn't. When I tell him how you smashed the walls of the house up. Stripped the doors and tried to burn them. When I tell him how you almost shot your son accidentally. You'll be either in prison or penniless. Either works for me, as long as you're not here. Take your clothes and get out. Here's your work laptop."

"What about Stevie?"

"What about him?"

"I need to see him."

"I think a judge would give me sole custody. Maybe supervised visits."

Paul thought for a moment. "I need to see him. Who would supervise me?"

"I don't know. I don't trust you with him. You're an accidental terror," she shrieked.

"So, I can't see him, then?"

"I don't know. I guess so. We'll have to sort that out. I just need you out now. Out! Out! Out!"

"I'll see you later, then," Paul said.

❊❊❊

"Do you mind if I hang out at your house for a while? I've locked myself out again," Paul asked over an armload of belongings. "I have nowhere to go."

"Come on in, Paul," Angela offered. "Want a cup of tea?"

"That's not necessary," Paul replied.

"Not necessary, but would you enjoy it?"

He paused. "I would. That'd be nice."

She led him to the kitchen, where he took a seat at a small kitchen table. The kettle slowly exhaled until it struck a boil and then whistled. The two stole looks at one another. Paul's latest bruises wouldn't be obvious, except for what looked like a handprint on his left cheek. But Angela had a black eye again. And both wrists still had a thick bracelet of bruising.

Angela grinned. Listen," she said. "I've been thinking. You've been locked out a lot lately. Why don't I give you a key to my place, so if you're locked out at yours, you can get into mine, any time."

"Oh, no, no, no. That's too generous," Paul said. I should be able to handle it, generally. "I'm just having a …um…forgetful patch right now."

"Well, why don't you hang on to this key while you're going through your forgetful patch?"

Paul stewed silently for a moment. "It would be handy. I could, you know, pay you rent."

"Rent? Paul, my mom and step-dad own this place. I rent from them. Rent is cheap. Plus, you and I are friends." Silence stood for a moment or two.

"Well, um. If we're friends, I should tell you. Bonnie kicked me out. Sort of. Temporarily. Maybe not. So I'd like to pay rent."

Angela smiled. "I sort of wondered about that."

"If you had a spare room, I could, you know—rent it from you."

"I wouldn't hear of it, Paul. My daughter's moved out and won't be coming back." Old age flashed took her face for a moment before she returned to herself.

"I'd be gone lots of the time, at work, you know. It's just, I tried to live in my office at work, and they kicked me out. Can't live in my office."

"Live here, please," Angela said. "That would be great, actually. That would be a big help."

"Okay. Not sure about the helpful bit, but I'll contribute somehow."

"Sure you will."

# 68.

For the second time in his forty-two years, Paul found himself going up the stairs and into the vestibule of Holy Name Catholic church. This time, it was because he was invited to the Mass of Reconciliation for his Polish friend Michael Sobczak. Michael had insisted he attend, because of the profound role Paul had played in Michael's rapturous return to the mothership.

The community was all there: Bal and his Sunday-go-to-meetin' toupee (not his gardening one); Joan, who was praying devoutly on her knees, tears coursing from the corners of her eyes, in the middle of the row. Owen shuttled himself to the end of the pew where Joan wrestled in prayer, his eyes transfixed on her supplications. Beata bustled around the front of the church in a white, first-communion style dress. Had she ever appeared in public in such a display of religious style? She was obviously in her glory, long past the need to question the sincerity of her husband's desire to reconcile.

The priest entered the vestibule, precisely on time, ready for the parade forward to the altar, and the Mass began.

❋❋❋

After the gentle religious workout, the priest stepped up for his homily.

"Math is a metaphor," he began. "It stands in place for reality, and as a result it helps us understand that reality. The biblical text is also, to some unknown extent, a metaphor too, and is there to help us understand our reality.

"Pick any two sequential numbers. I'm going to pick one and two. Between those two numbers is infinity. I mean that the space between the numbers one and two can be infinitely divided into pieces. I can, at least theoretically, continue to divide the small numeric portions into smaller and smaller ones for the rest of my life, if I so choose.

"It is possible to run beyond a calculator's ability to calculate ever-smaller numbers. Such is the case with horizontal and vertical asymptotes, especially vertical asymptotes." The priest wrote an inscrutable formula on the board, then drew an elaborate graph. Then he drew a curved line that represented the formula. He dotted a vertical line down one side of the graph. "This is a vertical asymptote at x = 2. Another term for this is 'infinite discontinuity.' The number represented by the graph eternally approaches 2, draws closer and closer and closer. It will never meet 2, despite all its best attempts, because whatever the remaining space, it can be halved infinitely. Do you understand the idea?" The priest waited.

"Sort of," Paul said, a little too loudly.

The priest nodded, and continued, "We are so used to stepping on the planks between infinities that do not notice the gaps we step over any longer. There is one and there is two. This simplicity we use as a defence against the overwhelming complexity of truth. Infinity is not after death. Infinity is not a part of the beyond. Infinity walks among us, is all around us, right now.

"Now let me apply this to theology. This is the same idea as the idea of perfection. Perfection." The priest wiped off *x=2* and replaced it with *x = perfection*. "Humans, being what we are, can improve. They can improve a lot. They can work their whole lives towards perfection. But they will not touch perfection. It is an asymptote. We can halve the distance towards God, half it again, and again and again, and though we're so much closer, we will never quite get there.

"There is the Holocaust. There are the estimated forty million people Stalin wiped from the planet. Hurricane Katrina. There is the tsunami which took a hundred thousand souls. These ideas are offered as proof that the human existence is an accidental one, blind chance's lucky burp of life. Where was God in these moments? What can be said about these things?

"I'd suggest that these moments might be a discontinuity. Human beings are so simple, that what they understand is this—the truncated graph." He drew a sketch:

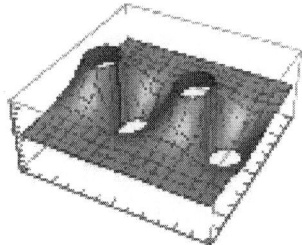

"When, in fact, life is far more complex—it goes off here to infinity, to regions we cannot see except as gaps or holes. And what happens when we use a simplified understanding in place of a fuller one? We get gaps. Holes. Once the complexity has been lost, it's impossible to regain it again."

"A larger idea of holes is suggested by Gödel's theorem, which must be discussed another time. One of its great implications is that there are a number of holes that cannot be systematically filled.

"Of course, there is also quite a bit on the other side—like Nature's exact and precise fit. I am always surprised by the mosquito at this time of year. A tiny, tenacious and rather sturdy creature whose composition and construction defies the imagination. And yet, what do I see when they visit? Nothing but annoyance." The priest shook his head.

"In our quest for perfection, we must be careful to allow things that confound our understanding. We cannot know all. The original formula has been simplified to the point where information is missing and not recoverable. There are holes. There are gaps. But this does not mean we need quit our quest.

"Why can we not get there? Why does perfection elude us? It seems we are not even able to understand all that happens around us. I would suggest the concept of removable discontinuities, or holes, might aid us here. Please forgive the simplicity, but more complex maths would likely make this point less clear to most of you."

The priest scribbled another formula on the board and worked it through, and graphed it, roughly circling spots on the flawless, upward sweep of a curve.

"These are gaps, absences, vacuums in our understanding things for which we have no understanding, or understanding seems impossible."

"Michael Sobczak has chosen to step closer to the church today, and this can be a step closer to perfection. It is one step among an infinite number each of us can take. Of course, the intention of a step is only known in the heart, so closer is sometimes not obvious, but closer is better. This can be a profound step, Michael, if you want it to be."

※※※

Again the bells rang, as the priest lifted the elements into the air. Paul looked at Bal, who seemed to feel Paul's question.

"Same as last time," Bal whispered. "It was just a wafer and wine before the bells rung, and now it's not. There was an absence, now there's a presence. At least that's how we used to think of it."

Paul nodded and frowned with thought and turned his attention back to the altar.

# 69.

Paul arrived at Angela's house shortly after one on Friday, ready to begin his weekend. He tried the front door, which was locked, so he used the key around his neck to let himself in.

"Hello? Angela?" He heard nothing, so took his briefcase full of final exams to his room and tossed them on the bed. Friday was a busy day for Angela, so it would be no surprise if she went out, Paul thought.

He headed to the kitchen to make a cup of tea.

As he headed up the hallway, he heard what sounded like a groan. So he stopped.

"Angela?" he called. A long, muffled groan. "You okay?" A smaller, staccato groan. The groan was coming from the master bedroom. The door was closed. He knuckled the door gently. "Angela?" It now sounded like soft, muffled sobbing. He knocked again. The sobbing continued. Paul put his hand on the bedroom door's glass knob.

"I'm coming in, Angela. Stop me now if it's not the right time." Huff. Sob. Huff. He opened the door slowly. And there, restrained to the bed hand and foot, stretched out like a sky-born star, lay a battered, bruised Angela. Naked. Blindfolded. A ball gag in her mouth. Bloody mouth. Bruised neck. Hands handcuffed to the bedposts. Feet tied to the foot of the bed.

"Oh, Angela. Oh, my dear Lord." Paul fumbled with a buckle on the leather strap of the ball gag, and gently pulled it out of her mouth.

"Paul?" she asked. Her white teeth were painted rose with blood. Paul pushed the blindfold from her eyes. "Oh God. Oh God. Oh God."

"It's okay, honey. It'll be okay." Paul stroked the side of her head tenderly. "Where do I find the key to these cuffs?" He studied the situation for a moment. "Oh!" he exclaimed and visited the bedroom closet, which was filled with all kinds of specialized equipment. On the top shelf there was a plain old blanket. Paul took it down, unfolded it, and covered her body up to her chin.

"I don't know," Angela replied, and began to cry again. She heaved a lungful of air. "Those bastards left me here to die," she screamed. She sobbed and thrashed.

"Hold still a minute," Paul requested. "I'm slow at this."

Paul worked on the knotted ropes holding each of her legs in place, until they were free. When they were, she brought her knees together. Paul rummaged through the bedside tables and looked under the bed, everywhere he could think of, to find the key or keys.

He returned to Angela's side. "It's okay, Angela. You're alive. I'm going to look for keys. Maybe you need a drink of water or something?"

"Key," she said between sobs.

Paul strode through the house looking for a key on any surface anywhere. No key anywhere. He returned to Angela.

"No key."

"Paper clip."

"Huh?"

"Find a paper clip, bobby pin," she ordered. She sniffed. "Kitchen drawer, just below the microwave on the right." Paul jogged to the kitchen. "Big one," she yelled. "Not a small one." Paul found a big paper clip and returned with that, as well as a glass of water and a box of tissues.

"I'll tell you what to do," she said. Paul nodded and listened as she spoke. After a few tries, the cuffs were off. Paul left without saying a word. Angela banged around the bedroom for a while before a long shower.

Paul marked three essays before he went to the kitchen and put on the kettle. The kettle whistled as Paul dropped a couple of orange pekoe bags into a stained brown teapot. He pulled two cups down from the cupboard. Angela trudged into the kitchen in her PJs, housecoat, and fuzzy slippers, dabbing the corners of her eyes.

"Tea?" Paul asked, and passed her a steaming mug. She nodded her thanks, and slumped at the kitchen table. The two sat in silence.

"Ah, this is a bit awkward," Angela began. "I should probably tell you, I'm a sex worker. Ah, a prostitute."

"I sorta wondered about that," Paul said, with a grin.

"I'm so glad you had a key. How long would I have had to wait for help? I don't think help would have come. Fortunately, I'm just humiliated." She gestured to Paul.

"Was that those fat fellas?"

"Yes. Ow." She ran a finger along her lower lip, until she found the split. "They're brothers. They've been escalating. Thought I would be okay." She sighed and smoothed her forehead with a hand. "They're twins. Blake's the one who is sort of the boss. Jake, he just does whatever his brother tells him to do. Bastards. They just left me. I might have...." She set her cup down and inspected her wrists.

"Thank you, Paul. Sorry you had to see me like that."

"You saved me twice," Paul reminded her. "Glad I could return the favour."

# 70.

THE OLD CAMRY WAS TUCKED into the garage of the million-dollar home. It was certainly the car. A man in a black tracksuit, with a spice stocking over his head, waited hunched behind it. The overhead light popped on, the garage opener engine engaged and the door opened. A nearly new black Land Rover Range Rover rolled just inside the garage, leaving ample space around the sides and front of the vehicle.

The man waited until the garage door closed and the two men got out.

"Oh God! Call the cops!" The passenger side man grabbed a phone from the console and fumbled it, but it dropped to the garage floor. The man with the bat gave it a boot and it skidded to the far garage wall beneath the Camry.

"I lost my phone. Do you have yours?" The man on the passenger side asked.

"It's in the house," the standing man spat. He faced his attacker. "What do you want?"

"Good question. A difficult question to answer. There's what you think you want. Then there's what is best. I want what's best. Ignore the tinsel of desire."

"Ah. All right. Okay. Why are you here?"

"Also a good question. Unanswerable, though."

The man shrugged. "What am I supposed to say?"

"Maybe you should stop asking questions, and let me deliver my message."

The fat man looked around and nodded.

"If you ever, ever hurt my friend again. Ever."

"What friend? We didn't hurt anyone." The driver seemed genuinely puzzled.

The attacker shook his head. "You did. You tied her to a bed, and left her there."

"Oh. Her!" Standing man responded. A beat. "Right. She said we could. She's a whore."

"Don't talk about her like that. Now which one of you is Blake?"

"He is," both boys said, pointing at the other.

"Fine," the man said, raising a bat. "Same message twice." And he began to swing.

When the attacker swung at the male on the passenger side, he dodged the feeble swing and bummed to the floor. But as the spice-nylon-hooded man threatened to bring the bat to bear on the problem, the man lay down and began to whimper. Easy pickins. The attacker checked his swing before making contact. He took another attempt at a swing. This time there seemed much less intention behind the swing; more like a golfer lining up a ball for a tee shot.

"Wow. This is harder than it looks," the attacker muttered.

The attacker adjusted his stance. Fidgeted with his grip. Swayed to get a good feel for the bat. Practice swing. The bat's end whistled over the fallen man's head. The man on the cement floor cried out. Practice swing. Again a loud moan.

"He's right. I can't do this. I can't begin a revolution."

The driver side man began to walk around the hood of the Range Rover. As the attacker lined up another good practice and brought the bat back to work on his swing, the driver side man caught the bat in his hand and wrenched it from his grip.

"You can't do it, can you," he mocked. "But I can. Let me show you how it's done."

And with that he took the bat and brought it down. The attacker leapt back but the bat still grazed his shoulder.

"Ow. Ow. French fried shistfit." The attacker grabbed his injured shoulder and stepped backward over the man cowering on the concrete, just as the bat came down again. This time the bat went full force into the floor man's gut, and just as that happened, the attacker accidentally stepped on fallen man's hand. Something crunched.

The man on the floor howled.

"Sorry, Jakey," the standing man said.

"Sorry. Didn't mean to step on your hand," the attacker apologized.

"Get up, Jake," the standing man said. "Let's teach this guy some respect."

The attacker stepped back once. Back again, between the Camry and the Range Rover. Jake squirmed on the floor like a celeried jelly salad.

"I can't get up, Blakey. I'm stuck."

"Sokay, Jake. I got this." He stepped carefully around his brother and stepped towards the attacker, circling the bat in the air. When he got close enough he let go a full swing. The man ducked. The bat sank into the tinted back panel window of the Range Rover, sending a hail cloud of dark glass around the garage.

The attacker backed around the corner of the Range Rover.

"Open door," the attacker muttered. "It's always the answer."

The entrance door lay at the far end of the garage. The attacker backed around the Range Rover's end and the garage door. He paused to catch his breath. Hard to swing a bat in this space. Blake appeared at the rear of the vehicle and the attacker slid to the opposite side, the driver's side, checking to see if Jake had taken to his feet.

Blake followed him slowly, though he had a little bit of an issue as his torso wouldn't slide as neatly between the back end of the Range Rove and the garage door. He had squeezed himself about halfway around the back of the Rover.

"Door," the attacker muttered. "Door." By this time, the attacker stood by the garage door opener button, which he hammered with his fist. The door started to rise. Blake yowled.

The garage door locking mechanism's latch had caught under his belt, and began to hitch his britches. It tugged his chinos upward, giving him a mighty, grade-school wedgie. Then the motor, feeling every one of the 534 pounds of resistance Blake offered, changed direction. The door came down and chopped against the shelf of his butt. Meeting resistance, it again changed direction. It headed higher, and hiked Jake's pants with them. The door repeated its motions several times.

Finally, after a few good tugs, the chain stitching that held the waistband and beltloops to the top of the trousers gave out in the strain. A soft ripping sound marked the separation of waistband from top of trousers. The door mechanism slowly lumped the belt up Blake's body, over the balls and rolls of fat, until it stopped with the belt under his armpits. There the door jammed, hiking higher, and sticking, then heading lower and jamming.

"Oh, oh, please!" Blake roared as the door tugged him up.

"Ungghh," he wheezed as the door's downward squeezed him against the end of the Rover, forcing the air from his lungs.

Blake yelled and groaned as the door jittered up and down. Jake walrused around the floor, trying to get himself up. The attacker waited by the front of the Rover for one of the two of them to come forward.

The garage door seemed open enough for a lunge. The attacker waited until it was headed up and dived through the half-open entrance. He stood out front until he was sure he was safe, then with a quick look around removed his spice headgear.

Blake's pants, in a final act of humiliation, without a belt to champion their placement, obeyed gravity and dropped away. Exposed to the night air were a pair of hairy legs and butt cheeks and the purple silk waistband of what might have been a thong, which tracked downward a few inches before being enfolded in flesh.

The door finally quit. The light inside the garage blinked a few times to register its complaint.

Paul checked to make sure he hadn't dropped his bus transfer, which was still good for another twenty minutes, and walked up the street.

# 71.

IT WAS A SIMPLE PLAN. And perfectly set. Old Man Sobczak giggled in anticipation. The house blessing was only a half hour away. Beata came into the bedroom where he sat on his edge of the bed, walked past him and slid her hand over his shoulder as she passed to her dresser, where she continued to finish her look, popping large clusters of fake diamonds on to the lobe of her ear. She wore a black and white skirt and jacket, a brand new one because the situation seemed to warrant it. She had even paid retail. The sales clerk had recommended a black skirt to "slim her figure," which did interfere successfully with the perception of her ampleness. The coat was black and white checkerboard, like the game she felt she'd just won. She swung her head to the left to check the look of the right side of her head. Then to the right to check the opposite side.

Michael Sobczak giggled to himself. She smiled contentedly into the mirror. "You had me worried," she said to Michael. The sound of her voice sobered him up. He turned to look at the two of her. "I thought I might have wasted my life marrying you. I thought I would never be happy. I did not think I'd have a reason to dress up again." Michael's initial focus had backed away, and though his eyes were looking at her, his mind was elsewhere. "I've made five hundred of your favourite perogies." Michael still seemed blank. But his unresponsiveness seemed tolerable now. Her public disgrace was ended. Her home seemed heated now. She wouldn't ask much more of him than this. This already had the feel of a miracle.

The clock ticked away. The smell of sizzling butter and onions pressed itself into the furniture and clothes, the smell of a Polish household ready for a party.

The perogi filling used five cheeses. One cheese she'd bought at a cheese shop on 26$^{th}$ Street; another from a Polish deli where the proprietor had commended her excellent taste. Special Polish sausage, smoked in a real smokehouse. The priest was going to eat after he blessed the house, and she was going to make sure he could taste his own blessing. She reviewed her kitchen preparation, gently placing her hand on the counter where each item lay ready. She navigated the counters and headed into the living room where the TV blared. She shut it off, and the house fell into an unusual silence. The clock ticked ever closer to 11:30. The house was spotless.

She sat in her chair near the window and waited. The glorious sun of day blasted through the window. The priest appeared, walking briskly, about a block away.

"He's coming, Michael," she shrieked with delight. "He's on his way. Are you ready?" She jumped out of her chair and began to dither.

"I'm ready," Michael called in a come-hither voice. He walked out of the bedroom and started pacing in between the living room and bedroom. She smiled at his nervousness. The priest headed down the sidewalk, juggling an armload of trinkets, stopped and juggled to read a piece of paper and check the house number. Then he turned up the walk, and jogged up the front door. She stood and waited to hear the ring of the doorbell. The doorbell rang. She counted to three, then opened the wooden door.

"Michael," she said, pronouncing his name with the softer Polish pronunciation. "He's here. Come and greet him with me."

She pushed the latch on the screen door and pushed it outward. The priest was carrying a few things and couldn't help her with the door. She felt Michael use his foot to open the door further. The priest looked up and she met his gaze, which flickered with a smile at her, but then moved from her face over her left shoulder. The priest's pleasant smile registered a fleshy confusion, then shock, then terror.

"You killer, son-of-a-bitch, no good, math-loving priest," Michael yelled. Beata turned to look over her shoulder and saw the grey polish of 30.06 hunting rifle with scope suspended over her shoulder. Time felt thick and slow, like molasses. She saw a flower of smoke hurtle forward, blooming from the barrel of the rifle, and the barrel disappeared; from the corner of her eye, she watch the priest leave the steps of her home with an abrupt grace, his arms slowly spread wide like wings, his two small boxes (in one box was the cross he planned to leave at the house, which he had pre-blessed in a box with another forty-nine crosses) rolling like dice in the air. Rising, floating, he flew backwards away from the steps, like a man pushing off of the edge of the pool into an airborne back crawl. In her ears a sick buzz. Gravity finally took those spinning dice down onto the top of the stairs, where one tumbled down and another broke open, spilling trinkets down the stairs. The priest's backstroke brought him close to the trunk of a weeping willow, where his forward motion was overtaken by a downward one. He planted himself like a bloody seed at the base of the tree.

He made a small bloody crater in the middle of his clerical robes, his mouth open, eyes agape with surprise. She turned to her husband,

Michael, who was slowly pulling the rifle back into the house. On his face was a wide grin, a look of release, of genuine happiness. He was saying something to her, and she could not hear. The gun dropped to the ground, and Michael grabbed her hand. In his eyes sparkled a kindling vitality. He pulled her to him in a hug. The world slowly turned checkerboard, then black.

❖❖❖

WHEN SHE AWOKE THE WORLD was abuzz. The sound of the world was thin and tinny. Stereo turned mono. FM gone, AM in. She was now lying on the couch. The world seemed tolerable and comfortable. The low-volume world seemed to intensify the glorious smell of perogies. Uniformed police officers swarmed around the house. No one was paying any attention to her as she lay there. The cackle and static of radio conversations, people lifting the bottoms of shirt pockets, speaking into devices pinned there in low tones. Confusion. Then she glanced down at her skirt. $42.50, she remembered. And by a sort of tragic miracle of memory, the previous moments resurrected themselves in her mind. The priest flew back from the trunk of the willow to her steps, and flew away to the tree again, and flew back, because she willed him back, and flew away again.

The flying cleric, she thought. Oh, my God.

Then she thought about her thought, and after thinking about it ever so briefly, leaned over the edge of her couch and threw up.

❖❖❖

MICHAEL, AFTER HE HAD HELPED the priest to fly and die, after the rifle had kicked him back on his ass on the hardwood in his hallway, stood and set down the gun. After he had clasped his wife's hand, and she had fainted, sprawled oddly on the top of the step, he went to the kitchen. It was true, he discovered. She had made five hundred perogies. He pulled one from the parchment paper on the counter and bit into it. There was water boiling on the stove, and he shoveled a couple dozen of the crescent moons into the boiling water. The perogi he was tasting seemed to taste of a quintessential peroginess. The flavours flounced over his tongue, seducing his taste buds. These were the best perogies he had ever tasted, and they hadn't even been properly cooked. His nerve endings seemed suddenly new and sizzling. He could feel the column of humidity boiling up out of the pot around the stove. He had a fit of laughter as he stood there, feeling his frame lighten in his shoes. A few feathers, he thought, and I could fly. He flapped his arms while he waited, laughing. A few of the moons poked up from the bottom of the pot and bobbed at the top of the boil. He scrambled for a plate.

A faint siren. Growing. He heaped his plate full, spooned a generous layer of butter-fried onions over the mountain, and peaked it all with a generous helping of sour cream. Siren heading this way. A fork. He walked into the living room and watched out the front window. The siren stopped in front of his house. An ambulance. An attendant leapt out of the vehicle, with his eye on the woman on the steps. He bounded up the walk, and as he did so, noticed the priest. Michael laughed to himself, as the man seemed almost to lose bodily control. Finger to the neck. Nothing. Michael walked over to the door, his mouth full of perogi. The attendant yelled back to the other who was gathering something from a compartment on the side of the ambulance. He disappeared. Michael walked outside. The screen door open, held open by his wife's unconscious body.

The attendant looked at him first with terror, backing away, then confusion stopped him in his tracks.

"I killed him," Michael said, waving the white, sour-creamed ends of the fork at the priest with a smile. He pointed to Beata with the same fork. "She just fainted." The attendant seemed uncertain. "She'll get better in a few minutes," he elaborated. The fork he wiggled above her released a globe of sour cream, which splotted onto her new black dress. The attendant began to back away again, holding up both hands in a "don't shoot" pose.

"Do not worry. I've seen this happen to her before," Michael said. The attendant turned around and ran to the ambulance. Michael sat on the steps and dug into the perogies, which demanded all his attention. It seemed as if he had not been able to taste anything before, and his hunger was deep and voracious. When he looked up from his plate, there were two police cars in front of his home, now three and four, and the ambulance had moved partway up the block.

"Drop your weapon and come out with your hands in the air," said a man with neatly trimmed short hair.

"The gun," Michael said, glancing down to his plate and forking another moon up to his mouth, "is in the house." He looked up and smiled. But the policemen did not seem impressed. "I only wanted to kill the priest," he said simply, grease glistening on his lips, sputtering a blend of potato and five types of cheese out of his over-full mouth.

"Please, sir. Put your plate down. Put it on the steps. Raise your hands, and stand still." Michael nodded his cheerful understanding, and complied. "Is there anyone else in the house?"

"Just my wife," he said, motioning to her sprawled form, holding open the screen door with her monolithic ass. His hands in the air.

He was ushered into a police cruiser, where he sat uncomfortably, his hands behind his back.

The media vans showed up, set up and ran around for interviews. The door nearest Michael opened quickly, and an interviewer stuck his head inside with a microphone. "Did you kill the priest?" she asked, ripping the microphone from her mouth and thrusting it before Michael's lips.

"Yes, I did," Michael answered, smiling.

"Why did you do it?"

"A dream is a wish your heart makes," he replied. "My friend Dr. Paul Shreeve told me to kill him, so I did. Dr. Paul teaches at the university," he added proudly. He shrugged. "It was a good idea." A police officer approached the car, and closed the door on the interviewer's hands. "Follow your dreams," Michael shrieked, as the camera pulled away. "Follow them."

※※※

THE WORM HAD BROWNED IN the heat of the sun, but its cylindrical form hadn't collapsed or dented, which, to Paul, indicated that it was still alive. He gently separated it from the sidewalk slab where it was slowly frying. He studied it closely. It needed moisture. It did not move. Death was near. Paul looked around. No visible sign of a visit, but it was close. He considered spitting on it, but spit sometimes interfered with a worm's breathing. It gummed the flow of air through its skin, especially when the skin was leathery. A puddle? The land was dry. He walked and scanned the ground as he went. Around the base of a willow tree, there was a gardened circle of dirt, recently watered. He walked onto the lawn and scooped a fist of wet earth, nearly mud, and gently pressed the earth onto the worm's skin, burying it in his hand. He stood and waited to let the moisture do its work for several minutes. With the index finger from his other hand, he slowly brushed the soil from the worm's head. The worm lay, it seemed, basking in the moisture. It seemed partly revived. So he took the mound of earth, and gently placed it on the circle of earth under the tree. He heaped more earth upon that creature until it seemed safe. Then he walked on.

# 72.

PAUL GOT UP TO MAKE a pot of tea. It had been a long day of interrogation at the police station. It was just 12:30. Angela was in the living room with the materials from her Real Estate Broker course spread around her. She looked up as he entered the room. "You hardly ever sleep," she commented.

Paul nodded. "I can't."

"You think way too much."

"Three months ago, I didn't think that was possible. But now …" The kettle whistled. "Tea?"

"Please," she responded. "Caffeine please, for me."

Paul returned moments later with two china cups, passing her one.

"I'm nervous about tomorrow's test. It's just on this week's chapter, but I haven't written a test in years. And even then, I did so poorly."

"You'll be fine. Do the work, the test will go well."

"Your mind's in knots."

"Tatters and tangles."

"Maybe you could let all that go, you know."

"Love to. Can't."

"Why not? You're only stuck because you can't let go of these thoughts."

Paul nodded and pursed his lips.

"What if you're not a Marxist? What would happen?"

"Couldn't drop that. That's how I make my living."

"It's killing you, you know."

Paul sat motionless for a moment, then nodded. "You might be right about that."

"I am right," she said, as he shlorped a gob of tea.

"I'll keep that in mind."

"Could we have Stevie in for a cup of tea?"

"Sure. Why not?"

Paul made a call and after some vigorous discussion, returned with a grin on his face. "He's coming over tomorrow afternoon."

# 73.

"Nice to meet you, Stevie," Angela said, offering a hand for a handshake. Stevie slapped it, high-five style.

"Mom says you're a prosetoot."

Angela belly laughed. "I was a prosetoot. But now I'm going to be a person who sells houses."

The Buddha nodded as if he understood.

"I'm going to school to learn," she added.

"I go to school," Lou says.

"I know you do," Angela replied.

"It's fuckin' hard," he commented.

Angela laughed loudly again.

❋❋❋

Paul returned Lou an hour later to the front door of his house. Bonnie opened the front door, letting Lou in. "Paul, would you mind stepping in for a moment. I have a couple of questions." Paul stepped into the tiled entrance.

A blur in his peripheral vision. A sudden huge pain in his groin area, and he crumpled immediately. Bonnie's classic boot to the balls. He should have expected it. His face near a rack of shoes and a rubber mat. Paul was completely out of breath and lay on the brick-red tiles.

"I'm going to Solandro's place for the Easter break. I'm taking Lou with me. You're taking care of the house while we're gone. If you do anything else to our house while I'm gone..." She made a fist over his supine figure, then turned and left.

# 74.

VADIM FINALLY STEPPED INTO THE examining room, some twenty minutes late.

"Oh, you are back again." He closed the door and tromboned a colossal fart. Within seconds, the air in the small examination room ripened.

"Oh, God," Paul said. "I can't believe you did that."

Vadim smiled contentedly. "It's important to let it out." He inspected Paul briefly. "You seem improved." He gestured an open hand around his neck. "Except for the neck. That looks awful. Like you tried to hang yourself or something."

"That belongs in your office, maybe, or the bathroom."

Vadim nodded in agreement. "But I offer my air biscuit to make a point."

"Typical first move with Russian diplomacy."

"I trump to remind you that you and I are full of shit." Vadim sniffed his own smell deeply. "That's the smell of humility, my friend."

"Speaking of humility, I think you're right," Paul began.

"Thank you. I'm glad to hear this. What am I right about?"

"I'm not a good Marxist."

"How could you be? I've never met one. They're either holding a gun, or making ridiculous assertions."

"I can't do it. I'm not a Marxist."

"And you look much healthier, maybe happier as a result."

"Sort of, but I'm not sure what to do now."

"Fly. Be free. Tap dance. I don't know."

"I've got to somehow move forward, but everything I've built is connected to Marxism. What do I teach?"

"Part of the problem is your desire to rely on a system. It's never the system, it's always the person. Think of the detective show. If the system did the work, then we would watch a show where the system solves the crime. It wouldn't depend on who the investigators were. Moscow had TV like that back in the day. No one watched."

"But the North American myth is not the system, but the person. So you have the system, one that is guilty of both justice and injustice, but in the hands of the right detective, a person of the right character, intellect, resolve, and drive, the system works. It is not the system, friend. It is the person, or at least a system with a decent person," a gesture toward Paul, "perhaps a man, working with a system."

"But the right system is at least helpful."

"Yes. Helpful. But a bad person with a good system and things can be horrible. But a bad system in the hands of a good person and all is well. Consider the business of knowing. The knowledge of something is not itself enough. The person has to bring something to the equation: morality. It is not what you know; it is how you know it. One fundamental aspect of knowledge, for example, is humility. One must be humble, humble enough to move from a worse version of an idea to a better one. One must be brave enough to hold one's own ideas to account. To simply cling with certainty to one's perspective is immoral. To lie to oneself or to others about the best of the perspective is fatal to understanding, of course.

"If one is so fortunate to encounter one idea that has some correspondence with life, one has to hold it carefully, and when that idea leads to a better one, one has to be humble enough to leave the old idea behind and move to the next one. The new idea has to be held in the same way. Doubt must be romantically involved with every single certainty. On the positive side, we can call humility. On the negative side, if doubt overwhelms the balance, is neurosis. There are many threats to this tender morality. Certainty. Pride. Ego in all its manifestations. Lack of awareness. Inability to empathise. Thought stranded purely in the mind. Give that up, and your life improves."

"So this was your diagnosis? Terminal Marxism?"

He nodded. "It's only terminal if you make it so. I could have called it neurasthenia. Maybe, myalgic encephalomyelitis. Terminal Marxism."

"And there is no medication for it, I guess. "

"It's a long and difficult process. More like detox than an ailment. One must always doubt what one knows. It's a problem with your way of knowing and you have been most fortunate to stumble in this way. But to be fair, you've had it coming since grad school, haven't you? A colonic cleanse and inspection of those inner passages which seem so useful. A balancing of the teetertotter, if you will."

# 75.

She left on the Wednesday. Paul could have enjoyed her absence more, except he needed her to keep him from thinking too much. A good chuck in the groin stopped any thought in its track. Maybe that was the point of the penis. An emergency stop-thought button. So as she left the car with Lou and headed to the airport, his head began the slow frenzied decent into insanity. His rational thoughts began to fight and feed on one another.

Tires screeched and someone leaned on the horn as Paul cut across two lanes of traffic without so much as a shoulder check, to make the first right turn after leaving the airport. The horn scared the hell out of him and he swerved and hit the curb of the right hand turn, flattening the two front tires instantly and slamming into the thin pole of a directional sign. Paul's head smashed the steering wheel as the vehicle stopped. Then the airbag inflated, slamming him back against the back of his seat.

\*\*\*

As he walked he listened to the song of the city. The hum of rubber on roads rippling over the curb. The mutter of matter and machine performed a fugue over the unending gasp of the city. The never-ending gasp of the city, a sound that could sound like a sigh, a sigh motivated by any number of reasons. Here and there birds dared to mark time and added certified-organics to the mechanics of city life sounds.

Everyone in this city, even those living in homes together, driving together, on the same bus, is heading in different directions. Most barrel. Some shuffle. No two people are heading the same direction at the same speed. Paths intersect on the street, in buildings, in homes, in cars, in elevators, electronically. One of the most conspicuously absent sounds is the sound of collision, crisscrossing; cutoff lives ought to collide or come close to collision more frequently than they do. This sometimes surprised Paul, that city folk so seldom honked at one another, that so few vehicles were smithereen-smashed, so few people yelling at court, and that the sound of collision in all its various forms didn't make a mark on the overall sound of the city.

※※※

MARX MADE THE DEVIL THE rich, the poor into gods. Really an extension of romantic thought, the noble labourer. Perhaps a bent extension of the Sermon on the Mount: blessed are the meek, for they shall inherit the means of production. But as a religion it bore one systemic gap: the inner person. It included no personal theology, no idea of the individual, and how the individual was positioned relative to the grand scheme of things. That's why behaviourism teamed up with Marxism for a good while to try and explain the individual in the light of the grand scheme.

"Marx, you partial god, a god who only partly revealed a theology," Paul muttered to the city, maybe. "A god who accounted for the grand scheme, but failed at reading the individual. Who, in my estimation, should never have tried to be a god at all."

He was disgusted to realize that he believed he had lost his soul. He rationalized and tried to sear the thought from his mind, scrub the stain from his grey matter. Bleach it. Blot it.

"I didn't decide to believe this. Flack me. I am an atheist," he yelled at the wall. "I am master of my own mind." He raged in a small circle, holding his fists in close as he looked for something to pound. "I do not believe in a soul. I do not believe in a God. And this is all barging bridgeshipmet." Before he knew it his fists were raised skyward, and he shook his threat upwards. "You can't do this to me, you bastard. You have no right." Then he realized as he spoke that he had just acted as if he believed in God. "Oh, my God, I'm going fucking nuts. These head injuries are doing something to my brain." He looked up at the roof of the basement. "Hah. It's medical. Flay off, you fast-wasting hallucination. Flap-nappies. Go away, please."

※※※

THIS BLUBBERING MAN, POISONED ONLY with his own thoughts, this saviour of worms, wandered up his own block, past Sobczak's house where the police tape still hung, banded to keep people out of the spot that the priest's body once lay. He stopped for a moment, interrupting his own thoughts as he analyzed.

Funny what police did to the place where someone died. It was the reverse of the church's blessing of a place. A place can be blessed, and too holy for a man off the street to approach without ritual, a priest, an intermediary. And a place can be so cursed, that it too cannot be approached without ritual, and the regular man on the street is prevented, too, from entering what amounts to a kind of holy ground, ground made sacred by the detectives, sign readers, who must come and read the meaning of the curse, and once they've read the land, they can return it to the regular person. Like the church, who won't let the common person enter holy ground until they've desanctified a place, removed the blessing through the vacuum power of the holy kiss, one given while drawing one's breath. And zoop! Into the priest's body goes the blessing. On one side religion, on the other side the law. Ground sacred, ground cursed. All in the same neighbourhood.

In his grasp he held the police tape, the barrier between the crime and the nieghbourhood. And he carefully broke the tape. In the late-night rain, he wound the tape in his hands, unwinding it around the trunk of a tree and from the handrail descending from the front door. From the edge of the miniature wooden windmill. And from the gate post at the corner. As he did so, he cried. This balled nest of police tape he held in his arms. He did not notice Mrs. Sobczak's pale face in her living room window, looking out at him, as he finished his work and wandered up the street. The tears were nothing more than the rats deserting an already empty ship. There was nothing more inside, nothing but mechanical, analytical, psychological, physiological, digestive processes that consumed any good thing, all good things, and turned the goodness to shit.

As he staggered up his own soggy lawn, he sat down in the middle of it. The emptiness had overwhelmed him entirely, and started to consume Paul's external world before and through his own eyes.

"Karl, Karl, are you there?" he asked loudly enough that he thought he should be heard. "Karl, if you're out there, come into my heart, I invite you to be my personal saviour." He waited in the sodden silence. "Karl, I know you had planned to be a saviour. I know it. You had plans for heaven, you defined your sin. But it's all gone horribly wrong, you need to come again. You need to come and save us." His rib cage ached, as it heaved, muscles worn by emotional expansion and compression. "Karl!" he yelled. "Come to me, come and be my saviour. Please. I beg you. Come into me. If you will." He waited several minutes longer. The night rain dibbled on his head, pattering a call for him to leave his thinking and join them on the outside of thought. Unfortunately, his thoughts were waterproof.

"Karl?" he screamed. "Karl, you fog-water bastard. All my life I've been trying to summon you. I've introduced your thinking to places who'd never considered you before. I've been your missionary, converted unbelievers to your cause. You owe me something here." He left space enough for a reply, and then continued, "I've laid down my life for you. Now you come and save me. I need you now!" The trembling of his body ceased, the cold wet no longer bothered him. He stood up and shook his fist at the sky and spun in a circle fisting the rest of the world. "What? Was I not a good enough scholar? Do you only inhabit the finest of thinkers?" The sound of the rain drubbing the ground filled the empty moment. "Fine then. Fine. Wherever the flab you are, damn you. Floob doodle off. Fast-walk completely away."

He turned to face his house. "All right, I've given you, Karl, the right of first refusal. If there is anything out there, anything at all, I invite anyone to come into my life." He paused and dropped his head for a moment to think. He turned to the two-trunked spruce tree in his front yard, and preached with a final gusto. "I am empty. I am alone. Fill me up. Pick me up, off this god-damned sidewalk of life." He looked to the side at the black-eyed windows of the house. "Save me. Someone pick me up.Something. Anything. Pick me up."

He screamed headlong into a gust of wind that came down off the roof of the house, stealing the authority and anger from his voice. "How about any products? Since you are ideas with a physical presence, I invite any products that will have me to come into my life." He looked up into absorbing blackness of the sky. "Okay, send a coupon then?" The rain biddled the skin around his face, and began to pool in the depressions of his eyes. "I'm giving myself away for free, to any cause, to anything. Just show up." He wheeled around to the sidewalk and street and whispered, "Save me. Please, save me." Then looking to the ground, his voice grew to a mighty shout. "Save me." He waited for a moment. The silence served its answer. "Just as I thought. Not one will have me." And he slowly crumpled to the ground.

This man, wet and hopeless, lay on his darkened lawn, lay there until another idea gave him the impetus to move again. So, he lifted himself with all remaining strength, trudged around the side of the house, his step gaining force and lightness as he went. He realized as he stepped up to the back step that he really had no idea where his keys were any more. He searched himself, and when he couldn't find them, he took the handle of the broom next to the door and broke the window in the back door. He reached in to unlock the knob, accidentally poking a shard of broken window through the palm of his hand. In the rain, he couldn't distinguish the blood and the rain. Everything dripped darkly.

Once the door was unlocked, he opened it and stepped inside. The rain poured through the broken glass. He didn't switch on a light, or take off his shoes, or remove his coat. He headed straight to the basement. As he headed down the stairs, he found his keys in the left coat pocket. He pulled them out with a laugh. He stopped and dangled the keys in front of his face. He gurgled with laughter again, before he turned and threw the keys out the broken window of the house. But with the discovery of his keys, he found a new energy.

He rushed to the basement, into his office, and punched on the office light. He strode over to a pile of boxes along the far wall headed over, kicking furniture and stuff out of the way. He tore open the first box, looked inside, pawed through the first layer in the box, and threw the box to the opposite corner of the room. The cut on his hand, which he eventually noticed, he marked with only a passing interest, though it bled profusely. Spinning through the air, dropping some of its contents, the box smashed through the drywall, but Paul didn't notice. The flaps of the second box he tore off as they resisted his attempts to open them. He sunk a fist into the contents and threw the box aside. After several boxes, he found a length of yellow polypropylene rope.

"Aha," he exclaimed to himself. "Just what the doctor ordered." He stepped out of the office, punching the light switch out on his way by. He sunk into his favourite reading chair, whacked the reading light on, and set about tying a noose. It must be said, however, that knots were not his forte, just as fire seemed to elude him. He measured and folded a couple of lengths of rope and began slowly to roll the yellow braid into tight coiled loops. The noose he finished, surprised at his own handiwork. One try and it seemed perfect. He stretched the knot between his hands, and it held.

Into the bedroom he ran, excited, eager. He looped the rope over the home's supporting beam, between two joists on the upper floor, and secured the noose in place. He heaved the bed up on its side against the wall, and made a space where he could dangle to death. He whistled as he worked. In the other room he found a short stool in front of the electric piano and, returning to his bedroom, set it under the yellow noose. Then, without hesitation, he carefully stood on the stool, put the noose over his neck.

"These are words that shall not be heard, a suicide speech that will never be known." He laughed and the tears returned, like hot and cold faucets, each running full. "There is not an idea worth dying for. Not one. All the ideas I've ever known have only interfered with life. All the thinking I've ever done has ruined me. Ideas and thinking will be the ruin of us all. Therefore, as a mark on the impotence my own thoughts, on all ideas, on all ideas' inherent dysfunction, I now die." And with that, he leapt from the stool. For a moment the noose held, and he thrashed wildly, but then slowly, very slowly the noose relaxed its grip, until his feet touched the ground. After gasping for a few moments, he caught his breath again.

"Fallnug this! I can't even die properly." He laughed, he cried. "I am entirely inept. If ever such a being was so pathetic, if ever someone was so inhuman, it is me. I cannot live. I cannot die." He hopped on the stool again, undid the noose. "The knot shall not be pretty. Fawn-cut pretty. It shall work." And so he improvised a simple slipknot and placed the loop over his neck. "Fram filter me," he said, and jumped off the stool. As he thrashed about, his hands at the rope around his throat, his feet kicking around desperate for ground to stand on, he noticed that he'd left the light on in the room.

*Should have turned it off.*

And all went dark.

# 76.

He woke in a pastel yellow blur, a room filled with light, too bright to meet his eyes.

*Heaven? Yes. No. Don't know.*

He fell asleep again and dreamed he awakened and a man with muddy fingers was standing over him, smiling, pleased with himself. The man's muddied hands were slick with wet, grey clay. Around him a grove of trees thrilled with spring. The man's face he only glimpsed briefly and in shadow, his head backlit by the sun. The grove faded, but the sun did not. He blinked his eyes, sipping the brilliance flooding around him. Directly above him. His eyes came to recognize a bulb protruding from the ceiling like a bubble of gum from the mouth of a teenaged girl.

He came to, slowly, and it was not heaven. First he noticed an intense thirst. Then a foul smell. The rope, the foolproof slipknot had slipped from the beam he'd tied it to, and he lay on the floor with it hugging his neck. He sat up and loosened the rope around his neckline and pulled the noose off like necktie after a hard day at the office. Somehow there was blood all around him, the carpet soaked with it. He had fouled his pants. And probably pissed them, but it had dried.

He got up. Slowly. A little unstable, he stumbled forward, and caught a dresser with his hands to steady himself. His right hand gave him a mild pain. He flipped his hand up before his face, and his hand was brown and flaked with dried blood. In the center a scab.

A large something slid down a pant leg. He waited until that something cleared his ankle. In a careful weave, he headed to the basement's bathroom. In the full-length mirror he examined himself again. He looked like shit. Lightheaded too. He shed his coat and carefully stripped. Started the shower. The water was a little cool, but drinkable, and he guzzled the shower's first water. As he stood in the shower, he felt like he was smiling. He patted the front of his face, and it seemed to be true. He rinsed down, soaped up, and rinsed again, and the smile still felt like it was there. He stuck his head out of the shower, and saw his face in a mirror. Truly, he was grinning like an idiot. His smile sat on the middle of his face, which sat on top of a purple and black ring around his neck. He felt his insides stir and waken, and waken, and waken. His senses began to hum as if they had just been turned on for the first time. He faced the showerhead and let the water beat against his forehead, trickle down his temples; he opened his mouth and let the warm water dry his tongue as he took another drink. He turned the temperature up as hot as he could stand.

Climbed out. Dried off and dressed. First put his old clothes into a garbage bag and took them out to the trash can. Then he returned to his bedroom. A big belly laugh as he shut the light off and the bedroom light's absence did not diminish the room's sunlit glow. He surveyed his bedroom. He laughed to himself and righted the stool.

He stepped up to the rope, and a deep belly laugh set in. The noose was very difficult to undo. He picked at it with some joy until it yielded. He looped up the rope and put it back in the office. Then the tin church speaker parroted the ring of an invite to mass. The ring drew him to attention. Up the stairs. Into the holy glow of a Sunday morning.

Fridge. He felt the cold spill out of the shelves as he opened the door, as he touched each shelf, considering something to eat. He picked up a murky, smudged packaged of hotdogs, and selected four, one at a time, knocking them out of the package as if each was a cigarette, downing the lengths in horse bites. He noticed their puckered texture, and chalk texture they left on his teeth as he bit down on them. Relying entirely on routine, he made a cup of coffee in the French press and held it in his hand, near the back window where the spring light warmed the outside of his hands, and the coffee the inside. His heart whirled and rose with in steam, fading into unity with the air around him.

He followed the sick ringing up the alleyway and up the steps of the cinderblock church. Inside the church was packed. There were flowers everywhere. Plastic. Real. A huge purple sheet covered the crucifix. The church was jammed with bodies. The procession was about to begin. There was a clear spot in a pew in the front row, so he headed up and slid into the empty place. Purple bolts of cloth hung from the ceiling on both sides of the crucifix. Christ himself was covered with a purple shawl, preventing anyone from seeing his crucified figure. Above the hanging, draped Christ there was a small roof, sheltering the crucifix inside the church. Paul found himself staring at that roof and contemplating it.

The interior of the building was austere and blank, underneath the Lenten stripes.

He hadn't known why he had come to the church. Except he needed to come out of his house, out of himself somewhere. If he'd been a little less transfixed by the surroundings he might have noticed a little stir he'd created in the pew. He was seated in the end of the pew, on the left-hand side of the church, his shoulder propped against the pew's end on the center aisle. Those sitting to the left of him—an older woman who would obviously be grey-haired if she didn't dye her hair blond, dolled up in a pristine brown business suit, and a short, young blonde floor installer next to her—whispered in excited tones, pointing to him, both noticing the black and purple ring around his neck, though not referring to it directly in their whispers.

But the organ began and a choir sang, reverberating around the cinderblock and brick interior. And the priestly procession glided up the aisle. First the brass cross, followed by the scriptures, held high overhead, a host of robed children, then two men clad in purple priestly robes, and followed by a host of others, most bearing Easter lilies and flowered decoration. The group ascended the platform and the horde laid the plants and decoration around the building, filling the building with the smell of fresh potted earth and the dust of newly opened buds. Two men pulled the shroud off the crucifix, though one side got stuck on Christ's hand, and the two men could not bring the purple covering down. Paul smiled.

The sight of the cross, mostly uncovered, brought a joyous sorrow to Paul's throat. Christ's sagging head, his hands, each seemed to hold the nail in place, poised in the palm of the saviour's hand. The feet, pinned to the wood with a single spike. The thorns circling the head. Christ, with his feet coming together in a sharp point, looked like a sad dagger, the head and shoulders the handle. The outstretched hands, the hilt. The feet, the blade. The dying dagger-god.

He gazed away for a moment, then back at the figure. Then a song lyric, half-remembered.

*Wait, maybe the answer's looking for you.*

The program commenced. Paul was caught standing a couple of times when he should have been seated. And he could not hear most of what was being said. The church, the priest, himself, these things were marvellously new to him again, and every sense vibrated as it collected as much information as it could and pumped it to Paul's brain. All that could happen in his thoughts was a general sense of electric euphoria, bordering on giddiness.

Father Bal came by, waving a small object that looked something between a baseball bat and a pestle. Purple. Green. Pied yellow light blotched on brown brick. He dipped it in something and his first dip he swung the object right at Paul, spattering him with spatters of water that seemed to sear his skin as they hit.

After the choir and congregation stood and sang and sat and knelt, Paul heard a trio of bells sound like a single chord. He watched the priest genuflect and kiss the table in front of him. The priest broke a round wafer and twiddled his fingers free of crumbs over the chalice before him.

Shoes and granite. A wonderfully tight sock hugged his foot. The hair of his eyebrow suddenly visible. All was alight. Everything verb.

*In him, through him, by him. In the unity of the Spirit.*

Paul curled slightly as the priest's words assaulted him.

Then after some other words were spoken, the people in the pew beside him suddenly stood. Paul after a couple of seconds of processing, also stood, and as he stood he became aware that the entire church was seated except for his row. The woman beside him crowded close to him. He continued to stand. The lady crowded closer, and pointed to a spot in front of the Bal the priest. Paul stepped forward, and Bal handed a wafer to Paul. "Just because we're friends." Paul didn't know what to do with it. "Stick your tongue out and put the wafer on it." Paul didn't respond. "Pretend your tongue is a CD player, and the wafer is a disk. Put your CD in the player." Paul stuck his tongue out placed the wafer on the end, and retracted it inside. Satisfied, Bal waved him aside.

"Thank you," he said, falling back on his childhood politeness. Bal looked past him at the next person in line.

He waited for the group to push him to the side of the church, to the wine. A woman held the cup up to him and muttered something under her breath. Paul took the cup and took a healthy swig from the chalice and handed it back. Then he filed back to his seat.

Eating an idea is better than studying it, he thought.

For the rest of the service, he searched for effects within himself, wondering if he could see what the wafer had done within him. Was this the Christ? What kind of saviour appeared to his people as a cracker?

Mind you, however slight the cracker may be, Karl Marx's presence had not the substance to match it. Blessed or not, it seemed a little odd. The wine, the blood, an old drink of an idea, gaining an intoxicating strength with the age of itself, this made more sense. A swiggable, drinkable deity. Liquid, solid. Gas, of course, the Holy Spirit—all three forms covered. A drinkable, edible dagger.

What kind of a saviour need a roof within his own church? Sure, this idea had been nailed to a cross, but was it substantial enough to sustain him? What was Christ doing in him now, now that he had eaten him in and drank him in? Was the god-cracker, cracker-god mad to find himself in a person who had not been made ready to receive? Was Sally Field Catholic? These thoughts to which he could not have an answer. Perhaps he'd just committed suicide again.

*I'm a living suicide. Dead-not dead.*

And somehow, this inkling pleased him. And without another thought, he bounced out of himself and dissolved into crackling and buzz of the church.

What happens when Christ mixes with hotdogs and 18 percent meat protein? He wondered. It's profanity, he concluded. But how much holier the hotdog than himself. How little meat protein he himself contained, but how profane his bumbling, blunt, inarticulate existence.

How can a hotdog be holier than a human? he wondered. The wafer will be fine with the hot dog, but I hope it doesn't burn a hole in my stomach lining.

*Last night I didn't have a dream so much as I had a vision. Once in a while, instead of a dream, I just see things as they are. Last night, the cosmic abyss opened up before me, all space, all time, and I saw myself, and the world in the light of the cosmos. I was in dark, surrounded by points of light, looking at my own life and the lives of those I live with. My existence, as I moved away from my own body, and out towards space, began to shift. And I became the cosmos, looking down at my own life and culture. Time slowed to time as the cosmos experiences it, and I watched my life race forward and vapourize into a steam cloud, and absorb into the universe. The lives of those around me vapourized one by one, each on its own time, into nothing, and suddenly after each life had popped out of existence, there was nothing more. And the earth itself, after a few moments, vapourized into nothing. And the universe was not gone. Somehow, I was able to rewind this vision and, so I did so until I was able to see myself on the earth again. I paused the vision and examined all my dearest things in the light of what I'd just seen. What, for instance, does it mean to love your children, against such a vision? Nothing. What does it mean to not love your children? Nothing. What did writing mean in the light of this vision? Nothing. What did it mean to not write? Nothing. Vanity of vanities, says the preacher. And the preacher, bent over kissed the cloth on which the elements, the body and blood stood, and kissed the cloth. He kissed the cloth, inhaling deeply as his lips met the cloth, consuming all particles of the holy host, leaving behind just a cloth. All meaning, all symbol vanished in the sucking kiss of this perspective. Is this the kiss of wisdom? I'd have rather seen a ghost, thank you.*

*I saw the oblivion, my individual self saw it, and stood in terror. This terror hit me like food poisoning, and I felt nausea. In the black, in the dark, in the middle of the night, when one is alone with a terrifying idea, one's whole life, whole being can become unhinged, unclasped, and swing wide open, as mine did. The darkness dims the world enough to let a person see the truth, and I find truth hits full force at night. In the day, with the birds singing, the sunlight laying itself out on the lawn in angular yellow sheets, and the pendulum of progress swinging, one can still see the truth, but it only visits at a distance,* like a knife-wielding assassin. In the day, the assassin visits as if it is part of a show on TV. In the night, one meets the assassin face-to-face.

The I was terrified. It has worked very hard, and I can vouch for it here, very hard to achieve itself. But individuality is nothing. I woke in terror. I laid there in terror, my mind scrambling for a foothold, some kind of security in the vision. What antidote might I apply against this truth, so that I can live with it in some sense of peace? I reviewed my life, looking for a mental weapon or tool to fight this. I wanted to find what existed on a computer, some 'save' feature that would take my preferences and choices, the disagreements that have come to constitute me, and preserve them somewhere, somehow. There was nothing to save. Worse still, there was nothing to write on.

In this moment, there was only one thing to cling to—the possibility that there was a God and that he might, as ridiculous as it sounds, care for me, or if not me personally, as an individual, the collective lives of those on this planet. And, once again, I am left clinging, dangling from a preposterous idea: what could be more outrageous than God? And, God doesn't commit himself to preserving the me I am in the business of creating.

# 77.

It was a regular Sunday morning, the sort of day that if one added the last ten years of Sundays, and divided by 520, one could understand this day well. Mass began. Father Bal was leading the service for a group that was half-filled the church. Like students in a classroom, most seemed glazed and only there out of duty.

Father Bal wormed his way through the liturgy, and the congregation, though sluggish, kept its end of the antiphonal teetertotter.

About the time when communion began, a lone man, wearing a classic spice nylon head covering and a black tracksuit, ran from the back of the church to the front. Waving a substantial kitchen carving knife, he directed it at the altar girl with the pageboy haircut. She flinched.

"Sorry," he growled. When the attacker saw the priest, he did a doubletake.

"Bells," he growled, and motioned to the bells on a cushioned seat beside the young girl. "And there'll be no shenanigans," he growled.

The young woman looked at the priest, wide-eyed. "The bells, Keera. Give him what he wants!" ordered the priest. She lifted them from the cushion and held them to the robber, who gently received them.

"Thank you," he rumbled. And then he sprinted to the emergency exit, next to the electric organ, and out of the church.

# 78.

"Paul!" Bal yelled.

Paul quickened his step and acted like he hadn't heard.

"Paul!" Bal jogged to catch him and touched his shoulder. Paul turned with a groan.

"I'm sorry, Bal. I didn't mean to give you bad advice."

"I should apologise and thank you." Paul stopped and faced the older man. "I blamed you for something that wasn't your fault. When my wife left, I lashed out. It's been a while since I've practice a more disciplined outlook. But I've begun to practice it again. In fact, I am going to be a priest again."

"What?" Paul replied, with a feigned incredulity. "You were a priest?"

"Yes. Yes, I was. I was a priest at Holy Name Church for twenty-two years. I left the priesthood when I met Virgina, my wife. She was this young woman. I heard her confession and long story short, she'd been assaulted by someone in the neighbourhood."

"Let me guess," Paul interjected. "The first Paul Shreeve."

Bal's eyes widened. "Yes. He's the one." He shook his head. "She was too ashamed to bring charges, and through the whole process I counselled her and we grew quite close. I chose to leave the ministry to marry her. We stayed close to the church and rented this house together. That's what we wanted." He paused and swallowed. "But she outgrew me.

"I forgot myself when I yelled at you. I was off my game. You see, there's really only one connection in the monastic mind," Bal said. "In this sense, there really are no good or bad things, there's only expressions of the other, or God, which is cause for contemplation. Everything that happens to me isn't you, or Virginia, or the people I meet or the circumstances around me. I get fooled into thinking that way. But it's all an expression of God. That's the proper monastic viewpoint. There's just the two of us. Me and God as he expresses himself through people and circumstance.

"So the point isn't to react and blame you, anyone, or anything else. All the people and events that make up a life, they're a gift and part of an ongoing conversation with God himself, of my conversation with God. You see, I need to act as if you are God speaking to me. I didn't do that.

The mystics didn't believe in people, but that the world was an expression of God to them. So they didn't get upset by things as they unfolded. So when you speak, I should regard you as part of the unfolding."

"Bal, I think this is an apology, and thank you. Apology accepted. I am sorry for the way things went. And please never regard me as God."

"That's just what God would say," Bal giggled. "The bishop will be running Father Joachim's funeral. I'll be going, of course, now that I'm a priest again. Anyhow, my real reason for speaking today is to ask forgiveness, but also to invite you to my First Mass. I've been offering masses already, though. This Friday, 10 a.m.. I'm now a Father again. And it feels great. Please come. I'll even allow you to ask questions. And I promise to keep your secret about the bells."

Paul felt his face go red. "Bells?"

"Come on, Paul. You stole the sanctum bells, didn't you? It looked like you. It smelled like you. You asked all those questions."

"I don't know what you're talking about," Paul said.

"And neither do I," Bal said with a wink.

## 79.

"You got some mail," she said, and she frisbeed a letter to him, which to his surprise, he caught. It was a card-shaped envelope. Return address, Holy Name Catholic Church. His name in perfect block lettering.

"Can I have Stevie over for a visit in a couple of days?"

"NO! It's a disgusting, unhealthy environment. You're sleeping with a prostitute, and you want your son to visit?"

"I'm not sleeping with anyone. After what you did to me, I'm practically a eunuch."

"Right. And the Pope is Polish."

"I'm renting a room from her. That's it. And she's a pretty good person, it turns out."

Bonnie shook her head. "You're not safe." She gestured to Paul and the house. "Unhinged. Wingnutted."

"I agree. I don't think I've been well for a while, and I've come close to hurting our son, and that disturbs me, and I know it disturbs you. But I just want him to visit for a cup of tea, just an hour or so. He'll get pretty bored here, I think. Nothing to do."

"Could you have tea in the back yard? So I can keep an eye on you two?"

# 80.

PAUL TORE OPEN THE ENVELOPE. Inside was another, older envelope, which Paul recognised. Immediately a chill thrilled through his system. Inside a note.

Dear Paul,

Despite any objection you may raise, this letter is for you.

Joachim

The note offered no cushion of comfort. Paul lay on his bed. Nausea pumped against the back of his throat. But what good was a fourth-wave Marxist if he would not look truth in the eye? So with a trembling hand, he carefully tore open the envelope and unfolded a yellowed letter.

Dearest Paul,

It's your fault. You pretentious, lovely windbag. You charm anyone in or out of anything, which is what I fell in love with when we first met. It didn't hurt that you had money, too.

But I wasn't enough. I was never enough. And you had to sleep with anything, anyone that moved.

I suspect I only knew about a few of your escapades. There was a rumour that you might have deflowered a young teen from church. There were the women from work. Four that I heard about. But the one that hurt the most was Joan. Her son was yours, wasn't it? That's what Joan claimed. The morning you died. She needed money to help her son. She came over to look for you, to ask. She was beside herself. But she found me, and we had an argument. And in the middle of that argument she blurted the facts. All she knew. She knew a lot.

You were so stingy after you got what you wanted. You were with Joan. You were with me.

So, when I think of what happened the day you died, I don't think so much that I was at fault. I didn't mean it. Yes, the knife was in my hand. Sorry, my love. But the neighbours helped cover the facts, and I don't think they figured it out.

Ashes to ashes; dust to dust and all that. My new life begins today.

All my love,

Bess

# 81.

**H**E OPENED OWEN'S BACK DOOR. Owen was sitting with his little glass of Pepsi rolled up to his table.

"I know why you've come."

"Why am I here?" Paul asked.

"Torment. You're a ghost."

"I came to talk to you about something," Paul said, waving a letter in his hand.

"Talk. Torment. What's the difference?"

"You old bastard! What are you talking about? You sit here alone in your house day after day. I come over here to pay you a visit and you treat me like this? How am I a ghost? What have I ever done to you?"

Owen's wrinkled face trembled and slowly began to twist with emotion. In a matter of three minutes he was weeping openly. Large tears rolled like stones. each running in different folds of the map of his face. He pulled a long manually operated claw-cane from his side. When he squeezed the grip at the handle end, the far end would pinch together like two clumsy fingers. He poked the cane at the Kleenex box at the far end of the kitchen table, and pulled. One Kleenex. Then another extension and pinch.

Paul had no idea what to do, but he didn't sense any urge to leave either. So he stood staring at the floor.

"I've got some news for you, maybe even good news," Paul said, waving the letter.

"Okay. Okay," Owen finally conceded. "I will tell you what really happened. Not that other funk-bunker I laid on you. I'll tell you why I'm strapped in this chair." He plucked another tissue from the box and dabbed his cheeks, and screwed it into his eyes. "You had been a true neighbour, a very good friend to me. Especially after my wife left, you know. Those were difficult days. And I got going with some new work—I got a job driving new motorhomes from the manufacturer to the place where they were to be sold. I loved it. I loved the road. And you came to me. I remember the night, and you told me how bad life was getting for you. How Bess seemed to be smothering you. You were drinking, of course, and after a couple you started to cry, just like I am now. And I knew I was supposed to do something. I knew I was supposed to help you."

The story started to gush out, with speed and force. Paul removed his shoes and stepped into the kitchen, on to the indoor-outdoor carpeting, to the far end of the table, just as Owen's claw plucked another tissue from the box. Paul slid the box down toward Owen and took a seat, tingling slightly as he sat. "But I didn't want to help you. I didn't want to stop what I was doing. So I tried to get you to buck up and take it. I remember telling you that any man would be happy to be married to Bess, and happy to live in his bungalow, and own so many homes, including this one. He was the envy of everyone in the neighbourhood. I remember the dark light in your eyes fading to flat black. You stopped talking. You stopped because I asked you to. Then," Owen said with a tearful laugh, "to fill up the sudden silence, I told you about the trip I was taking in the morning, driving a beautiful brand new motor home to Bakersfield.

"The next morning I came to visit you, and I found you on the floor. Bleeding badly from your wrist. Above your head swung a noose. Bess was there, bawling. She had the knife you'd used. You were dead, but still warm. I remember. I took the knife from her. She was worried that the police would think she'd killed you. So we set you up in the noose. Bess and I couldn't lift the body, so I got Joan's son to help. He owed the Shreeves a lot, too. You did so much to help that poor, tormented boy."

"Let me guess," Paul interjected. "The knife is in my house, somewhere."

"Actually, no. Come to think of it, I don't know where it went."

"I left the next morning. Leaving Bess. But we didn't tell the police about what we'd done. I gave them a statement on our conversation the day before. I'm sorry, Paul. I didn't know you'd do this to yourself. I let you down." He stared at the floor, unwilling to meet Paul's gaze. "Church wouldn't give you a funeral. Couldn't bury the body in the cemetery. It was my fault. I wasn't there to help.

"And then, two weeks later I was standing over my sink," he pointed to the far end of the kitchen, "I was getting something to drink in the middle of the night in a wicked whale of a lightning storm. And lightning struck a spruce tree, followed the roots, and came up in my sink and threw me across the room, and I've been in my wheelchair ever since." He shook his fist at the sky. "It was God judging me for my failure."

"You believe in God?" Paul interjected quickly.

"No, I don't. At least, I don't think I ever agreed to believe in him. But choice has almost nothing to do with this."

"And so when I moved in next door?"

"I was terrified. What could you do to me to equal what I had done to you?"

"I don't think it was as unbalanced as you think."

"You know when I found Paul's remains in my house, it included a letter." Paul held the letter up, for Owen to see. "Bess says she killed her husband here. I wasn't suicide."

Owen sat stone-faced for a moment. "Liar. Goddamned liar."

"Why don't you read the letter, Owen." Paul passed it across the table.

"May 29th, 1982. Date's right." Owen muttered, as he settled into the letter.

"Oh my Lord!" Owen exclaimed. Suddenly, he looked years younger. He looked at Paul. "You're not making this up?"

"Owen, how could I? I am not the same guy. I don't know what happened." Owen's eyes narrowed as he assessed.

"So it would mean…" Owen hesitated. "It would mean that instead of me being responsible for your death, I helped cover up a murder. Bess murdered you, and I helped her get away with it." Owen frowned at Paul.

"Can you lighten up, man? I'm not trying to find a new angle to snooker you into guilt. I'm trying to help you off the hook here. Your death wish is unfounded. You didn't murder or hurt anyone. You can let it go."

Owen harrumphed. His face registered a barrage of emotion.

"Maybe you can get into a seniors' residence and enjoy the last years somehow."

"I don't know how to feel," Owen finally said. "I've lived all these years thinking I was responsible for your death. Now I learn that I helped the murderer to get away. I don't think I'm out of the swamp yet. I don't think so." He paused. "I can't afford those fancy retirement places. I got cheap rent right here. Speaking of, I see you're living with Angela now. Angela Gager."

"Yeah, I'm renting a room from her while Bonnie and I sort some things out."

"A room. Right." A beat. "I can't go to one of those seniors' residences. I want to be close to Joan. I've loved her since the day I've met her. I couldn't leave her. I couldn't. She was so kind to me when my wife left. I couldn't help it. I fell for her. Ever since you died, she can't stand me. Won't talk to me. But I won't leave now. Too late."

"Anyway, I don't think I'd like it. At best they'll patronize me when I tell them about my dog, Sandy, the way she used to bring my slippers. They'll smile at me and pat my head, but they'll hate their job, and I'll hate them, too, and there won't be a thing to do about it except, if I'm lucky, lose my mind."

"What about going for a bath with the help of a young nurse?"

"What is that to me? My homecare help is all I need to live."

"I know someone in one of those homes and it was something he looked forward to."

Owen winced. "He must have been mighty desperate."

Paul nodded his agreement. "It's hard to be more desperate than he was. What about the taste of roast beef?"

"That means nothing to me."

"Why not?"

"My thoughts chase me. Every waking moment. All I've done traps me in a living hell." His point began to carry him away. "All beef does is hold me alive for another day of torture. You know that, that's why you don't let me go, that's why you come over to talk to me." The tears started to flow again, sinking into the wrinkles on his face, his age seeming to absorb his sorrow. "I hurt you so long ago. I made my mistake, and you're going to make me live with it the rest of my life. I'm a bastard. I know. But do I deserve to live like this?" He made some soft crying noises, and lifted a stiff finger to his cheeks and dabbed the wet spots.

"I came to check." Muffled dingle.

"You came to check. To poke a stick at man who let you down so long ago." He made an effort to pull himself together. "This is my punishment. I'll take it. But I want to die."

# 82.

Moody, Owen's home-care nurse, had been to help that morning and had just left. Owen settled into his morning routine of crossword puzzles, television, and looking out his rear-view mirror. And there was a knock at the back door. Owen grinned and waved them in out of the rain.

※※※

"This isn't going to hurt, Owen. But now that you know, you have to go."

"Okay. It's not like I can get away from you now, is it?" He laughed a little. "Now, that I'm staring at the gates, not sure I wanna go."

"You're gonna go. You're gonna go now." On the plate a rum and Pepsi, and an Oreo. Beside the glass, more than enough pills to do the job. Owen stared at the plate, overcome by a sense of horror. Horror that he had been wrong about his desire to die. Horror that death did not come in a way he'd expected.

"I don't want to go now," he said. "And I don't want to die by my own hand."

"You brought me over here to help you. I'm here. I'll help. It'll be painless. You won't feel a thing. I've now made the case plain, and it's time."

Owen met the menacing gaze. Nodded. Removed the Pepsi and rum, with the Oreo first from the plate. Sugared Eucharist first. Then the pills. Downed them with a slap, and swiggered the rum and Pepsi. "See you in hell."

# 83.

THE MORNING RAIN SEEMED TO Paul to renew the world. The ominous clouds shared the sky with a piercing sunlight. The lawn seemed to glow. Paul stepped out into the briskness, out to the street, and picked up eight or nine worms, putting them in a used yogurt container, wandered through the back alley to Joan's house, and knocked on the back door.

Joan answered, and as soon as she saw Paul, glowered. "What do you want?"

Paul held the tub of worms out toward her. A quiet dingle from somewhere under his coat.

"Oh, thank you!" She seemed surprised by his gift. "Good idea. My robin might love these. Maybe they'll help."

"May I come in Joan?" he asked. "I have something to show you."

※※※

"I WANTED DRAMA IN MY life. I wanted something to happen. And you happened. But you were only the beginning of things to happen in my life. After you died, my husband left. My son became a drug addict. And I couldn't shut the drama off. And now my robin is dying. It's God's judgment on me." On the table in front of Joan languished the little robin she'd been nursing. The box stank with food remnants. Paul sat next to her. Joan strung one of the worms out, against its will, and with a kitchen knife chopped it into robin-sized pieces and offered them to the bird.

"You believe in God?"

"Obviously. I go to church. I'm a good Catholic. I'm so tired of the drama I've lived with. I just want jig-saw puzzle boring again."

"Joan, I need you to hear me out," Paul said softly. "I found a letter. You remember when you told me that Paul's remains were in the wall?"

Joan wouldn't meet his gaze.

"I went home and found them. And with them was a letter. It was from someone named Bess."

"Bess," Joan agreed. "Yes."

"In the letter, she confesses to killing her husband, Paul."

"Damn you, Paul. Damn you!" She backed her chair away from the table. "Why do you have to stir things up? That's not what happened. Not at all! Liar!" Anger offered her a power with which she could tackle the Paul and what he represented. She met his gaze and tapped his chest with her kitchen knife clarted with worm bits and blood. Worm flesh fumbled down the front of Paul's coat. Paul reached inside to a breast pocket and wiggled his hand. A quiet dingle rang out.

Joan realised suddenly what she'd done and pulled her hand away.

"Do you want to read the letter?" he asked.

"You're lying," she growled, with an ungodly growl.

Paul pulled the letter out of his pocket and gingerly slipped it from the envelope, unfolding its tea-coloured pages. "Joan, I have no stake in this story. I'm just another guy with the same name. I'm not lying. I'm just telling you what the letter said." He paused as she rested the trowel on her hips. "Do you want to read it for yourself?" He held the letter toward her. The distraction meant she didn't notice the robin take a small nip of worm.

"You better not be joking." She set her knife on the table, and took the letter out of Paul's hands. "That looks like her handwriting," she said. When she'd gotten through a portion of the letter, her face registered a deep confusion. "But…" She said aloud. Paul tracked her vision. It look like she'd begun the letter again. "So that would mean… my John didn't do it?"

"John didn't do it?" Paul repeated.

"My John. My son. I always thought he murdered you… ah … the first Paul." Emotion clouded her features for a moment. "I already told you what I remember." She cupped her chin between a thumb and forefinger with her free hand. "I heard a hullaballoo over at the Shreeves. So I set down what I was doing and went over. On my way there, John passed me, coming back home. He was covered in blood. When I went over there, Bess was in the back yard looking for you."

"Not me, Joan. Another guy with the same name." Joan glared at him for a moment. "And I'm not sure she was looking for him, me."

"She could hardly speak. So I went into the house and found you hanging, downstairs." She didn't bother to describe the scene as she had the first time. But the look on her face suggested she was looking at it again.

"Why did you think it was murder?" Paul asked.

"The whole scene seemed funny. I mean, who cuts their wrists and hangs themselves? Seemed a bit, I don't know, overdone." Tears jumped to her eyes. "Johnny was wearing a white t-shirt and jeans. He was soaked with blood when he passed me. And out of his mind."

"Owen said that he and Bess were worried that the police would think it was murder, because Paul had fallen from the noose. So Owen enlisted the help of your son to hoist him into the noose and arrange the scene to look more like a suicide. And I'd be pretty panicked if I'd just help lift a dead man into a noose. I'd be blue bricked and beyond."

"True. But I didn't see Owen around."

"He probably left when your son did, and I bet he went straight home because he was covered in blood."

The conversation fell to silence for a long minute.

"I thought he murdered you—Paul—and then we got lucky with the suicide verdict."

"You never talked to Owen afterward?"

"I couldn't. And my John, he couldn't talk about it. I felt like Owen knew. And I didn't want him to bring it up." She eyed Paul again. "And the letter is right. My Johnny was Paul's son. My husband was away up north a lot. And Paul, well, he was quite a man. I don't think my Reggie ever knew. He was a trusting soul. Paul had a lot of fun knocking me up. But I couldn't get him to help with anything, because John, he was a handful. Schizophrenia. Not easy to deal with. He overdosed a year after Paul's … ah… death." A frown. Deepening frown. "Murder? Bess. Owen. How…?" She snapped the letter up and devoured the text again. Her mouth worked up and down as she puzzled it out. Then tears. "Bess."

"Listen, Joan. If this letter isn't enough for you, go talk to Owen. He's fifty yards from you right now and he can't go anywhere. At the risk of sounding like a teenager, I believe he loves you."

"Really?" She pulled her head back and pouted.

"Ask him about his story. He knows enough and you know enough that you'll be able to see that the stories don't jive." He paused. "Any idea where Bess went after Paul's death?"

"No idea. We talked just after she got him cremated. She didn't know what she was going to do. She wanted to sell the house, of course. Who would want to live with those memories?" She looked at Paul. "No disrespect."

"None taken."

"I could probably follow up, though. I still rent from her."

"Right, because she inherited all the first Paul's land when he passed."

# 84.

"911. WHAT IS YOUR EMERGENCY?"

"I need an ambulance to 2420 35th Street. A man named Owen has taken too many pills," Joan sobbed.

"Can you stay on the phone with me?" the operator asked.

"I won't hang up, but I'm going to be with him in case these are his last moments," she shrieked.

She dropped the olive handset of the ancient rotary-dial landline, and went to the table where Owen lay slumped. "Owen, don't you die on me. We're just getting to the bottom of things. Just getting it sorted. Don't you dare." She alternated between thumping and rubbing his back between his shoulder blades with an arthritic hand.

"The ambulance has arrived," the operator said. Joan couldn't hear it from the kitchen. But she did hear the loud knock at the front door.

# 85.

After a long slurp of tea, Paul worked up the nerve to ask the question. "Did you tell me once that you rent from your mom?"

Angela looked up from her binder of class materials. She pulled her cup from a coaster and took a sip. "Yeah, my mom. Why?"

"Does she own a bunch of the homes on this block?"

"Yep. She owns all of them, 'cept yours."

"Ah. Okay. So what's your Mom's name?"

"Elizabeth."

"Okay. Well. That's interesting."

"What? What is it?"

"Does my name mean anything to you?"

"Yes." She added a nervous laugh between more sips of peppermint tea. "It's yours."

"Did you know another Paul Shreeve?"

"I don't think so," she replied.

"Can I interrupt you for a while? I have a story to tell you."

Paul began where the story did and told her the story.

"The letter," he finished. "I finally found enough gum to open it. I have it here. He took it from his lap and placed it on the table.

"I think your Mom gives Owen a deal on rent because he helped her stage the scene. I think she gives Bal a deal on rent because the first Paul assaulted the young woman Bal married. I think she gives Joan a deal on rent because Paul fathered a child with Joan, a guy named John, and John helped stage the scene, too. But you should read this letter, because I think your Mom admits to murder in it."

# 86.

PAUL ANSWERED THE KNOCK AT his front door. There stood Angela's dad with a tin-foiled Pyrex baking pan. Paul opened the front door.

"Hi! Didn't know you were visiting," Paul began. "Come in, sir." He used the word *sir* because he hadn't learned Angela's dad's name.

"Just a quick drop-off," he said, holding up the pan of food. "It's still hot."

"Oh, that's very kind of you!"

"Angela was telling us you were on your own this week. Made a little extra. So here you go."

"Thank you!" Paul replied. "Be right back." He retrieved a pair of oven mitts from the kitchen and returned to receive the dish.

"It's a lasagna," the man said. "And I didn't cook it, so you should be fine."

"Your timing is perfect," Paul said. "To be cliché, I could eat a horse."

***

PAUL LICKED HIS LIPS AFTER eating almost half the lasagna right out of the pan. The meat and pasta held down his insides with a gravity that felt right. It would help keep his feet on the ground. And his neck hurt. Probably from being hunched over the pan of lasagna and eating like a proverbial pig. Hot lasagna as opposed to a pan-warmed hotdog. A pang of nausea. "Ate too fast," he said to himself. "Again, I cause my own problems."

Then began a dizzy headache, and an overwhelming desire to take a nap. He swaggered like a drunk man to the living room couch and collapsed on the cushions. "Sleep." As he lay there, a white-haired man with a huge beard and an old suit wandered over and stood beside him.

"Thank you for your service to the proletariat," he said. "We've had a lot of calls about how you've helped. We don't usually give awards for being a good communist, but in your case, I think we must begin. It begins as always with a lasagna, but will end with our highest award. You just wait and see. You've been such a good boy this year. Ho, ho, ho," he laughed, grabbing his belly, thumbs through the suspenders of his red velvet pants. "You just wait and see." And with that Paul succumbed to slumber.

⁂

Bonnie and Stevie walked through the front door, which they found unlocked. Inside, on the couch, they found Paul lying on his side, in a puddle of Italian-smelling vomit.

"Paul, you jerk. I told you to be gone when we arrived home." She strode to the couch. She slugged him where he lay. "Have you been drinking, you useless slob?"

Stevie giggled. "Daddy's a slob."

"Paul? Paul? Paul?" she yelled. "Get up." She noticed, then, the vomit. "Paul," she yelled again, this time far more anger. "You didn't kill yourself here, did you? That's just evil. And you've ruined the couch. It's garbage now. Trying to make a statement of trauma? Trying to martyr yourself? Well, I'll show you, you self-murdering drama queen." In a supreme effort to undermine Paul's apparent attempt at a last word, she pulled out her cell phone and called 911.

# 87.

"WHAT A SURPRISE!" ANGELA YELPED, and surprised she was. She had a one o'clock with an accountant she'd have to cancel. "Come on in. what brings you to town?"

Her parents stepped into the house. "Wait here for a second. I was in the middle of something." Angela swept through her house, and in the middle bedroom set aside a number of contraptions that she had prepared for this afternoon's session. She put them in the closet, carefully, and covered them with a blanket. A few she set in a lockbox.

"You should have told me you were coming," she yelled to the front door as she tidied up. "I could have prepared a thing or two for you."

She joined them in the living room where they were seated on a couch, making themselves at home. It was their house after all. So not hard to do.

"We just felt the need to come to the big city. We have a few things to get at Costco and a few other errands."

"Oh, great. You want to stay here."

"No. You've rented a room to your neighbour, so it'd be cramped and a little awkward. We're staying at the casino hotel, so it's not too far."

"He's house-sitting next door for the week."

"Well we wouldn't want to be a bother. But I'll do a little meal prep, if you like. I'm going to make some of my world-famous lasagna."

"Oh, yeah. Wouldn't say no to that."

***

"THAT WAS FANTASTIC," ANGELA GLOWED. "You haven't lost your touch, Mom. Sad we couldn't eat with Dad around."

"So good to hear. I hardly have the opportunity to make it any more."

"Dad took a little over to Paul, your friend next door, if that's okay. Men aren't that good as bachelors."

"That's nice, Mom," Angela slurred. "He'd like that." Her head lolled to her chest. Her mouth tasted of metal.

"You dirty whore," Liz said. "You think I'm stupid and don't know what you're up to? If your father knew, he'd be humiliated. I've let you freeload off me for a long time, now. But like all rentals, you pay first and last up front."

"Real Esssstaate," Angela hissed, as she listed to starboard and fell off her chair to the floor.

"I should never have written that letter. I was so distressed at the time that I needed to for mental health reasons. I never thought anyone would find it, not 'til much, much later. Stupid mistake. Stupid, stupid, stupid. It has given me the chance to tie up some loose ends."

Drool and phlegm poured from Angela's mouth and nose, which sputtered once in awhile as she began to snore.

\*\*\*

In a fit of inspiration, Angela's dad strung a route together in the traffic-choked afternoon rush. It was just one of those days. Everything flowed, especially the banks. There used to be more trouble when it came to moving big amounts of money. But today was different. Everyone was ready for him. He'd be home early, just a little late for supper.

When he walked through the front door, he was surprised to find Liz dragging something down the steps into the basement. Bunk, bunk, bunk one end of the package knocked on the steps.

"Hi Honey," he sang. "What you up to?"

# 88.

THE WHOLE BLOCK WAS THERE. Down at the station, all of them. Waiting in the waiting room. Officers poached them one by one and they were led away to make their statements. But the case was clear enough.

"It was Owen, I think," Joan said. "He'd never say it, or claim anything. He saved the lot of you. When I found him, he was not well, but he'd left a pill in his hand. And it saved his life, and probably the both of you as well."

"Good thinking on his part," Paul chirped. Bonnie nodded to him as she bounced Stevie on her lap.

"She'll go to jail for the rest of her life," Angela's dad sniffled. "Zolpidem. I thought she just had trouble sleeping."

"It sure blended well with the lasagna."

Paul nodded. "It was bloody good lasagna."

# 89.

"THERE ISN'T MUCH OF AN agenda," the chair said after the business was complete. "So if anyone has anything they'd like to discuss, we have time now." Paul raised his hand.

"Paul, you have the floor," the chair sighed. The room groaned, except for Veto who was drooling in a chair closest to the boardroom door. Paul reached inside his briefcase. A small triangle of dingles rang out. He sat back up.

"Ah, well. I am tired of living with ghosts. I can't do it any longer. I read ghosts. I teach ghosts. I promote ghosts. Can't do it." Paul shrugged.

"What does that mean?" Krandall asked.

"I don't know. I just can do this work anymore. It requires belief, like most things do. And I don't believe any more. I don't think I'm a Marxist. I don't think I ever was. I don't think I could ever be one. I don't even want to be one any longer.

"My theories are not held to account at all. A mechanic might have a theory about what makes a car stutter before it accelerates. If that mechanic's theory is correct, the car has an improved performance. In other words, it's held to account.

"My ideas—I think they're promoting a better world, but there's no objective proof of that, is there? I have ideas on gender, race, creed and value. Am I right? I think so. What do my ideas do? The same thing that all theories do. They push people out and bring people in. Somebody's excluded. Someone's included. Bully people unless they convert. Not a rifle: the soft, social gun.

"Marx was right about one thing. Religion is the opiate of the masses. But he was wrong on his idea of religion. He was too specific. He thought it referred to the institution of religion itself, which I don't think works. But if you think of religion as a cultish adherence to an idea, a system, a degree of devotion to something, then I agree with him entirely. Religion is the opiate of the masses.

"Unthinking, unexamined adherence to an idea is religious, and it is the opiate of the masses. If I use this definition, I'd suggest that theories are always inherently religious, depending on how they are held by the theorist. They create insiders and push people outside. They create doors. I've thought that this is what education is all about. I've been religious, a religious Marxist.

"Religion is lazy. It's what happens when a person gets tired of interrogating what they know. They begin to become unwilling to change, sure of their rightness. Sometimes ideas ossify not because we're still sure, it happens because we make our living from a particular perspective. It's just easier not to change. And knowing turns from a life-giving journey to a dead-end death-dealing dark. I've been that kind of knower. I've made a living from it. But I'm done.

"A few months ago, I thought that doors were something that needed to be removed, because humanity interfered with the success of theories. Which, by the way, was absolutely correct.

"So I removed doors. Which was, in effect, asking those I lived with to deny their humanity, and my attempt to deny my own. And what has happened? My marriage has ended. I've nearly killed everything I've loved. If my mental health was anything but a curious visitor, it has left.

"But tail wags the dog here. Humanity is the only essential part of what are. I lived without doors for as long as I could stand it. And my humanity was not erased. None of it. Ironically, I could alter my theories to suit my humanity, but not the other way around. So I've decided to live with my humanity and give up theory. Since this job is all about theory, I'm going to give up this job, to favour my life and mental health. I'm going to live with doors. I'm going to live with fences. I'm going to be a Walmart greeter.

"I'm an analytical freak! My analysis prevents me from achieving any useful thought. What if there is more to a job than how many holidays you get? What if meaning matters?"

"Me." He shook his head in disgust. "I'm as empty as any of you. I am as vacuous as any of you. Most people pass my course the way they would pass a gallstone. And no wonder. What have I to offer them?

"The plastic sticks of thought, little logical connectors, I build these little plastic homes and cars. They are good for nothing. No one can live in them, nor are they good for anything. They're toys. They have doors and windows that open and close. I can even put little plastic people in them, and they fit in the seats. But my ideas are nothing more than toys. In reality, I can't get Marx to be useful or real. So I posture. I like his ideas, they seem to hold a certain truth. But I can't make them apply anywhere. And they have such important holes.

"It's like I was pretending to be a canoeist. I drive around with a rack on the top of my car, and tell everyone how much I like to canoe. The rack is there always and people find it easy to imagine that one would fit, and that I likely use it, given how I talk. But the rack, for me, is just a sign of an absence. For me it's a constant reminder of how useless the support structure I've built is. I'm tired of acting as though I canoe. I'm tired of this constant absence. I am empty. I am done.

"Just because a person has legs, pays taxes, and makes a car payment, don't assume that he or she is real. Most people I know, with the exception of one, weren't born the day they were born. Their bodies began to function. For the first few years, a person has visiting rights for their bodies. They come, stay a short while, and leave. They're just checking up on things, making sure all is developing well. And then, years later, after the body seems ready to handle their person, they joined up with their body, if they're lucky.

"If they're not so lucky, the body isn't such a good home for the person. The person visits the body, and every time is less impressed with the accommodations. The person starts to visit the body less often. Once in a while, the person checks back in with the body. And, then, often in a fit of anger, the person will leave that body, never to return. My father-in-law was like that. His person demanded a five-star stay, and his body could only provide a two-star motel: stained curtains, and an old TV with horizontal hold problems."

He paused, and the tears began to flow. As he fought to stem the flow, the pain resting in his loins jumped up and rushed to his chest and head, and he began to weep openly. Fortunately, he had also ceased to care for his decorum. The room sat in silence. No motion. After a few minutes he began to gain control. Mucous from his nose glubbed slug trails from his philtrum over his lip and into his mouth. He looked around the room at a group of people who shrank into their chairs. If the chair cushioning had been absorbent enough, all of them would have disappeared. "As I suspected, there is not the wherewithal in this room to cope with this most disgusting display." He looked up, and wiped his nose onto his sleeve. "I quit. I quit. I cannot do this any longer. Consider this my resignation." The room gasped, suddenly awake. "I'm going to clean out my office."

He stopped in to use the washroom before his walk home. He waved his hands under the sink, and the tap poured forth immediately. "It makes sense," he muttered.

# 90.

PAUL WALKED HOME SLOWLY. ALONE. Instead of bringing his books home after he quit, he simply moved everything out into the hallway and let the magpies carry away what they wanted. On his face was a grin that seemed unable to quit. As he walked up the steps to Angela's house, Angela was just leaving.

She was dressed professionally in a skirt, blouse, and blazer. Her skirt was still as short as her whoring days, but about her buzzed a new sense of business and professionalism.

"Hello Paul," she said, with a new aggression. Her jaw strained and relaxed, strained and relaxed, toiling over a piece of gum. "How are you doing?" She held her hand out. "I'm a real estate associate now. Got the job this morning. And I have a listing, too!" She squealed in delight. "My dad's letting me sell Bal's place, since he doesn't need it anymore."

Paul opened his mouth but no words filled his mouth for a few seconds, as he adjusted to the changes. "Ah, wow." He met her hand and shook it. "Congratulations. That's an important change."

"Yeah," she said shyly. "I think this is going to be a good move for me."

"You know," Paul said, releasing her hand, "I think I'm making a career change too. But I don't know what it is, yet." He smiled. "Good for you for finding your way. That's not an easy thing to do."

She grinned her reply. "But when you're desperate and you find something that works, it is a sweet, sweet thing," she said. Her eyes shone, and she swallowed hard, fighting off a desire to weep—weep for joy, perhaps.

"I hope I find it. I hope I can." He dropped his eyes to the hedge. "Actually, for me, getting out of the old line of work was sweet enough. I could probably go on welfare now and be the better for it all."

"I hear ya," the realtor said. "Getting out alive is more than half of it."

"Yeah. It is."

"Good luck on your search, huh."

"Thank you. I think I'll need it."

She nodded. Her cellphone suddenly began to play a fugue in her pocket. She held it up and looked at the number and grinned. "It might be a buyer. I gotta take this. See you around suppertime."

"Suppertime," Paul parroted.

He entered the house, walked straight to the kitchen and made a pot of tea with a handful of fresh mint he found on the counter. He looped the china cup handle over the spout of the teapot, grabbed a handful of cookies and headed to the back yard. As he stepped through the back door, a little boy screamed.

"Daddy!"

## About the Author

Bill Bunn is a professor of English at Mount Royal University in Alberta, Canada. He is the author of 3 novels for young adults and a collection of essays. Though this story is a work of fiction, much of it sprang from actual occurrences, though the names, dates, and places have been changed, to protect the innocent, guilty, and those in between.

## Books by Bill Bunn

young adult fiction
*Duck Boy*
*Kill Shot*
*Out on the Drink*

adult non-fiction
*Hymns of Home,* a collection of essays